Meet Aurora. A human born into ruin, forged in brutality, on the poverty-stricken streets of London. Skilled foot soldier and expert at gang warfare. A trained killer.

Tragedy strikes, a series of strange occurrences leads Aurora to cross over into the forbidden lands of the Immortals, to save her sister. Encountering a vampire, who saves her from certain death, by sharing his infected blood and turning her. Destiny whispers from the shadows and Aurora hears its call. Prophecy comes into being, The Elder return and vengeance comes for those with no soul to call their own. The Elder - Lights of the Seven Kingdoms Series begins.

Trained to protect the innocent and kill from an early age, Aurora has accepted her life of brutality on the poverty-stricken streets of London– *to Fight or Die.* An unfortunate accident takes place. Strange occurrences begin, starting a sequence of events that see her cross over to the Outer Realms; Lands of the Immortals, to save her little sister.
Her sister has been taken as part of an ancient Rite to uphold the Clandestine Agreement, sacrifices must be made to appease Earth and the rest of The Seven Kingdoms – to prevent war. An Agreement was made between humans and immortals, that divided civilisation, a long

time ago, separating those with magical abilities from those without. The magics, called Immortals, left Earth, and migrated to the outer dimensions of the Seven Kingdoms, establishing a planetary system of home worlds for each of the immortal tribes.

This happened a long time ago, humans have forgotten their history, the Clandestine Agreement, includes a pact of secrecy, the details are just only becoming known. But this is no fairy tale and Aurora knows *Happily Ever After* doesn't happen for people like her, people who have lived a life of violence. The best she can hope for is making these worlds safe for others and gaining some semblance of control over her dark demons, in the process.

Aurora learns, a little too late, monsters and immortal beings are real. Polluted by the ancient curse of the vampires, leaves Aurora immortal and conflicted. Aurora must learn all the secrets of the ancient Rite and solve the riddle of The Elder, to save Earth and return home, with her sister.

If that is what she is destined to do. . .

The Elder – Lights of the Seven Kingdoms

By Phillipa Albion

The Elder – Lights of the Seven Kingdoms

The Elder – Lights of the Seven Kingdoms

A fantasy story about a young woman, forged in brutality, who crosses over to the lands of the immortals to save her little sister. Becoming a living fable herself and beginning an ancient prophecy, which is all part of her Destiny . . . .

Book Cover Design by 100 Covers

L Newton Editorial

ISBN: 9798325394867
EAN

Fiction > reference > Independently published / self-publishing.

Other fantasy books by the author

A young adult fantasy series about a warrior with a heart and an undiscovered destiny, Pollux:

Polly and the Tome of Herne - Book One
The Heart of the Dragon – Book Two

The Elder – Lights of the Seven Kingdoms

Table of Contents

The Elder – Lights of the Seven Kingdoms

To all the **dreamers** and those with big hearts, who feel the **world** and all its pain. Too much at times. Know we stand **united**. Terrified of growing hard, but equally, wanting to stop the ache - lamenting for a bygone time, waiting for **something better**, something new.

The return to the **magic of the universe**.

I see you.

PROLOGUE

There is a place. A strange place, on the outer edges, where time and space behave differently; multiple dimensions converge at a single point in time here, drawn, by the immense pull of power. A grouping of seven planets circle this part of space.

The immortals govern the planets that makeup part of the Seven Kingdoms. Six of the Kingdoms belong to the race of Immortals. Each one is a home world – a realm, of sorts, to one of the immortal tribes.

The significance of the naming of each of the planets has been lost in the midst of time now, but most are believed to have been named after conquering warriors of old. Let us start with the names and tribes that inhabit these other worlds, which are so vastly different from the Earth that we know. First, the Kingdom of Vulldune for the Vampires, fearless and cunning. The Kingdom of Attraides for the werewolves, loyal and fierce. Nimbuu for the witches and warlocks, symbiotes of nature and protectors of the balance of the universe. Tylerine is the home world for the High Elf Lords, lovers of treasure, and culture - longing to be rulers of all. Toova the lands of the Celestial Guardians of Time and Space, clever physicians, and masters of Lore, - too inward-looking, to care about the others, - now ruined, lamenting for times long past. Then, there is Pericullious, a world that divides the immortal tribes. Integrated, it is the pinnacle of all the home worlds, uniting the tribes, to an extent, under one banner. Governed by one king of the Immortals, at a time, a steward king – an elected Ruler sits on the Amber throne. Pericullious is the very heart of the universe, it sits at the axis point of the Seven Kingdoms, – the point of all creation. Abundant in resources and the core of all magical powers – highly prized indeed. The last and the

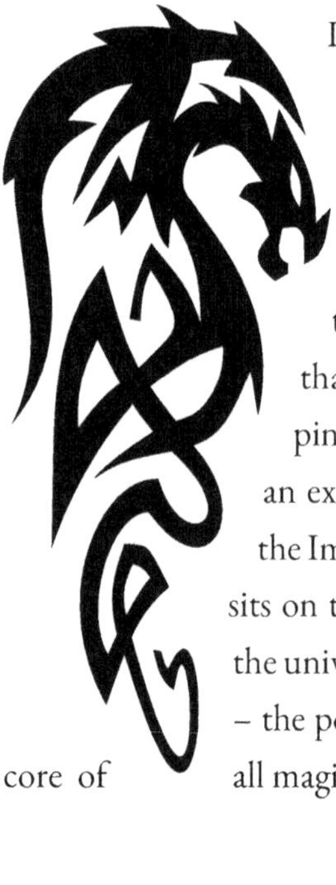

most complicated of the Seven Kingdoms is Earth. Lands of the humans, once the Immortals lived alongside us and we shared the planet, Earth.
Most humans are unaware, blissfully oblivious of the other worlds circling them, just at the edge of their own reality. Humans are left alone but observed from a distance. They are a plague on the immortal's minds, where war is coming soon, - to take back what is owed.
Earth is named as a part of the Seven Kingdoms because it is located in a stretch of space known as the Inner Dimension. The other six home worlds reside in the Outer Dimensions. These dimensions are separated by a kind of disillusionment, a fracture in space called The Void.
It was not always this way, centuries ago, the immortals lived amongst humans and humans had a kind of magic of their own. The Immortals became very powerful and were, eventually, brutally persecuted on Earth.
It was a violent time, not any different from the rest of Earth's history, until the immortals became organised, coordinated, and begun to defend themselves against human hatred for being different.
The humans declared civil war on the immortals in 2036 BC. The magical folk were too few in number back then and were easily overrun. A great many were slaughtered.
Immortal leaders had conceded, at the time, knowing they stood no chance of winning, and the Clandestine Agreement was created between the immortals and Earth. All to protect their own people and keep magic from being erased, from stopping everything they held dear from moving forward into the oblivion of extinction. A deal was struck and the Immortals agreed to migrate, with magic, to the outer dimensions of the Seven Kingdoms and created the six home worlds separate from Earth and in truth, from each other.
History was made and history was forgotten. Things, that should have perhaps remained remembered, were lost in the mists of time and space. Only pored over by the celestials, who look to the past more than the future

and find great comfort whispering over ancient history. A case of *once upon a time, a long time ago. . .*
Before all of this unsettlement, an ancient race of celestial beings, immense in power, called The Elder, held The Seven Kingdoms once, - before the immortal and human wars, and the first grappling's for power.
I am only learning about this history myself.
Once upon a time, I was a human, but now I am something else, something that the immortals fear to name. A prophecy there is, of one that will come to walk between the Light and Darkness, with the ability to break space and time – to restore the universe. To unite the Realms. A new order, a new pattern will emerge to take forward life across the universe. The Elder will return when The One comes forth, to restore all.

Chapter One - The Sacrifices Well Made.

I am sat here, and while I waited, I picked up a brittle, plastic

pen, rolled it between my hands, and let the smooth outer casing slide through my fingers, bouncing a little when it hits the blunt surface of the table, in the police station. Making a small '*puck,*' sound.

I watched the pen lazily, through eyes hooded in concentration.

How do I explain my story to this police officer?

He won't believe me, what's the point?

"So, Aurora, that your real name or your gangland name or somethin'? Either way, sounds stupid and made up to me. Not the right sort of name for a wanted *killer,*" The police officer scoffs, with a toothy grin. He's trying to get a rise out of me.

I responded with the sharpness of a withering look. Debating whether or not, to levitate the pointed end of the pen into his neck. My eyes flicked towards the door. I could do it, y'know, and it would give me a chance to make my escape, as well as some pay back for the insult about my name, but I take a second to pause and realised I didn't want to. I sighed, wondering if I had lost my nerve.

Glancing around the room instead. I'm looking for something that's making that weird buzzing sound, or is it a sensation, rolling round the inside of my head – a sense of *déjà vu* is growing upon me, perhaps.

I sigh and lean back in my chair. There is no one here on Earth, who could come to help me in a situation like this. I have no one. I am alone in these worlds; it makes me feel like I am *far away* from the place I once called home - Earth.

I fear nothing. I have nothing except for my freedom; a freedom from being human that is.

The Elder – Lights of the Seven Kingdoms

I drew in a tight breath; my two hearts are pounding out a symphony in my ears. Building up the nerve, getting ready to tell my story to this irritating Police Officer. He will be shocked but what else is there to do? I'm tapping the plastic pen on the table while I clear my throat. Oh, what the hell. Here goes nothing.

"It didn't start out this way for me. A human I was in the beginning, but I lost my humanity a long time ago before I had left Earth if truth be told. With a sometimes mother, a little sister I'm desperate to protect; and no father that I can remember or no father that is memorable to me would be a better way to describe it, you would too. To hear my story is to listen to a fable. To speak of something that is unimaginable, too spectacular, too unreal. But to speak of the unimaginable, the unthinkable, we must.

There were years before the beginning, there always are, no? But sometimes they are too mundane to bother to describe, but this is sadly not the case for me. Recalling my beginning would be a waste of my thought, a waste of words to me now, but I fear that's what I am going to have to do. My beginning was miserable, but still, I don't hold it accurately in my mind anymore. To my expansive memory the past is but a blot in time, now I am immortal.

Maybe my beginning is even too tragic for your ears to hear; to those of you who have no experience of a hard life. For those of you who are more accustomed, well, my beginning is no different from your own, my dear friend. Too painful for me to speak of at times, I must admit. I am the storyteller, and I get to decide what gets left in, please give me that much, at least. To decide how to tell my own story. It is my very last dignity."

The Police officer is not listening, he's scribbling away on a form, not quite ready yet, so I lean forward and make a point of grabbing his attention, "You will want to know something about my early years that will explain my character, I suppose? Very well."

I stir, sitting in my orange plastic chair, rigid, hard and unforgiving on the curvature of my back. My injured dog, Poppy, sat on my lap – recovering from her ordeal, thank goodness. I can't help but keep fidgeting, trying to find a comfortable spot. I needed this police officer to believe me, but I can't seem to find the right words to begin, so I start looking around the place that seems so dull and ordinary to my eyes. While the large clock on the wall keeps tick, tick, ticking, reminding me time is running out.

13

The Elder – Lights of the Seven Kingdoms

The police station we are in is rather barren and austere. Made that way, by the environment, but also, by the dead of eye humans, who work in this place. Losing their souls, wading through the human condition day after day, just to police these cesspits of streets, riddled with poverty and crime. I take in the flaking white-washed walls, the blinking strip light overhead and hide-all-the-stains, cheap, brown carpets – all reek of despair. But I sit in this plastic seat, and I am embarrassed, made painfully aware that I have become too unaccustomed to such brutal furnishings.

The Lands of the Seven Kingdoms, I inhabit, affords me nothing but luxury these days.

I am fidgeting quite wildly now at my disgust for the primitive plastic seat, while the detective inspector's cigarette smoke, curls upwards into magnificent, transparent whirls. Drawing my eyes to the beautiful ribbon of smoke, which announces pending death and disease to these humans. Not to me, not anymore.

The police station is in the backwaters of London somewhere.

I squint under the glare from a torturous, raw spotlight aimed at me, in the hope of intimidation – it is unsuccessful. It is, however, lighting up the small translucent hairs on my face. Each follicle prickles, flexing, testing the environment to feedback information to my senses. My inner eyes are tormented by the harsh light, but I do not blink nor look away, showing grit. Determination. Instead, allowing dots to swim like gnats over the surface of my eyes.

The detective inspector is sitting before me in deep shadow, the outline of his tall frame folded into a plastic seat like mine. He is bent over writing. His name is Lloyd, he introduced himself when he walked into this little box room. Lloyd is under the misguided belief he can contain me in here and that makes him feel safe, but I'm afraid he is wrong. Very wrong.

I can keenly hear the scratching of his bitten-down pencil on the small pages of a rough, cheap notepad. Uniquely attuned is my hearing to my hunting environment – casually looking for a feast.

He is distracted, not paying attention again.

"I said… you will want to know something of my early years that will explain my character, I suppose. Perhaps, why I am in this mess? *Hmm.*" he does not respond, nor look up, but curtly nods, in a bored fashion. "Very well," I say.

14

The Elder – Lights of the Seven Kingdoms

A sudden screeching of the police officer's chair legs sliding across the floor, announced his desire to pay more attention now that the paperwork was done – he takes his time to make himself comfortable and shuffles under the desk. The oblong table was positioned between us. His large face pushed forward into the light of the lamp, to join mine. Facing me he says, "Tell it 'Ow you want to, and I'll ask questions along the way."

Now he's near to me, I closed my eyes and deeply inhaled the sweet scent of his skin, deliciously close to mine.

My eyes glinted dangerously, with the luminous, glow of the predator I really am inside. My pupils expanding out to take in every dimple, every line on the officer's face. Glowing, my eyes shine bright when I pulled my head back into the dimness of the shadows left by the flare of the spotlight — taking refuge in the darker corners of the room. His smile slipped a little from his face. With the brief blinking gesture from me, he had caught a glimpse of my true self. Fear drenched his glistening face. I smiled.

He glanced at the door momentarily, gulping in his disbelief. But he knows something is not quite right, looking in alarm between me and the door, searching for an exit, after seeing the cold one within me for the first time. I watched his reaction, I enjoyed it, but I did not want to reveal myself just yet, so I set about adjusting myself to my best advantage. Making a point of sprinkling a softness to my next words - all honey and saccharine - quite sure my words will snake out and whisper to him of tranquil summer meadows. Easing him, befriending him, caressing his ears, coaxing him with a familiarity, until he is defenceless. That is what my kind do, after all. The creature in me like a rattlesnake shaking its tantalising tail. I licked my lips and then I began.

"So let us start at the very beginning. Let's say that I was forged in the brutal backstreets of London. . . right here.

Aurora is my human birth name. Named after some forgotten screen siren my mother had admired. The 1980s is where I will start my tale. I was living where the poor of London were shepherded by the wealthy to the low-rent districts; to share damp holes and live in cramped, warren-like spaces. Multiple breaths, in the same room, where dank, fetid black mould builds up in corners. I used to see the mould as large black, bloated spider nests, as a small child growing up in those places, - the mould was allowed to feed on the weak. Forcing the poor to breathe in its ruining decay.

The Elder – Lights of the Seven Kingdoms

Poor families, and the decrepit, and the villains of the world, and whatnot, who can't afford to stop the spread of the black mould, as it seeps through the ramshackle houses - consuming the poor and taking their young in the bitter cold winter nights.

Those people who can't afford to use their heating or dry their wet clothes anywhere more suitable; you know the ones I mean. While the wind continues to howl on, whistling through bones and making teeth chatter, all the while ice forms on dilapidated rooftops, as punishment for not having any money.

Six to a room at least. No privacy for mum or dad or lovers. Everything is seen. Then everyone pretends to have not seen the truth in their comrades in arms - in the futile defence against a life of poverty.

The mind-bending violence, and the addicts, and the invasive misery, not to mention the assaults. The embarrassment of being done in, done over and the exuberance of being the alpha, the winner for a night - the power taken from others in the same situation as you. You know something, it doesn't last that long, that type of power - taken from the weak. Even the desperate rise up against the oppressor in the end. I noticed that even in my younger years. That type of power, taken from the vulnerable, turns to a greasy, queasy feeling that whispers in the perpetrator's ear telling them: that they are no good. So, I watched with a distant stare as the perps and the victims all kill themselves slowly; with drink, drugs and screwing; just to not be that person anymore. While bits of their soul abandoned them a piece at a time. They only wanted to escape the putrid person they had become to survive. It happens to all of us who remain in places like that, even if you have just been a helpless observer, like me.

Needless to say, I grew up where crime was rife. Even the do-gooders' were afraid. Primary school teachers and volunteers and the like, who did find the stomach to venture into the interior of this urban hell to help the young and innocent; either were broken down by developing the same mental afflictions as us or ran as fast as they could the hell out of there.

Oh, I didn't blame them; I would have done the same thing given half a chance. So, there you have it. Got it? My childhood wasn't the best. I don't want your pity. Grateful I am for that beginning and you'll see why when we get nearer to the end of this tale – my witness statement after the facts, if you like.

The Elder – Lights of the Seven Kingdoms

A cold skin slowly grew over me. It hardened and I floated further away from my own surface as a child. Plunging into my darkest depths. Hidden, I was suffocating inside, could only peek out through my large, hazel eyes. Watching the horror unfold around me.

I didn't have any friends growing up. I was described, and, shown, in a multitude of different ways, that I was someone who was thought of as antisocial. Sometimes it came out as I was 'quiet'. Other times 'withdrawn', 'a little odd' and my personal favourite of them all was 'In my own world half of the time'. People can silently show you what they *really* think of you too - the recoiling arm was always a dead giveaway that they thought I had a screw loose.

I escaped into my own brain whenever I could. I wanted to live there.

In actual fact, I was resigned to a life of chaos, of poverty and I wasn't letting anyone in or get close enough to break me - I was determined to survive.

Let me tell you a secret. Come closer.

Do you know how I kept myself in that state of unbreakable resolve? I'd made a pact with myself as a little girl; to get to the age of thirty years old and if my life had not improved by then, well, I would end it, and on my own terms. That's tragic, you say. Yes, but also no, it's a very practical way of looking at things. This was the reality of my life - abysmal.

This promise I made to myself, was a curse, of course, keeping me in a state of waiting. I unknowingly cursed myself that day because I didn't understand the power I had back then. My power and abilities were nestled inside of me, incubating. Waiting for the right conditions to be released, but I'll come to that in a bit. Everything changed for me, you see, and I want you to know things can change for you too. You've just got to hang in there.

Now, where was I? Oh, yes, I was withdrawn back then. The only thing that roused any type of loss of control or emotion in me, was the thought of my little sister being hurt. Anyone, and I mean literally anyone, even looking at my sister sideways would get my knife in their belly and my fists pummelling their face.

My little sister was the sweetest, most gentle being that ever graced this foul earth. Sometimes, I just sat there and watched her playing on our threadbare rug, which covered the dusty, unvarnished, termite riddled floors – she didn't deserve the desolation of poverty.

Through all the tough times, my sister remained unaffected. She would glow like an angel; singing and smiling, and I would see that she belonged somewhere else, somewhere better. Inside a fairytale, where good triumphed over evil - *always.* Not in our grim reality of a life, where we shared one meal a day of unheated, jellified luncheon meat from the tin and a plain, stale piece of mouldy old bread; where our 'uncles' regularly turned from saviours to sinners overnight; and my mum would drink away her sorrows until we were so poor again. She'd spruce herself up and go out to find another horror story waiting to emerge. All for a bottle of drink.

The scientific community say alcohol is used to remove the essence of something from another form of matter. This is exactly right. I watched my own Mother's soul removed one unit at a time until there was nothing left but a dead eyed stare – wiped away. Gone.

On the good days when we were left alone, me and my sister would sit down peacefully for hours, her making dolls from old wooden clothes pegs, and me practising throwing with knives – both in our elements.

Unrelentingly, I protected my sister because she was good and pure of spirit. Not cut out for the world we found ourselves in. Sacrificing myself, I became what I needed to, to protect her - it was all for her. Not really caring about what happened to me in the process – but even I was shocked at how dark I would eventually become.

I collected comic books and became fascinated with heroes, the ones mostly dark themselves and used their shadows to dispense justice. Turning their disappointment with the world into a light of hope for others. "Altruism," a teacher once said to me, "Revenge," had been my reply.

I mentioned that I grew up in the 1980s, later referred to as the decade that style forgot. I started dressing my tall, lanky gamine frame in shapeless black clothes. My long dark thick hair greased down into a ponytail, which sat limp at the base of my skinny neck. My intense, death-wish eyes, were rimmed with a black kohl pencil, stolen from a nearby chemist - on the regular. The cashier not daring to show she was a witness to my theft.

My outfit and my scowl were all carefully put together to warn others off. To not draw attention to my frail femininity. Too hardened on the inside of my scrawny body, to be seen as soft.

So now, I have set the scene; best to get on with it and tell you about the journey to the outer dimensions of the Seven Kingdoms. What's that you've never heard them? Oh, well, you soon will because they are coming, the immortals, and there is nothing humanity can do to stop them.

Me and my sister used to spend hours on a Saturday morning combing the flea markets at Whitechapel, with our dog, Poppy - a stray just like us. Now, Whitechapel is best known for the brutal murders committed by the notorious Jack the Ripper. The area still carried a menacing quality because of it; like he was hovering over us, lingering, still there somewhere watching us all. Me and my sister loved looking around the market at all the things we couldn't afford.

On one thunderstorm of a godless grey day, between the leaking plastic sheeting of the market stalls, I saw something that stirred my heart, but also, jolted me to pay attention - a sense of *déjà vu* stole over me. It was a memory from a long time ago, that I couldn't recall in my lifetime or make much sense of.

But what I did know, the déjà vu had been brought on by something that had caught my eye. A long, battered, old tan leather trench coat, with dull golden military buttons - it had all of them still stitched in – a small miracle in that second-hand marketplace.

Mesmerised by the coat and the imagined armour it would provide me. My frozen fingers flexed involuntarily, to touch the soft leather – I was strangely drawn to it.

My sister kept looking between me and the coat, recognising the longing on my face, while we stood semi-covered, under the plastic roofing of the tarpaulin.

Freezing, slanted rain hit us hard, finding every entrance point onto our frigid cold bodies.

"Clear off riff raff or I'll choke your mingy mutt," snarled the street trader, leering at Poppy. He covered up half his face with a cloth cap pulled down over his pock-marked skin. He had an ill look about him and a horrifying sneer, - he terrified us. We wanted to escape his glare, so we decided to leave. As we did so, I touched the sleeve of the leather coat once more,

with a subtlety, breathing in the leather then I let go and we moved on. I hadn't wanted to leave it behind, but what could I do? I couldn't afford something as beautiful as that fine coat.
The rain was torrential, driving down as hard as hammers, beating on our flesh. Drenching every item of clothing we had on.
Walking further on, we looked in the window of a Chinese restaurant, steamy and warm from the cooking inside, where fragrant smells of garlic, ginger, fried onions, and exotic pastes made its way out onto the pavement, making our mouths water. The requisite Peking ducks strung up by the dozens, on display, in the front window.
My pockets were empty; save for a crumpled and pitifully damp one pound note, in the same sorrowful state as my sodden black jeans.
I turned to look at my sister. Hand stretched out to offer the money to her – gifting her the purchase of a tub of rice to fill a small hole. When I looked down, just past my shoulder to catch a glimpse of the smile that was sure to be there - I was in fact, staring down at a space absent of her glow. *Where was she? She must not be left alone in this neighbourhood, where devils lurk around every corner.*
My heart started hammering in my chest. A sickness slid inside my belly as tight as a clenched fist.
All the warmth from the fragrant spices gone, in an instant. Replaced with a taste of bile from the heavy, restricting sickness, growing in my chest.
I called her name and ran, darting in and out between the market stalls, while the torrential rain got even heavier. The bounce back of that rain, hitting the pavement - leaping two feet in the air. The roar of it was deafening, I was barely able to hear myself think. The wind blew unabated into my face. I held my frozen hand up, protecting my searching and beseeching eyes from the onslaught of the gale.
I screamed her name and kept on screaming it. I threw-over stalls and pulled plastic sheeting down in my frantic search for her. A gaggle of people followed me, shouting at me to 'Clear out. Get lost'. I was already lost, until I saw her shiny face come darting out from between the bones of the metal stalls of the market.
Running, she was running towards me - thick and fast. And with each heavy step, her feet exploded in the pools of mucky, black water collecting

on the pavements. Loyal Poppy at her heels, tongue lolling playfully. Barking with joy, in the thrill of that moment.
In my sister's arms, a flash of that tan leather coat I'd admired. She had stolen it.
Her mouth wide open, screaming at me with a huge adrenaline-fuelled grin on her face, while she was crouched low, dashing forward quicker than the pitter patter of the bullet-sized rain.
"Come back 'ere with that coat, ya' repulsive little street urchin."
Looming behind her was the very tall, exceptionally large, and very red-faced bellowing market trader. His rheumy eyes, and belly protruded, with too much beer drinking, on the regular, but it was something else that made him sinister in appearance. He caught my eyes and started darting towards me, aiming to head off my sister - fist clenched over a wooden bat.
I knew straight away what he intended to do to us. The look on his face said it all. Not to call the police but hand down his own form of punishment; with his fists and his steel-toe-capped clobbered feet. He lunged to punch her in the back of her head.
"*I don't think so Mister, not my sister, you don't,*" I spitted out.
Racing forward, I came at him. With a forceful momentum of my own, I leaped through the air and landed my fist on his leg, at the outside of the knee joint. Cracking the bones, which splintered and pierced through the skin - it only takes two pounds of pressure at this point of the human body to annihilate and break a leg. Did you know that? Well, I did. The school of hard knocks taught me every dirty trick in the book. I learned them all a little too well.
The street trader howled and collapsed in on himself. Down he fell on his back, flailing about. Surrounded by filthy rainwater, and even murkier looking Eastend passersby.
To the crowd he began appealing, wheezing out his screams of pain. The crowds gathered around him for the sport. Casual pity was offered but no practical help - they were only glad it wasn't them this time laying helpless on the pavement.
All I could hear when I picked up my sister in my arms and run with her towards safety, Poppy in tow, were the screeching of the police sirens, coming after me in the background, accompanied by the odd screamed out, "No, it was those shitty girls, feral they are, I tell ya'."

Now, the dizzy excitement of the theft made me and my sister giggle out loud - eyes glistening from our shared ordeal being over. I smoothed down the back of hair making sure he hadn't landed a punch. The streets of London darkened. We slowed down to a gentle jog, the nearer we got to the place we called home. Not drawing attention to ourselves was drummed into us from an early age. We had learnt early on in life; the more people took notice in my neighbourhood, the greater the risk you found yourself in.

We came to a stop at the corner of our street. My sister took the opportunity in this quiet moment to hold out the coat in her little freezing hands,

"For you," she had proudly said – holding up the coat like it was a trophy, like she had won that day.

Leaning down to face her, my eyes travelled downwards to admire the coat and I gasped out my astonishment,

"But we can sell it and buy some decent food for once," I tried not to gaze longingly at the long trench coat in her outstretched hands. She gently moved a sopping wet tendril away from my forehead, leaving behind rivulets of water to drip down my skin, unencumbered, and off my long aquiline nose.

"Not this time. This is for you and when you wear it, you will remember me."

She touched my cheek with her tiny frozen fingers, which felt raised and wrinkled at the tips, then pulled my chin closer towards her. My gaze looked at the tiny little face of my sister. A sad ache settled in the pit of my stomach. I did not move my hazel eyes away from her aquamarine ones, currently so very bright. Framed by her wringing wet blonde hair. Our breath was frozen together, mingling in a mist in front of our faces being in close proximity to one another. We listened to the whistling of the wind, crushed together like that for a while. There were no other sounds apart from our own breath keeping us alive. I wanted us to remain that way forever – frozen together for all time. We were safe together like that.

Three heart beats past, while we looked at each other tenderly. Her last words had settled and caught in the back of my throat,

"That's a really bloody odd thing to say," I managed to choke-out angrily, my eyebrows as heavy as my words, but all I felt was a deep sadness. Lifting up, shrugging the moment off, scared of losing her. I finally moved away. Not wanting her to see me as I grabbed at my tears with a ferocity - damn them for trying to betray me.

She held my arm back, in her little hand.

"Okay, okay, well, happy birthday then. It is your birthday next month. Take it for that reason then, or for being like the Robin Hood of London, always looking after the poor and don't ask for nothing for yourself," she said, her own eyes welling with tears, little drops forming at the corners. The deep, dark circles of neglect under her eyes; held onto those tears within her tiny face.

It wasn't fair, none of this was fair.

". . .Robin Hood, you say? I'm glad you see me like that and not . . . well." I looked away, letting out a long sigh, but I could see my sister sadly smile, stretching up to place a tiny finger over my lips to stop me from saying the words. The words we both were thinking but saying them out loud would be admitting to what I was becoming.

Begrudgingly, I took the coat, and it made a neat *swooshing* sound, as I pulled it through her outstretched hands. I shrugged it on, it made me stand up a little taller, a little prouder. That was when I decided there and then that I needed money for us both and fast. No more taking risks just for crumbs to survive. The greater the risk the greater the gain would be.

Well, the only way you can make massive quantities of easy money on these streets is to sell something, your body, or drugs. I knew which one I was prepared to do. My sister was sent home, unceremoniously, with a barking order. Poppy trailing behind her - looking back at me with those sad, canine eyes, every now and again. I watched them go. Waiting, until they had turned a corner, before I moved a little further into the shadows that day. Casing the outside of a notorious barber's shop. Doing up the gold buttons on the coat, twirling around like a caped crusader, I went inside. The bell above the door went *ding-a-ling* as I entered that felonious den and all the hardened narrowed eyes behind the door were on me, and I stared each pair down, a snarl on my face.

I went inside that shop a sixteen-year-old girl and came out a foot soldier, with a hocked gun and a kilo of gear to sell to get me a cut. My hazel eyes were like flint, ready to hustle as if my life depended on it - it did in a way. I didn't use the gun; in case you were wondering. Blades have always been my weapons of choice. On these streets, you have to learn that there are only two choices in life - *fight or die.* Which one would you have chosen placed in my position?

Oh, I did have some rules. You always do. Kidding yourself you're one of the *good ones.* Lying to yourself that you're not totally going *all in.*

I didn't like selling the drugs, the thought of adding to the misery all around me was inconceivable to me, but eventually, I did find I had an aptitude to act as muscle for the gang: a courier at first, but a few incidences later, that came and went, and the gang saw something in me. I was a natural enforcer and an executioner I would become. Dispensing justice to criminals when they stepped out of line.

To judge, to execute, to clean up the streets. I had a thirst for rage. It made me feel powerful, and the executions made me feel cleansed – well, for a while, at least.

Four years passed me by, and I exacted justice more times than you've had hot dinners, and the street gangs I worked for noticed I had a natural affinity for gangland warfare too; for strategizing, for politics and 'Brainology', as the gang called it. I had taken easily to training daily too, honing my body to become a weapon. Now that I had regular meals inside of me, training had become part of my ritual. To honour thy self and all of that. I never took my health for granted. It was my weapon. My instrument. My tool. I had street smarts, and martial arts skills, and was given respect, mostly due to my tendency towards explosive uncontrollable, savage, rage. Money that was owed - people paid. Turf that was breached - people paid. Drugs that were cut - people paid. People saw the tan leather trench coat and stepped aside to let me pass. The big and the small players avoided my gaze.

For the first time, my family had money for food, meals out, and recreational activities – the small pleasures that make life worth living. For gifts and toys, that sort of thing. My little sister, Button, as I called her, but her real name was Dawn, never looked happy about any of it. She hated it. I was becoming something she couldn't understand just to keep it all.

Button would look solemnly at me on evenings spent before the warmth of the fire hearth, and would remind me that I could get a job, go to college, and earn the same with fewer risks if I applied my intellect in the right places. Whereas our mother, dear old mum, that bastion of hope for us girls, would scoff and take a swig of the finest single malt whiskey, slurring out,

"Get real Button, people like us don't get those sorts of chances. Nothin' ever happens for us. There's no happily ever after in this life, *you mark my words.*".

Then one night, everything in my world changed.

Chapter Two – Those that hunt demons.

***R**ing, ring, ring'* goes the telephone, on the stairwell, such a distinguished, thrilling sound in the 1980s. The phone sat in the middle of our small, terraced house, situated on the wrong side of town. I knew it was for me and in connection with my freelance work.

My dear old mum didn't know anyone who could afford the upkeep of a landline, so we knew none of the calls were for her.
Only once did I have to warn Mum to never answer that phone. She had nodded and shivered at the time – skin crawling. Knowing full well, what type of monsters are hooking a phone under their chin at the other end of the line, whispering for me to partake in nefarious activities.
'Ring ring ring' the phone was persistent and continued to trill, as I speedily climbed the stairs flicking the light switches on as I went by. There wasn't much light coming from the dark flowery patterned shade swinging sadly in the hallway landing. *Why had my mum liked fringing so much back then?* The shade is covered in thick strands of fabric, completely impractical and offers no light whatsoever, it was like standing in a long dark tunnel, for all the good it did. I sighed, and unhooked the hard, red Bakelite phone from its moulded cradle and waited in silence for the caller to begin to speak – better that way, lest I don't incriminate myself with aimless chatter.
The loud rasping breathing, whistling down my earpiece, indicated it was Fat Tony, notorious Kingpin, and leader of London's biggest drug cartel. I pinned my ear closer, waiting for the hot wax to swirl in the canal of my ear – melting from the blast of Mr FT's booming voice.
"Listen, we have a . . . *situation*, which requires your very special skillsssh." False front teeth leaving a hissing speech impediment in my ear.
"Yeah? Go ahead I'm listening."
"There's this cook. He don't wanna cook no more. He's in trouble with the law and wants to do a runner to South America. Thing is he knows too much about the business. *My* business. Cooked a lot of meth for us and if

he gets caught, well, he will sing like a little birdie to reduce his sentence, understand? He is a liability and has to go," a pause, then a wheeze, "-Questions?"

"None. All clear my end. Get Little Jimmy to drop over the details. I'll book him in."

"No, tonight. It has to be done tonight. The Old Bill are onto him, not the police under our control either. My snout told me so," He growls, making himself understood, with a chilling menace like I could be next.

"I'm taking my little sister to the cinema tonight. I promised her-, erm, what's the emergency? What's *he done*? This time limit, it's unusual."

"Nothing, in my view, a couple of hookers got feisty with him, and he enjoyed sorting 'em out a bit *too* much – if you catch my drift. Killed the girls accidentally, like. Boys getting excitable is all." Fat Tony chuckles, snorting with laughter.

My knuckles whitened, as I clenched the cord of the phone, a little bit too hard. Imagining stopping that laughter – for good.

"Rory, you still there? I'll send round Little Jimmy with the address. Listen, make sure it looks like an accident. No drama, no witnesses, got that? None of that, what you call it? . . . *vengeance* type stuff. Last time you frightened the boys like, we all good?" He says the word vengeance with a tinge of fear, which makes me smile to myself.

I steadied my breath, Fat Tony only called me by my nickname, Rory, when he wanted something outside of the norm, "*Yeah*, we all good," I said.

The phone clicked dead. I headed to get my blades, shrugged on my tan leather coat, and slipped a mask into my pocket. I stood for a while taking my time screwing on a silencer to my gun, but knew I wouldn't use it, even though I promised myself I would. *It's got to be a clean hit this time.*

I stand for a while, taking my time to sharpen my blades – they glint at me lovingly, while I wait for Little Jimmy to arrive. *Yeah, it's all good.*

A little later, Little Jimmy, who could fill a doorway twice over, had dropped off the address where I'd find The Cook. Looking down at the crumpled piece of paper, I could see the job was in Knightsbridge. I set alight to the slip of paper, once I'd memorised the address. I watched with a kind of dread, as the blackening folds of the paper flutter to the floor like a dying firefly.

27

The Elder – Lights of the Seven Kingdoms

Arriving at the location, I walked through the gates of a four-storey block of apartments. Very posh and clean. No graffiti. Manicured lawns and clipped hedgerows, styled into fancy designs. No rubbish. All gated. Keep Out the Poor – screamed from every lavishly lit pathway and polished, twinkly light. *How utterly divine.*

I walked through this alien environment, like I owned it. Knowing I don't belong in this world and I'm just passing through.

The Cook was doing well for himself. He must be a trained chemist or something – a rarity in the drug world. Usually, Cooks are street kids trained by other criminals – disposable, every single one of them. The kids understood how to make the formula of the drugs, by being shown and going through the motions of cooking a batch of meth or heroin, but not fully understanding the process – the infusions of chemicals, minerals, and the like. The magic of the alchemy, of taking separate compounds and creating something new. Something different. Something valuable.

I shrugged – *makes no difference in the end.* Be him a street cook or a professional chemist, he was hurting women. He had to go.

The plan was for me to 'take out' The Cook and then, call in the clean-up crew, who would wait outside until I had done the job and completed the mission for Fat Tony. The words 'cleanup crew' is a kind of grand way of describing: two shifty members of our gang, on the boss's payroll, clean up the crime scene – it's no more complicated than that.

They had already arrived, slouching against the wall in the underground carpark, when I got there. Carrying tubs of hydrofluoric acid mixed with caustic soda and other chemicals, to dissolve the body in the bathroom – clearing The Cook's drains, at the same time. A public service in my view.

The clean-up crew stood together – hooded, obscured by the brickwork of the tall buildings. I nodded to them, as I silently walked across the pristine tarmac of the underground carpark – slipping the mask over my face as soon as I had reached the back entrance door. Hidden, dressed all in black apart from my tan leather coat with my hair up in a tight ponytail, keeping it out of my way.

Calling the lift by punching a gold-coloured button with my gloved fingers – no prints, no evidence would be left behind. I am a shadow.

The doors of the lift slide open, and I slipped in. The lift starts jerking and churning on creaking pulleys, lifting me up to the penthouse apartment. A loud *"ding"* announcing my arrival. I step out, face up, but only to quickly glance into each corner – one camera on the far-right hand side, above The Cook's front door.

Head back down, I hugged the wall, briskly walking towards the camera and jumped up the wall, holding there perched like a cat. Gripping the outer casing of the camera, I disconnected a wire in the blink of an eye, knocking the surveillance equipment out and dropped down. I brushed my hands and dust flew off my gloves as they clang together. The camera was dusty as hell. I doubted it even worked.

I pulled out a key kit and with a click of the front door of the penthouse - I'm inside.

It was dark, there were no lights on in the hallway. My soft leather soles gently gliding along fine herring-bone wooden floors, as I slivered and slinked down the corridors swiftly, at a pace. My arms lifted with both blades in my hands, so they don't make a sound rubbing against the material of my coat.

There was a bright light on up ahead, glowing, interrupting the darkness all around. An old crackling radio was playing, the tune blaring out, recognisable to me. An old French song 'Non, Je ne regrette rien' by Edith Piaf, "*No regrets,"* I whispered in English to the darkness. My mum had told me once I was half French and half Londoner, something about my dad's family not being from, 'round here'. Mum would only tell me about my beginning when she was blind drunk and even then, wouldn't say that much and refused to talk about it any other time, so it was hard to know if it was true or not. I became fascinated with French culture as a result of that revelation, using pidgin French when I'm very stressed or angry. It gives my brain something else to focus on – a welcome distraction at the times I need it most.

I used the beats of the music to cover my footfalls, walking in the rhythm of the song – I danced out a terrible ballet, with a twirling grace, prancing forward, knives slicing through air as I go. Deeper into the darkness - closing in on my prey.

As I get closer to the door, where the light is coming from, I heard a man's cackling laughter closely followed by muffled screams. A teenager with something shoved in her mouth to keep her from screaming out in her terror.

The Elder - Lights of the Seven Kingdoms

I froze. The sound of my own breathing heavy in my ears. This was unexpected. I hadn't planned for anyone else to be here. Slowing my breathing down, I tried to concentrate and take in all the smaller details to help me form a plan. I tell myself not to let the rage in, but it's coming on in waves, anyway.

My heart raced; my veins throbbed with barely contained anger.

I pressed my back up against the outer wall, nearest to the room, and with a flash of movement, I peered around the corner into the occupied room. My head darting about and then I returned to my position – back pressed up against the wall.

I gulped in air, steadying my breathing and closed my eyes to build a mental image of the scene.

He had her tied up in her underwear using sharp objects on her. Blood fell like rain to the floor – there was a pool of it nearest to the shower tray. It would be slippery when I entered. Her eyes were wide, pleading and petrified but she hadn't seen me while he stood over her hysterically laughing at his 'artwork'.

My eyes were unblinking at the trauma written across her face. My breath was short and coming in little bursts. I was shaking with uncontrollable rage.

My hand reached up to remove the mask covering my disgusted face, slowly pulling off the balaclava revealing who I am, what I'm prepared to accept.

He would see my face as I come for him.

I would watch vengeance being enacted, as it stalked him.

He would see my glaring eyes as I ended him.

She would see my face. The last line of defence against people like him.

Folding up the mask in my tight fist, I shoved the mask back into my pocket and got ready with my blades. They are welded to my hands like claws. I weighed them up – heavy they felt. It's the price I pay for what I do. For what I am good at. I take a moment to accept the weight of the guilt from what I am about to do next – staring at the glinting, shiny blades in my hands.

Non, je ne regrette rien

I breathed in- and out- and in- and out-, letting out a slow breath, which turned into a long sigh at the end.

I was ready, pushing myself off the wall. I rounded on the half-open door before kicking it forward with a hard swing. It came off its hinges as I smashed my way into the room – announcing my wrath.

At first, a look of relief flashed across the hostage's face, followed closely by a shadow of fear. She watched, terrified, as the door was being smashed to smithereens by one swing of my foot.

The Cook started bellowing, screaming out in anger as soon as I entered the bathroom. A withered little sick man stood before my judgement.

It was not long before I had kicked him onto his knees into the prayer position with the type of strength that only my rage can muster or, at least, that's where I thought my strength was coming from at this point in time. He looked up at me, neck craning to see who had come, his eyes take in the swirl of the folds of my tan leather coat and widen.

He knew.

"I-I-I can explain. Please – please -" he lifted the palms of his hands up to me submissively, dropping the Stanley blade in one swift movement, but he knew who I was – what I do. My eyes glared down at him in disgust at what he had done to the girl, while I moved around him like a snake looking for the best position to strike. There was nothing else to be done. He would not learn; his type never do, but I must try anyway to save him. Executing The Cook was the easy part. Taking a life is a bit too easy, in fact, but it is the aftermath that sorts the angels from the sinners. The termites of wriggling guilt that make the dark, dreamless nights never ending – you are alone in the night when your own demons come. Only the strong survive the process.

So, it's the fight for my own soul that made me lean forward, prepared to ask him and to hear his final words.

"Tell me something, why'd you, do it? What's it all for?"

My face was impassive, curious even, set that way by the questioning gleam in my eyes. They shone with a type of hope too, hoping my questions would release something salvageable in him. You know, something that would have an impact and he would respond in a way that meant he was somewhat redeemable. However, it was not going to be the way of it for The Cook. He laughed; the sound gave out a cruel edge.

"They're slags, nothing but flesh to be cut and thrown away down the gutter." His grey cold eyes met mine, even colder.

A smile slid across my lips, detached from the ice glinting across my gaze. "Thank you," I leaned in his ear to whisper and pushed him to face forward, "thank you, for giving me this absolution from what I'm about to do next."

The laughter stopped, he flinched back and the fear leaked out of him like water from his gut.

"I'll cook for you, make you millions. What do you say?", an oily smile plastered on his face. This may have worked for the Cook if I'd been someone else. Someone different.

I stared at him. Just kept staring raising my blades up.

"Whatever you offer, it will never be enough, I'm the one that has to keep these streets safe from the likes of you. I'm sorry you are not able to save yourself, I don't get any enjoyment out of this and I want you to know that before you depart."

"Depart. . .?" he whispered, panting.

I knew it was time, I darted forward to stand behind him – he was bent down before me. Taking my blades, I cross them over until they converged over his bobbing Adams-apple and then I pulled back my shoulder blades,– with full force. All the while, I clenched my teeth and a *thud, thud* on the tiled floor indicated his head had separated from his body - hitting the hard, tiled floor one at a time.

Silence fell. It was done. I watched the bathroom floor change from dark tiles to crimson liquid – spreading out from his open neck. The bathroom smelt of metallic blood and artificially sweet strawberry lip gloss, a most confusing combination.

The girl started screaming, but I tuned it all out.

I stood in stillness, face up to the ceiling – blades hanging down either side of me like I was a terrible Marionette puppet loosely hanging there – limp. A mess inside of me I needed to untangle, but I couldn't find the knots to start to unpick them properly - there were just too many to try to pull loose. For a minute or two I stood frozen to the spot with a ringing between my ears. All my senses had gone blank. A veil had dropped over me. I couldn't hear anything, I couldn't smell anything, I couldn't see anything – I was numb. I stood there staring up at the ceiling listening to the sound of my

chest rising and falling – nothing else, just the sound of life beating within me. In that blankness, I asked myself . . .
When did it come to this?
When people began treating others like objects, my brain replied. *The vulnerable need protection, the police are too busy to save them all.*
Non, je ne regrette rien is all I said in a hushed whisper to myself. It did the trick and broke the spell – my brain just needed a distraction.
In an instant, all my senses were reactivated. I was back in the room, in charge of myself and in control of my rage, once more. I needed those few moments to myself - of forgiveness, to remember who I am, and what I do it for.

I hear a croaky whisper, the young girl had screamed herself hoarse, but she was steadily finding her voice again,
"The l-l-lights. What are those lights coming out of you? You literally had superhuman strength. There is no way a human could have done what you just did. What are you? What are you? That ain't normal. It just ain't normal."
The girl says to me, covering her ears with her freezing, white-beyond-pale fingers. Looking up at me from a crouched position in the corner of the shower she occupies. A teenager, her wide eyes blistered into mine with the weight of her terror.
I am confused by her questions.
"You're okay. You're okay. *Shush now*, I'm going to get you out of here,"
But as I extended my hand towards her, she cowered away from me – shrinking back even further into her corner – into herself.
"Get away. Get away from me. I don't know what you are but you're not human. You're a monster," she screams out hysterically.
"Of course I'm human. I think you might be a little bit *stressed* -, what lights, huh?" My head swivelled about, looking around the room. Out of the corner of my vision, something moved.
I can see amber glowing balls hovering in the air. I blinked a few times – checking my vision is working properly.
I turned my face in the direction of the lights – stunned.
Catching a glimpse of my own reflection in the bathroom mirror, I can see there are some last embers of light particles hovering above my head, pulsating. They glowed unnaturally, as large as Christmas baubles for the

tree. The balls of light are merging with me - seeping into my skin. Disappearing. I am frozen to the spot, staring into the mirror watching my own reflection with my mouth hanging wide open. *The lights disappeared into me.*
I blinked not quite believing what I was seeing, the lights had all gone when I had gathered myself and managed to snap out of my trance. I looked down into the corner of the shower and the girl had vanished too.
Wet bloody footprints on the floor that lead out to the hallway, then into the lift and then there was nothing. She had disappeared '*poof*' into the urban jungle of Knightsbridge. Just. Like. That.
As much as I tried, I couldn't explain the lights at the time, so I gave myself a shake and shrugged it off. Telling myself that my mind was playing tricks on me and the girl was in distress from her ordeal. Or something worse like drugs or some sort of shared delirium, maybe? I was starting to feel dizzy. I needed to sit down. I crouched over and breathed in deeply.
Non, je ne regrette rien
Right, focus on the practical stuff, then get the hell out of here. Tonight, has been too odd.
I washed my hands off, blood diluting under the flow of the running water. I stripped out of my clothes and handed these to the clean-up crew, who would ensure they would be incinerated, along with any other items that couldn't be chemically destroyed. I had scrubbed every inch of myself using the kitchen sink, while the crew were hosing down the bathroom of all evidence. I got dressed, while they were busy grafting hard to clear the crime scene quickly.
The only bits of evidence left were tiny spots of blood splatter in my ears– a DNA test kit would've been the only way to find it on me. The Old Bill weren't going to do that. Most of them were on the payroll like me.
I felt an itch, this insatiable need to go and see Leon, my casual hook-up. I needed a release in this heightened emotional state I was in – a distraction. This itch hung over me, like a cloud. The itch was one that I just couldn't scratch by myself. I consider swinging by Leon's place and then afterwards, picking up a pizza on the way home for Button and Mum - as a way to say sorry for not taking them to the cinema as promised.
I let out a long sigh. I hated needing Leon in this way. I hated feeling vulnerable with anyone. Leon criticised me every time for leaving

straightaway after the deed was done but was always happy to let me in the next time, anyway.

I pager him. "You at home?" This was code for can I come round and screw away my guilt and shame for the way I live my horrible life.

"Beep, beep,"

The reply came through as soon as I had finished sending my message.

"Cum round tonight, but I'm hoping to meet someone who cares about me too."

I rolled my eyes – *was it worth it or am I just adding to my strain?*

An inner debate started and raged within me, but I didn't have long to nurse my anguish, my angry scorpion jabbing me in the head. I was shocked into paying attention to what's happening in the room when the crew walk into the kitchen to confront me. I snap out a sharp, "What?" at them.

The crew grumbled out, "This is gonna take ages to clean up for fucks sake. Why are you such a psycho?"

I glared at them in silence, as they continued to shout at me.

"You gonna find that witness we saw running out of here, then and kill her? We don't leave any stone unturned on this mission. That's what Fat Tony said. Did you hear?"

Still glaring at them, I made a show of pretending to feel for my weapons and they backed off – averting their eyes. Stepping aside as I shrugged on my coat, pretending, I was on it, ready to chase the witness down – to hunt her. I was not going to do any of those things, but she was a witness to my murderous rage. I heaved out another loud sigh. *What a mess,* but I already knew I would not harm a hair on her head. It's not my style.

But that was not the only thing that went wrong that night. The next thing that happened was far, far worse.

Chapter Three - The Silence that I can't stand.

I had finished the job for Fat Tony. You'd do well to remember you always prioritise the demands of a real high-up boss, like Mr FT. I was somewhere in Knightsbridge, down in the car park with the rest of the gang, after everything was wrapped up, when I got a message on my pager, "Blue lights down your street, outside your house," a police snout tapped out, then the message blinked dead.

A cold shiver running down my spine had told me to get home, fast.

The gang shouted at me as my wheels screeched away,

"How we gonna get home," is all I heard them bemoaning, into the night – arms flinging in the air laying their petty trivia on me. The car spun wildly out of the private underground carpark and my fingernails dug deep into the steering-wheel, driving at high speed, to get home.

Arriving at the end of my road had been like watching an old horror movie in black and white. There were lots of different things happening at once so I pretended it was all happening to someone else, and I was observing – allowing me to stay numb. That was all I wanted, just to stay numb.

"Lord, please let Button be safe," is what I kept mouthing over and over again to myself. I had never spoken to Him before. I wondered if it would make a difference.

I stood silently in amongst the police cars. A despondency crept over me; my hand was thrumming on my thigh, tapping out my distress to myself in signals to my numb body.

The blue light flashed on and off, streaking across my face. I blinked in time with it. My ragged breath slowed down. There was a ringing sound in my ears. On the side of the road, was my scrawny, wretched mum mouthing something to the ambulance crew. I watched her, my vision slowing everything down, like I was looking in at a fishbowl of activity – removed. Removed from myself.

But I was alone, locked up in my own head – it was horrible.

The Elder – Lights of the Seven Kingdoms

The blue lights continued to blink on and off.

Blue, nothing. Blue, nothing. Blue, nothing.
My focus is on the nothing.
Standing blinking in despair.
Through wetted eyelashes
I see myself standing there.
Alone, the shadows of my life creeping into sight . . .

Suddenly, and without warning, the sound switched back on in my vulnerable head – everything was loud – too loud.

I was standing there, and my mum was screaming in a horrifying timelapse against the backdrop of the silently flashing blue lights of the emergency vehicles while spittle flew from her mouth. Lashing out - she was deranged, screaming, yelling out "*nooooooooooo*".

I stood frozen in stillness as she threw herself at a small body laid out on a stretcher. Poppy was walking around with her tail between her legs, confused and looking for Button. Silently, walking, lost and alone. I wanted to go to Poppy but my feet wouldn't move.

While all the time, my mum wailed and scratched at her own face. Large welts had formed from her forehead to her chin. She had raked her nails down both cheeks; taking off a layer of flesh, offering it in exchange for events to be reversed.

Small dots of blood slowly seeped through the cheap pastel green, over-boiled and rough textured, hospital blanket, which covered the lifeless small body. Faceless that body was to me, and I wouldn't acknowledge who it was underneath.

The glass at the front of the house was smashed in and there was police tape stretched around temporary poles across the gate. I remember hyper-fixating on the tape, it didn't look real, it looked too squeaky clean in the environment – one of death.

A small white shape was drawn on the ground in the front garden and there were the telltale signs of gunshots fired randomly. Some of the bullets were embedded in the big black plastic bin. The one I drag to the front of the house every Tuesday, leaving it on the curb side. On a Tuesday.

Tuesday, that is three days away, such a normal routine. It's amazing the intricate details that a brain in shock will take in. Anything and everything instead of what is happening on the inside.

The Elder - Lights of the Seven Kingdoms

The denial held sway over me. The ringing in my ears was telling me like an announcing siren in my head that I may not have done it myself. . .but I had killed. . .

. . . my baby sister. The words did not come out easily for me.

"Who was she to you?" a police officer had said, dipping his head to study me more closely, under the light of the streetlamp, on the pavement outside my house.

"My reason for everything" I had replied - unflinchingly true.

He looked away, embarrassed at my weakness and what it meant for me in a neighbourhood like this.

My mum had been admitted under a legal detainment order of the Mental Health Act. Compulsorily, she was conveyed to a psychiatric ward on that night. Whisked away from me, she was my only chance of support. She had spiralled with uncontrollable grief and rage. Her alcoholic brain was too addled to cope with the trauma - half eaten with abuse.

She was threatening to kill herself and others.

Come up to me, screaming in my face with her rancid nicotine-breath, that I had killed my sister - in front of the squad of police constables. Luckily for me, the police had dismissed her accusations as a mother who was "*highly strung given the circumstances*", but I knew what she had meant. I wholeheartedly agreed with her.

"Where were you tonight?" one of the younger constables had said, in a soft voice, but I could see the mistrust written across his face, the suspicion hard in his eyes.

My brain screamed "*alibi*".

Rubbing my nose, "At a friend's house," I mumbled.

He left, convinced, while the guilt ate me – ate me up alive.

Keeping one eye on the pastel green blanket on the stretcher, it was throwing silent accusations at me and seemed to move.

I stood as a sentinel outside of the house in the wake of the sirens. I was there when all the statutory services had departed, and I was still standing there when the sun had set the next day. I trembled through it all, but I remained standing on the pavement allowing the grey London rain to wash over me. It was punishing me for my inability to protect my sister. I had

never had faith, but that day I lost hope too, and any sense of God. The Divine wasn't real. It hadn't protected those who needed it most.
"People gotta live with death. It's an unpleasant fact of life," is what my crabby old neighbour had muttered to me when she had eventually come out of her house, took me by the hand with her yellow stained fingers and walked me back inside the house I had rented – breaking the line of the police tape.
"Don't take responsibility for others, if you can't handle the rejection when they are let down by you'se too, sweetheart," My neighbour said. Funny, I hadn't understood what she had meant at the time, I disregarded her words as mad ramblings. It was only years later that I truly understood what she was saying and came to a type of regrettable peace with those words; with myself even.
We walked through the house I didn't want to enter, paid for with the drug running money, which had killed my little sister. I couldn't stand it. There was no air in there – suffocating me with my shame. A cloud of poison blackness seeped into my lungs and choked me - choked me on my own guilt.
So, I grabbed my things and left, preferring to sleep rough in the park nearby then spend another moment in that prison-house. The bricks and mortar had promised safety, I had convinced myself that was all we needed to be safe, but that house had left me with death. *Life's final blow.*
I don't remember the days afterwards; I had switched off – gone blank. Walking through life behind staring eyes, I willed the tears to come, searching for any emotion. I wanted something to finally break within my body, so I could die, but life is cruel. It makes you relive the small important moments over and over again, thinking that you could have changed the outcome by being a little softer, or listening a little harder, or have taken a different road. But ultimately I know, the choices I had made were Button's undoing.

A couple of days had passed. Standing around for hours on end is a theme for organising the mundane things after a death. I had an appointment to arrange the burial. Standing outside the funeral parlour this time, I looked around the dark moonlit streets before entering. It was dusk but unusually dark, like time had sped up. *Odd.*

The Elder – Lights of the Seven Kingdoms

The funeral parlour was painted white on the outside. Fake orchids and patterned silk whorls were artistically placed at angles in the shop's front window – in simple decorative form. On closer inspection, the white paint was chipping and yellowing round the edges. The fake orchids and white silk folds were covered in a fine, almost indistinguishable layer of dust. My new skill is detail that distracts me from how I'm feeling inside. The condition of the place was making the overall effect of the funeral parlour, dirty and distasteful – uncared for.

My sister's body had been transported from the hospital morgue to the chapel of rest. I was here to pay the fees and agree on the date for the burial. I was late of course. I was twenty years old when it happened. In my line of work, working hours were somewhat unpredictable.

It's true I was late and maybe this was the reason I wasn't paying enough attention. There was something different about this night, but I couldn't put my finger on it. It was like being watched by a thousand eyes attached to salivating faces. My skin kept goose bumping like something cold and dead was crossing over it, but I was alone – no one around. The night was too black at the edges. I was on alert, but not paying enough attention to that feeling of being watched by something I would describe as 'other', not of this world.

On the approach to the funeral parlour, a slight creaking of a roof tile had made me peer up into the darkness of the open night sky. My eyes darted and squinted to get a better look at something. I could see a solid shadow moving strangely, over the roof - gliding against the wind. The moon peaked behind the figure- lighting the thing dimly.

"Hello, who is there?", I called out.

The figure bended down and I saw the outline of a shape that was human, but not at the same time. The outline was blurred, almost furry at the edges. Gulping, I leaned forward to get a better look, so very dense was the darkness. An inky blackness, like a wall, slid down and partially blocked my sight. On my face was an intense pressure like an invisible flat iron was pushing against my face. What I could see however, made me shudder. Two glowing eyes stared directly at me then blinked, accompanied by a rolling growl from the shadows, as the empty thing moved by. I stood frozen to the spot, and then the sound of a cat scrabbling up a fence nearby made me look elsewhere. When I turned back, the thing was gone -

disappeared. Misguidedly, I had linked the two occurrences: the cat and the shadow. I believed the riddle to be solved so I relaxed, the strange shadow already forgotten about.
I'd say now, that may have been my first mistake on that night.
I rang the doorbell, and a few minutes past and when no one came to answer the door, I started to case around the place and could see a faint glow of light coming from the weed-strewn backyard. They mustn't be able to hear the doorbell so I decided to let myself in and if anyone asked me, I would just say the door had been left unlocked. I picked the lock with ease, a knack I had developed when I was a little girl. Learning to pick locks with a hairpin and a piece of card, it gave me access to anywhere, such a sense of freedom this ability gave me. The clunk of the release mechanism inside the heavy door sounded and I closed it behind me with a clang. All was in pitch black darkness inside the funeral parlour. There was a strange smell, of mothballs and decay, hanging in the stale windowless air. The impression given of a place neglected over time, not cared for. *Maybe crooks run this place?*
A light was on at the back of the shop, gleaming out from under the doorframe. Silently, I crept forward drawn to the amber glow. It was like it was a beacon - calling me on. The strain of the last few days was heavy upon me, so, I made an unwise choice, not knowing it at the time; I continued to walk forward.
The Rainbow Cottage, where my sister's body was laid out in her final rest, was at the end of the hallway. That was when I heard someone speaking and the words made my skin crawl.
". . . we 'ave got the little girl and the ten adults to ship tonight. I don't know where the Twelfth has got to. I've bagged 'em up ready to go in the coffins, so it's just a case now of transporting the shipment through the portal. They gotta go tonight, you say?" A frustrated sounding, angry, middle-aged man could be heard saying these horrendous words behind the door of the strangely lit room. *They wanted to ship the bodies?*
I stood quietly on the other side, listening in with my ear pressed against the cool, hard wooden door, which didn't quite fit the frame - I noticed these tiny details. To keep me safe, you understand.
A chug and a churn could be heard from the other side of that door like a sizeable machine was starting up, then a strange tinkling, whooshing sound

of bells. *A gigantic vacuum of some sort, maybe?* I asked of the enveloping darkness surrounding me.

I kept getting this weird urge to look round behind me, like there was something inside the hallway watching me, but I shook it off – paranoia must be setting in, in this creepy place.

The conversation behind the door continued and took my focus away from the hallway.

"Yes, well, that will have to do I suppose. We usually have twelve by now, but the last one didn't turn up to her appointment for some reason. There is nothing to be done about it, eh what, Carter?", said a voice, terribly well-spoken and erudite, precise in its pronunciation. A stark contrast to the first speaker, who sounded like a burley street boxer, and I imagined he had cauliflower ears and broken front teeth.

"Bloody hell governor, what do you want? Me to go out with a crowbar and rustle up some more victims? They will have to feed on what is here, the eleven bodies and make do, My Lord."

The other man tutted with irritation, "Not *feeding* Carter, no one eats the bodies. The bodies are given to the immortals as part of The Offering. You know, part of The Clandestine Agreement between humans and Immortals to uphold our end of the deal. They are not chosen at random, these people have been carefully selected, so your crude crowbar method is no good here. *Bloody hell man*, how many times must I tell you all this," sniffed the terribly proper one.

Shaking my head a little, at the terrible words being spoken and pressing my ear closer to the door - a bit too hard maybe, my cartilage popped inwards. I clenched my tongue between my teeth and took a silent intake of breath.

Could I have been mistaken about what I had just heard? Who was feeding on the bodies? What's an Offering? Had they been planning to kill me?

With trembling hands, I pulled the machete blade out of its holder; underneath my coat then pursed my lips into a small circle to make sure my breathing couldn't be heard.

While I readied myself, the gruesome conversation behind the door continued, in what I assumed the mortuary to be. The intense cold was seeping through the door, my ear was frozen solid against it. The floor underneath was covered in a fine powder of glistening ice particles.

Were they planning on eating my sister? I looked back behind me towards the exit, shrugged and decided there and then, my sister would not be eaten, my sister would have a dignified burial, even if I had to kill everyone here tonight to do it. Resolve spread across my face.

What were they planning on doing with these bodies, some sort of sacrifice of some kind? That's what it had sounded like. With a suppressed yelp in my throat, I stepped backwards. Shoving the ugliest thought ever imagined from my mind away. Hand on my heart and my other hand wrapped around the handle of the large knife, I prepared myself to kick open the door and kick in the two men behind it.

A rage had settled over me, at long last, I shivered, fully embraced it, and an exhilaration set in. I smiled to myself, baring my teeth, psyching myself up, before all hell broke loose the other side of that door.

Chapter Four - Ice is cold, but vengeance is colder.

Taking a deep steadying breath and tracing an imaginary bullseye on the part of the door nearest to the lock, I take a running jump and kicked in the key chamber, - on target - knocking it completely out of its cradle.

The thick, door shuddered inwards, bouncing back on its hinges. My knife was drawn, held upwards and my eyes were black, heavy with rage, when I burst through. Flying through the air, landing on agile feet straight into the middle of the two conversing gentlemen *for want of a better word*, I got a better look at the situation inside the room.

The large coarsely spoken man had a rugby nose and broken front teeth – *I knew it.* He threw down the small coffin with a loud '*thud*', onto a conveyor belt contraption in the centre of the room. Then, started to make his way over towards me. The rollers that the belt moved along, were performing a piston-motion. The casket jerked up and down, rumbling along, tethered to a long, large rubber belt. The rollers were moving the small coffin and my sister's body, away from me and into something I had never seen before - I doubt many people had.

An effervescent vortex over ten feet in circumference was spinning around in the centre of the room. Yes, you heard me the first time. A large gaping, chasm of a hole-like-mouth was sucking everything into it in the room. *Bloody hell.* The sound of tinkling bells was coming from somewhere inside of the monstrous gateway.

Motionless and in shock, I stood with my blade hanging uselessly at my side, while my brain reeled – I felt demented. My eyes were staring and dry with a kind of fear that I had never experienced before either.

My wide eyes were fixed on the vortex, trying to deny the thing in front of me. My mind could not accept it, but I could not deny it either, as I was watching my own long dark ponytail, behaving in a most peculiar way. My

hair was being tugged away from my face and trying to escape into the black hole of an abyss in front of me, while I just stood there, flummoxed and mouth hanging open in confusion - the bottom had quite literally fallen out of my entire world.
The force of the damn thing was lifting me physically off my feet, at that moment in time and if I didn't do something fast, I was going to be sucked into the gateway – into the unknown. "*Ugh,*" I yelled.
I was on my tiptoes, barely able to hold on. Scrunching up my toes, I tried to anchor myself to this world and, somehow, managed to force the heels of my feet back down, onto the ice-covered solid ground of the mortuary. *What the hell is going on here? Why was there a vortex to another dimension in the middle of the funeral parlour?*
You must understand that was not my only problem at this point. Out of the periphery of my vision, I could see the large man with the broken teeth moving in slow motion towards me, also trying to break himself free of the force pulling him into the black hole.
With all his strength, he was slowly inching his way towards me, fighting against the pull. My eyes drifted downwards; he was busy shoving a knuckle duster onto his large hand. It was a good weapon of choice, practical and lethal - I couldn't help but to admire his choice.
Blowing out my cheeks, I let out a sigh that cleared my head of the rage that had built within me. My calming breath let me focus on my attacker and the situation I was presently in instead. Time to *Fight or die.*
I chose to fight. Straightaway, I pivoted around on one leg, grabbed hold of the doorframe, and used it like an anchor to jump up against the door with two feet. Clinging on with my fingers, I used the solid mass to project me full force into the man with the broken teeth. I flipped over, fists-first, barrelling into the large man's chest. As he skittled over, I drove my machete downwards stabbing him straight through the centre of his chest cavity with all the strength I could muster.
We both fell to the ground with me on top of him. Blood splattered up into my face, cascading off my forehead in long rivulets into my angry, staring eyes, and with a vicious sneer on my lips, I cast my gaze over to the second man in the room. Well, the only living man in the room now, that is.

A peaky paleness consumed the posh man's pallor – I love rhymes and forming them in my head.

The dead man had referred to him as Lord. *Lord of what I wondered.*

His waxed moustache twitched upon his upper lip. On closer inspection, he did not look like he belonged in this time-period. He had on an immaculate Harris tweed suit. His eye monocle glinted, balanced in his socket, connected to an extravagantly wrought and decorated, thick gold chain.

The man stood in high brown riding boots, a set of breeches wrapped into them with neat matching socks and a well-fitted jacket. The ensemble appeared handmade. He looked like he should have a pipe and a hunting hat a la Sherlock Holmes to complete the look.

"Tally Ho," I wanted to shout, to ridicule him some, but he had the kind of face that could heap scorn upon me until my skin blistered, without moving so much as a hair of his well-defined eyebrows.

He stood there tall and slim. In the Victorian era he would have been described as dashing. A crocodile smile plastered across his well-arranged face. His eyes darted away from me and looked into the black hole.

He held out his hand, flourished his fingers, conjuring a long thin brass rod the size of a rolled-up newspaper. It was quite literally out of nowhere. I thought that it could've been my imagination, but then I watched him, he seemed to grip it tightly, like the object had a secret purpose. In his hand, the rod sprang into the shape of a javelin – as long as he was tall - and without further hesitation, he said, "Offered you are the Twelfth." and threw the javelin at my head.

I closed my eyes as it was on course to collide with me in the killing sense. I felt a pinprick on my forehead then a clanging sound directly behind me, as the metal object hit the back wall and I opened my eyes.

A deep-rooted fear shot across his snobbish face. "What in the blazes . . .did you just use magic, by Jove?" His chin shot up and he was staring at something above my head.

". . . What?" I replied, scrunching up my face in confusion. I peered upwards, and you wouldn't believe it, but the bloody, glowing balls of light were back. "What the hell?" I screamed at the balls as they hovered above my face. "What the *fucking* hell . . ." I shouted this time, with more feeling, accusing the lights of making me feel crazy.

His eyes were wide, deranged, staring at the balls that had appeared out of nowhere. He didn't seem to want to ask any more questions or wait for an answer. Looking in the direction of the growing vortex, he gave a concise and well-practised two-footed hop and slipped inside, whipping from view within seconds – he had disappeared. He yelled something to me over the loud rushing sound as he jumped inside the black hole.

Sacre-bleu Is all I could think.

In the eerie silence left by his departure, my mind started to calm and try to work out what his exact words had been before he flung himself full force, through the vortex. Upon reflection, I thought I had heard him shout,

"You silly little scruffy urchin. You don't realise what you have done to Earth." However, that didn't make a great deal of sense, so I shrugged it off; given the circumstances.

Putting my foot on the dead man's chest, I tugged my blade free.

Springing upright, I allowed myself to get sucked along under the force of the vortex, feet scraping across the floor, until I was close enough to grab hold of the coffin. Grabbing at the handles to stop me from falling into the black hole. I try to lift the heavy oblong box off the conveyor belt – feverishly, I grabbed at the handlebars pulling it with all my might. But the bloody black hole had hold of the coffin too, sucking it in towards oblivion. Placing my knife in between my teeth, the nerves in my incisures reacted intensely against the cold steel. I wrapped my legs around the pulley machine to anchor me to the room. Over half of the pine box had already gone through the vortex by now. It was disintegrating into tiny dust particles. I couldn't stop it from being sucked further inside. I was trying with everything I had left to pull the coffin back into the room.

"She is not being eaten. You can't have her. You can't have my sister. She is mine. Do you understand me?", I screamed out into the void - demented and small - playing a terrible game of tug-of-war with the universe's smaller version of a black hole.

The muscles on my arms twitched violently at the strain. My teeth were aching under the pressure of being clenched tightly over the ice-cold metal. My hair flew about wildly, whipping about my face, but still, I would not yield. I held on, not giving an inch. My eyes fixed firmly ahead; fixed on the insanity before me – the Vortex was winning; slowly consuming all.

Most of the time, the universe has a plan for its inhabitants, and it did not like one bit that I was resisting my fate as much as I was.

I did not know it at the time that I had a fate. We all do. Destiny is strange like that.

A huge metal urn came tumbling off a shelf behind me, pulled through the air by the suction of the great swirling gateway. Lumping me with a metallic *'twang'* on the back of my thick skull, it knocked me forward, completely unconscious.

When I managed to finally flick my eyes open, I couldn't keep them up, they wanted to be sealed shut and in denial. I was just about able to take in the details of the grainy wood of the casket at close range. I fixated on the tender lifelines of the raw tree trunk that had been used to make the coffin, while the room spun around me, getting darker.

Sprawled out in a heap, hands and legs hanging over the sides, I laid on top of my dead's sister's coffin - defeated. My last words to the world were of grateful release.

"I'm coming, Button. I'm coming. I'll be with you soon . . .that's all I've ever wanted . . ."

The eyes of 'Aurora the human' completely shut and opened no more on Earth.

All the while, my body and the coffin were slowly being dragged into the blackness of the vortex, straight into the cosmic beginning of the abyss. A fancy way of saying I was out of luck.

At this point, and rather ominously, ten more bodies, encased in heavy-duty plastic zip bags, glided over my head rustling at the bottom as they clumsily, bumped into and skimmed over my hair. All twelve of us, the bodies, me, and my dead sister, were pulled into the mystical portal before us and where we would eventually end up was anyone's guess.

Chapter Five - of myths and legends we daren't speak.

This place was strange. The moon was not alone in the sky. It was accompanied by another moon and a large array of planetary systems – all cringingly, far too close to the planet's surface for comfort. There were stars so big and dazzling, the dark blue light from them was as powerful as the Earth's sun. It was like nothing I had seen before. They radiated like blue beacons in the dark sky. Black star dust fell in great clumps, and speckled over everything it touched. . .

Everything was coated in this perpetual darkness, but those strange beacons managed to pierce it. The outline of the landscape illuminated with a blue bioluminescence; it gave out an odd glow.

One of the moons, the furthest away of the two, had a circling meteorite storm around it, but it was a moon, nonetheless. Faintly, I could hear the cosmos above crackling with a terrifying power. It was emitting an energy that could be drawn on – like a power source drawn on by immortals. The inhabitants of this planet.

I wasn't aware of any of this at that time, it just looked alien and terrifying to me. I lifted my hands up to the sky and the dazzling power clung to my fingertips. It zipped between my fingers. Coldness was all I felt. A faint blue glow lit my upturned face. I gasped out in terror.

At first, I didn't realise that we were no longer on Earth. The red comets and green shooting stars streaking through the night sky, just above my head, were a dead giveaway but hey, I didn't do school that much after the age of twelve years old. Anyway, I'm leaping ahead of myself, let me take you a step back . . .

I awoke with a start. Slumped forward on top of my sister's coffin, my face was affixed to the wood with dried patches of my drool.

What a beautiful way to describe the beginning.

The Elder – Lights of the Seven Kingdoms

My limbs were cold and stiff. I felt discombobulated, as my old Uncle Jack used to say. It was the only word he knew with more than four syllables. Gave him a sense of "class" he'd say.

Drenched in a fine layer of moisture from the chilly air, it was as if frozen lips smothered me with cold kisses and bite at my flesh. My ears pricked up at the howling of a chill wind. A black glistening stardust fell on my goose bumped flesh – covered it. Disquietingly alien. Snow was falling too. The air was filled with the white from the snow and glittering black from the stardust.

My head was swimming in the blinding glow of the too-bright twin moons, it was disorientating. I could smell natural pine trees. Real, living pine trees over a hundred feet tall, densely spread-out and growing in the ground. Not like the ones sold cheaply in the alley ways of London to celebrate the Christmas season or the Pine Fresh car fresheners bouncing on my windscreen back home. No, these smelt like a forest – deep and beautiful, and abundant.

On a lonely hilltop, we had landed. The '*We*' in this instance was me, my dead sister and the ten other dead bodies wrapped in thick plastic body bags. Just in case you were wondering.

Deep in the valley below, I could see millions of pointed steeples of furry pine trees growing tall, luxurious, and thick, with their cones nestled deep into their branches. Snow was settling on the ground and over the tall trees. Further up the hill, rose a vast mountain range and more pine trees, which were larger, taller than the ones below.

My senses were taking in every new sight, smell, and sound. An abundance of small forest mammals chattered away and birds sung harmoniously from every direction. I could hear the cacophony, the rising of their voices, and it lightened my heart - a little.

Sounds such as these were preciously rare in London, so much so, that I stood still just listening to the chirping. I had forgotten the beauty of nature's chorus. Blinking back tears, I sat up to survey my environment start finding the risks.

Button would have loved this.

My eyes were unsettled, swivelling from new sight to sight, drinking in the wide expansive space of the forest. Breathtaking. It had an alpine quality.

"Hello", I shouted, my echo bounced back to me *hello, hello, hello,* like my voice was filling a vast chasm and singing to the great, open wilderness, and far beyond.

I didn't fully appreciate the forests beauty at the time. In my grief I only had eyes for the desolate pains of its emptiness – the lack of other voices. I found myself alone. Or so I thought.

I wish . . .oh, not to worry. I think you can guess what I had wished I could have seen, but she was dead. On the floor, in the coffin.

I shook my head and brushed my hand over the back of my hair to take hold of my long-plaited ponytail, this simple gesture offered me a little bit of small comfort. My hand struggled to reach the end of my ponytail - it hung just below my waist. I was thinking to myself I must get it cut here, where I didn't know. *Where even is here?* I continued grasping my hair a little harder, because the strands reassured me, allowing my fingers to send messages back to my brain, confirming that I was *actually* really standing here. I felt terribly small. Lost.

Right, first things first - orientation.

The last thing I remembered was the inside of the funeral parlour with a throbbing vortex swallowing me whole and now. . . well, now, here I am, transported deep in the wilderness with the coffin of my dead sister strewn on the path and ten body bags covering the forest floor.

Gruesome thoughts clouded my brain. My skin started crawling, and it's like a living nightmare was unfolding itself before my raw, dry eyes. The wind and the snow, mixed with black stardust, kept on gusting, trying to push me over. My eyes darted this way and that. I noticed a prickling sensation, a strange spiral of fear circling me – building with an alarming tension. I felt eyes on me and I shuddered. *Something is watching me from with the forest.*

That is precisely when a howl unfurled itself across the shadows in the valley below. The sound made me jump out of my skin, but then stand still, waiting, listening for what would come next.

I had no time to waste. Leaping up, I staggered forward on my legs grown weak by pins and needles. Collapsing back down, making a split-second decision to crawl on all-fours. I searched around in the darkness of the night, for my blade. Fingers wriggling like tentacles, searching through the freezing snow, "Shit," I stuttered out, "where the hell is it?"

In the distance, I could hear the wolves answering one another. Each howl came closer than the previous one.

I stopped, chills running up and down my arms. Snow falling thick and fast. There is something about the howl of a wolf that taps into a primal fear in the survival part of the mind. The brain is quick to assume that at the end of the drawn-out howl and the beginning of seeing the glowing eyes of the wolf, you will be running for your life, before the pack – chased down like a wretched thing. I shivered in the realisation the pack is on the move and I am the hunted.

"Where's my bloody coat?" *where's my bloody armour, I was really asking.*

The moons cast ghostly beams of light down on the path. I spotted a faint glow of metal on the ground underneath one of those wretched plastic body bags. It was the hilt of my blade glinting in the distance up ahead. Unsteadily, I stood up, pushing my knees off the floor and slowly, I make my way towards the plastic-covered, rigid human form. The snow getting even thicker.

The thick plastic bag obscured the outline of the dead man underneath, but I knew he was there. I was knee deep in death.

Snow was drifting down, feathery, and full. Over one foot deep now, I had to kick my way through it.

Gulping down quick-rising frothy bile, I shivered and bent down trying not look in the direction of the outline of the dead body, covered in plastic. Grasping blindly for the hilt of my blade, I kept my face turned the other way. My fingers were numb from rooting around in the shocking snow. It covered the floor and covered the bodies, but I still knew they were there.

What were they going to do with the bodies?

Shockingly, a thick tuberous leech-like creature, the size of a rat, latched on to my hand and immediately started guzzling. Ripping it off my skin and yowling out in pain, I flung it on the path and stamped it into nothing – my legs are now working at last. Reaching down with more urgency to find my knife now, I'm getting the impression the environment was hostile and I need to be able to protect myself.

Slowly, I pulled the machete from underneath the dead weight - in the literal sense. *Hey, I still have my humour, right?*

A rock catches at the blade and the metal made a slick, drawn out '*chinging*' sound bringing comfort to my ears as I pulled it and gripped it with my hand.

Peering through the blackness under the thickly set trees, I could see shadows moving. Grey and tawny brown fur coats with amber eyes hanging in the air, the beasts were trotting forward – circling round me.

Let them come. I lifted my chin stubbornly.

As the wolf pack got nearer, I could see them all better. The size of those amber eyes were larger, and they stood taller than any wolves that I had ever seen. Each wolf was the size of a great grizzly bear.

One of them stepped a huge paw out of the treeline. It was bigger than the others. The wolf's coat was thickly set in a ridge at its back and its snout was crinkled back, teeth fully bared. It's incisures were the same size as my hand.

We stared at each other; the wolf and me. The leader was growling aggressively as he stridently, walked out towards me leading the pack in an arrow formation behind him. They were gaining ground.

I started stumbling back. The snow and ice were slippery, catching at my core making me wobble and lose balance. Looking around me to assess the landscape, I took on the environment from the wolf's point of view. If I were a hungry wolf in the cold, I'd see the ground was strewn with fresh meat - an all you can eat buffet for a predator. I had to move.

Light on my feet, I started pulling the body bags to a centre point around my sister's coffin. The animals could have the dead bodies first, but not my sister. Then I stood up tall on top of the wooden box – legs naturally organised into a power stance – a show of dominance to hide how scared I am. My hand was extended out with my machete tightly in my sweaty palm. The blade tip wobbled in my fearful hand, but still, I held it there, standing alone, bouncing on the balls of my feet to warm them up and holding my trembling frame in my thighs. Defiant.

"I'm ready when you are, *ya' filthy animals!*"

Damn, that felt good, I always wanted to say that line. Fist pumping the air in the drama of it all, I was giddy with adrenaline… or psychosis? One of the two.

I was ready to go out in a blaze of glory, protecting the memory of the only thing that ever mattered to me - my sister.

I clenched my teeth and emitted a low, guttural growl to show them they should expect a fight to the death. This was a warning to my encroaching foe.

Gangland warfare strategy and psychology, even against animals, is still effective. Beast and human alike, all the same really. Nothing but tribal animals the lot of us. The sooner you realise this, the easier life is to work out.

The wolves were all crouching low, casing the environment with their eyes locked on me. Padding forwards, they growled and snapped their huge jaws. Two of the leader's shaggy-haired foot soldiers, walked out before the giant beast - separating as they both slinked past him, twitching their enormous tails.

The two wolf foot soldiers were both flanking me. Saliva, dripping venom from their canine fangs, it hissed as it hit the snow. The smell of wet dog was overwhelming. I knew it was not long now for me and these two were to be the killing tools, sealing my fate. I hoped for a quick death. I welcomed it in a way. I made a show of moving my machete backwards and forwards between my outstretched hands, but I already knew I am no match for the wolfpack.

With an eerie synchronisation, the wolves all lifted their giant heads and stopped dead in their tracks. Sniffing at the oncoming wind, the wolves started to whine like new cubs and club their paws to their great snouts. My nerves were standing on end. I was straining with my veins popping. I cried out for them to fight and let me expend the energy building within me, but there they stood, ignoring me, staring into the strange black-blue light behind me.

The wolf-pack leader leapt forward and started pacing, sideways on to me. Up and down. Up and down and growling - head bent low.

Then it occurred to me with a dizzying shock like an electric current to my brain that the wolf was watching something *behind me.* His fearful eyes were fixed upon it, but there was a challenge in them – a challenge to fight, to determine who would get me as their prize.

I've been hunted before, you see. I know the look.

I daren't turn round, lest the beasts before me, jump at me – but look, I absolutely must when the chance arises. Gradually, I could feel the hairs prickle at the back of my neck.

Something solid was rising behind me – unfolding itself. A cold whispering gust of a breath announced the thing. A foul smell lingered in the air. A creeping sensation slithering down my spine. My skin twitched and shivered like someone had pushed in my funny bone, but no one had touched me. . .*had not touched me, yet.* I corrected myself.

I shook my head, raising my blade to eye level and pointing it at the wolves in front of me, still viciously baring my teeth in a threatening show. I kept an eye on the wolves before me but then shifting my attention to my periphery.

That's when I saw a monster out of the corner of my eye. It hadn't quite solidified just yet. The shadows began merging, striving to take hideous, solid form. To the side of me, it grouped, furling itself into an odd human shape. Red eyes glowing in its head, the sound coming off the thing was like a million wriggling maggots, slithering, latching, crawling over one another and putrefying flesh.

My legs buckled under me at the gruesome sound, but I lurched onto my haunches, forcing myself to stay upright.

"Hell no, what the fuck is this new madness?" I screamed out into the land of walking fables, walking in the snow and star dust before me. My thick, grotesquely comical London accent more pronounced in the strangeness of this land.

Not exactly appropriate language to use, I know, while I am on an unexplored alien world. Teaching the aliens swear words and street slang, to communicate, am I? Usually, they send the well-educated members of polite society to explore new planets.

In that instant I imagined the first aliens greeting the Prime Minister and Cabinet members, shouting "Wotcha, alright?" I giggled to myself, a strange, wild sound inside that moment of imminent death. All these thoughts came simultaneously, rushing to my mind. My brain tried desperately to grasp at reality and was not winning because I was spiralling and fast. Was I going mad like my dear old mum? I think I may have hit my head a little bit harder than I had first thought. . . or the air is thinner here. Why am I debating this now?

Run, run, run, run, run, run, run, run, run, run, run, run, run!

Mad inner debate shoved aside; my survival instincts kicked in finally. Adrenaline had suppressed my fear. Concussion be damned!

The Elder - Lights of the Seven Kingdoms

I jumped forward, landing heavily on the ground with a dull thud. My right ankle cracked under the weight of my ambition to flee. I refused to acknowledge the pain, but my teeth did, clenching so hard together to the point of fracturing in my mouth.

The wolf took a swipe at me with his huge claws but missed. I flinched back just in time.

In that fumbled moment, while I tried to regain my balance, I risked a quick glance behind. Instantly, regretting that I had. Gasping out in horror, I saw the full image of the monster. It was hideous.

Darting sideways and then folding back on myself out into the open, I ran steering well clear of the monster at my back and the bear-like wolves to my front. I made a last-minute mad dash for the tree line further up the mountain and further into the deep, cement-like snow. My tendons were painfully cracking as I ran full-pelt up the hill. My footsteps were crunching in the dense snow, leaving tracks in my wake: a little map for them to find me with.

My gut felt wrenched open, with painful awareness, I was leaving behind the body of my sister, she would be alone with the monsters of fables below.

I was looking left, then right and back again, searching with eyes shaking with a dizzying fear. Taking in my surroundings, the newness of the landscape was pictured in my mind in lurid technicolour like a 1970s film. I was watching with the sound turned off and my vision made everything look alarming; primary colours throwing dominance over the lesser hues. Fear was taking hold.

My head searched for an escape route, my body found none, but my eyes kept feverishly searching for one regardless.

Hope is an ardent friend.

I needed to find a tree with low branches. There were so many but I could not even contemplate stopping to climb one. It was too risky when the monster was clinging to my footsteps just behind me - hunting me down.

Running flat out up a hill, pain was searing in the backs of my legs. My lungs were at bursting point. I risked a quick glance behind me. The tall shadow creature was following me at a lumbering pace but somehow still gaining ground. It was floating, feet dragging along the ground. Do the laws of gravity not apply here?

The wolves were howling and shrieking, no doubt feasting on the flesh of the fallen – my sister. I imagined it in my mind, and I turned cold. I cried out a wretched sob that clung to the back of my throat. There was no quick retort or smart-arse comment to make. Just the sombre knowledge that I was being hunted to the death, while my sister's body was mauled and eaten below.

"*Button,*" I choked out and urgently covered my mouth with my hand to stop anymore outbursts.

The thing is, I knew my punishment would find me eventually for the kind of life I had lived, and I was resigned to it, but it would come on my terms. I decided the quickest way out of this mess was to climb a tree and throw myself off into the blessed Last Sleep on my own terms.

"On my own terms," I shrieked into the bitter night air and my echo rebounded back to me with a shrillness that reminded me how deranged I sounded.

Scanning the desolate horizon before me in my desperation, I noticed a slightly smaller tree some way off in the distance. The lower hanging branches and the abundance of fallen pinecones at the foot of the trunk created a sort of wobbly step. Deciding, to try, if I jump high enough, I just might make it.

Zigzagging through the trees to get to the smaller one, the bristles stab and grab at my bare arms. My feet kicked up a thick layer of pine needles, which carpeted over the snow in this part of the forest.

The trees were densely packed here, giant, and unyielding to outsiders, the steeples reached up for miles, stabbing the sky and I am the size of a squirrel, compared to these great tall giants, scurrying around on the forest floor. They smelt fresh, and strangely calming but I was too panicked at this point, for the scent to have much of an effect.

The trees own these lands with their silent guardianship, that much I could tell.

Maybe it wouldn't see me. Maybe the monster would not be able to track me through this dense wood and the snow. I paused and then scoffed. *Fool.* I have never lied to myself or pretended to be self-compassionate, and there I was mocking myself at the supposed end of my life. *Typical just bloody typical.*

I ran at the tree, that just might shield me, with the momentum of a freight train. Pinecone step not as sturdy as I had hoped. Quickly, I sure-foot it up the trunk and make a running grab for the lowest branch to catch it. Hoisting myself up, through my honed muscles, I chaotically flung myself from one branch to the next, making my way through the lower branches. They stabbed and grabbed at me lecherously. Scraping my skin raw.

Nearing the middle of the tree, I changed tactics. Using my body, I created a makeshift vertical tunnel through the closed, brush-like branches.

For a moment or two, I rested my head against the bark, catching my breath, until I realised, there was sap dripping down my cheek, covering one side of my face. I started climbing further on, pushing my head and body up along the bark of the trunk, through the thick brushes of pine needles, debris was sticking and collecting on my face.

My body wasn't fairing much better with each push upwards I took, I was grazing the top layer of skin off my belly, but I had no choice, I continued to slide upwards against the rough and lethal bark. I didn't feel a thing mind you. I was numb and dizzy from shock. My head was ringing like spiralling tinnitus, my terror was making the environment spiral around me making the landscape strobe in my fear. I couldn't adjust my vision; it flicked on and off, like my brain just couldn't take in what was happening to me.

Carrying on and climbing further up, I managed to get forty feet above the ground clinging to the pine tree. Slick sweat was dripping off me but still I climbed until I was shaking wretchedly with weariness. The huge spasms of adrenaline had left my body ragged. I began to lose focus and energy fast. I started slowing down, I lost my grip on a smooth branch and dropped. My body was tumbling, freefalling, downwards through the air. Stomach acid burning the back of my throat as my chest dips lower than my legs.

I hit a thick branch at full force, my head smacking down painfully with a '*crunch*'. I had landed, resting precariously, on a thick branch, the width of my body, but I was balancing at a haphazard angle.

I hadn't noticed my stomach was impaled on a protruding, jagged piece of branch, not straight away anyway. The pain came on slowly, that was when I noticed I could feel the branch piercing my intestines and the tip scratching at the inside of my spine. Crying out, I snapped open my eyes and surveyed my surroundings. What I saw filled me with an ice-cold dread - the creature was coming.

It was standing at the base of the tree, directly below and it was assessing the situation. It seemed …pleased.

Silently floating upwards, it had its face turned upwards to me. Its red eyes were fixed on me, boring into my own. There was nothing I could do.

It was coming. It couldn't be stopped. It was coming.

I tried to pull myself up, but I was impaled on the sharp splints of a tree. A sickening pain ripped through my stomach. The branch was holding me in place, like it wanted the monster to have me.

I laid in stillness on the branch, desperate not to move.

A terrible exhaustion had set in and my breath was laboured. I accepted it, the realisation settled over me that I could not execute my plan and make my own choice to end it … so I succumbed.

Consciously making a choice to be still to the last, I hoped my death would be a gentle undoing, not like the life I had lived.

Listening to the yelping of the wolf-pack some way off in the distance, I waited for the dark shadow creature to come flying towards me and devour me whole. I watched, frozen with shock – numb but incredibly peaceful.

The gentle undoing of life always is.

My blood was drip, drip, dripping from my broken body onto a branch directly below. I watched it with a curious intensity. My blood was dark, and I noticed it was congealing at the edges - a survival reaction. Even though it was outside of my body, my blood was still trying to save my life.

I smiled, weakly, as I rested my head on the tree.

"Thank you," I simply said. I was grateful in my death throes to that plasma. It was the only part of me that had ever shown me any love.

My breath was slowing down now - ebbing away. My body slowly settled.

The shadow creature, tall and spindly, with eyes that are searching out and craving my flesh, landed on a branch next to me so lightly as if it were made of air. I heard a slurping sound as it extended its fangs, readying itself to eat me.

A cold, lecherous finger prodded at the blood seeping out of my temple. Shifting its weight forward, I saw it greedily lick its hands of my blood. Its red eyes grew wild and brighter like my taste was a particular delicacy to it.

The creature leaned forward greedily, holding my inconvenient head to the side before it clamped down on the artery of my neck and began draining me. It inflicted a searing pain as it transferred something and the blackness took me for its own.

Chapter Six - When the twilight comes for me.

In the blackness of my coming death, I could just make out a sound. There was a whooshing, then a loud bang, like a million fireworks exploding into the sky above me. I was floating, bodiless in the stillness of time - peaceful. Alongside the elemental gases and the star makers, I was nestled into the beauty of the universe, watching myself being consumed by the terrible creature of darkness below. The creature had stopped feeding on my broken body and was now staring up into the sky.

It could see the exploding lights too – the monster. The brilliant lights were reflected in its cold black eyes. A shadow of uncertainty turned into fear on the creature's upturned face. A pounding of footfalls drumming out below. The creature lifted its monstrous head to watch something moving fast down in the forest underneath the trees.

An unusually tall, athletic man came running through the trees, nimble and quick, streaking through the forest like a prancing deer. He was a blur to my eyes as he ran, I could just about make out he had jet-black, tightly cropped hair, as he came bounding along. Coming nearer, I could see he was dressed from head to toe in a dark military uniform of sorts, an armoured bodysuit. He was terrifyingly strong and bounded up the tree like a wild bear, straight up, to confront the creature. His taut frame drew out a sword with runes etched along the blade and he swung it upwards in an attack formation. He muttered something and the sword burst into brilliant golden flames.

The creature emitted a high-pitched shriek, that made my ears quiver painfully. Exposing the webbing at the sides of its foul mouth, giving it the ability to disjoint and extend its jaw like that of a giant snake – some sort of evolutionary advantage to devour larger prey. It roared out a warning across the frozen treetops, my dried blood flaking at the corners of its mouth. It jumped off the branch and flew at the man with its crooked talons outstretched before it. Lethal and ready to kill.

The man pivoted out of the way and quickly threw a light in the air that combusted with the brightness of a thousand stars. The creature recoiled back, unable to withstand the quick flashes of light. I could see the creature properly now, the thing had pearly white skin, which made its eyes stand out, redder round the edges and opal black inside. The man swiped with his sword still aflame, missing its body by a hair's width. The creature, valuing its own skin over that of its prey, lurched out of the way and tumbled to the ground, when it landed it looked back up at my broken body hungrily – leaving its meal half-eaten and not through choice clearly had upset it.

A second man, tall – seven foot or so, stepped out from under the trees. He was only slightly smaller than the first, with long blonde hair, plaited in strange patterns at the front. He was holding a mighty silver axe; clenched between his strong, broad hands. Swinging and slicing at the creature, he took aim and threw it with a practised ease, at the monster's torso. They were both oddly dressed, these two males. I wouldn't describe them as human – they were too tall, too perfect to be one of us. Their DNA screamed out '*other*' or '*alien*' to my eyes.

A loud crack sounded below. The creature had created a dense cocoon of smoke and swaddled itself within, like a chrysalis; a death moth, it shrouded itself in a cloak of cloud. As the smoke cleared, the creature was no longer visible and had vanished into thin air. The axe had passed straight through the smoke and landed heavy, with a dull thud, on the snowy ground.

The threat was over, or was it? *Is it ever?*

That was when the first man with cropped hair, swung up through the trees and steadily dropped onto the branch I was impaled on. My body muffled out a cry as my intestines were wrenched forward, with the motion of his landing. He strode along the branch on quick feet and crouched low beside me. His chiselled chin was now above the back of my head and we were both at an awkward angle.

His stubble grazed the tip of my nose. I felt a tugging sensation. I felt myself floating between two places: above and rejoining my body – *an astral projection of some kind?*

He was leaning over me fully now; I could smell him. The sweet smell of honeysuckle circled my nostrils. It brought on a dizziness I couldn't quite explain. *A sense of Déjà vu? I'd had a lot of these recently.*

"Oh no, oh no", the stranger exclaimed, in a deep melodic voice. His eyes glowed like an animal in the darkness, but I could see they were filled with a type of sadness, a deep concern. The two glowing disks for eyes reminded me of the wolves – more animal than human - blinking down at me in the dark. I wanted to reel back, away from him, but my body wouldn't allow me to. Not while I was affixed to the spot by the terrible, jagged branch. Working quickly on nimble fingers, he managed to release the branch from my abdomen - like he had used magic of some kind. I saw flashing lights, with each swell of pain that hit me. He helped me to turn over onto my back and my blood pumped, spilt out from the open tear; my guts exposed - steam curled up into the freezing night air.

I felt the stranger hesitate, holding his breath in for a long while before he reluctantly pressed a large hand down on the open wound – he stared at my blood, as it dripped onto the tree branch and slowly froze.

A pause before he spoke, the sounds chaotically pulled together like he was practising speaking English, "You have lost a lot of - blood. I am sorry. We arrived too late."

The stranger dipped his head to get a proper look at me in the light beams coming from the stars in the heavens above and I could see him more clearly now. He had beautiful large green eyes and a ridiculously handsome face. I studied the details; tiny freckles across his perfect nose, the fullness of his lips, and his prominent cheekbones, then I let out a gasp.

"Pointy ears, like a beautiful elf," I heard myself say, quite certain I was delirious and hallucinating. Anything I said wouldn't be heard anyway. I thought he was an apparition of some kind, a pretend-being. That it was all a dream.

He whispered, "No, not an elf, but I am . . .one of the immortals."

"Oh, I see," I didn't see at all, but I am just being polite at this point.

"You are a *hu-man*?", he questioned and I nodded.

I felt myself slowly slipping away. The golden light I always imagined to be my soul in my belly was fading. I knew I was dying, it's this that made me want to reach out for connection for the first time in my miserable life.

I looked at him, this stranger before me, but I'm not really talking to him, I'm talking to the unfairness of the universe when I say,

"It's okay. I am ready. You win, Life. You win. I am defeated. Now, let me depart in peace," I croaked out, with a resigned whimper and a defiant

laugh, trying to shout these words to the looming sky. But then I shifted my gaze to the stranger, peering directly into his eyes and added, like the warm person I could've been if circumstances had been different for me,
"Thank you, thank you whoever you are. I didn't want those red eyes to be the last thing I ever saw in this life. Even though I deserve it for killing my sister. I am glad that I got to see your open and loving green eyes . . .I didn't quite reach the age of thirty, but still . . .," I was rambling.
The stranger reeled back in shock,
"You didn't kill your sister. You mustn't really believe that. She was Offered."
His eyes illuminated, nodding his head like I was supposed to understand what this meant. He took my tiny hands in his huge ones. Scrunching up his forehead lost in deep thought, his large green eyes were distant in the strange blue light of the night sky above.
I am going to die in this strange alien land.
The wolves were no longer howling. The Trees were waiting, even the rustling of the wind through the green leaves was quiet and listening. All was in silence apart from the snow. It glided down like feathers and gently settled with a *plop* on my face – then evaporated like it hadn't existed at all, mixing with the saline of my hot tears.
My heart was slowing down. The last beats of it came on in erratic spurts. You know those people who are all romantic and tell you that you see your life flash before your eyes before you die? *What* a load of codswallop. I just urgently wanted to go to the toilet. *Typical.*
But I wasn't here alone, I took a moment to see the grief etched into the strangers beautiful, open face. The sad look told me all I needed to know about him, he was a caring soul. He didn't want to witness my end; it was upsetting him.
"It's ok, you can go now. I am at peace, I am done . . ."
We wait and let the air swell, to breath between us, this stranger and me.
When suddenly, at my last, strange green and gold flecks of light start flying from my body. I was dying, so I didn't care that much about the display, in all honesty, but these lights were insistent. They pulsated between me and the stranger like brightly burning butterflies fluttering past our faces. He watched them with a keenness that I couldn't describe. As the embers

floated past his face, he read them as if they held a coded message that only he could see. His eyes grew wide.
"The last light of the Elder," he gasped.
I didn't understand. It was gibberish to me.
Not speaking another word, he leaned forward. His eyes darkened. A flash and sharp fangs slid down out of his perfect mouth. The realisation hit me - he was a monster too. I was going to be eaten anyway. The stranger leaned forward a bit further getting too close and staring at my neck - ready to bite down.
"Please no, please no, don't bite me, don't eat me. I don't want to die in pain, in violence. Let me go peacefully. I beg, you take me after I die."
I was closing my eyes; shaking my head; and screaming out hysterically. Lifting my arms, I struggled to push him away causing my blood to pump out of me faster.
He looked at me like a craven thing, blinking back his predator-like eyes.
"No, you are right, I cannot bite a celestial being, even one in *hu-man* form. I dare not bite an Elder. It won't work, only an Elder can change an Elder if the legends are true, but if you drink my blood, now, that just might work to change you. To save you."
He regained control of himself, closing his eyes to concentrate, not speaking another word, and then slashed his blade along his own wrist. Pulling back my head, he dropped some thick, freezing cold liquid into the back of my throat from his wound. His blood was smoking like nitrogen. Spluttering, I gagged. Convulsions constrict the back of my throat and I spit out the liquid, gasping for air.
Tense was his face as he gripped my nose once more, "You must drink my blood it is the only chance to save you.", and the thick substance was once again dropped into my mouth. This time my throat opened up. Taking it in, the freezing liquid burned. Burned. BURNED. My skin was crawling, and I was on fire. A white-hot fire danced within me – a battle between ice and flame.
I am The Damned.
"Rhyiathe, tell me right now why is she screaming like that? What have you done?" The other man yelled at him from where he was stood on the floor of the forest, "I command you to tell me now, what have you done? She is an *Offering*." There was a kind of hysteria in the other's voice. I sensed

something, a nervousness, that Rhyiathe had given something that could not be taken back so easily. Immortality. My skin prickled with the unknown.
I was no longer split, hovering above myself in the trees, with the bright lights above me. I was being funnelled forward with a fullness of energy, rejoining my broken body below. When I re-entered that place, the belly of my body, I was aflame. A burning, wildfire illuminated the dismal light that I once was, and I was Reborn.
Writhing in pain, my fangs slid down out of my mouth cutting the sides of my chin. My new predator eyes blinked in the light – my vision enhanced. It was terrible, flickering chaotically and forged out of Darkness and Light.

Chapter Seven - Awakening

I woke up horizontally, laid on a soft four poster bed made of cloud and slumber. That is how it felt to me, anyway. There was movement in the far corner of the room along with a rustling sound that let me know not to open my eyes. The memory of the forest and being impaled in a tree swam into my mind's eye. *Remember* my mind whispered.

My fingers slowly crept towards my stomach, waiting to find the wounds but all I felt was my soft, supple skin stretched over my sunken belly. My fingers tried to find any reminisce of a wound, be it scarred skin or open sores. There was nothing.

Rhyiathe, the name rang in my ears. *"What have you done?"* The question was left unanswered by the tall blonde-haired man in the forest. What have you done indeed?

I flexed both my feet to test the muscles in my legs, preparing them should I find the opportunity to run – to escape. My legs were weak but moved under my control, nonetheless. Thank goodness.

"I will leave you now my lady and come back with some food and drink, maybe find you some fruit too," a female voice called out from across the room in my direction. I listened but scrunched up my eyes and didn't dare to say a word, as her feet pattered out a gentle rhythm over a soft ground. A door is opened and then it is closed, tightly shut. I waited anxiously to hear any sound of it being locked – of me being locked in. None came. The sounds from the hallway were slowly growing fainter, the person is moving away - gone.

There was a pure white, blinding light in this room. I felt the brightness of it flickering across my closed lids. It shimmered like a dancing warmth of sunlight across my face. A window was open somewhere in the room, I found myself in. The sun was out and gently coaxing me up.

The Elder - Lights of the Seven Kingdoms

Before I fully opened my eyes or consider rising, my fingers urgently explored my body to see if I was clothed. A light linen fabric of some kind covered me.

I opened my eyes and darted my head all the way around the apartment I found myself in, then closed them back up and laid back down to assess the situation, what had I seen?

My host or jailer rather, had a penchant for white, that's for sure. *Now let me see.* There were white natural stone walls, and white wisps of long linens hanging over the floor-to-ceiling windows. One of the windows led to a balcony, where the doors had been left open. Outside, I caught a glimpse of a mountain range and to the side of this building, a rockface covered in greenery. There was an ocean in the distance. Everything was very bright and very warm like the Mediterranean but there were two suns. *Two Suns*! Two suns in the sky and a large red planet clung in the background, so extremely near to here. Wherever here is. What the hell?

Don't panic. Don't panic. What did I see in the apartment? Keep to the apartment for now, don't let your mind wander.

I took a deep steadying breath. Okay, here goes.

No, two or three more breaths should do it. My heart was racing against my chest, so hard that my pulse was drumming in the back of my throat, pushing at my windpipe. Hey, hang on, that's not just one loud heart racing, there are two pulses I can feel in my chest. I gaze down at my chest feeling faint. Two hearts?

Don't panic, don't panic.

I started again.

The room was mostly made up of windows and they were all exceptionally large. There was a cleanness, a cared for tendering that I struggled to describe. Each detail of the room was lovingly thought out. Huge paintings with extravagant and ornamental gilded frames were hanging on the walls. On the floor were intricate and immeasurably large rugs, laid to cushion the feet in clouds of luxury. There were four fireplaces and sizeable chandeliers dripping from the ridiculously lofty ceilings. One of the fireplaces nearest to me had a fire aglow and some fireplace pokers. Metal and hard equals lethal to my wanton eyes – looking for weapons. If I can't find my knife, then they would have to do.

This place felt wholesome, and I couldn't spot any details of concern or terror. '*Yet*' my mind adds. *You haven't found any yet.* Okay, good point I answer my own brain as I have done since I was a small child.

I slowly lifted and pinched my legs into action. The crisp cotton sheets slide with a whooshing sound over my legs, onto the bed, and the thick silk eiderdown-topper fell to the floor, rigidly, folding into its own heaviness.

I stretched out a leg, placed my foot on the plush rug and wriggled my toes, noting, with disgust, that my feet had been pampered and my toes painted. Whoever chose this colour picked a vile one. It was a nude colour, prissy and stupid. It would have been a cold day in hell before I allowed someone to put this kind of shade on me. I would have chosen red or black for myself. I looked at my hands, yes those too. "*What has my jailer done to me?*" However, I must admit that it did suit the creaminess of the colour of my skin. "Ugh."

Moving my fingers to my hair, the last remnants of my slicked down ponytail was gone. Instead, my hair was washed, brushed, full and luscious. It was as soft as silk. I had been well taken care of while I was asleep, unconscious, or drugged. I didn't know which one yet. Maybe I was being prepared for a sacrifice?

"She is an offering" screamed a demented voice in memory form.

It served as a reminder to stay on my guard.

I stood up, but I was weak, I was thin too. Feeling my ribs, bony, and the gauntness of my angular cheeks, I wondered how long I was out for and what this place was. I gulped. *Where is this place?* The vortex spirals in my mind.

The two suns swam into view on the horizon.

"What the hell. . .," I stood open mouthed.

Hyperventilating now, the room spun wretchedly. My eyes cannot focus, and the blackness swallowed me whole.

"My lady, my lady, please wake up!" I opened my eyes and stretched out my arm gingerly. I was in a crumpled heap on the floor, my legs were under me, bent at an awkward angle. I investigated the woman's face. I took a glimpse; my brain organised some details. Her eyes were turquoise and held in them, a look of concern. Hair like silken honey, she had feline-shaped eyes and ears that were defined and pointed – like my rescuer's but only smaller, I gulped, they were elf-ears and make no mistake about that.

"Let me help you back onto the bed. I have brought you some fresh water and some soup and sauteed vegetables to rebuild your strength. The bread is freshly baked here at the castle."

She towered over me with unnaturally long limbs and she was shapely too. She lifted me up with incredible ease. I was terrified and begun grasping at my chest, my hearts pounded painfully again. Are they all super strong here, wherever here is?

I did not speak or look her directly in the eyes. She lifted me up and perched me on the bed. Scrambling to get under the covers like a naughty child, I hid myself away.

Unfazed by my cowering away, she placed a breakfast tray, with solid wooden legs, over my lap. The wood was lovingly carved, polished and refined. But I didn't take much notice of the craftmanship, I saw it as a weapon, my fingers latched onto the sturdy legs, holding them firmly in case I needed to fling it at her. All of this took place quietly, in secret, without her seeing.

I smelt the food and my stomach ached with emptiness. The chicken soup was a little red, it had a fine shine on the surface. I could smell it was a homemade wholesome soup, accompanied by a dish of buttery sauteed vegetables on a porcelain side plate, and lightly toasted bread, and an orange dip next to the silverware – it smelt like a marmalade dessert. To the side was a stiff, fine napkin and porcelain condiment holders. All were well presented and arranged with care.

Ravenous, my stomach growled, but I would not move to eat until she left. She leaned forward, and I fretfully lurched backwards and cowered down some more. Looking upset, she made a point of unfolding the napkin slowly and placing it on the side and tried to remain casual when she said, "Would you feel more comfortable if I left?"

A discernible nod from me and her shoulders slumped forward. With a sniff, she was gone. Only the sun motes in the air moved slightly to indicate that she was even there at all.

I was shaking, as I watched the door. I picked up the soup bowl on trembling fingers and drank the soup down in a few mouthfuls directly from the lip. Liquid dribbled down the sides of my mouth in my haste to get food in me. I needed the energy. Grabbing at the buttery vegetables with my hands, I shoved them all in my mouth in one go, the butter dripping down my chin. Turning my attention to the bread, I tore at it brutally barely taking in the intricate designs plaited into the sourdough crust. This kind of care and attention to detail is absolutely wasted on the starving.

Gulping it down, skipping over the tastebud experience and storing the food in my cheeks until I could shovel it into my food pipe, I was done with the tray.

I threw the pretty wooden tray over the other side of the bed and got up. It had inexplicably smashed into the wall, even though I had hardly touched it and I was left staring down at the tiny pieces of splintered wood. *Strange.* No time to waste musing.

"Prioritise looking for my knife", I urgently whispered to myself, while I sprinted around the room looking for a weapon of some kind. I needed to be doing anything other than sitting down waiting to be a victim.

Curling my fingers reassuringly around the hard metal of the poker, lifted from next to the fireplace, I held it out in front of me giving it a swing it to test it out, then twirled it in my hand, expertly. This would do until I found my machete.

I am darting around the place with more energy now that I had some warm food inside me.

A warm gush of air made me look through the floor to ceiling glazing. Outside, I could hear people talking in the crowded spaces, below the balcony. Drifting over to the window, seductive sunbeams dance across the floor and the swirling little shifts of the curtains looked inviting. The poker drops to the floor with a loud clang, but I barely notice it.

The golden haze drew me in. It was tantalising to me – obsession dropped over my eyes.

Drawing aside the rich fabric curtains, they glide, bunching up on the rail, I stepped out onto the large balcony. The sound of voices instantly rushed upwards into my ears. The sun kissed each part of my skin. My thin white cotton nightgown was lit with a glow. The warm winds swayed the light fabric softly around my legs. I closed my eyes; the suns beating down and seducing me, lolling me into a calm state, like a murmuring lover in my ear. With the warmth touching my cheeks and the inside of my upper arms like

it needed to caress every part of me, urgently loving me, I hugged myself and touched the tender parts of the inside of my elbows. I was hypnotised by the elements of this unfamiliar environment and yielded to the scenery. A deep contentment fell over me like I was under a spell of some kind. The sea-drenched salty air promised cleansing and renewal.
The scent of the green of the forests surrounding me; stretched out to me with an offering of peace.
The mountains in the distance were my anchor - unshakable, majestic, and reminded me of my strength, whenever I would need it.
The wind swirled around me, lifting me a little lightly off my feet.
"This place, what is it? It restores me," I murmured companionably to the wind, to the sun, to the greatness of the universe above me.
A large, colourful parrot flourished its wings nearby on the breeze and then swung around to circle back and around me, landing with a gentle hop on the balcony wall. It tilted its head at me and yelled in its little cracked imitation of a voice. "Pretty, pretty," it said with its large grey pebble-like tongue on display.
For the first time in my life, a smile of innocence broke across my mouth, I had no control over this simple joy, that I felt. I stepped forward, giggling and held my fingers to cover my abashed happiness. I looked up at the vast walls of the building I am in and am astonished to realise I am standing on one of a great many balconies of a colossal castle, multiple levels rearing up out of the blue sky. A real, fairytale castle, with golden turrets and sturdy battlements and immense, towering statues built into the moulded walls, and terrifying gargoyles and fluttering banners, with regal symbols of power and strength. The outer walls gleamed and stood proud, under the glow of the Suns. I am swept away into my imagination, of tales long ago, told to me at school about heroes, myths, and legends. *Am I dreaming?*
Birds of all kinds hovered on warm gusts of wind near to my eyeline, the gulls squawked at me, which served to shake me out of my reverie at the time.
Remembering I had a visitor and approaching the colourful parrot on my balcony, I reached out a hand to touch its vibrant red feathers and it let out a *squawk,* flapping its wings in warning and flew away.

Leaning over the stone wall, I glimpsed down into the bustling square below. The city centre was miles below me, far away. A green stream ran through it – a tiny line to my eyes.

"Impossible -," I said in a hushed tone full of awe and wonder, "- how can I hear their conversations so clearly?" Then my heartbeats stopped in my chest and all I could see was his face upturned towards me – so vividly, he looked back at me. It was the man from the forest, who shared his blood with me.

Watching me, with a curiosity like he was reading my soul, my secrets were all laid bare to him. My eyes prickled with tears for some unknown reason. There were crowds around him. It was a festival of some kind in full swing. Tall elves and other beings were smiling and laughing, dancing, and cavorting, but everything was blotted out, everything was in darkness and he was drenched in a spotlight of gold from the suns and my attention was caught only by him. I could not look away.

The brilliance of his shine left all else in different shades of the same darkness, like shadows moving around him, glorifying the vibrance of his beauty. His green eyes were luminous and fixed on me. I could not breathe. In his eyes, there was an intensity, unfathomable.

He was devouring me, drinking me all in. We were locked together by a golden thread, sharing the same air and I could not breathe. I could not.

The hairs were standing up on my arms and my goose-bumped flesh shuddered. All over I felt him. A strong waft of honeysuckle floated up towards me and my memory stirred of a time long ago. I blinked, not fully understanding.

I was abandoned. My whole self was exposed, naked and my armour was gone. I was adrift in the sea and don't know how to act or where to hold on to for safety from the intensity of that stare. There was no raft that can hold me, but him.

"A spell, he has placed a spell on me and that's why I can't control myself." My hands were grasping at my forehead. I fumbled with my foot to take a step backwards and bolted for the safety of the room. Panting, I was trembling, trying to gasp oxygen into my crushed lungs.

"What was in that cold liquid that he gave me?" I fumbled out in distress.

I slumped down on a cushioned chair next to the balcony doors and held my fingers to my temple to regain myself to some semblance of control.

There was a click of a door opening.

"My lady, I have come to collect the tray. Did you - enjoy it?" She was politely pretending not to notice my angst-ridden state, or the tray smashed to smithereens by the bed. Instead, her eyes dropped to my butter-smeared, glistening chin and the droplets of solidified butter hardening on my chest.

"Hmm? It was okay," I murmured. My eyes not lifting to meet hers. My stomach was churning and I felt sick.

"Would you like some more?"

"No, no . . . I...", I fumbled, serving staff were a bit of a mystery to me so I sat, reclined holding my stomach, in awkward silence waiting for her to guide me, my eyes turned away.

"Are you sure you are, okay? You look a little peaky." She walked past me out onto the balcony and looked down. She smiled as she spotted something, waved, and then returned to the room.

I nodded and blinked at the strangeness of the exchange.

When will she tell me what I am doing here?

"Oh, you have a visitor coming soon. My Lord Tennison. The Elf King's son and heir. He is the Crown Prince, Heir Apparent to two thrones of the kingdoms. The Amber Throne of Pericullious under the one-hundred-year stewardship and the other, the High Seat of the Elf Home world of Tylerine. Do you know why he has requested to see you? It is most unusual." Her eyes gleaming, her expression deeply serious.

I shook my head, my forehead scrunched up in confusion.

She looked me up and down.

"Never mind then, we better get you dressed into something else. Something more suitable. You can see straight through that nightdress. Definitely, do *not* go out on the balcony. A sunny day like this will not save your modesty, my lady," she said with a smile, knowing full well I had been outside already. The colouring of my cheeks said so.

"What would you like to wear? A silk dress or something lighter in this heat. Perhaps a charming cotton one? We have some lovely colours of red that will accentuate your beautiful raven hair."

"Erm, do you have anything a bit more *practical,* like a bodysuit?" I ventured, quite interested in an attire that would be practical for my escape. She raised her eyebrows into her hairline, and I couldn't help but like her.

"What is your name?" I blurted out, I did not mean for it to sound like a command. My voice becomes sturdier when I am worried and anxious, it's a defence mechanism since I was a child.

"Lliandria, but you can call me Lilly. All my friends do." she smiled warmly; a look passed over her open face. A hint of expectation and something else, that I couldn't quite fathom.

"Lilly," I let the sound roll around in my mouth like it was familiar to me somehow, "Lilly, please may I have a bodysuit." I had noticed those strange males in the forest and the people in the city below, wore them "I feel. . . I would like to wear something more. . . suitable is all."

She nodded, again a look of expectation spreads across her face.

"I know exactly what you describe. *The* suit. I will find it for you. It will need adjusting to make it smaller now that you are a . . .," There was a pregnant pause, and then she whisked out of the room without so much as a backward glance. With the door closed, I waited. It was not locked once again. My freedom I still had, but I didn't know enough yet just to make a run for it.

Why did she use such a strange term, as 'I will find it for you'. . . I watched the door with an apprehension that I could not explain.

Walking over to the balcony doors, I slowly closed them on the bright rosiness of the Two Suns of this strange alien world. The noise of the crowds below ceased abruptly once the edges click shut together. I stood not knowing what to do. My nerves were jangling in my veins. I was lost, I was nothing, I was a ghost without my sister, Button.

Chapter Eight – The Armour that covers me.

I took a great deal of care pulling the curtains over to make doubly sure, the Immortal Worlds were locked out – not a glimpse would be let in. After fumbling to push deep folds of material into every corner of the window, covering every crack, a darkness consumed the room. I rest my back against the balcony doors. Relief flooded through each inch of my body, as a pain, a burning sensation gripped hold of me, coming on in shredding waves.

I screamed and yelled, accepting the pain – it was my punishment. It was what I deserved, and I was glad it had arrived finally – this pain was mine to bear alone. Writhing in agony, I found it was comforting because at least I could feel something other than the numbness that had attached itself to me since Button had died. I would finally allow myself to fall apart in the hope that the gusts of time would blow my old self away, bringing me back together, anew - stronger. Better able to cope with the hand that life had dealt me.

With this perspective holding like a vice to my fragile mind, it was at this moment I allowed myself to slide into the pit of my despair – to finally give in.

My legs became heavy. I drifted down to sit on the sturdy, but most definitely steadying, hardness of the floor – crawling into a child's pose. My back crushed up against the solidness of the wall. I was hugged in on myself in a little tight ball - I began to cry. I had been strong and disciplined, so ridiculously hard all my life. I just couldn't carry on in this life of brutality without the reason why I do the things I do anymore.

Wading through life, holding my nose against the putrid cesspit of humanity, and precariously leaping from one jagged rock face of trouble, to the next – to hold everything in, '*to show my grit*'- was pointless without her. My everything. my excuse for all the terrible things I had done.

That was where Lilly found me, on the floor, in a catatonic state with my eyes staring forward and my pupils barely there – just little pinpricks of blankness. I was temporarily gone. Disconnected from myself and my

reality – from my burning pain. Her face was full of empathy and compassion, images flashed before my eyes but my vision was blurred. I saw nothing, just faces. Everything was at a distance – distorted, like watching the pixelated snow on a TV screen that was not working.
"It's okay, it's okay, it is your grief but also, the toll on your body of changing into a vampire. I'm sorry, it's the last phase and the most painful part. It's the physical changes to your DNA, let's get you to bed and I'll get a potion to ease your suffering, for the pain and the bloodlust, while your body heals itself," Lilly said, with a tender softness.
Lilly silently lifted me in her strong arms without saying another word, she gently carried me to the bed. As she placed me with such tenderness under the covers, I could tell she was trying to tell me that Lord Tennison was on his way and she would need to leave to send an urgent message, advising him we would rearrange due to a sudden bout of sickness. The door clicked shut and I remembered nothing else.

I slept. I slept forever. The endless days passed by in a loop and a type of monastic silence; only cut open with my shrieking due to the pain of turning into a monster – being ripped apart. I had hours to stare inward, I endlessly searched within myself for something to cling on to. I had to find my reason for continuing to want to live.
Lilly was there – always. She did not leave my side for very long, during that time, if at all, but I don't remember those days clearly enough to tell you this part of my story. I remember snippets and pictures that came vividly to my mind in the middle of the night, some months later, but I have no memory of those days, which is the scariest thing about it all.
Lilly served as my carer for those long days and nights of oblivion; I would not have had the will to survive if it weren't for her. I owed my life to her in truth, to an elf that I hardly knew. She would bring in on rotations food and potions, to ease the fire burning in my veins. Glasses of clean, clear water and fresh flowers, and other things in tow, just to try to cheer me up.
I could hear the echoes of her busyness all around me, clearly at times, on the good days and on those other occasions, muffled like I was submerged under water, gasping to swim for the shore of my own skin. She was always doing something for me, like taking out plates of half-eaten food or sitting

in the corner of my room, reading one of her favourite stories of heroism, and of courage; to remind me I wasn't such a hopeless case. The book would fall from her hands, when she fell asleep upright in the chair; covered in a shawl made from the soft wool from an animal from her world, that I had never heard of. On the seldom nights she did venture back to her bed chamber, on those odd occasions, she would return at daybreak to fluff up my pillows or stoke the fire back into life. All the things that I seemed incapable of doing – for myself. I didn't think I was worthy of any self-care at all. I allowed my sister to die, that was the song on repeat in my haunted head. Hammering me down into nothing.
My cocoon hardened around me, all ugly, all cobwebs and bones and made from the dust of my skin falling off me. I laid there day after day, staring, starving, searching for my light. There was nothing there for me. The suns and moons took their turns to cross the colossal sky, and I sat, staring out of the window – all the while, a darkness grew inside me.
But then one day, a day like any other, when I awoke something in me had changed. . . I noticed a glimmer of hope, a growing steadiness. I peered inside my emptiness, and for the first time in my life, there was something there for me to find. Just for me, only for me. Not because I needed to be or do something for someone else, but just for me.
A candle was held up against the darkness of my soul. It glimmered and a small, tiny flame, twitched into being. It was at risk of going out, on a knife edge at all times, but I had found it. I found that tiny flame of purpose deep within me . . . and that's always the first step. It's so strange how something so small can be the very centre of the beginning of everything – a catalyst.
One bright morning, Lilly was reading from a book and I was gazing at the Suns's pink glow as it was cresting over the fluffy clouds of the sky above, and she said to me.
"What would make it right for *you*? What would make *you* feel better?" she closed her book patiently waiting for an answer.
I had already found an answer but didn't know how to voice it until that moment. "To take back the body of my dead sister to Earth, so she is with me, so I can bury her, so she can finally find peace, and then I will complete a promise to myself that I made a very long time ago when I was a little girl."

My face still upturned to the sky, I shared the oath that I had cursed myself with as a little girl, but this time the Suns of the Seven Kingdoms wouldn't allow it. The brightest of Sunshine beamed down upon my face, so bright that I could not open my eyes against its warmth through fear of being blinded.

Lilly watched the impressive rays light up my face and gave me a solemn look, a curiosity in her bright elven, feline-shaped eyes.

"Your sister's body is part of the Offering, and you need to see the Rite, it is beautiful. She will be part of something greater. It might give you more than the closure that you seek, more than what you ask for – but my Lady Aurora, you don't think that there is something else. . . more out there for you? Something more that you may need to do. Perhaps, to help more people like your sister be free of misery, from the desperation of oppression?"

She watched me carefully, eyes wide with a secret knowledge, like a great big tawny owl.

I sat up, suddenly and a little straighter. My eyes were focussed for the first time in days, that I had lost count of. They were still swollen and slitted from crying, bruised in places, but her words had ignited something with me, helped me to find a purpose to see me through, to give me back my strength.

"Either way, I have found something to focus on. You say that the Rite involves my sister's body, and you know when this is going to happen and where she is? Where are the clothes I asked for please? And may I have a little food?"

Lilly smiled at me; a joy spread across her kind face. She was getting ready to answer my questions, but I squeezed my eyebrows together before impatiently asking another question, the one that had bothered me for a while, "My sister's body, it's been a few weeks, will it have decomposed?" I feared the response but still I had to ask.

"No, the bodies of the Offered are preserved and you will see why-." She looked at me to see if this brought any comfort and then continued "- and, yes, the Rite will take place soon. I do not know when it will be or where it will be held, but this is a start. A good start. You look better than what you have in days. The clothes you asked for are waiting for you in your dressing room, my lady."

Immediately, I moved to get up. I placed a weak foot on the floor and stood up, wobbling at first like a toddler, but eventually, with a little persistence becoming more stable. I was concentrating really hard on my footsteps and I refused to acknowledge that I had undergone some physical changes too, in my deep hibernation. My eyes could see more clearly than ever before and when I run the tip of my tongue across my teeth, I felt the sharp edges of fangs that nipped at my flesh and made my tongue bleed, but for now I just silently walked on, pretending everything is fine.

I walked out of that room and into the dressing room to find my armour, so I could face down these worlds.

Chapter Nine - The Twelfth

Standing before my reflection, I was looking at a warrior poured into a tan coloured, bodysuit of military design, oddly similar to my tan leather trench coat back home. I was still exhausted, my muscles felt weak, but I was finding my old strength hadn't left me so easily – it had stuck to me even when I abandoned myself.

The bodysuit fitted perfectly to my body. Every line was a perfect, exact match. It hugged every part of my anatomy like it was custom-made for me, yet it was not new and was somewhat battered-looking and worn out in places from being worn.

The material looked like leather but it was not, it was made of scales, but I was more taken by the fit. I wanted to ask Lilly where it had come from, who did it belong to before, but I dared not utter these words. They filled me with an inexplicable dread – too close for comfort. Lilly would not look at me, just kept her hands held before her in a clasp. We continued to pretend, co-conspiratorially, that there was no strangeness about this dressing occasion. My fingers glided to touch the material. There were lots of sly pockets to conceal weapons within. I knew where each one was with a practised accuracy. My fingers moved intuitively, through the motions of placing an array of daggers, and swords and throwing death-stars into places, that I could not have possibly known were there.

When Lilly had brought in the bodysuit, she also presented a pouch of weapons fashioned from the same material as the suit. She watched me intently as I dressed and placed my weapons in the right holders within seconds. It was like being in a trance, my mind recalling from a place of familiarity something that my memory was too terrified to reveal to me just yet.

"Lilly?"

She looked away, determined not to talk about this, "I will get your brush. I'll be back soon.". Then she exited the room.

I stood tall, upright and I gazed at the woman I was in the mirror. I looked like a celestial warrior of old. It sounded arrogant to say such a thing, about oneself, so I denied it, but I could see it still the same.

Lilly came back in. "I will do your hair the way you like it, and then help you on with your boots," she said with a smile that made her eyes bright, "I want to see you in all your battle regalia."

She set to work, brushing, and plaiting my hair into patterns at the front and pulling it up into a high ponytail at the back.

"It's exactly as I wanted it. erm, . . . Thank you," I said.

She nodded knowingly then turned to leave.

"Lord Tennison will be here in a few moments," she gazed at my reflection for a long while then shook herself a little before leaving.

I stood alone before the mirror. My outline and hair were strangely familiar to me in these odd, exotic clothes. I brushed my hands down the creamy, rich material of my bodysuit. Standing taut and poised, I bit down on my bottom lip hard, trying to reel in the chaos of my mind through the pain of this action.

"Good afternoon. Aurora, is it?"

Looking up into the mirror, I see the tall blonde-haired man who fought the monster in the pine tree forest. He was standing behind me taller than I remembered. I had to stretch my neck to see him fully.

A small nod I gave. I would observe and mirror his gestures and talk in the way that Lilly and Lord Tennison do. To fit into any environment is my skill - The Chameleon. All my life.

"How do you find your quarters? To your liking, I hope. You have one of the best views in the castle. May I tempt you into the living room and out of the confines of your dressing room for some sweet tea and baked treats?" He looked out of the window over the splendour of his city and then flourished his hand at the door of the room.

Staring at him, I gave another small nod,

"You first," is all I said. I'd rather have him in full sight. There was something about him – I felt it.

He slowly bowed, his bright golden long hair slipped forward, while a gleam danced in the depths of his brilliant blue eyes and a smile played lazily across his full, red, sensuous lips.

"But of course my lady", he turned his broad muscular back on me, and I watched as his tall, impressive frame ducked under a doorframe and disappeared into the next room. The sheer size of these beings was staggering.

Turning back to the mirror, I addressed the street soldier in me and silently mouthed, "Be careful, go lightly. He is wicked. It is there in his eyes." Then, I left the comfortable, soft furnishings of my dressing room and entered the game with a solid step forward in my high, polished, heavy boots.

Lord Tennison was wearing a royal sash pinned with a gold and diamond broach to a custom-made shirt. He had his strong legs stretched out before him, seated in a grand high-backed, dining chair and had pulled out its twin for me to sit opposite - gently nodding to me to take my place. His blonde hair shined with golden haze in the light coming in from the tall windows. He was sat, glistening from the rays of the early morning suns. There was a six-seater table made of dark wood between us. I slide in and tuck myself neatly under the smooth surface. Flicking my eyes up, I noticed he had undone the top two diamond buttons of his frilly shirt, exposing smooth skin underneath.

My gaze flicked up to his face. He smiled back, parting his generous lips and his eyes roamed over me with a curious interest.

The Courtiers he had with him stepped forward, a busyness of servitude unfolded in the room while Lord Tennison kept his gaze averted from his own butlers. Lord Tennison's men were practised at remaining unseen – flinching back whenever he made a movement. They placed miniature pastries on dainty side plates and poured steaming tea from a large silver teapot, adorned with silver and gold leaves that looked realistic, apart from the metal they were wrought from and they were a little *too* perfect to be real. Lord Tennison was busy snatching glances at me throughout the tea ritual, his bright blue eyes had changed to a foreboding artic-blue and they were piercing and probing, trying to silently solicit mine for information, but I knew I had to resist, not to utter a word. Allowing him to begin to feel uncomfortable and pressured to fill the silence, then, eventually give some small details away.

I watched him with great care, hawkishly from under my eyelashes, tipping my pinkie finger out delicately while I took a sip of freshly brewed tea. The

black dried leaves spun and twirled at the surface of the cup. I let them settle and then stirred them up again.
"You may leave us now," Lord Tennison commands the courtiers. The courtiers bow to the prince and then, to me and shuffle out of the room, closing the ornamental doors as they leave, without meeting my eyes.
We are alone and the silence stretches out between us, pinching me like needles pressing on my face.
After several minutes, Lord Tennison lost his composure and red dots formed on his high cheeks, while I quietly slurped my tea, swilling it over my tongue. He glared at my pinkie finger – its daintiness offended him somehow.
Very seriously he studied me now. All his painted-on smiles had slipped from his handsome face. He cracked first, it was inevitable.
"You look well rested, but I fear you need filling out after your ordeal. Eat, eat," he said, throwing up his hand, with a rehearsed playful laugh. It was a politician's cold, practised keen stare looking back at me.
I took a delicate bite of the delicious pastry. It flaked and dots of the pastry spun down lightly, towards the table. It was not a question, so I waited patiently, strumming my fingers on the table. Drumming out morse code for, "get on with it, I am no fool," to myself.
"Are your wounds healed? But of course, they are, with superior elvish potions and spells in you." I fluttered my eyelashes and nodded in response politely.
He looked irritated. A male as beautiful as him is not used to doing all the work and it irritates him, that much I can see.
"The monster was a wild vampire, quite feral and untamed, no longer able to turn back into its humanoid form. They roam these lands unchecked, mongrels, all of them. The werewolves too." He stamped a foot on the floor; the sound stunted the quiet of the room.
My mind reeled with the shock of these inconceivable words, telling me fairytales are real, but I forced myself to remain quite calm. I was solid with composure when I asked,
"Vampires? And those other creatures in the woods were . . . were they werewolves then?"
He shook his head, saying,

"Those were just wolves. *Hu-man*, have you forgotten your lessons? All wolves are werewolves who have become too wild to change back. The feral vampire too, it's what becomes of those who end up too wild and . . . primal," The Prince said these last words and his gaze fell to my lips, resting there for too long. It made my cheeks warm.

I replied, "Oh, they were excessively big. What lands do you speak of my Lord Tennison?"

He gazed at me and waited a while, lingering on my face with one eye squinted suspiciously. I just smiled back, looking vacant at him. Minutes passed by and I continued to smile sweetly in that tense silence. The trick is in gang warfare to make the exchange a little uncomfortable but allow them to wrongly assess that you are not a fret, even better if you get them to think they are smarter than you and won't understand a word they say - that's when they usually impart their secrets. That's when you have them.

I folded my hands in my lap, prim and proper – a delicate flower, waiting patiently to be plucked.

"Well, I shouldn't be telling you this, but I suppose it won't do any *harm*," he smiled broadly and patted me on the hand like I was a lap dog.

"You are on Pericullious, one of the worlds that are part of the Seven Kingdoms. All of them, governed by Immortals, except for Earth. Tribes of elves, vampires, werewolves, Goddesses, witches, celestials, you know, people with magical abilities and that sort of thing. My father, the King, well, he governs this kingdom and the Elf home world of Tylerine, but it is not always an easy alliance between the tribes. They don't accept their places. Elves, well, we are the only ones fit to rule," he averted his eyes for a second or two, an angry expression passed over his sharp features and then he composed himself before he continued,

". . .humans are forbidden here so we are just trying to figure out how you got through the barrier . . . *alive*. Do you know? Are you able to tell me?"

There it was - what he had really come here to ask me. He was straining now to listen to my response. His body was just a little bit too far forward to give a convincing impression of feigned uninterest.

I pursed my lips and was careful to mirror his body language with a practised ease, then let out,

"Wow, incredible. Magical beings are real? The stories are real. And I have wandered uninvited into a dream, so what will you do with me, my lord?

He gazed at my profile, assessing me again, "Well, we are working that out now. We cannot very well let you leave, but my father extends you an invitation as his guest. So, you are free to go anywhere, but well, you will be escorted by Lilly for your own *protection*. Humans are thought of as little more than vermin here. You will not be safe going about alone." He looked at me rather grandly, like I am less than him. His words were intended to land a blow. He patted me on my hand again. A reassuring gesture perhaps? *No, he thinks I'm a simpleton.*

Anger rose in me, "Vermin are not a threat. Why would I be in danger if humans are not considered a threat?"

"Well, there's the Clandestine Agreement that was agreed between Immortals and Humans, centuries ago. Immortals agreed to take their magical abilities and live alongside each other in this realm and humans remain with their science and strange customs on Earth. You should not be here, you, see? That was part of the Agreement. We don't cross over into each other's territories. It is considered an act of war. Your leaders have been contacted." He pursed his lips.

"Forgive me, but I have a question. Vermin don't usually have the wits to negotiate a peace treaty. That is what I assume this Clandestine Agreement, really is?, -" he hesitated and gulped down a glug of sweet tea - he looked like he had burnt the inside of his mouth in the process, eyes agog or my question was a little too near the mark. "- which would imply that Immortals and humans were once at war. I wonder who was winning. I have my suspicions considering you referred to humans as vermin. Spite is loaded on the Victors by those that have lost after the battle is over, would you not say? What has the Offering got to do with all of this?", I said, talking as if I already knew the answer.

He jumped up out of his seat, legs stood firmly apart.

"*Well,* really. I came here to see how you were doing and responding to The Change inflicted on you by Rhyiathe . . . I'm not here to discuss politics and bandy crooked words with a *female hu-man,*" Lord Tennison spoke with a haughty, spitefulness and ended with a sniff, "do not mention the Clandestine Agreement. It is forbidden. You have only just got away with saying those words because I am with you. Do you understand, *female hu-man?*" He glared down at me.

I was not frightened of the prince, but my breathing wasn't as easy as it perhaps could have been and there was the sensation of bugs crawling underneath my skin when he ventured too close or touched me, so it was brave of me to have said,

"My lord prince, I did not mean to offend you. I have a naturally curious mind. One of the bodies taken for the Rite is my dead sister. I followed her here, but I did not realise where '*here*' was at the time. I wonder if Lilly could take me to see her, to say goodbye?"

He stood up a little taller, straightening his cape, appeased by me acknowledging him by his proper title and offering him an explanation. "So, you say, you do not have any magical secrets, do you? A way of getting through the vortex undetected perhaps," He broods on this before adding "and if I grant you this request, to say your final goodbyes to your dead sister, then you will leave it and accept the Ritual of the Offering, if we agree to do this thing for you?" the gleam in his eye, an expression came over his fine features like he was weighing up the advantages of my request – he looked perplexed.

I stirred. What he asked of me I could not promise. I didn't know anything yet. I didn't know if there had been some sort of foul play. I sensed something was not right here, so I held in my breath and looked down at my teacup. The porcelain was intricately detailed, gold leaf was bonded to the rim and I enjoyed studying the patterns of the design.

"Very well, you will *not* be visiting the chambers below anytime soon… and one other detail. You were meant to be the Twelfth Offering. You were supposed to have been dead like your little sister. Rhyiathe changed you. You are to be questioned and examined about how you got through the barrier and if you did knowingly enter, you will be hung until you are dead. We do not take too kindly to humans wandering into our territories. Or anyone or any*thing* for that matter," with a coldness to his last words, he spun around on his heeled boots, white cape rippling behind him, his shirt ruffled and his face disgruntled. He stalked out of the room on his polished shiny boots. I was left panting by the abruptness of his departure. I was also left sitting there with a thousand unanswered questions, spinning around in my muffled head. One of them being, would it be a fair trial if I am to be the Twelfth and they need me to complete some foul sacrifice?

But then I was slightly encouraged by the fact that he had mentioned that my sister's body was to be found somewhere called The Chamber.

Lilly rushed in, her cheeks were glowing pink and her brow line sweaty.

"What happened? What did you say to annoy him? *He* is no one to be trifled with. In time, you will realise this or be dead. Either way, you will learn to hold your tongue."

"*He* was playing games and I played *him* back . . . *he* got annoyed. What was I supposed to do? Just pretend that they are not holding my sister's body captive?" I shrugged and turned away. A terror slipped inside my belly, but I refused to show it. I couldn't make out the rules of this place but I would. That is what I am good at.

"What did he tell you? Speak now," Lilly said, in a harsh voice, that I had not heard her use before now. Lilly was clutching my arm to hold me still – standing up straight, all seven feet of her. I looked up at her and suddenly felt like I was in a world that I did not belong in nor understand. I closed my eyes, like a small child wanting to go home. My second skin grew as webbing over me – I needed its protection.

I began to speak more boldly than I felt sure of,

"Nothing that I really understood. I'm to be put on trial I think, and he told me a bit about the, ah, Agreement and that I should be dead, and something about being the Twelfth. Does that mean anything to you? Why *AM* I here?" I said with a boiling-over anger and frustration, it was seeping into each word as I spoke, "I didn't ask to be here." I petulantly turned away.

She flinched back at my innocent questions.

"We need to get you up to speed and fast. You will accompany me tomorrow doing chores with me throughout the day and I will tell you what I can, but there is a powerful spell on these Lands that means we cannot talk freely of the *Agreement,* about the secrecy surrounding it. Anyone who utters certain words is located by this spell, and put to death, by order of the Elf King. Are you willing to risk your life for this knowledge about the Seven Kingdoms, knowing what I have just told you?"

I looked at her grave face and her bravery, her expression was piercing, like she was challenging me to be as brave as her. There was something important happening here that I needed to understand, so I took in a large gulp of breath and replied,

"Yes, I think I do, but know this. As soon as I have found the body of my sister, I will be leaving with her and returning to Earth. The rest is up to the Immortals. This is not my fight,"

Lilly relaxed her shoulders and smiled, brightly. Her next words were a lie because her voice was very high when she said,

"As it should be. We will begin tomorrow." With a knowing glance and a smirk on her face, I trusted her expressions more than her words somehow, she believed this is my fight and does not want to challenge me just yet. I sighed.

Chapter Ten – Stories of the Seven Kingdoms

"Slop, slop, slop", went the mop on the hard flagstones of the courtyard – a relaxing sound to my ears. Normal even, I could be back on earth, while my mum attempts her annual cleaning up of whichever house we were living in. But I was not on Earth, and the mop travelling around, did so of its own accord, autonomously - confirmed this very starkly to me.

True to Lilly's words, we were up at the crack of dawn to start her day as a servant in the biggest castle in the Seven Kingdoms. She had riled me awake, insisted I get dressed in a servant's attire for the day – a simple cotton dress and my hair held back in a piece of silk. "Very fetching," she had whistled through her teeth and giggled, I had tried to remain grumpy, and sullen, insisting that I looked like an idiot and this outfit was torturous for me, but I couldn't help but laugh too.

"Now, see, you don't need to wear your bodysuit around me."

I quietly smiled in the way that you do when someone says something, and you realise you are seen and understood by them.

Lilly walked me down to the kitchens, which were unfathomably vast. Magic was in the air; the pots were hot on the stoves busily cooking lots of delicious food, the water piping through, and the mops and brushes cleaning and twirling into all the nooks and picking up any sign of dirt. Everything was made of copper, rose-coloured, gleaming, and beautiful – I gasped.

"Haven't you seen a kitchen before, Aurora?" Lilly said with a tinkle of laughter, poking fun at me.

"Not one like this, this is beautiful," I replied. My hands touched the smooth natural stone walls, the granite worktops, the copper pans, the living plants, and herbs. All the items made up a great big space that honoured nature, reflecting of the give and take cycles, in the natural world. Simple and divine.

The further I walked into that great cavernous room and the nearer I got to the magic being performed, I felt like I was wading through wet cement, a pressing sensation on my face. I reached my fingers up, arms stretched out before me, to feel the air. It felt like a metal plate was being pressed against the skin of my face, I described the sensation to Lilly.

"Ahhh, yes, that is the residue of magic being performed. You will feel it whenever a spell is being used, it's a useful indicator to know. Sometimes people will try to use magic on you, and you will know it from this pressured sensation. When you learn how to use your own powers, you can place a shield charm around you that stops the sensation and stops any spells too. Let's try some magic this afternoon, but for now, let's eat and then get to work."

I nodded, eyes wide with wonder, I had heard the words but not really taken them in, they floated before me. Lilly thought I would be able to perform magic. A childlike excitement bubbled up in me, but I tried to remain sullen on the outside – I didn't want to get attached to this place, to these people, I felt myself starting to trust, which I had never done before. Shaking my head, my resolve slipped over my hearts, reminding myself, I had to find my sister and go, return to Earth. I would play along for now.

Lilly shared some snippets of information with me about the Seven Kingdoms, in a very rushed way the night before.

She had called it, "The foundations," and asked me to sleep on it. There are seven planets, drifting in the same gravitational field, but in different dimensions - home worlds for the immortals. There is Vulldune for the Vampires, Attraides for the Werewolves, Tylerine for the High Elves, Nimbuu for the Witches and Warlocks, Toova for the Celestial beings of Time and Space, Earth is one of the planets of the Seven Kingdoms and Pericullious, the planet we were on, sits at the very centre of the universe and because of this, is rich, abundant in the resources of creation – matter, magic, power, that sort of thing. The air is crackling, full of it and the Immortals can draw it to themselves and perform great deeds of magic with it. The Immortal tribes fought over Pericullious at one time, many years ago and then reached an agreement, before they had all became extinct – from warring amongst themselves. The agreement was that a different ruler, one of the Kings of the Home worlds, would sit on the

Amber Throne and rule all the Kingdoms, for one hundred consecutive years as the Steward King. Earth had never taken their turn to rule. Its leaders have removed themselves from the business of running or even being a part of the Seven Kingdoms – living in quiet oblivion and ignoring the Immortals and their place in the histories of the Seven Kingdoms for a few millennia, or even longer. The Elf King had ten more years to serve as Steward King, before he must hand the Amber Throne over to the next Steward King to rule – most of the immortals were pleased that the Elf stewardship was nearing its end, and the elves would be handing the Amber seat over to the Vampires of Vulldune. I listened to Lilly with such a fierce intensity that my face ached from my eyebrows being permanently fixed up to my hairline and I didn't even realise when she had stopped talking – I was rehearing her words in my mind, echoing of the history, coveting the very thought of the beauty of what I was hearing, this story was a gift to my ears and I never wanted her to stop – I was mesmerised. I felt special just hearing all of this. Button would love it. Would have loved it all – I corrected myself and a sob had caught the back of my throat.
Lilly was serving breakfast. We sat together, side-by-side, at a large, wooden table, smooth and natural, without any varnish or shaping, the circles of the aged tree spiralled out to greet me. I flicked my head down to see more of the design, and I was stunned to note the tree roots and trunk were still attached to the ground.
"It is living" I blinked, with wonder.
"Yes, the immortals are caretakers, guardians of nature. We never cut down or kill anything we care for, unless we must, to protect the forests, oceans, or sky. Earth must be like that surely. We are nothing without honour to life, no?"
I sat back in the chair made of living tree roots and rubbery green curling leaves, - very comfortable. The living tree moulded itself to my unique posture and I sat there reflecting quietly, deep in thought.
"Right, you will need some blood soon or otherwise, your Cold One will jump out on us and eat me alive," Lilly said with a chuckle, busily loading plates made of natural clay, but I was left stunned.
"What do you mean eat blood and my Cold One, what's that?" I was barely able to keep the concern out of my voice. "Have I been changed by being here? Breathing in the air or something. Am I a feral monster that Lord

Tennison told me about?" The living tree roots tightened around me, feeling the vibration of my panic.

Lilly ran over to me, placing the plate with red blood blisters down in front of me. She looked me in the eyes and then cuddled me.

"I'm sorry, I didn't mean to scare you. I thought you had figured it out already. I put some blood in your soup these past few weeks, so maybe you haven't felt it yet, the bloodlust, the thirst, I mean, The quickening of the vampires?"

I started to tremble, and she squeezed me closer. I pulled away – suffocated, not used to being comforted. Usually, I was the one who offered comfort to others – the caretaker, not the cared for. I didn't need anyone. I stayed seated but moved away from her arms.

"Tell me, what did that man do to me in the forest? I have not been the same since and I demand to know."

Lilly's elf ears pricked up; her face ashen with disappointment, "*Demand?* You demand nothing here. This is *not* the way we immortals behave. We are not primates growling with aggression. Only those that have lost sight of themselves, think that they can be cruel, violent, and demanding. No, you will ask me to explain kindly or you will not be told *anything at all.* Do you understand?" Lilly's eyes flashed with disappointment and there was a gleam there of concern, she sat down heavily and began eating her breakfast, but I could tell it was hard for her to swallow, - the food and my outburst.

A shame crawled over me; an embarrassed silence fell. My cheeks coloured warmly. The black bloated spiders of my childhood whispered in my ears and began knitting, clicking, covering me with a fine cocoon of webbing separating me from the outside world, isolating me, but I didn't want to hide in the cocoon anymore – something had changed since I had nearly died.

We both turned to each other at the same time and spoke urgently, "I am sorry, Lilly. I'm not used to all this, having…*someone* to guide me, I've looked after myself for so long..." I looked down, embarrassed I had hurt her feelings, while she said, "I am sorry, you've been through a lot, of course, you are scared. I should have been more understanding, but the way you spoke triggered me, you sounded like one of those haughty, vile High Elf Lords."

We both looked at each other and smiled. She leaned forward and hugged me. I let her, but I still found all this uncomfortable, this connection that was forming – '*I must stay guarded*', my spiders said, and my hearts beat louder, my smile broadened, and the spiders' whispering appeared lessened to my ears, somehow. We continued eating while Lilly explained.

"So, Rhyiathe, a vampire, and my friend, had to change you, to share his blood with you, to save you. He didn't want to, but it was the only way. I am sorry."

"Rhyiathe is the vampire from the woods when I first arrived here? How do you know him? Can he be trusted? What will become of me, now that I-I-I'm a . . ." I couldn't say the word, but curiously, I didn't care that I had become a vampire, a creature of the night. I just wanted to keep talking about Rhyiathe. He fascinated me and I sat up straighter in my seat, leaning in."

"A vampire, yes, you are a vampire. You will need to feed on blood taken from the animals, they give it freely. Some of the vampires still kill living beings and drink their blood, the feral ones, but Rhyiathe doesn't do that. Now let me see, along with the thirst, the bloodlust, you have special powers now of the Vampires. Strength, sight, hearing, sharp teeth, self-protective magic, that type of thing. Now eat before, you get too hungry and cannot control yourself. Rhyiathe is going to drop by today. He will tell you a bit more." My head was spinning, but I did not question her any further. I began spooning the blood onto the utensil and sniffing it. It smelt like honey to my acutely tuned olfactory senses and I slurped it down in one go.

We cleared up the kitchen and the castle began to come to life with the sounds of hundreds of people or beings rather, rising from their slumber. Lilly told me that Vampires mostly sleep during the day, but the blood blisters change the arcadian rhythm.

She took us out of the castle to the stables to give the stable hands some breakfast and help with the mucking out of the creatures housed or rather, living there. Lilly didn't like the term housed when I used it. She said the creatures can leave when they want to – freedom is theirs, but the immortals make it so comfortable for them that they don't want to leave and are happy with the arrangement. It was all very confusing and so

different from Earth, where we just take and take and take from nature. I was too embarrassed to tell her this.
I took a shovel from one of the sheds, heavy and practical in my hands, and walked into the stables. The smell of raw wood and clean hay, of animal husbandry of all aspects, hit my senses. It was a good smell. Wholesome.
As soon as I entered, I was made to stop dead in my tracks, shovel clanging to the golden straw-covered floor. My hands bumped at my sides, pinching myself to make sure I was real.
A large white unicorn stood tall and proud, on its own, shimmering in the rays of sunlight, peeking through the scattered, gauze-like clouds.
The clang of the shovel had made her turn her great head towards me. I had no choice but to move towards the dream-like creature and she allowed me to stroke the platinum strands of her course mane and touch the patterns of her golden horn - after I introduced myself of course. Nuzzling me with her large, long nose, I was dumbfounded. I just stood staring up at the beautiful creature of myth with awe and wonder. The beauty and majesty of the beast took my breath away, its polished hooves pawed the ground and its lithe and taut torso danced in the rhythm of its swaying movement. I leaned forward, hesitating before I flung my arms around the unicorn's wide neck and began to cry – to sob. She snorted then laid her head on top of my own.
"I didn't want to touch you. I didn't know if I am worthy enough," The unicorn snorted and licked my hair and my confessions were spilling out of me and I didn't know how to stop, "Am I allowed to confess to the life I have led? I did it for others, I hated the hardening cold of what it was doing to me. What I had become. I resented and loved my sister in equal measures because of what I had to do to keep us alive, but there is something else. I always knew there was more. That I was different. That I was meant to look after them all not just Button, I mean to say Dawn my sister. Do you see? Do you understand? Am I forgiven? What do I do now? Please tell me, I don't know what to do now."
Great hot tears were running down my cheeks and as they touched the skin of the Unicorn, they turned to crystals and dropped onto the floor, with the sound of bells.

We stood together in that way for what felt like forever, being comforted by the majestic beast. I was a maiden, and she was my saviour.
A cool wind blew, and I saw her looking out into the distance as if guiding my eyes to look out too. I found my eyes were caught by the mountains looming on the horizon, but I never left her side. I stood there for a long time while my sorrow was understood and lessened somehow by just being in her presence. She gave me the gift of forgiveness that day and it came a little easier to start forgiving myself.
He was present with a suddenness, standing behind me and introduced himself by gently saying, "Aurora, I came to see you. To see how you are doing." It was Rhyiathe, the vampire who changed me.
I knew it was him, before I even looked, or turned around. Before he had even entered the barn, the stables, or the cobbled pathways leading up to the castle, he was with me and I felt him wherever we both were, even if we were a million miles away. I felt him always.
I released my arms from the Unicorn. She reacted by snorting, stamping, she looked down gently on me, with clear bright eyes, crested with beauty – nudging me forward, gifting me back control over my own hearts once more. I brushed my fingers down her long fine nose as I turned to Rhyiathe.
We stood facing each other, the cool breeze drifted over our skin, and I watched his lips as I bit down on my own. I felt drunk standing there in his presence – an urgent angst was upon me, and I don't know how I managed to stop myself from running into his arms, but I did. I willed my legs to stay pinned to the ground.
"What have you done to me," I heard myself quietly say.
Standing up into his fine legs, I hadn't realised how tall, muscular, broad-shouldered, and completely aligned to his proud posture, he really was. So handsome, physically he had presence. He could be misconstrued as domineering, due to his impressiveness, but he was too kind. I saw it all in the way he moved and the shape of each expression. He was not nervous, rather solemn, and tongue-tied maybe, but not nervous like I was. He smiled, and with each opening of his mouth to speak words to me, my painful hearts soared. I cared not how his words were formed, just that he spoke to me, only to me.

"I'm sorry, I'm sorry, I turned you into a part of me. I had no choice, you were dying and, well, I had no choice. . ." Rhyiathe closed his mouth. His eyes spelt out his anguish, but there was something else there – he was covering something up.
I brushed my nose, my fingers glided over my eyes – trying to hide myself away from what I was about to say next,
"I understand that, but what have you done *to me*, are you now my, what is it called, my *sire*? Am I your *slave*?" I managed to fumble out – deadly serious.
"What? No," he warmly laughed, "I don't know *where* you've gotten that strange idea from, but no. There is no consequence other than, you are now part vampire, part something else -" there it is again, a fleeting glance of secrecy, he looked at me with a deep curiosity for a microsecond, "- and I am sorry for that. I couldn't ask you for your permission, you were dying. . .I made the decision, I am hoping it was the right one, I saw the Elder Lights . . ." his eyebrows set in a line, and I couldn't read his expression or what he was referring to by this reference to the lights. The words were weighty and had another meaning of some kind, I was sure of that.
"Yes, I am sorry, where are my manners. Of course I must say thank you, thank you for saving me, so these feelings between us, they are not anything to do with the vampire's bite?" I mumbled, scared to look at him, but I do.
What if he feels nothing? What if I am nothing to him? I am trembling why can't I stop trembling. Can he see?
"Feelings?" He stood still – blinking, then his face softened, he begun stepping closer, lifting his hand to reach out and touch my upper arm. His breathing became heavier, as he removed his gloves first, then he placed a fingertip gently on my skin, to trace down my arm. Lights explode behind my eyes and I quivered under his gentle touch, warming my very core. My pulse was racing, a shaky hope was rising within me. His eyes looked deeply into mine and darkened, his lips open by centimetres, as if he wanted to partake of me, to devour me and quench his thirst. Obsession gleamed in his green eyes.
"I, I, . . . You are incredibly beautiful. I struggle to breathe around you if that's what you mean." He did not take his eyes off me; he was talking to me like we were both wandering in a dream. Our speech is not real. I

couldn't explain it, like we had known each other since the beginning of time. It was odd and I was scared.
"I am made of cobwebs and despair." Is all I could think to say.
He replied with the most intense look on his face,
"You are wrong about yourself. I only see greatness and the light in you. It is there you just haven't learnt how to fan it into life yet. It will put out the darkness, in time, you will see."
I suddenly felt very afraid, exposed, I stood there, but I drew back and huddled myself away, afraid of letting myself go. Desperately, abruptly, I tried to keep myself locked in, shut down – holding on to what I am used to. Rhyiathe quietly leaned towards me, gazing at my lips and his eyes were feverish with longing.
I pulled myself back, *"I want this so much, but I just can't, don't ask me why. I just can't,"* I murmured, forgetting that I was speaking out loud. His eyes flickered and held within them an intense pain.
"Rhyiathe, oh, you are here? When did you arrive?" It was Lilly and we both took this as a silent cue to jump back from one another.
"Oh, I'm terribly sorry, I clearly interrupted . . . something." Her eyes flicked towards Rhyiathe then swivelled extremely fast towards me, taking in my folded in posture, which is most unusual for me,
"Aurora, are you feeling, okay?" Lilly said with concern marking her face.
"Have you eaten enough? Enough blood that is?" Rhyiathe asked, spun towards me, "You'll need to feed regularly for the first few weeks or so. Has the burning gone or at least dulled yet?"
I folded my arms over myself, a protective shell in the absence of my bodysuit, and nodded, without looking at him, moved towards Lilly, to stand just behind her, where I felt safer from this overwhelm and his searching, befuddling gaze. *How can I trust that I am not under his spell?*
"Rhyiathe, while you are here, please take Aurora to the more secluded courtyard to show her how to use the vampire magic, and be quick about it, we haven't got much time."
Before I had time to object, Rhyiathe had my hand in his and he led me to a more secluded, emptier section of the castle – the walled secret garden was wild and overgrown. Meadow flowers overran the place and the bees were busy pollinating them, the bluebirds sung, tweeting out a kind of joy and the place is alive, like my hearts. The wind blew gently on my skin and

I felt this adventurous spirit in me awaken from a deep sleep. Pericullious brings out my lightness.

My strange new two hearts were thudding deeply in my chest cavity – making my legs tremble from the heavy rush of blood. He stood behind me, I sank back into his chest a little too obviously. He whispered softly in my ear.

"Now, concentrate, think of something you wish to protect and then visualise a wall around it. You are immensely powerful, more powerful than a vampire, more powerful than you realise – trust it. It will respond to you. The Lights are *yours*," he blew on the back of my neck, near my ear. I shivered from the sensation; while the energy shifted and moved between us and it was intoxicating, in the heat of the afternoon suns. I did as he guided me. I was astonished when I eventually managed to conjure a shield charm, shimmering pink under the glare of the Two Suns. Rhyiathe threw spells at it, to test it and none of them penetrated the shimmering surface. We continued with a great many lessons that warm afternoon, Rhyiathe showed me how to build and harness a lightning bolt by calling it with my mind and pulling the power from the ionised atmosphere above us. There were other lessons too, such as, how to lift objects off the ground – making them vanish into thin air. Then, he showed me how to use my new strength, my speed, my vision, my hearing and all the advantages of being part vampire. It was fun and he was enjoying sharing the marvel of his gifts, that he had bestowed on me. I was careful to stay out of his reach as much as I could, but I struggled to remove my eyes from his pillow soft lips, the shape of his torso and the brilliance of his eyes. He caught me gazing at him very often. He was funny, and warm, tender, and charming – easy to be around. Everything I was not. I am the exact opposite. I stayed quiet, withdrawn and hardly uttered a word. He must have thought I was a simpleton. Maybe I am, I was ruining everything – unable to show him how I feel. How I feel about *him*.

When he readied himself to leave Lilly and I that afternoon, my powerful hearts started to hurt in the centre of my chest. I watched him put on his cape and turn to exit the castle; my longing was displayed on my face. I wanted to scream hysterically, to lose control, to tell him he must not leave, he must stay with me. We stared longingly at each other. He was waiting for something and I just didn't know how to ask for reciprocation of

something so precious as what I myself, felt for him. It was unimaginable to me that anyone would be able to give it back as intensely, as ferociously, as I wished to give to him.
But I was lying to myself, I did not know how to stop feeling scared. I had no experience of this type of love. How I could show him and still feel safe in a world that had always let me down. I am a coward. So, I just didn't say anything at all. That day, he looked sad as he leaned down to kiss my hand and I blushed at his touch, all the while my toes curled in my hard boots.
"Anything you need, Aurora, just let me know. I will be here for you. Always." His last words I carried with me for a long time – in truth, forever – they were imprinted on my soul for the rest of all time, but I just would not admit it to myself back then.
He left, green eyes fixed on me, looking back over his shoulder as he rounded a corner. When he had finally gone, my hearts missed a few beats. A fear slid into my belly, but I didn't speak openly of my anxiety and tried to swallow it down into my bobbing neck – fists clenched. I was getting too close to him, to them all. I brooded on this. It felt dangerous to trust.
"Here, he left you this," Lilly had in her outstretched hand a ring made of silver, with a large creamy, translucent stone at the centre, the glint of it shimmered across my face as I tried it on.
"What is it? Is he coming back?" I said, petrified of the answer.
"It is a moonstone, the wearer can walk freely in the sunshine, even at High noon, when the vampires are at their weakest, due to the fact they draw their energy from the moon."
It glittered as I positioned it on my left hand, where a wedding ring would traditionally be.
"He will be back. Rhyiathe is an old friend of mine. You will see him again soon, *I promise*," Lilly said carefully, watching me out of the corner of her eye as my head drooped down to my heavy chest.
I straightened up and sniffed, "I care not," I lied and petulantly turned around, spinning on my heels to run away with the intention of crying in my rooms, where no one else could see me. I wanted to be alone, I felt lost. This was all new to me and I was scared.
When suddenly, a voice calls out. "Lilly, I am dropping off the strawberries picked this morning from the fields, I gave half of them to the field mice, but kept the really juicy one's for you," A tall golden-haired man entered

the courtyard, wriggling his eyebrows at Lilly – a shared joke. I laughed aloud and he warmly crinkled his chocolate brown eyes in appreciation of my laughter. His presence was sparklingly shiny like the Suns overhead.
"Dillion, you wicked dog, werewolves are all the same. Feeding the pack, even if they are the smallest of us all. How will the chef make the strawberry cakes now for the festival?" Lilly says, hooting with laughter and shouts over to a very young stable hand, who was busy brushing down a winged creature, with fire rolling out of its hooves. "*Youngling*, please come here. Get the rest of the strawberries down to the kitchen, before this wayward werewolf gives them away to more beggars, who can very well find their own food. This kingdom is abundant with plants of every kind and life," Lilly said to a stable hand, who smiled with a nod, before rushing off to unload a cart of fresh food. I could smell the scent of the crops, soaked with fresh rain, wafting up into the bright blue sky.
I yawned; a nap is very much overdue. My mind wandered, recalling the events of the day; today had been a long one of mucking out stables, cleaning floors, polishing silver, learning how to use my new skills, and trying not to throw myself at Rhyiathe.
Before I left the courtyard, I turned to Lilly and shouted with not a care, "What about this Clandestine Agreement, what about the history of these worlds and its warfare?".
I didn't even get to close my mouth or get to the end of the sentence before Lilly and this Dillion fellow jumped up, heads darting around. They both lifted their hands simultaneously and caught my words in the translucent webbing of a spell – casting this together with practised ease. The sky darkened, the wind picked up and the clouds overhead began to sizzle with a jagged edge of magic.
Dillion yelled, "Domino, dominion," into the sky and then suddenly, the black clouds disappeared, the sky turned back to a calm blue and the crackling, bleak, moody atmosphere had gone - vanished. Dillion ran to jump into the driver's seat of the cart and disappeared without a backward glance.
Lilly ran over to me, urgently taking me by the hand, running us up the castle stairs two at a time, dragging me up behind her. We reached my apartment very quickly, where she locked the door shut from the inside,

listening behind it for a while, before she spun round to face me, with an expression that was dark.
I fumbled out, "I don't understand. Why were Lord Tennison and others, allowed to say . . . *those* words and not me?" I said in shock, my face ghostly pale. Lilly replied, in temper, "Because royalty is exempt from the laws of these Lands, but as much as you think you are above the law, you are not. Not here. You can behave how you want on Earth, there are a different set of rules here. Can't you see? They are waiting for a chance to execute you in front of the Kingdoms. Do you understand? I could not bear watching that happen to you . . .not seeing another person I care for being executed again."
I studied her face; a pain was there that I did not want to touch upon – to open. It frightened me, in truth. She was so strong so whatever had hurt her must have been unbelievably bad indeed.
"There is a banned book of immortal history that you can read. It is in Lord Tennison's library. There is a sword tournament this evening in honour of the Festival of Freya. You will enter the competition as a distraction, and I will steal the book for one night only. Do you understand? You have one night to read as much of it as you can. You will be given that book of history to read and you will read it from cover to cover in this room tonight. You will eat, read, and sleep and then read some more. Until you understand the danger you are in, you will be stupidly walking into the Hydro's den willingly, like a fool."
Darkness settled in the room when she mentioned the Hydro. Black clouds crowded over the sunny view on the balcony, and I slinked back in horror. Not from my telling off, but because she had a terrible shadow over her eyes that unsettled me.
"What makes you think I can fight with swords and be any good at it? Lord Tennison said that I am not safe here and you want me to enter a tournament with weapons and violent Immortals, well over seven foot tall, all of you. What makes you think I will survive?"
She took hold of both my shoulders. "Because I know you and I know you can do this even if you don't. Rhyiathe has shown you the ways of the vampires and how to use your magic. You will win."
She left to place my name in the competition, and I stood holding my chest, listening to the flutter of two hearts in there, unable to breathe.

Chapter Eleven - Queen of Shiv, rises victorious.

When Lilly came back, an older woman accompanied her. On earth this woman would have been about seventy years old but who knew what age she was in this blasted dimension. Introduced as Callen the Wise, after I was introduced to her as Aurora the Dim, Vexer of Princes, Callen commented with a mischievous grin, "it suits her," with a gleam in her eyes.

The two women laughed at their own jokes, and I stood there scowling, adjusting my throwing knives at first, hoping to look menacing and failing miserably, while a laughter formed in the back of my throat and I started to begrudgingly giggle along with them.

"Right, the tournament starts in an hour. Callen is a witch, and she is going to unlock your fighting abilities by brewing a potion, like a spell yet more potent," Lilly said, all matter of fact, like she was talking about ordering in a pizza.

"Unlock my abilities, what does that mean? What does it involve?" I asked but no one was listening. They were standing together before me, conferring about the best root vegetable to include in the magical spell to make the potion, which is going to enhance my fighting prowess or trigger something, I couldn't quite keep up, with what they were planning, I listened to them.

". . .Tarnen root is best, I'd say Lilly."

"But doesn't that cause diarrhoea for a bit? Wouldn't sage and key pine root be better? Less symptoms afterwards, Callen?"

"Erm, can someone tell me how this is going to work please? I'm a bit unsure about the symptoms part of this spell. Will I be ill after I drink it?" They both look at me questioningly and '*tsk*' then continue talking like I was not there at all. I pinch myself. *Maybe I'm not here after all. Maybe this is all a dream.*

"Right, sit down over there. I'll mix this up. Lilly, do you have a pewter pot and river water, or should I conjure them up?"
"Oh, conjure them please. I don't think we have time for me to dash back to my apartment, Callen."
"Good point."
I sat down and placed a cushion in front of me like that would be enough to protect me from my mind bending. Listening to the way they were casually describing magic and that I was entering a sword tournament on an alien planet within the hour made my head swim and I felt like I was going to vomit.
"Have I got time for a lie down?"
"No," they both shouted over at me in unison.
"I'm going to be sick." I placed my hand over my mouth.
"Do it over there then," Callen said gruffly with a stern glare in her brilliant blue eyes and folding her arms at me – giving me the impression I was an inconvenience, without saying a word.
She turned to face the pewter pot she had just conjured, and a fire sprung up underneath it. The flames lit up the Witch's craggy, lined face, strange lights of orange, pink and gold glow under her prominent chin – flames licked at the bottom of the pot, liquid bubbling inside. She is hideous, but strong lined and beautiful at the same time, a face of unending restraint and sorrow. Dressed simply, yet her clothes are well-cared for, like she has precious few. Muttering words over the contents of the pot that I didn't understand, she started adding ingredients, which were appearing from nowhere into her hands and she was throwing them into the pot. It hissed with steam. A pink smoke started curling upwards from the mixture and she sniffed at it. When she was finally satisfied, the witch spooned some of the potion into a small wooden cup, that looked like a birds nest. Holding it out, Callen called me over to drink it. I stood, slowly taking uncertain steps forward on legs weak with fright. I didn't want anyone to see my weakness. Taking the cup in my shaking hands, I peered inside the rim and down at the strange liquid. Callen placed her hand on mine to steady my fingers and she smiled at me, and softly said,
"It will be okay. You are going to be magnificent, believe you can do this and you will. Now, drink it down in one go."

I peered at her; the kindness stunned me for a moment. It was the first time in a long while that someone had offered me softness and encouragement like that. I felt like I was stepping out of a parched desert into the warmth of a cooling sea. I was grateful for her words. It spurred me to take a deep breath and I gulped it down in one go.

An hour later, Lilly was guiding me down a long, stone, spiral of a stairwell within the castle and she was striding down before me. I was running to keep up. All the way down she shouted instructions at me.

"It starts with eight fighting pairs in the arena for the first stage and there are three rounds in total. The winners will move on to the next stage then there will be two contestants left for the final stage. There is only one point to win in each battle. It is a quick tournament. Although the immortals like showing off in front of one another, we prefer the eating, drinking, and dancing parts of this particular festival more than anything. Also, the Goddess Freya is one of the Goddesses of love and joy. The fighting will include making fun of one another so isn't taken as seriously as our other . . .*contests* but because you are human, I would guess the competitors will want to humiliate you. Be careful. Stay vigilant," Lilly said bitterly, "Oh, and the other thing is don't acknowledge Callen. We don't want *them* to know she has helped you. Okay? One last thing, I will sneak out once it begins and I will leave the book in your dressing room and collect it before dawn in the morning. Right, got all that? Try not to draw attention to yourself and try not to get too hurt. I will be back as soon as I can. And don't slouch it makes you look weak. . ."

I had stopped on the steps and Lilly had continued running down the stairs for a while but must have realised that my footfalls had gone quiet. She ran back up the stone stairs, her face came around the proud, solid wall of well-designed masonry, and when she saw me standing there adrift and alone, on the steps of a strange castle, a look of pity passed across her features.

"Why are you helping me," I said in a low hush, frightened of the answer.

Her turquoise eyes were a glow of determination, "Because I am meant to and that is all you need to know for the time being, now come on. We are running out of time."

She stepped up another stair, moving closer to me, and held out her upturned hand, and I leaned forward to take it gladly. We walked down the steps, side by side in silence, leaving echoes behind us with the surety of our feet, while I contemplated the enormity of her words *"because I am meant to"*. Does that mean some sort of foretelling?

The roar of the crowds was deafening in my ears, as we walked down the deep stone steps, built for Elf strides not for my human legs, we came out near to the entrance of the main arena. Lilly still accompanied me, we or rather I started jogging through a long dark tunnel, covered in straw, and it smelt strongly of animal sweat and manure. There were other contestants walking before us and a small gathering at our back. A murmuring whisper rippled through the immortals participating in the games, as we stepped through the first set of doors of the tunnel. Hearing them urgently whisper behind their hands, calling me names that I did not fully understand, but I could tell they were an insult to me, just by the way they were spat out of their awful mouths with a sneer, "Shiv'doress", was said on more than one occasion.

"What does Shitedress mean?" I said in a bemused tone to Lilly, not able to fully pronounce the word as the 'vd' part was being rolled in a guttural way, so I improvised, somewhat. A shocked expression crossed Lilly's face, she flushed with embarrassment, I had even dared try to pronounce such a word.

Flustered, Lilly thought about it then said, "The closest translation to your language is 'infested *Hu-man* whore of no value, which has relationships with low class animals' I think, that's what it is in your language."

I nodded thoughtfully. "A very precise insult. I am most impressed," I laughed out and Lilly laughed back at my light-hearted reaction.

A stone came skimming over the walking crowd, landing with a thick, dull thud on the back of my head. Blood pooled and dripped on my shoulder, but I felt no pain. A hand roughly gripped at that same shoulder, squashing the blood into my bodysuit, roughly grabbing at me, pulling me backwards. A male elf was standing before me. He had long brown hair and dark chocolate-brown eyes. He was very tall. I was staring at his chest rather than his face. Muscular too, he had the look of battle on his well-defined features. The braids in the front of his hair were the same pattern as Lord Tennison's. "Greetings Shiv'doress Queen. I am Eiderlan, Bringer of your Pain," he bowed, mockingly. The crowd of elves started to laugh and jeer.

He looked around at the crowd, holding his muscular arms up in the air, the size of barrels, drinking in their adulation.

"Not now Eiderlan. Go back to your Master, little monkey and tell him that we are not afraid." Lilly stepped forward, nose to nose with the male elf. They were staring angrily into each other's eyes.

"Good to see you, Llillandria of Collendale, keeping the company of lowborn, are we? Does it make you feel important like you have recaptured your father's royal title again?" the large elf laughed in her face.

Lilly curled her lip viciously and reached for her sword pinned to the side of her leg. She twirled it expertly between her hands and threw it up in the air with a practiced grace. Somersaulting through the space in the tunnel, landing into a standing position and catching the glinting sword on the tumble, she held the point deadly straight to Eiderlan's thick neck.

"You will not mention my father and you will take back your insults, mongrel or I will. . ."

Stunned by the expertise of the swordplay displayed by Lilly, I stepped forward pulling the two great Elves apart from one another with a kind of strength that I did not know I possessed. These were seven-foot-tall elves, immense in stature, powerful and I was pulling them apart like they were made of tissue paper. My knees trembled together in confusion.

I cleared my throat, "Eiderdown, let's take this to the arena and we will see what happens in there," I say boldly - bolder than I felt at that precise moment in time, knowing I hadn't trained a day in my life with a sword or combat drills with immortals before.

Eiderlan glared at Lilly and then down at me.

"It's Lord Eiderlan to you, Shiv. Neither of you are worthy of my time." and then shoved past me, slamming into my shoulder on his way to stalk into the bright, openness of the torch-lit arena. He was greeted by an almighty thunderous applause, that rung in my ears. His silver chainmail clinking like little bells over his broad shoulders. The spotlights illuminated him while we were stood in the gloom of the tunnel, shrouded in darkness.

"Not a big fan of mine, is he?" I said peering inside the arena.

"Eiderlan is nobody's fan. Filled with hate and spite, and excrement. He is part of Lord Tennison's guard. Try to avoid him in the arena, Aurora."

"But what if he is in the final with me?" I smirked.

Lilly laughed again, all tension leaving her sweet face. "I like your confidence. Well then, best him. Here, take my father's sword and try to stay alive. I will be back soon." She hugged me tightly then left.

Looking down at the sword shoved roughly into my hands, I began turning it over, it was made from a king's weight of silver and gold, large, glittering with precious gems, studded into the hilt – highly polished, as well, as loved. I go to shout to Lilly, to say thank you for such a fine weapon and honour to fight with her family's heirloom; even if this was my last battle, but I would have been talking to myself. Alone, I was the last person standing in the tunnel, so I straightened up, threw back my shoulders and strode out under the flood lights, ready to put on a show.

There were about one hundred thousand spectators in the arena, seated on tiered platforms, leading up towards the sky – the noise from the crowds like a roaring tsunami. The Suns were beating down on the grainy sand of the ground. The wind was picking up and there were dark brooding clouds rolling in, it would soon be overcast and stormy. The ambience electrified. Those that had come to watch the tournament were small dots to my eyes, busy bumbling about in the distance, screaming, and chanting the names of their favourite champion. *Clue:* this wasn't me.

Waving flags and toasting with pints of frothy drinks, their faces were alight with happy expectation.

All went quiet when I stepped into the arena. A shocked hush rippled throughout the crowds. It throbbed in my ears, so profoundly deafening that I stumbled under the weight of it, but only for a microsecond before regaining my composure. It did not pay to show weakness in places like this. The frisson of hate for humans was palpable. I took my time to scan the place.

An elf dressed in chainmail with a black arm band on, an umpire of sorts, was on the sidelines to ensure the rules were obeyed, that I didn't even know yet. In the distance, on a platform hovering over the oval shaped arena, was where the Elf King and his family were seated, each on regal golden thrones. The King dressed in emerald, green armour, with a heavy-set battle plate, leaned forward to get a better look at me, he openly stared, and our eyes were locked together. He grinned malevolently, but I would not break his gaze.

A commentator's voice echoed out into the vast space of the arena.

"Well, here we have our final contestant. . . what's on the card. Oh yes, here it is. Aurora the . . . Twelfth? Here as a special guest of our illustrious King to celebrate this day. An emissary from . . . Earth. . . Is that right?" A shocked pause and then a muffled conversation in haste, "Well, we hope to be able to return her whole and not on a stretcher my good folks of the realms, but you never can tell how this tournament will go."

There was a roar of laughter from the crowd and the tension broke open. "She's so small, are you sure they've not sent a child by mistake?", the big oaf Eiderlan shouted out, his voice amplified, while he rallied the crowds with his peacock walk. The Elf King could be seen chuckling and wiping at his eyes. This sparked off some of the crowd, they began to catcall and jeer at me, with insults.

I tuned out all the noise and concentrated on my own breath, sizing up the seven other contestants in the arena. A few were elves, but there were others too. A couple of werewolf type of creatures, A witch with an elaborate headdress and matching cape, and a humanoid looking tree. It could be my imagination, but he looked very scared. I wondered what his story was, why he was here. Not for long mind as I found myself quickly shoved towards a female elf, I am matched with in this contest, and then we were both roughly pushed into a circle etched into the ground – it's glowing. As soon as we were both inside, a shimmering pink and white translucent force field wall, shot up through the ground with a '*zip*' it encircled us – closing us into a fighting arena, with fresh, course-sand and large rocks positioned on the floor. The translucent, glowing wall was making a strange buzzing sound. Whoever had made it had charged it with enough electricity to knock out an elephant. I waved my hand as near as I dared to it and the wall crackled out to shock me - no escape then. Our images were being projected onto huge screens, positioned around the arena. My opponent was watching her own humongous projection, clapping, and smiling, and waving to endear herself to the crowds. Quite a show she was putting on.

I turned, to study the Elf more closely, who was to be my opponent. The female elf had jet black hair and large, bird like staring amber eyes, light with knowledge, currently staring at me with a hard shine of hatred. She had gold rings in her hair and on her pointy ears and she was dressed in a black body suit, like the tan one I was wearing, but hers was of military design – motifs and hard-won medals adorn her chest. Her suit is made from individual scales, that move and change, autonomously. Presently, they were spiking up. I looked down at my own and see my suit is the same – I picked up a single scale and the rest moved to close the gap. The scale in my hand wriggles away from my grip and snapped back into another part of the suit – curious. I'm conscious that I don't have time to study the suit, peering back up at the elf. The braids in her hair are patterned in tribal shapes like Eiderlan's, they are a team.

"Hey, good luck," I said and extended out my hand, with a warm smile. Hey, I was trying something new, like I said, something had changed since I almost died in the tree.

Gripping my fingers vicelike, she bent them back roughly and said, "Fuck you, Shiv."

I had to grit my teeth, to suppress the yelp, but I managed to pull my hand away. Shaking my hand slowly, I deliberately took a step back and shouted over to my opponent, wondering at the same time if she was forced into this competition too.

"Nice. Thanks for the welcome. Hello to you too!" It doesn't get to me – nothing does. I've had to put up with a lot worse in my life. I grimly assumed a defensive stance and held up the sword to my eyeline. My opponent was taller than I'd like, so I gently pulled out a blade from inside of my bodysuit – two blades to take her down.

"No mercy," I growled, getting ready and bounced on the balls of my feet to warm up my legs, ready to skip out, to administer the first blow. She would be confused as I had adopted a position of defence - London style. The whistle blew and I box-jumped high into the air, leaping forward, lifting my arms, readying myself to perform a difficult manoeuvre, - leaping over the top of my opponent. Driving my sword and blade downwards, as I skittle-balled into her and froze both her shoulder blades by pinning them down into the flesh of her back, thrusting them through her skin, with the brutal sharpness of my sword and blade. The elf couldn't move her arms and helplessly, she staggered forward. I finished by taking a somersault over her, landing lightly on the turn. Standing behind her with a dark glint of a smirk on my face, I kicked her forward, face first into the ground – her face eating dust.

The grit flew up in her eyes as she slid over the sand-covered floor on her stomach. I walked slowly over to her and took my time for the glory of the performance. Kneeling, I pulled my blades out of her back, then I lifted her large head by the plaits in her hair,

"My name is Aurora, and you would do well to use it next time we meet, She-Elf . . ." I spoke to her through clenched teeth, throwing her head back down after I had finished. She had lost a lot of life essence but not enough to kill her. The blood of elves is green like tree moss, it glows illuminous like the yellow green sponge plants on a silver birch tree.

I stood up. A stunned silence settled over the crowd. I stood a bit taller to shoulder the shocked edge to that deep silence and took the chance to wipe my blades on my thighs, trying to ignore the spiralling confusion coming from the crowds. Minutes passed by and murmurs had started to erupt in the stadium and grew louder. A discontent brimmed over and rushed to the fore. I shrugged and smiled at the crowds.

"She can't do that. Can she do that? Is she actually *hu-man*?" a shout from one of the spectators.

"Nuala was tricked. You won't be as lucky with the next contestant, Shiv," clearly one of the female elf's more ardent fans.

The commentator fumbled, "Okay, okay, settle down. Watch and enjoy the other battles and we will see who Aurora will fight next."

The clouds darkened overhead and the wind was picking up, the ominous cracking of thunder rolling in, didn't do much to lighten the mood in the arena either. My next battle was over quicker than the first one and the crows cawing for my demise in the crowds got even angrier. The potion in my veins was working well or was it the strength from being a vampire? - it's all very confusing.

I was paired with the Witch for the second round. She vanished as the whistle sounded. Intuitively, my mind homed in on where she would be reappearing next, like I had a sixth sense. I saw the faint particles of smoke of her emerging, I aimed three small silver throwing daggers at the smoke centre. As she solidified into her form, they landed on target neatly pinned along the line of her stomach. The Witch stood in shock, staring down at the knives and I hoped she was not a friend of Callen's. The Witch was not mortally hurt - I had made sure of that. She raised her hands and aimed a crackling, red beam of energy at me. It hit me square in the chest and I was thrown backwards, flying through the air to the opposite side of the arena and landed with a loud, '*crack,*' on the stone walls, dividing the main arena from the spectators. I slumped forward, dazed, but I felt nothing – no real pain. Leaping back on my feet, I ran forward in the blink of an eye. Swinging my sword and darting to the side of my opponent, I took a chance and glanced up at her. The Witch was petrified, watching me with apprehension, the folds of her deep maroon cloak fluttering behind her as she spun to face me, and I am wrath and ruin, as I took the hilt of my sword and with my full strength, bashed in her temple, it was the Witch's turn to slump like a dead weight to the floor, but I did this as lightly as was possible, so she would be rising again, but with a very sore head the next morning. I must keep sight of who the real villains are here and it wasn't the contestants.

This time there was an uproar, a commotion.

"She is cheating somehow. Umpires, stop her," screamed half the crowd but the other spectators were clapping and calling out my name. Although I did not need their support, I was not going to lie to myself, their cheers of support did boost my morale some.

I didn't watch the battle of the remaining two contestants because I knew Eiderlan would win, and he would play with his victim, to toy viciously to show me what he had in store for me. I wouldn't give him that pleasure.

Eiderlan, Eiderlan, Eiderlan, Eiderlan, Eiderlan, Eiderlan. . . The Crowds chanted and there were a few seldom Aurora's mixed in there too if I strained hard enough to catch them.

The commentator's voice floated in the air, explaining the losers were being stretchered out of the arena by healers, which I assumed were like some kind of medics. Eiderlan's last opponent was scraped off the floor.

I felt myself being shoved onto a glass step that lurched upwards from the ground. I held on with the shaky strength of my core muscles to prevent me from falling, but nothing could stop my stomach from churning as we climbed to the top of the arena on that flimsy glass step. Both I and Eiderlan were transported around opposite sides of the arena, towering above the yelling crowds as we completed a lap of honour. We were then deposited, unceremoniously, barely able to keep steady in my case, onto a glass platform that had appeared in the centre of the arena hovering a hundred foot in the air, above the excited crowds.

The icy wind at that height, battered at my body. Blinking back the coldness whipping across my eyes from the gale-force wind, whirling around me, I stared, stood tall and pulled out my sword. Alone, just the two of us in the sky. It was deafening, the silence between us, even at that height, when we faced each other down.

The frigid wind blew hard. My braid worked loose. Ice had formed on the hairs on my head and the band holding it had become brittle and fell apart. His forehead drooped forward, a primitive look forming on his sneering face, and I could tell he was going to use this battle to slaughter me. No doubt using me as the Twelfth Offering to further his own career in some way or for some type of diabolical political gain of his own making. He planned to beat my skull in with the heavy club like axe, bouncing in his large hands.

He viciously smiled at me, and I knew there were no rules that applied on this platform. Fight or Die. Fight or Die. Fight or Die. Fight or Die - ran through my mind once again. My nerves were numbed by the screeching winds. My hair flew about my face in the drama of the height of the platform.

The whistle blew in the distance, and he ran at me without a second's pause. Smashing down his hammer and it made a sickly sound as the glass crunched and fractures split open. Creaking cracks appeared in front of me, reaching towards me like spindly arms ready to thrust me to my doom. I had no choice but to join him on his side of the platform or plunge to my death.

I made the choice and jumped over to his side, while he waited there with a dagger dripping in venom, hissing as it dropped, melting the floor. He drove the sharp blade into my shoulder when I landed. Metal hit bone, that's how far he shoved it in, and I whimpered back. Half of the glass platform fell away. I counted five heartbeats before I heard the crash on the ground below. Holding my left hand to my right shoulder I pressed hard on the opening, but the blood pumped still freely between my fingers. The searing pain was ravaging the whole of my body. Rage filled my vision; red covered my eyes and that was when it happened.

Fangs sprang forward and I heard myself hiss out my descent into the wild. My tongue slipped in between my incisures. The sinew of the bone, the muscle and blood rebuilding in my shoulder, in some sort of horrific sped-up time lapse. Not for one second did I take my eyes off him as my shoulder rebuilt itself more quickly than is possible – rapid healing powers of some kind. When the pain stopped, I rolled my shoulder in all angles, to test it and then I stood erect before him. Concentrating, I floated upwards, hair blowing about in the gusts of icy winds. Levitating like the coming of an ungodly messiah, he cowered back trying to wipe his own vision clean in case this was a nightmare he needed to try to wake up from, sweat glistening heavily on his brow. He wiped his fluids across his chest and that is when I caught the sweet, delicious scent of my opponent's lifeblood.

"How can this be? This doesn't make any sense," he screamed out in terror.

A terrible thirst caressed the back of my throat. My irises illuminated under the dark clouds forming overhead, I blinked at him like a wild thing, in the mist that was rising before me. My throat was parched, and I flew across the remainder of the platform, to drink my fill.

Chapter Twelve - the history that governs the future.

"**W**hat happened? Where is Eiderlan and where are we?" I emerged from a black fogginess, heavy headed. Laying on my front, Lilly was holding a forest-fragrant compress to my back. It was cooling my aching bones, but my spine felt bruised and tender, as I went to lift myself up.

A thunderous gushing sound of running water bounced through the space I was in. Nature was honoured here and all around me. It was soothing. This place was intoxicating, it appeased all of my senses. I was in a large cave like dwelling with natural stone rock walls. Plant life of every kind was growing in between each crack and crevice, the rocks jeered out in unencumbered celebration of the natural world. A gentle waterfall gushed along one side of the cave; encouraging light green moss to grow over the rocks. Stalactites hung down in the most beautiful formations, covered with a bioluminescence. Glow worms crawled over the rock-face, joining the shimmering motions of nature's luminosity. Vegetables grew in rows of clay pots and chickens and geese waddled and roamed freely, in the distance, gathering around smooth, sandstone fountains of spraying fresh water making a comforting sound that could soothe the soul of both devils and angels alike.

"Where are we?" I managed to croak out shaking my head a little, checking I am fully awake.

"We are at Rhyiathe's home. It is quite the spectacle, is it not? Listen, I am sorry, I went to the library, but the book was not there, so it was all for nothing. I am terribly sorry, your powers were revealed, Aurora. The council are deliberating over what should be done with you, now they know you are not . . . *hu-man*, and how they will obtain a Twelfth hu-man for the Rite. You are immortal, a vampire even, so they cannot very well hold a trial against you now or examine your case as a hu-man, or even use you for the Offering. But they want to know how you got through the vortex to Periculliouis and undetected. You have *shiv'ved* off a lot of powerful people, so you better stay low for a while. Silent even," Lilly raised an eyebrow, a small smile played on her lips like I was incapable of doing this – being quiet.

I heard all the words as they formed themselves into neat little slots, which were pushed inside my mind for processing but the only word that clung to my ears like a tick, getting engorged; was the word, "Rhyiathe." I shuddered, the *spell placer*. I still didn't trust that he had not put a powerful spell on me somehow, so I sat quietly, not saying anything.

I was told later that when I had attacked Eiderlan in a state of blood lust, I was shot with a tranquiliser dart in the back and that it had taken four or five more shots to bring me down - which was an unheard-of amount even in this great magical world. I had stumbled back, unconscious, falling off the platform backwards and had been plunging headfirst into the great abyss. Rhyiathe had flown across the arena and caught me in his arms. There was an uproar. The King had openly announced that there would be no trial to examine me on how I came through the vortex and he had declared me to be a Vampire, seeing as I had changed into one before the crowds. Lilly had said this was strange and that the announcement had been rushed, and the King had left straight afterwards, while the Council were pleading with him to change his mind. Although, I had shrugged it off at the time, I was immensely relieved, in truth, I didn't have to stand trial, so I didn't really want to ask anymore questions about it.

At this moment, Rhyiathe strode into the room carrying an enormous ancient looking leather-bound book; it hung over his broad chest. He tried to look at me under the cover of his thick, black eyelashes. I flushed and muttered something about not feeling well. They both ignored me – the story of my life here in the realms.

Lilly stood there, mouth opening and closing soundlessly before she said, "The Tome of Cold Ones. Where did you get it Rhyiathe? I broke into Lord Tennison's . . ." she abruptly stopped, remembering her place, and straightened up.

"Go on. What did you say, *lawbreaker*?" Rhyiathe burst out with laughter and muttered, 'criminal,' under his breath. His laughter was a beautiful sound, full of sunshine. He spread a type of summer haze wherever he was

and I coveted him from a distance in that atrium in a cave inside a mountain.
He continued joking with Lilly, "I know all about your little plot anyway, that's why I am going to leave my old family heirloom, that *I* have permission to have, by the way, in the more intimate little reading room off this very hallway and if *someone* were to come here in the afternoon each day to read it for an hour or so, then I doubt I would notice it to have to report it to the authorities." He looked around Lilly, directly at me and wriggled his eyebrows, playfully.
I pulled myself up and back out of his eyeline, embarrassed that I was injured, and half undressed. His expression was one of hurt upset. A queasy feeling gripped me. I hated seeing the hurt dim his usually vibrant green eyes, but I felt awkward around him. Self-conscious even.
"Well, I'll leave you two to your- . . .*administrations*." He turned and I couldn't help but notice his slender back and muscular shoulders were very taut and fine. Spinning back around, he looked at me and it was just the two of us focussed on each other, drawn into one another's gaze and my stomach flipped over again. I watched the pertness of his mouth as he said, "Aurora, you are welcome here each day. I will be here waiting for you . . . let yourself in." There was that intense gaze, again. He stepped into the shadows by the rock wall and disappeared from my view – I kept forgetting he's a vampire and made from the stuff of shadows and mist. It frightened me that I am one of them too, well, in part.
A few moments passed.
"*What* was that?" Lilly yelled out, waving the compress around in the air with a frantic kind of energy.
"What was what?" I flipped my hair across my face, my bare shoulder grazed my chin and I pouted sulkily. I was going for sultry, but I looked like I was chewing a wasp, I could feel it and started blushing. My face coloured and I burned.
"Don't you pretend that I didn't see what I saw . . . you and Rhyiathe." The shock dripped from each syllable of Lilly's words. No doubt her eyes were popping out of her head too.
I muttered under my breath about pushing her own feelings onto me and she squeezed the compress harder than necessary on my back, making me scream out with an "*ouch*."

"Fine, keep your secrets," Lilly pouted, digging me in the ribs, "right, you grab some time with the Tome, and you can read a few chapters before I take you back to the castle." This was not a request but more of a command.

There was no point arguing with her. Sliding off the table, holding my back, I walked gingerly over to the small room indicated as a reading room and let myself in. It was actually the size of a small library and there was floor to ceiling shelves of books that covered each wall. Sitting myself down at a chunky neat wooden table in the darkness of a corner, I lit a candle. The flame spat into life, sharing its glow with me and the thick darkness of the surroundings of the little library. My fingers caressed the smooth wooden surface of the table. I ached to see the open blue of the sky but knew it would not happen today. The heavy plush red curtains were drawn in secrecy over the strange twin suns and frothy cotton wool clouds outside. I was a trespasser here in the immortal lands, hunched over a large golden tome of ancient immortal history, stealing their stories, weighing the narrative in my mind to get to the truth – the very heart of their troubles. The history was all in this forbidden book of the Seven Kingdoms. I run my finger over the letters of the embossed title, called Book One: The Tome of the Cold Ones. Here to devour each word, so that those that wrote these hand scribed texts could speak to me over the sands of time, I got a swift chill thinking about the fact I was reading the words of the long dead. They were here with me, standing in the shadows, whispering from the gloom all around, leaving a legacy of truth about cobweb covered days, best left forgotten. I held my heart cavity and took a deep breath. My senses were open, ready, and waiting to take in their wisdom and I was gone. . .

Book one: The Tome of Cold Ones

The first recordings of the existence of magical beings were believed to be through the telling of fables that were then translated into a range of different texts across the world. Before the Clandestine Agreement of 2026 BC on Earth, it was a time of discovery; development of empire states and colonisation of the discovered continents of Earth. Each country on this planet was organised around a set of natural resources and minerals, and these natural occurring elements were traded for equal value between nations in early 3000bc. This Free Trade enabled the setting up of transport links connecting the globe

through trade routes. Specific countries in the West, like Briton, developed skills and crafts that enabled great expeditions, which included vast armies and weaponry. Ship building and engineering was the centre of Empire-building civilisations, during this period, with one mission in mind; to colonise. Colonising and expanding territories through the treaties of offering education, sanitation and infrastructure to smaller countries and tribes. Whenever smaller groups resisted this offer and wanted to continue arrangements of fair and equal trade, then the empire would become aggressors and occupy lands in territories, organising campaigns to subdue resistance. The British Empire colonised many parts of the known world from 2860 BC through to more recent years, AD, creating systems of control such as mass slavery, oppression, and death penalties for those that did not cooperate. Although this was a dark time in the history of the world, it also connected smaller communities and tribes to one another. This is when it became apparent that magical beings existed and, due to the established transport links, these communities started to gravitate to specific areas of the globe and consolidate.
Magical beings were already organised and more secretive about their own abilities, due to the real threat of persecution, and were often found settled in regions of the planet that were considered as less hospitable plains of Earth – away from their human counterparts. Magical beings lived together in peace and harmony, often finding safety in their combined numbers. As a society, they had cause to become more militarised in response to colonialism.

The beginning of the world finding out about the existence of magical beings on Earth was brutal, during a barbaric time in the history of the world. It is recorded that magical beings could not be distinguished from humans without them being in the act of performing magic in some way. Their abilities were unique to each of them - no two had exactly the same powers, but elemental and celestial groupings were evident. For example, all the immortals were able to channel and draw on nature to conjure fire from their hands and manipulate the elements. Most Immortals were discovered when they were in a heightened emotional state or provoked or trying to protect themselves in some way. Immortals looked exactly like humans at the beginning, and it was not until much later, until they crossed over to the other planets that make up the Seven Kingdoms, that they grew in tallness and strength. It is typical for an immortal to grow to be over seven feet high. In the beginning, their discovery rate was minimal, so their existence was interwoven with folklore, myth, and legends. As their numbers grew, along with a tendency to converge into settlements more commonplace, Leaders and kings of humans became very wary of their potential. Humans believed they could absorb the powers by eating the flesh of a magical person. A gruesome underground-economy trade started, and stone tablets have been discovered on archaeological digs of evidence of sales of immortals and their body parts. Those who were not killed were enslaved, performing magic for Kings, Queens, and leaders, and supporting armies through performing spells. Immortal children were kept as pets on occasion.

Disorientated, I emerged blinking from the pages of the ancient words. Lilly had come in at some point and opened the curtains a little. Slivers of the light danced across the table - oddly bright to eyes grown accustomed to the dark. The last sentence of the text still prodded at my brain. The ancient words whispered from my lips - soundlessly. Slamming the book closed, my fingers involuntarily flexing on the gold, embossed cover of the book. It was studded with precious stones, and I scrapped my knuckles over the raised, cut diamonds.

The heavy pages had fallen, brushed in thick wedges against the softer underside of my hand, as I slammed the book shut, causing little shockwaves to course through my fingertips. It dawned on me, *It's real, it's all real. The immortals lived on Earth, were part of the human race and treated like chattel* I cried out into the gloom of the small room, while the foundations of reality that I had built my whole worldview on came crashing down. It's a comfort in a way, I just thought I was going crazy, waiting to snap out of this episode of psychosis, but . . .

Monsters did exist after all and they were human and the immortals were real.

No longer able to question my own sanity, my hearts quickened. Was it all real? Including the twelve that needed to be sacrificed? What did that now mean for my sister? I meant my sister's body. Oh god damn it. I don't know what I mean anymore.

A fear gripped me. My sister's body. What were they going to do with her? I knew the book contained the answers, but I needed to find out now, today, this very instant. I became panicked.

Running over to the plush curtains, I wrenched them open. The thick velvet folds clanged heavily on polished rings of pure gold.

Blistering sunlight flooded into the room and the power of the two suns in the sky shocked me once more but reaffirmed that magic was real, that I was made from particles of it and that my abilities were here with me in

each atom of consciousness that I hosted in this room. What was I becoming?
I stared out of the window trying to find something to focus on other than my dread. A wolf of a man strode past, hair long and teeth on display. He did a double take of me standing framed behind the glass of the window and laughed. He stuck out his lolling dog-like tongue and growled playfully, revealing canine teeth. My hands automatically covered my lips and as I stepped away from the glass pane, his growl turned to a throaty laugh. *It cannot be.* A scream curdled at the back of my throat.
Living fables were walking around and most humans are unaware of their existence.
It is all real, it is all real, it is all real, it is all real, it is all real, my mind was telling me. It was in shock and I couldn't focus at all, on anything else.
Turning away from the blinding sunlight, I looked at the door that served as a reminder that I needed to plan an excursion that night. I must find the sword and throwing daggers Lilly gave to me and locate the place where my sister's body is housed that Lord Tennison called The Chamber.

Later that afternoon, Lilly walked me back over to the castle, weaving our way through the baking hot cobblestone streets, the partygoers of the festival of Freya danced playfully by us, giggling and singing. Depictions of a beautiful flame-haired Goddess with blue eyes, covered every surface, her kind heart-shaped face peered down at me from everywhere, every angle. Cat symbols were everywhere too. Kittens mostly, gifted on bonding nights to soulmates. Lilly had told me not to get involved with the festival, to stay away. That bonding nights were a part of the immortal culture; to find and bond with a fated soul mate. This was customary. The immortals were few in number many years ago and it was decreed that to preserve their species, an ancient spell would be invoked that enabled each immortal to find the strongest match, a soulmate, and to have as many offspring as possible to grow the population to such a size, that they could protect themselves from any external threat – that of humans or any other outside influences that threatened their existence.
It seemed strange to me, but it was an inherent part of their immortal culture – to find a soulmate and raise a family for the survival of their species. There was no discrimination, nothing was frowned upon. Males could bond with males and females with females and those that didn't want

children of their own could still look after others' offspring or serve the community in some other way. Family and the community are at the centre of their worlds, it was a great honour to serve, in the immortal culture, and know that you were a part of a shared movement to protect the species and all living beings. Lilly had ended the explanation with an ominous,
"Well, for some families, community is at the centre of our worlds but not all Elves think the same way." I didn't want to ask what she had meant.

Tonight, the crowds wore intricately designed feline masks, hiding their identities from one another, to allow their senses to take over and intuitively find soulmates. There was a boisterous singing coming from the inebriated crowds. The atmosphere was charged and dream-like, mists were swirling round, covering the streets. It suddenly dawned on me, I stopped dead in my tracks, "So, how do they know when they have found their soulmate? How does the spell let them know?" I asked, trembling slightly.
"I think you already know the answer to that, Aurora, don't you?" Lilly gave me a knowing smile, her eyes full of happiness, "He is a good Vampire." Was all she said then dropped the subject, which I was glad of because my embarrassment wouldn't let me speak.
We strolled past strange shops and market stalls, which were everywhere in the city. There were apothecaries selling healing balms and remedies next to magic stores with magical wares and selling spells of every kind.
Great winged monsters that looked like large reptiles, sort of like more mild-mannered dinosaurs, stood guard outside large beautifully constructed houses and huge griffins flew overhead mounted by soldiers and keepers of the peace. Cats walked along the streets in little gangs, head butting immortal legs and hands for attention.
I stood staring and blinking in wonder and Lilly smiled and laughed.
The people were celebrating, throwing little pellets into the air in wild abandonment, that exploded, releasing twinkling lights and smoke, made of vibrant colours. The sky was crowned with shimmering golden lights. Breathless I was, in the awe-inspiring beauty of the magic of their world on display, but at the same time, a coldness settled on me, a distance. Focussing my intent, I knew what needed to be done. I was to find my sister's body and use this chaos as a veil to cloak me, while I navigated my way to The Chamber, Lord Tennison had mentioned.

But how to find it without asking, I did not quite know.
My subconscious brain was looking after me, scanning for solutions to my problem.
That's when I saw it, a shop displaying bottled spells stacked haphazardly on shelves in little neat rows upon rows. There was every spell imaginable there, my vision bounced between the baskets and shelving, my gaze found what it was looking for.
A little wicker basket was filled with lots of cobalt glass bottles labelled with handwritten notes on the top, "Locator spells".
Slyness of hand was easy for me. Quick and nimble were my fingers and the bottle was up my sleeve.
We made our way back to the apartment in the castle. Problem solved.

Chapter Thirteen - the lies that I have learned.

My hearts were bursting with a type of urgent turmoil. My throat was holding my breath in, suffocating me slowly with a strain. My hand was comfortingly wrapped around the hard glass of the locator spell bottle that I stole earlier. Waiting for Lilly to leave the apartment suite, I was stuck in this torturous state. I couldn't quite explain what was happening.

"Soon" I could hear myself murmur. I was desperate to get to my little sister, but I was in no fit state and a shadow was hovering over me.

I was in its grip. Hunger, such a wretched hunger. I trembled from it. Stifling out a sob from its coiling chokehold, my veins burned, and I was wretched. I was lost. Clammy. Incomplete. Wretchedness, when I needed my strength most.

"Where is she, my sister?" I wailed demented, screaming out in my despair but the sound doesn't pass my lips, I stood hunched over, leaning on the back of a chair a little too heavily. My throat swelling with desire.

"Are you okay M'Lady?"

The room spun, unsteadiness and trembling took hold of my body. All my control was lost. Dizziness tickled at the inside of my skull and my inner ear vibrated in my head. A loud buzzing in my ears. "An accursed bee of some kind in my skull?," I thought I had asked myself.

Shuddering to keep standing upright, Lilly stepped closer, "What bee? I see nothing?" and I lifted my eyes urgently, smelling her sweet, sweet lifeblood. The buzzing sound, the deep throbbing bass, was coming from her, and it was intoxicating to me. Her pulse made me sway, involuntarily dance. Leaning closer I could smell her essence and I was made wild by it.

Thrum, thrum, thrum, thrum, thrum.

The purest of elixir, the sweetest of scents. The fuel that I craved, calling to me from under her skin. My eyes were expanding and drinking her in. All eyes were upon her flesh, and I was consumed.

"Aurora, listen to me. Rhyiathe gave me something for you. Please take it. I am holding it in front of you. Please take it from my hands, now."

Her delicate hand was holding out a vial but all I could feel was the quickening pulse on the inside of her wrist, the dainty flutter. The delicious *Thrum, thrum, thrum, thrum, thrum, thrum.*

There was a singing of metal as she took out her sword carefully - an insurance policy.

My tongue protruded forward between my fast-growing incisures. Slithering down sharply, the needle pricks pinched at my drying out lips. It was sustenance I needed.

Lilly lunged to grab me with her strong hand, quite frantically, her vice like fingers pressed hard against my neck. Thrusting the vial in my mouth, I bit down passionately as if it was flesh. The liquid burst down my throat. I staggered backwards and Lilly released her hand away from my throat. Relief flooded her features, but her eyes were still avidly upon me. glistening with fear. She was leaning heavily on the thick, white wall of my rooms.

Kneeling, I suckled at the blood blister and I drained it without shame. Letting out a satisfied sigh when it was all finished, my eyesight returned to normal again. My incisures pulled back into my hard, stretched gums – returning back to normal, well, normal for me, now I am different.

"What was that?" I said with a fear bouncing between the words.

"The quickening. The frenzy for blood," Lilly said matter of fact, as if I was enquiring after the weather and she was telling me it was expected to be a fine, summer's day. None of this was normal.

"I lost all control…Will it…Will it happen again?"

She looked away and did not look at me directly. "I told you this would happen; you'll need these to keep your Cold One at bay. One every ten days or so, to remain . . . in control. Rhyiathe has more. He brews his own. Most vampires have their own family recipes. Here, take them. Here are three or four more for you to keep nearby. Sometimes you'll need one at random times. It will creep up on. The potion, it's not an exact science. Just try and stay in control and don't let it get beyond a certain point . . ."

"What happens if it does?"

"You've got a new kind of strength and power, I haven't seen before so, who knows. I just don't want to be around to find out . . ."

Lilly looked away again uncomfortably. I could tell there was something on her mind, something deep but she didn't want to talk about it.

"Thank you," I mumbled, "for staying and helping me to not . . ." I was struggling with the right words to describe it. 'To Turn.' *Will I know when I change? How will I change back?*
Her hands ran through her hair and she held the back of her neck stiffly as she said, "I better get going. You must be tired too."
It wasn't a question. I could tell she wanted to leave.
"Yeah, too much excitement for one day. I am so tired right now," I said, pretending to yawn a little bit too enthusiastically and immediately cringed at my terrible acting abilities.
Lilly hesitated and turned to me pulling me in for hug. "I'm so glad you're back," she said with a smile plainly on her lips and then let go, shimmering through the doorway, sadly, like a mist that I couldn't see or touch.
"Back?" I questioned the dust-speckled air, which circled around in her wake.
A few moments later, I was in the bathroom filling up the ornamental wash hand basin with warm water. Gold taps spurting out cool, fresh river water. Keenly I could smell the particles of the plant life and the riverbed it once washed over. Touching the glass bottle of the spell, I noticed a strange light in the contents that glowed from within.
On impulse, I poured the glowing liquid into the steam coming off the water. A huge reaction of blinding light knocked me to the floor and as I was blasted backwards, I shouted "The Chamber."

My eyes flickered open. I had been transported somewhere by the spell. I couldn't make out where I was, it was very dark, "Just great," I murmured to myself, while my hair fanned out behind me.
The floor was made of cold flagstones, corners and grooves pierced upwards into my tender back. There was a chill in the air, my bones ached from the cold of it. I hadn't quite recovered from the wounds received in the arena just yet. My eyes drawn upwards, following the shape of the freezing air holding onto the warmth of my breath. The ceiling was made of raw masonry, painstakingly tapped into shapes of gothic arches and imperial status motifs, heralding deeds from long ago. Hearing the trumpets of yesteryear in imagined blasts of memory, I get the sense that I had been here before but this environment was wholly unfamiliar to me.

Confused, I jumped up on my feet. The soft soles of my leather boots whispered on the floor as they glided across the cold slates, silently exploring this place, kicking up a fine layer of dust as I stepped through the halls. They were abandoned, little used, cobwebs and the scuttling of spiders told me so. I crept uneasily through the shadows, peering round corners and jumping at nothing but fat rats waddling away from the sound of my hushed feet.

The hallways were gloomy, a bleak labyrinth that spurred off into more hidden hallways - an odd type of grand warren. The smoke blackened walls glowing from torches dimly lighting the way. The ambience solemn and sacred, the place deserted. Quiet and in stillness as if waiting for something to begin. The Chamber must be a temple of some kind. Magic was in the air. I could feel the pressing sensation on my face, but I couldn't see where the magic was coming from or who was performing it. So, I continued on, moving like a snake from side to side – a little more guarded than before.

Closing my eyes and listening, I heard a low guttural humming coming from somewhere up ahead. Soft leather and muffled footfalls on hard stone were echoing towards me, gaining ground. Someone was coming.

There was nothing to hide behind in this bare hallway. Looking up for an escape route, a timber lintel overhead caught my eye and I jumped up to wrap my limbs around it.

As I sprung upwards, I bounded further than I thought I was capable of and hit the ceiling with the top of my skull. A deep *thud.* Eyes rattling. Head spinning slightly. This was when I cursed out loud. Gripping onto the stonework easily with loose fingertips, I found a tiny ledge to hold onto and hung there with hardly any effort at all. Choking back a gasp, I had no time to question these new abilities of mine, just appreciate them.

A tall man in a hooded robe made of rich cream fabric shuffled underneath me - a priest of some kind. Runes etched on a sash around his neck. He was holding a smoking metal ball, a thurible, on a thick linked chain of worship and was swinging it side to side, in a rhythm and murmuring in an ancient tongue.

The tendrils of incense and curling smoke, danced towards the ceiling. Earthy smells filled the dank air, of trees, and sage, and something else that I couldn't name.

The Elder – Lights of the Seven Kingdoms

My fingers perched in between the metal bolts and rivets, and tendons of the high beams in the ceiling, my body dangling arrow straight, over the walking priest. Muscles straining from waiting for him to leave the hallway. Sweat forming on my upper lip. I watched his lonely walk with some interest. He appeared to be on his own.

After a few moments had gone by and the Priest had moved from that hallway, I dropped down with a lightness of foot and held my core muscles taut, ready to fight if the need arose. But the hallway was clear, I was certain no one was before or behind me, except for the priest, so I followed the priest's footsteps made visible from the layer of dust. Along we both walked, me haunting his footsteps and him not realising – a studied game of cat and mouse we played for a while.

Eventually, he led me into a deep, dark cavern made from the inside of a mountain. Cream candles in the thousands lit all around, each had a golden flame that flickered, lighting up the thick gloom - offering up a wholesome light. I stood up a little taller.

The priest walked on and I darted into a fashioned-out chamber, hidden in the stone-hewn walls. I was up high looking down on a great, circular room with a centre stage and a glass ceiling held in place by the craggy, thick fingers of a jagged rock wall.

A great many robed priests and priestesses were standing on the floor below, a sea of cream folds, glittering chains of servitude and quiet reverence. All the drawn and pale faces, staring up, towards a fixed point. Their eyes were gleaming in the light of the flickering candles mounted on the floor, anticipation in their blank, monastic stares. The congregation were turned towards the raised platform in the centre of the chamber.

I witnessed the conflict within their religious faces. They were straining to subdue themselves, made guilty by the strength of their excitement. The vestiges of carefully avoided emotions, were bubbling back to the surface and as much as they tried to deny it, it was there written across each line of their reddening faces – like excited children waiting for something to begin, something special to start.

Each one of them were ritualistically swinging the smoking thuribles on thick, clinking chains, in a monstrous rhythm – to a loud beating of drums. Apprehension and a type of religious mania was slowly building. It clung

heavily to the room, announcing itself with a terrifying wringing energy. This was the night that sacrifices would be made.
A woman stepped out onto the raised platform. A Priestess of some kind. She lightly moved forward on feet clod in slippers, dressed in fine robes of spun wool and an armour of dull silver underneath, unadorned, but she distinguished herself from the other religious types by the wearing of a large crown upon her head. It was made with raw cut diamonds and wrought of gold spirals holding the gems in place. The High Priestess was lit up by lights. The source of which, was not easy for me to spot, if it was in fact, coming from anywhere external at all.
Up on the balcony, I slowly crept forward, crouching into the thickest of shadows, I remained hidden looking down on the spectacle below. It was easy to move and slink around unseen now that the Rite had begun – the drums banging. The noise drowning at all others.
On the raised platform, behind the priestess were twelve slabs of solid and golden veined marble and on the fourth slab along, was my sister's lifeless body. From the points of her toes to her forehead, she was covered by a white silk sheet, but I knew it was her. Smaller than the rest, but it was her soft bright, blonde hair cascading over the marble slab like waterfalls made from honey, which gave her away. I stared at her hair peaking over the edge of the white cloth, it reminded me of her small broken body on the stretcher that fateful day when she had died. My tears slide silently down my cheeks. "I'm coming for you, Button, and I will take you home," I whispered in a cracked voice, my eyes glowing in the soft light of the beacons lit near my head.
A hush settled over the cave as The High Priestess lifted her face and she began to speak in a melodic tone, clear and purposeful – setting out stepping stones of a story that would enable me to hear the truth – the truth of the Rite.

"We are here today, The Devout of The Light, to honour the Ritual. You, the faithful followers, who understand the history and wish to hold the Universe in peace." her hands, arms and chest are covered in a sparkling silver chainmail, which compliments the telling of this story - the magical forces in the air. Fingers pointing outwards, she was acknowledging the crowd as The Devout.

Thousands of voices rose up into the cold night air in unison, enough to give me chills as they all spoke,

"We are here to witness the Rite of the Offered."

"For centuries we have guarded The Void with the Offering of the Twelve, this Rite happens every thousandth year. We unite humans with immortals in one form, on this night, all to protect The Void and uphold The Clandestine Agreement, holding the universe intact and at peace. Sacred Agreement set by our ancestors to protect the Realms from the shedding of blood, covering all in a blanket of darkness. We will perform the Ritual, as is foretold, and resurrect those that are Offered. . ."

The High Priestess continued preaching her sermon to the crowds but I could not hear her any longer. I tuned out her next rhetoric. She was but a noise in the background as I twisted my mind around the words that seemed so very shocking to me. I repeated them in a whisper, *"Resurrect . . . resurrection, of my . . . my sister?"*

Abruptly, I woke up out of my grief. My grief cloak, the one that had been smothering me since the day Button died, that had been reducing me to a husk and driving my courage deep within me, well, the cloak was falling away.

Below the surface, a spark of light glowed at the words of resurrection. I coveted them – the words. Held them to me, my sister, Dawn can be saved. *I am coming Button.*

The lioness within me struggled forward on trembling haunches to push through, to rise. As her great claws latched on to the final barrier dividing me from the outside world, the animal within me let out an almighty roar of freedom. I stood up, erect and tall with purpose in the vast cavern where the Rite was being performed – finally able to breathe the free air.

I smashed my clenched fist into the palm of my hand and silently vowed to myself the Ritual must be allowed to go ahead and then I would return to Earth after the resurrection of my dead sister.

Here in the shadows of my grief, the light would rise again. I pledged that I would lead a different life if only she were allowed to come back to me.

The High Priestess's voice swam back into my ears and I concentrated hard so I could listen carefully to what would happen next.

". . . and so, we begin The Ritual to uphold the peace. Orderlies, please bring forth the sacred Staff of Indris, so we can begin."

A voice rung out unexpectedly through the crowd.
"Forgive my interruption, my dearest of High Priestesses, Bringer of the Suns to these realms. I have a question -" The smooth, confident voice of Lord Tennison echoed across the great vastness of The Chamber, he stood regal, dressed in gold armour and looking down on the crowd "- Why do we need to continue to police the Void? Why do we need to be afraid any longer? The Immortals are now many in number and powerful beyond human comprehension. Our powers are beyond anything the humans understand. Our weapons are lethal and cunning. Our people brave, wise, and just. Why do we still hold the Agreement true? When we can overrun and take back what is our birthright to restore balance to the Universe. To rid it of the race of *hu-mans*. Scourge of the natural laws, defilers of the planets and realms. Junk of space and crippler of sacred animals. What do we owe *them* I ask you?"
A great clatter of agreeing murmurs broke out across the crowds, following the High Lord's carefully, orchestrated words. A malevolent expression of pleasure glinted in Lord Tennison's eyes at the discord his words had caused. A sneer on his handsome face made him look disfigured in its coldness, in the flickering light from the vast array of candles positioned about the chamber. The High Priestess had no choice but to hesitate, looking around the room and assessing the intention of the crowd gathered there.
A large auburn-haired elf, covered in a well-used suit of copper-coloured armour, stepped out in front of the group of Elven Lords, he had been standing with. He held in his hands, what looked like an earth-boring tool, a gimlet. A heavy and cumbersome tool, but lethal in the large Elf Lord's calloused hands.
"Aye, I agree. We talk of the Ritual like it is a sacred Rite, but it is not. It is a reflection of the Immortals' cowardice. Our collective subjugation. It is our shame. SHAME. We must withstand it and tear apart the tools that uphold this Rite, The Offered. Death to humans and let us reclaim the Earth." He lifted the weapon, his hair flickered against the candlelight like it was made of living, precious metal. The great auburn-haired elf hurled these provocations outward into the middle of the room and onto the discontentment of the crowd. They are spellbound by his treasonous words.

The High Priestess cleared her throat and looked out over the gathered crowd, concerned. She addressed Lindon,

"Lindon, I understand your need for expression but not on this day. Not here in the Temple. Please address your politics to the Senate. To petition through diplomacy and within political arenas where our laws are set and governed. To bring such words of violence into this sacred space is not right and you know it. We are peaceful and devout."

She then turned to the other High Lord,

"Lord Tennison, my Crown Prince, why do you raise these questions in these sacred walls and at this time? What are you trying to achieve and for whose gain?"

Shocked murmurings from the crowd as all eyes wandered to gaze on the Crown Prince of Elf-kind.

Lord Tennison response was of disdain for the priestesses' words, he arranged himself by firstly pulling his cream silk cloak closely around his shoulders, like he was cold and weary, then lifted his proud chin, to address the room more than the high priestess,

"Forgive me, High Priestess, I did not realise that my question would be the spark that would ignite such a fuse of underlying discontent. I only asked a question, but I see that there are those who wish for change through whatever means necessary. I will go in peace, but I do not hold any store over *all* in this place," a wicked gleam crept across Lord Tennison's face as he said this. His eyes fell on Lindon and he grinned.

Looking around the room I noticed, amongst the thousands of unarmed priests and priestesses and worshippers, were about twenty elves that had the look of soldiers. Heavily armed under their cloaks of cream silk. They had carefully dressed as worshippers but silver chainmail peeped out from under comfortable tunics, to match their prince and his high elf lords. Easy to spot, they stood out, these were hired killers, rigid, hardened of expressions and keenness of eyes, but their sheep-like robes were more wolf than flock.

The large elf lord that the High Priestess had referred to as Lindon, started up the stairs of the raised platform, moving up each step with a purpose, armoured-metal feet scraping; clunking down hard on the stone steps, heading towards the marble slabs, where the Offered were laid out. Vulnerable and unconscious.

His weapon was drawn, bouncing in his huge hand. The pleasure of imminent violence set within Lindon's scarred and battle-hardened face. A dark grimace there.

The High Priestess raised her staff, long, dainty fingers curled around the outside of the soft wood. Quick-witted and sure, she moved swiftly to set a protective magical barrier across the platform, between Lindon and the Offered, with a wave of her hand. Her orderlies, fell back from the platform in a hurried worry. She was no match for a fighting elf lord, intent on destroying the platform. Lindon was pushed back by the protective spell at first, then he grinned at the challenge and raised his gimlet and came at it again. He grunted, thrust forward, and shoved the gimlet in both his hands, he charged at the barrier- he was not to be deterred. Blow after blow, he savagely landed on the barrier, with precision, he skewered through the spell with his twirling blade. Sparks rose and fell. The crowds fell further back. Shocked expressions on their faces. Huge chunks of the masonry were crumbling under the Elf Lord's will, as he set about disarming the magical barrier.

creaking and cracking filled the air of the cavern, the magical barrier was slowly giving way under the force of Lindon's hatred. The attack vicious and unrelenting. Deadly focussed was he on smashing his way through to the Offered and putting an end to the Rite. The gimlet shone and it showed signs the weapon had been enhanced in some way.

It was not long before a realisation settled on me that I needed the High Priestess to complete the Rite, otherwise my sister, Dawn, would not be resurrected nor brought back to me. I lowered my head, my lips curled back, Lindon was my enemy at that moment in time. I needed to get down there and fast.

Grabbing the solid high rocks nearest to me, I gripped them with my gloved fingers, using them as an anchor to hang down and freefall the fifty-foot drop to the ground, gliding like a spider's fine webbing. Legs struck out before me, landing lightly before a group of priests. Astonishment sparks in their eyes, they held onto each other in the way people do who are mortally afraid.

"Get out of my way, go on leave. This is no place for the likes of you priests," I said, with earnest, but it came out as a grim warning. Edging away from both me in the centre of the chamber and Lindon on the stage,

the priests drifted back towards the exit. When I pulled out my sword from its scabbard, I took a reconnaissance look at the platform above me. Pivoting on my back leg, I swung around – the elves' men in the crowd had spotted me. They changed direction and started towards me.
Darting and weaving through the crowds of beguiled worshippers, I ran towards the cracking sound ready to fight. I was running forward and the crowds were falling back, like the tide pulling in, offering a warning before the strike of a Tsunami.
"Lindon, stop." I shouted. The elf lord carried on not able to hear me over the deep shakes from the twirling gimlet blade. I did not wait one second longer, I jumped forward through the air with my sword drawn, approaching fast, sweeping into the brightly lit areas and onto the platform above. Drifting over the magical barrier, spinning in the air, to land face-to-face with the snarling face of Lindon.
My feet lightly thumped as they hit the platform. He stopped, standing straight, momentarily ceasing his attack to stare at me.
Shock passed over his reddened face. We stood still, my blade drawn to his neck. Unblinking we stared into each other's eyes, me above and him with his face raised to me knowing what was coming next. A grin crinkled at the corner of his eyes, mocking my challenge to him. His eyes were a warm brown with a hint of contempt, mine, well, I could care less how he described them but they were unblinking, unwavering as I crouched low, sword held upwards, readying myself for his next move.
"Come to play little she-human?" Lindon said with a callous laugh, swinging the gimlet up murderously onto his shoulder – holding it with intention.
"No, come to stop you so the Rite can go ahead," I said, with absolute conviction, while my blade tip was pointed at Lindon's thick, reddening skin covering his bobbing throat.
The chamber was steadily emptying but there were still whispers,
"It's the vampire-hybrid that killed Eiderlan in the arena."
It was not long before the last remaining worshippers could see this would end in blood shed, even the most hardy, stalwart priests started making their way out towards the exit, rushing to get through the arches and away from the looming battleground.

Lindon heard the murmurs, flicking his eyes between the crowd then back at me and there was an uncertainty upon him. Not to mention, the telltale little beads of sweat, sending me messages that he was concerned.
He managed a quick glance over to a darker part of the chamber and to where another elf lord stood, this one had hair as black as flocking ravens, as tall as he was beautiful, which was over seven feet. Towering above the other Elf lords in the middle of the group, he stood as their leader, straight backed and sure of himself. The dark-haired Elf Lord tried to remain anonymous, but it was too obvious with the way the others in the group looked at him for instruction, that it was him who had the real power here.
"Well, Gamone? Fighting a vampire witch wasn't part of our deal," Lindon shouted to the Elf Lord, losing all of his composure in the vibration of fear building.
Gamone looked interested, assessing me from the gloom of the balcony he stood upon,
"Have at it," a deep masculine voice, slithered out of his smirking mouth and a tinkling sound met me in my ears.
An energy pressed on my face. I paused to peer closer into the darkness at the one they called Gamone. He was submerged in dark shadow, made up of his own story but I could see him, physically powerful and intimidating in his taut body lines. I was fixed to the spot unable to move, the pressure was hammering me to the spot where I stood. His green glowing disk-like eyes searched me out as he keenly watched Lindon's gimlet, thick coils of sharp metal; being smashed into my ribs with an arc of his muscular arm, and then being withdrawn. It was in my back next, piercing my bones with extreme violence, while my attention had been temporarily elsewhere.

Chapter Fourteen - the gifts given to the chosen.

Falling forward, I landed heavily with a loud crack down on my knees - the joints shattering in a painful turmoil. That's when my adrenaline and vampire-quick reflexes kicked in. With a slightness, I jumped up and in one bound, somersaulted over the top of Lindon with my head bared down.

A strange thing was happening inside my body. My broken rib bones were fusing back together. Sinew and bone were re-knitting, and rebuilding themselves, and I could feel it all taking place inside of me like worms crawling over my wet, living skeleton.

With my blade in my hands, the top of my head brushed hard against Lindon's burning flames of auburn hair, I swung my sword down, the blade flashed. Cleanly cutting Lindon, mid-flight, neatly down the centre, his large head and body silently splitting into two separate parts.

I landed on one knee, my sword held up behind me, blood splattered on my face. Before the high Priestess, I crouched low – perhaps in an unplanned gesture of forgiveness. As Lindon's body, no longer whole, slumped lifelessly forward behind me onto the floor. The remainder of the crowd reeled back and begun to cry out in horror – "Demon, demon," was being howled out at me.

A look of outright disgust flashed across The High Priestesses' face. Sword still raised; my concern was not the High Priestess, there was still a small gathering of High Elves and their soldiers in this chamber to manage.

I tuned out her judgement, while my eyes darted into the shadows to see what my Lord Gamone would do now. The great elf lord, Gamone, stared at me with cold eyes, arching his heavy-set eyebrow – he was impressed. The Lords around him muttered in his ear, and with one final look at me of smirking amusement, he was gone. Gamone did not hang around, his boots clipped thunderously as he exited swiftly in the distance – woollen, prince-like cape, adorned with chains of gold, twirling behind him.

Lord Tennison was being pulled away by the other high Elf Lords, but he refused to move straightaway. Stiff and sullen, his head of bright golden hair rose out of the circle of Elf lord's and his eyes studied me closely. He was sizing me up, lip curled with venom, pontificating. Whatever he was plotting had been foiled, that much is clear from the tension – the obvious hatred, in his eyes aimed at me.

I smiled and winked, "I'll be ready, when you want to get even." I mouthed to Lord Tennison, twirling the hilt of my blade in my hands.

The High Priestess was stunned,

"No violence in this temple of the Light," she shouted into the centre of the cave. With a cautioning tone, she was turned towards Gamone's and Lord Tennison's group more than me. The High Priestess was clever – understanding politics more than she was letting on.

Circling around, I aimed the tip of my sword at the plainly dressed soldiers in the crowd that were edging, slowly creeping forward towards me. In a blink of an eye, they changed direction – wisdom gave them second thoughts, when they saw the furnace of rage burning on my face. Each of them started to move away from the platform. I relaxed my muscles and bowed deeply to The High Priestess.

"My apologies High Priestess. I had no choice. You were going to be attacked. Please continue." I bowed to her, leaning on my sword.

She stared down at me for a while questioningly and then softly said, "A vampire protecting The Rite and an Elf attacking the Holy, what are the realms coming to? What next is going to befall the Immortals and why do you help me, I wonder?" her eyes squinted trying to read my face.

I go to answer but all I heard her say is, "hold your silver tongue, vampire. I don't want to hear anymore lies this evening. Creature of darkness, get off my platform and I will begin."

I nodded and stepped back down into the crowd, eager to watch from the front row, The Rite and my sister's rebirth this night.

All the antagonists had left the Temple. I watched them as they went, hastening out discreetly. Then I pushed the loose strands of my hair behind my ears, that had worked its way free.

A werewolf came up behind me panting in my ear, standing a little too close. He transmogrified into his humanoid form, and he was beautiful, the human embodiment of a sleek dog. Blonde-haired, proud nose, loving

eyes and athletically built. I resisted the urge to pat his head and scratch him behind his ears.
"Hey, that was cool Vampyress. Dillion is my name, and you are Aurora. Do you remember? I saw you with Lilly the other day."
The lights that were lit when the ruckus started were now dimming. It was like the start of a play in a theatre when the narrator is outlining the introduction to the story and the lights are lowered so the audience can focus on the voice alone.
An excitement settled on me; the show was about to begin. My sister would soon be resurrected – I had such faith in the immortal's magical abilities already. It was inconceivable to me that she would not be back in my arms and smiling and breathing by the end of this spell. I whipped my head around and shushed him.
"Shush, it's about to begin," I whispered, stretching a hopeful smile across my manic face.
His eyes were chocolate brown, deep and soulful. In them was a loyalty and friendliness, that almost had me saying sorry for shushing him, but I didn't.
"Do I know you from somewhere?" I asked. The look on his face was unfathomable, intense – dark even.
"Listen, you are in danger...there is so much to tell you" And that's when I stepped back from him and gasped.
He grabbed both of my wrists and spun me around, my back pressed up against his torso. "don't draw attention to us. It's a lot to explain. Just not now, okay? Let's just watch The Rite together." His arms were still wrapped around me, and my hearts fluttered against my ribs.
"Okay," I let out as a whisper and stayed in the warmth of his embrace. It was comforting.
The whole temple turned to a rich black. A single shard of light beamed down. The golden light settled on the proud face of the High Priestess, presiding over this ceremony. Her crown glistened under the warm glare of the spotlights. Iridescent and ethereal she looked; her strong face turned up towards the ceiling ready to start the Rite.
My concentration was on the heartbeat of the werewolf standing behind me. All that was stopping our skin from touching was my bodysuit. I tried to move away, but he pinned me back to him. The heat was starting to

build between us. The tension before the Rite was palpable, and I am ashamed to say that in my emotional state, I started to warm to his enclosed arms, his sniffing at my neck and his nostrils urgently pressing on my skin. My body responded until The High Priestess's voice was echoing out into the cave, grabbing me, redirecting my concentration to the stage.

Dead languages mingled with the dank smell of the earth. A pulsating rhythm started to build in the centre of the stage, lights swirled in ribbons around the Platform – swooshing like clusters of invisible atoms circling in the air. The High Priestess was talking of a time long ago when humans hunted the Immortals like they were cattle - small and weak. Not yet fully formed, less than animals, seen as mutations of the human genetic code, children, adults, and the elderly were maimed and killed. Some were sold as slaves and livestock or maimed and left to die. My hearts wrenched with every word. Every single word. My sister and I both had known what it felt like to be considered less than, of nothing. Inhuman, is how we were both treated. Like worms underfoot.

I started to cry; warm saline tears, I was still human after all. The werewolf held me close.

I wanted my sister to rise – removing myself from Dillion's reach, I wanted her resurrection more than comfort; more than anything else. I felt the vibrations beating, coming from underground, from the planet's core. Lifting me up, making my atoms bounce within my veins.

That's when it happened. A loud crack of thunder sounded overhead, breaking the spell of the pulse. The ceiling was made of transparent glass. Lightning ripped through the darkness - great molten rivers of it and I watched it descend from the sky and ripple into the centre of the platform. Green glowing embers poured from the bolt and flooded the room, circling above each of the Offered and landing on them, emitting a heavenly glow.

The lights were coursing through the dead humans and linking their prone bodies to the immortal souls that had been put within them. The green lights were what Rhyiathe had called The Elder lights. They were twinkling and settling on me too, but I was too distracted to pay attention at the time. I trembled in silence as the souls of the chosen immortals were placed within the human bodies - returning her to me finally.

A thick blanket of blackness swarmed over the inside of the Temple. There was a collective intake of breath. The air was alive with the sound of the of a thousand gasps. Twelve small lights flickered into being and they steadily grew brighter in the middle of the stage. My legs become weak and my head spinning but as The High Priestess announces the words "*Arise, Arise, Arise.*" I focussed and lucidity slipped over my fragmented thoughts. Pushing my way through the remainder of the crowds. Every last one of them like zombies, the lot of them, not even realising I had touched them. They were so very fascinated with the Rite, verging on obsession. Frantic and tense was I, the lights were now blinding and calling me forth. One of my feet was resting on the raised stage, before I even knew what was happening. My blood was pounding in my ears – a queasy uneasiness was at my throat. I longed for Dawn, my sister to return.

The Temple lights came bursting on, - the shocking brightness of them leaving spots floating across the lenses of my efficient predator eyes. I, no longer needed the light to see now, with my enhanced vision, intended to track the slightest movements that stood out against any environment. Even though the lights hurt, I would not withdraw my gaze from its harshness. I wanted to see the rising of my dead sister.

When my blurred vision had settled and clarity had returned once more, I focussed a little harder. I could see her blonde hair moving, slipping off the pillow. Her upper body lifted itself up off the marble table, as rigid, as inhuman a gesture as a terrible reanimated Frankenstein.

Both of my feet were now on the platform. My body tripping forward. I fell onto my knees and let out a strangled sob,

"Please still be you. Please still be you," I cried out, hysterically, knowing that I asked too much as I was no longer me.

Chapter Fifteen - Arisen.

My forehead pressed against the cloth that covered my sister. The cover was wet. Small dark circles formed from the tears falling from my eyes. A large number of orderlies were moving around me, placing themselves between the marble slabs the Offered were laid on, lifting the bodies ready to support them through the next stage. They worked with purpose, trying to move me aside. They pushed and pulled at my sides, but I resembled a fly stuck in treacle.

A hand touched the back of my head, stroking my hair. I had goosebumps. I knew it was her. She was weaving my hair around her small, grasping fingers like she used to when she couldn't sleep as a toddler. It was a small hand. Small and achingly fragile.

"It's okay, I am awake," my sister's voice rang in my ears like an evangelical choir. All silken and honey, - hidden glory in each uttered word.

At first, I hesitated, but my bravery took over. Lifting my swollen lids and gazing through my moistened eyelashes, I was scared to look at her directly, lest she vanish like a wisp.

She was sitting bolt upright, and the orderlies were helping her get up onto her feet- Dawn, my Dawn was sitting there before me, blinking and breathing. She leaned over one of the arms of the orderlies to touch my fingers.

"Thank you for waking me up so gently, what is your name, and do you know what I am doing here? It's a strange place to wake up in."

Trembling, barely able to contain my emotions, I managed to say,

"Dawn is your name. We came here together. To the land of the Immortals," I softly said to my sister in a low, strangled voice. The cracked tempo of it betrayed me, but I tried to remain calm for my sister's sake. Searching her with my eyes to try to figure out if she had some sort of amnesia or if she was not my sister at all, I shoved that thought away to the back of mind. Dawn was being lifted off the marble slab with the help of the orderlies, but I couldn't take my eyes of her – it felt unreal. She had been dead and now she was alive.

"Okay, where am I going? Who are all these people?" Dawn said, scrunching up her forehead, looking out over the platform to the crowd below, while the orderlies take her by her arms trying to lead her away – away from me.
"Nowhere," I jolted to alertness, pulling my blade from its sheaf and held it up, moving it in a semicircle, deciding which one of the orderlies will be the first to die on my blade.
"Aurora, please no. They need to take her to do a check to make sure the body isn't rejecting the spell and the soul of the immortal Dawn is bonded with. If they don't then she is at significant risk and so is the Rite. Tell me please, who has Dawn been joined with? Who is her sponsor?" Dillion first addressed me then turned his attention to the elf and vampire orderlies who were assigned to Dawn.
One of the orderlies looked nervously at both me and Dillion. "Tayre has been joined with this one, Dawn. A female vampire of one moon cycle. Powerful in moon magic but she has no family so Rhyiathe will be the child's sponsor. We will do the checks then she will be sent to live with him as his ward because the *hu-man* part of her is but a child too. She will be trained and then sent to guard the Void. Now, move aside and let us go with the girl."
"Wait, please don't take my sister away from me. I've only just got her back." I swung my sword through the air in desperation.
"No, Aurora. We need to let them take her. We can see her at Rhyiathe 's dwelling later. Come with me. Now." Dillion grabbed both of my arms and physically lifted me off my feet. I struck my legs out trying to keep a foothold on the ground, but my arms were being held up. I was bounced in the air; held up by Dillion to cover the distance more rapidly away from the scene.
My sister was then calmly walked in the other direction. She gave me a weak smile as she followed the white-cloaked orderlies.
I looked at her and my eyes burned. I watched my little sister hungrily; my emotions bursting through my chest. All the pent-up rage, frustration, and confusion were surfacing like pools of itchy rashes on my skin.
Dillion half dragged; half carried me through the crowd as people silently watched me while they left the temple in organised lines. I was screaming and shouting, no one took any notice of my despair. They had obviously

seen this type of behaviour before from the immortal Families of the Offered. It doesn't make my humiliation any less.
Dillion took me to a quiet hallway and deposited me on the ground. It was dusty and a little dark. As soon as his hands were no longer pinning my arms to my sides, I jumped up with a fist pulled back and landed my knuckles firmly on his jawline. He crumpled inwards. Then lifted himself up, holding his jaw. I looked down at my hand and observed there was no pain in my wrists. Facing him, I noticed his soulful creamy brown loyal eyes and my knees buckled slightly.
"Better?" he raised his eyebrows. I didn't miss his hungry glance either at my parted lips. I felt this tug, this annoyed and frustrated tension course through me. The Animal. The Primal call.
I desperately searched out his eyes and stared back at his lips. I could feel this heat building between us, this physical intensity. I just wanted something. I wanted to feel anything but hurt and sad – it had been my daily life for so long now.
He paused, no doubt noticing the hunger in me and leaned in, closely. As he stared into my eyes with an intensity of his own, he placed his hands either side of me on the cool wall behind. He gently touched his thumb to my lower lip and rolled his fingers over my cheeks.
I was aching to be held.
Until. Until, well, until it was not all him on my mind.
Rhyiathe swam into my mind's eye and he was looking at me with a soulful expression.
The intensity I thought I felt with Dillion was a mere candle to the supernova of heat when I thought of Rhyiathe. My doubts about Rhyiathe still lingered. Again, I wondered if he had put some kind of hex on me.
Stepping back suddenly, out of the embrace of Dillion - all these complicated thoughts took over me and I just wanted to be sick.
Dillion's lips were on me, urgently kissing me and wanting more, but I began to feel suffocated. My lips detached first, then my energy withdrew, and my body slumped back away from him, and I hugged myself. A chasm formed between us, even though we were inches apart.
He stopped abruptly, drawing back his head to look at me.
"I don't think we should be doing this either. You're vulnerable right now. I tell you what, you still feel the same way in a few days then come and find

me and well, I would be more than happy to explore this but not now. It doesn't feel right. Not that I'm not feeling this because I am but . . . yeah, do you understand what I'm saying? The truth is immortals' pair for life and giving ourselves to each other means agreeing to that bond. God, I can't believe I'm saying this to you of all people. To me, you are like a goddess."

I stared at him blankly. *Wait, what's that about pairing for life? Impossible. Absurd.*

A rejection like that created a sudden wave of irrational anger in me and it filled my chest, even though I had been thinking about another man the whole time.

I stood pulling at my sleeve, pretending to be distracted, while a spark of misplaced anger and confusion settled on me like a fine layer of ash. My own inner demons began whispering of the cold rejection and the neglect I had experienced many years ago, and I became the beetles, the bloated black spiders of my childhood – I felt unsafe and wanted to lash out in my pain.

Is he playing with me?

"Fine. whatever you say," I heard myself mutter darkly. Not even sure if I wanted to go through with it. The thoughts of Rhyiathe were confusing for me, but to be rejected like this by the werewolf was just adding to this wild, out of control turmoil I was in - maddening.

My intimate life on earth had been a succession of one-night stands, or regular hook-ups with no emotional attachments and this had suited me just fine. In fact, it was me who had instigated the stipulation of no emotional attachment to the guys that I very occasionally was physically attracted to. However, to hear a man like Dillion telling me he didn't want to take advantage because I was 'too vulnerable' made my head spin.

"Hey, don't be like that. If you want me then I want it to be special is all I'm saying not some hook-up down a dark hallway because you're feeling upset and emotional. The bond is the bond in the Immortal culture. The act of lovemaking is a vow of commitment, and it is sacred to us, us immortals. We find our soul mate and that is it for us. You see, at one time the immortals were too few in number to defend themselves, so we created the Vow of Commitment to ensure that our offspring were prioritised to

build our population and to ensure the Immortals were no longer vulnerable to becoming extinct by warring tribes, and by humans."
I wasn't fully listening to his history lesson. My anger was clouding my better judgement *"Upset and emotional?"* I repeated back while rearranging my small throwing knives and looking down so he couldn't see my face colouring in a brilliant shade of red – I had been called out on my behaviour and I didn't like it one bit.
He stepped back and leaned on the wall staring at me in bewilderment.
"Okay, not upset and emotional then. But I *do* want it to be for the right reasons. Are you angry with me?" His soulful brown eyes held a strained look of confusion.
"Oh, I get it, so you just want me when you want me. Fine." I lifted up my chin stubbornly, intentionally making it difficult for him to discuss this, so I could hide my embarrassment about my outburst.
I finished placing my last throwing dagger into the lining of my bodysuit with a bit too much of a thrust and spun around to walk quite deliberately away - I would find my own way back.
It wasn't easy. Each step was agonising. All the while Dillion, the kind and bewildered werewolf was calling my name in a desperate kind of voice, he shouted,
"Listen Aurora, I need to tell you something important. It was a werewolf you saw that night above the funeral parlour. We were waiting for you, to protect you. To stop you from becoming the Twelfth Offered, but you arrived late, and we couldn't stop you coming through the vortex. . . Aurora, please? I need to talk to you. It's important. You are in danger."
As shocking as it was what Dillion had told me, I carried on walking away from him and that whole messy situation, at that moment, out of nothing more than my stubborn and embarrassed pride.
I did not look back around. I beat a hasty retreat not knowing what else to do.
You see, the thing is no one had ever treated me with that type of respect before and it freaked me out if I were to be completely honest. But also, why is it that whenever I thought of Rhyiathe I had no control over myself? I needed to get away from all these immortals, all their issues for a while and decided to head to my apartment in the Castle. There I would be able

to think, think about the werewolf plot that had just been revealed to me, think about my own fragile mind – unravelling. Think about Rhyiathe.
I walk at speed in a cloud of confusion.

Rushing to fling myself against the closed door inside of my apartment, I fully allowed the embarrassment and the surrealism of the last few hours to take a chokehold.
Dizzy from the number of things I had noticed, I began running through the events in chronological order. Sifting through, looking at the shape of each moment like trying to piece together a jigsaw puzzle that I was standing too close to, to be able to complete. I didn't have the full picture just yet. It was there but I hadn’t arranged the pieces.
A few things sprung to my mind.
I could have been imagining it but Lilly and now, Dillion seemed to know me somehow. Dillion had even shouted to me that the werewolves had tried to stop me from becoming the Twelfth Offered. How was this possible, how had they known I was to be the Twelfth Offered? Why did they need to stop it for?
Thinking about it some more, I realised that when I had put on the tan bodysuit it fitted like a glove and I automatically knew where each blade was carried. *But how?*
Something felt off and was not quite fitting together just yet.
The next thing I noticed was Lord Tennison wanting an uprising against the Rite of the Offering. It was him, who had instigated Lindon to draw his weapons in the first place and this elf lord called Gamone seemed to have struck some kind of a bargain with Lindon too.
I held my temples in an attempt to stop the confusion in my head then remembered the most important thing of all. The most important detail was that my sister, Dawn, was alive. Alive. ALIVE! What did they call it? Oh yes, Arisen. But what do the Arisen do exactly? Patrol the borders between the Earth and the immortal realm by the sounds of what I had heard today.
The shocking factor was our planet’s governments and leaders seem to know about this deal of the Offered. My mind was becoming foggy. It’s just too much information to take in in one go.

Will Dawn have changed now she is carrying the soul of an immortal called Tayre? I needed to find out so I could find a way to get her out of here, back to earth, through the vortex and home.

But in my current form, can I even go back through the vortex and return to Earth? Is there a cure for my affliction?

There were so many questions. I needed to read that book and visit Dawn at Rhyiathe's home too. And come to think of it, why was Rhyiathe Dawn's sponsor? My head was swimming with unanswered questions, but I was just too tired to think anymore so I stalked towards the balcony doors to open them, to let some fresh air in. The white linen curtains billowed inwards on the back of a cool breeze rising. Distracted, I was thinking about running a bath to luxuriate in, I needed to focus on something else for a while.

This is why I had not noticed the gold particles of magic accumulating over the balcony and seeping into my apartment through the now open doors, and the strange lights followed me as I walked across the floor to the bathroom – ready for a night of relaxation, so I can tackle things tomorrow with a clear head.

Chapter Sixteen - The Shadow of the Past, no more

I was in the bath when the golden particles of light descended rapidly upon me, and at first, I thought it was a swarm of fireflies, coming in through the window. Not realising what they were at first. The strangest thing happened next, which I couldn't quite believe my own eyes were witnessing. The particles started to brightly glow, landing on me, one by one and I was absorbing the energy through my skin.

The cells of my skin started to throb, vibrate, and I could tell I was being changed. Half the bath water was pooling on the floor in my efforts to escape the lights. I decided to jump out, get dressed fast.

The lights followed me through the apartment, through closed doors and wardrobes (*yes, I tried hiding from the lights in cupboards too*).

Hurriedly, I pulled on my tan body suit and fixed my shiny hair into a sweeping side plait. No time for careful placement of all of my daggers and knives in the little sheaves concealed within the armour on this occasion.

After dressing, only a few effervescent particles of light were left – bobbing along above me. Running away, I jumped down the sturdy stairs, a few at a time, towards the solid doors that led out onto the city streets. Deep booming bells of the temples, were clanging and chiming, ringing out the hour. Still, those lights followed me, snaking through the air to chase me down like a hunter.

My pulse was quick, fear gripped me. Shuddering, I started darting for a side alley, where well-structured and solid townhouses made from sturdy sandstone, lined the neat streets.

I stood finding cover under the canopy of one of the large and ancient Dogwood trees, the trees grow in harmony with the pavements here, which were beautiful and smooth to walk over, made from interwoven grass. My back pressed up against the trunk, while the last of the remaining lights descended and converged, infusing with me. The lights seemed unable to

leave me alone, like bees swarming on colourful flowers, irresistible I seemed to be.
The texture of the rough tree trunk dug into my back, full of angles, prodding me to take care. An unknown pressure across my face held me against the tree – from the lights or something else.
The continual physical force smashing against me told me someone close by was performing magic. This was what Lilly had meant when she told me that spells left a residue.
A woman, cloaked in a plush green heavy fabric that covered her face, on the opposite side of the road was watching me with a keenness. I tried to avoid the intensity of her gaze. She started walking across the bumpy cobbled street, intently watching the lights and then followed them, directing herself towards me.
"Are you ok?" a look flashed across her well-defined features; the eagerness of her eyes was like a hawk. She was had an expensiveness about her, haughty face, and intimidating style of dress. There was a dark air about her. It was not soft and kind like Lilly's, but deeper, darker, and shrewd. I was straightaway, on the defensive. The woman had an ill-look about her. I couldn't explain it.
Peering around, up and down the streets with a touch of the exaggerated theatre-acting upon my performance, pretending to look for the person she was talking to. Pretending not to know she was talking to me, I tried to act like nothing untoward had just happened. No alarming lights floating midair- an old defensive reflex of mine to pretend I don't understand a situation.
"Yes, why do you ask?" I said brightly.
"Those lights, what were they and where did they go?" she pulled me forward by my arm like they were concealed behind my back somehow. The pressure on my face released me. Her hand was smooth, but prickly on my skin. The smell of her was fuggy like she had been running for a thousand miles in the same clothes.
"What lights? Maybe you are mistaken, perhaps?"
The oddest feeling came over me. It was like I could see a darkness falling and it was shrouding over this person.

"Who are you?" my eyes betrayed me, showing my interest. I squinted at her, taking in the dark shadows that had suddenly collected like a fine gauze over her.

Her face moved from one of impatience to impassive, with a slight adjustment of her eyes and the tension left her face, it was replaced with a fake smile.

"My mistake, a trick of the light from the setting suns." she nodded her head and watched me as I adjusted the arms of my bodysuit. Slowly, I made my way out of the side alley, down the street and towards Rhyiathe's home still feeling her eyes on me.

A flick of her hand to her temple told me she had just communicated something about the encounter to someone else, for who knows what reason. Maybe law enforcement of some kind, but I doubted it.

She gave me a bad feeling like all the hope was sliding out of me and being removed from my world. Some kind of witch, maybe? *Yes,* my mind says. I daren't look back so I continued walking purposely forward. Striving further away – with each step away from her, the better I felt.

At the end of the street, out of her eyeline, I started to run to Rhyiathe's home. My legs charged forward in a piston-motion - extremely fast indeed. I needed to get to Rhyiathe's to see my sister, to see her with my own eyes and quickly too. Out of this sense of growing urgency brimming in my hearts, that everything was not well in the Seven Kingdoms. Plots and subterfuge were at every turn, barely seen, but held together like cobwebs over these corrupt lands. The air felt heavy with deceit and I wanted to be somewhere else and not dealing with these big issues anymore. I wanted to get my sister and take Dawn home – back to Earth where we belong.

I arrived, knocking on the solid oak door of Rhyiathe's home and it replied with a satisfying loud *boom* of an announcement. There was a pause, before the door opened by itself, as if an introduction had already been made and I am most welcome in. My feet treaded the path of the comfortable hallway. Intentionally, my eyes observed more details this time.

Rhyiathe was clearly interested in ancient history. A great deal of antiquities covered the walls and surfaces from different periods of Earth's history. Meticulously restored, and detailed notes with precious metals and gems framed and hung on the walls. Several wooden grandfather clocks were

stationed in the hallway ticking and gonging melodically, at separate times. Parchments written in long forgotten languages and fragile scrolls from ancient Egypt encased behind polished, gleaming glass.
He had some incredibly old relics from this realm too, well, I assumed they were at least. A strange fascination with old vampire lore is also present, alongside, celebrating nature and the marvels of the natural world – oil paintings of trees and the Suns rising that sort of thing. All were brightly coloured, all thrown together and arranged in chronological order of historical significance – put together carefully. Seeing his personal items filled me with a laughter and a type of wholesome warmth. Rhyiathe was a boffin. He was visible in every detail, every line – ornaments, books, and statues. I was reading into every little interest of his, wondering about his motives and if all this history filled him with a giddy kind of excitement, like most hobbies do. I was left studying each trinket, wondering what it meant to him and how he had acquired such treasures.
There were a few large tropical parrots casually sitting on golden perches high on the walls, with no sign of any cages in the house.
The hallway led out into a natural stone and rock made atrium with the open sky above and a waterfall was trickling down one of the rock faces – this was where I had recovered after the arena. The atrium was covered in large prehistoric ferns and succulent plants thriving in the tropical humidity of his home – he really enjoyed hydrophyte plants.
Dusk was settling upon his home. Deep orange and pink hues melted together in the sky above and the first glints of starlight could be seen. The pink faded into edges of the dark, velvety navy-blue night sky, where the sunlight fears to venture. A beauty and majesty all around. Comets and shooting stars begun to draw in, to travel across the night-sky and I was left mesmerised by the homely environment, but also the night sky, above us like a child at their first firework display, standing with my mouth drawn open in a satisfied, large 'O'.
"Aurora is that you?" a male voice called out, deep and honeyed with a ready smile that can be heard in its playful inflictions.
"Erm, yes?" Why did I answer as if I was questioning it was me? *Stupid, stupid, stupid, stupid.*

Rhyiathe appeared. There was a huge smile on his ridiculously handsome face, but his eyebrows were set in a quizzical fashion. He shrugged the look off as quickly as it had set in and began smiling again.

His green eyes were upon me giving me an appreciative look as he walked over to greet me. Coils of muscle enclosed me. I stopped, standing rigid, ready to feel the little electric pulses under his touch, but when he doesn't get a reaction from me, he changed to despondently bouncing his arms at his sides. I feel bad. I wish I was a hugger, but I am not.

Sadness crept over his face, and confusion settled there, which left me with a gaping wound. Seeing him hurt like that caused a burning pain that I could not describe, so I took his hand in mine. Instant relief lit up his affable face. His touch conveyed every feeling he was having – I was reading him. Laid open to me, he was and he seemed to know but didn't mind. He was afraid of nothing.

My breath came jagged, he stared into my eyes, and I felt the heat between us, but with an almighty effort, I broke the spell – the spell he has no doubt placed on me.

I am here for Dawn.

"So, where is Dawn?" I asked.

He placed his hand at my elbow and little pulses sent shockwaves through me. I was consumed and all I could see was him. I kept forgetting the reason I was here – here in The Seven Kingdoms, isn't for anything other than my sister and then, I would be returning to Earth with Dawn. Both of us alive. Both of us forever changed.

"Come through. She is being settled into her room, but I must warn you that she is not herself just yet. It takes a few weeks for the spell to adjust. The two beings, Dawn and Tayre, are trying to reconcile the order of things between themselves."

"What does that mean? Is she in pain?" I ran forward, looking at all the doors in my line of vision. There were so many. I would burst through each one to save her over and over again if need be.

"Hey, steady." His hand on my shoulder sent a warmth through my whole body, but I didn't pay attention to the feeling. The big surge of adrenaline was my only focus, ready to fight, clenching my fists, my vampire fangs begun to drop down out of my gums. My whole body was ready, even the

new parts. I removed his hand from my shoulder. I am here for Dawn and her alone.
"She is fine, absolutely nothing to worry about," a heavy sadness settled in his eyes, looking down at his removed hand. I cringed back, not wanting to see his pain, but it was the way of it, how it must be.
"But Aurora, she is no longer your Dawn. She died and she is now alive with two souls in her body. She has immense powers. It's a lot to take in for anyone. She is uncoordinated like a baby learning to walk in a new world. Dawn also is from a place where she was treated badly, I understand?" He nodded and looked at me searching, my eyes for confirmation. He waited patiently for me to answer, hands folded in front of him, trying to reduce his size so that he was not altering my answer.
A colouring spread across my cheeks and a single reluctant nod confirmed what he said was true. I stood up, tense and unsure of the question. His hand was placed on my shoulder again, a thumb brushing backwards and forwards in sympathy – he knew my answer applied to me too and not just Dawn.
". . .and now this new world holds many possibilities for her, and her potential is limitless. That's gotta be scary, right? She needs time to adjust. Lilly and I are working with her to slowly introduce her to the immortal's way of life. *You* of all people understand, right?"
Of course, I bloody understood. He had literally just described the situation I had fallen into, with a scary accuracy that made me think he was reading my mind. *Is he reading my mind? Oh god no, he'll know how unstable I am.* Nodding meekly, I felt self-conscious like he could see inside the core of my very being and at the vulnerability nesting within.
He smiled at me and held both my shoulders strongly while he manoeuvred me to a door. His broad chin, at times, bumped the top of my head with a gentle pounding. His presence of kindness and strength enveloped me, and I felt protected and cared for. It was like a sigh of warmth: a signal to put down my armour. I was not at war with the world anymore when I was with him. We walked along a window filled hallway; one side covered in old and frayed leather-bound books. The wooden floors were smooth and I stepped along listening to the sounds of the city outside, but in here, there was a lightness – a glow.
Finally, we reached the right door in the vastness of his home.

We, Rhyiathe and I, were like those building block board games that slid together and sealed themselves shut – locked together in our contentment to just be together.
Standing outside the room, we stood facing each other for a while. Apprehension shadowed his face and he quietly, reluctantly said,
"She won't remember you. Are you able to handle that because if not then I'm afraid I'm going to have to ask you not to see her . . . for a little bit. You'll cause her upset. She will be confused if you tell her of her past and she is my responsibility. You can still read the book in the reading room, and I'll help you with that but . . ." he waited for a reply.
"She's, my sister. And *my* responsibility." I bristled.
The heaviness of grief started to grow back like hard tree roots, taking hold in my chest – suffocating me. It felt like I was losing her all over again and I cannot let this happen. A snake coiled ready to spring, to defend myself against the sting of his words of protection for my sister, *from me.*
I was the one left confused. I understood why he was saying this, but I still reacted.
"Not while she is *my* ward, Aurora, I'm afraid. Dawn and Tayre are both *my* responsibility and I take this very seriously. *And* you didn't answer the question, Aurora. So, what's it to be? Are you able to play by the rules or not?" he leaned forward. His eyes were a vivid green and they had this ability to make me feel calm like swimming in a warm sea. I wondered if he was hypnotising me in some way. I didn't want to feel calm in that moment. I bunched my fists, digging my nails into my palm, my fangs hanging down, eyes blinking in the way of the predator. It wasn't fair none of this was anything to do with me and Dawn, yet we were the ones that suffered the most.
A realisation dawned on me; *fighting won't help me here.*
"Look, I'll do whatever is needed to keep Dawn safe,".
"Right," he blanched, biting his lip, "Except for one thing, Tayre is not your sister and both Dawn and Tayre are as equally important, so if you do have any wayward ideas about a rescue mission then please know that this won't happen. It cannot happen and I'm sorry to say, I won't let it happen. I'm sorry to be the bearer of unwelcome news, but it's just not possible. Dawn died. She was resurrected by magic, and she cannot return

to Earth in her condition. She will have a better life here. She is not technically Dawn now anyway."
I felt my eyes prickle with tears, and I physically felt my soul slump out of my body. The hurt of his honesty ripped a gaping hole in the confines of my chest.
"Have you read the extract of the book about the Rite yet or the lead-up to it? It explains it all in there."
I shook my head. "But I will," is all I could hear myself murmur. I placed my hand on the door and pushed it forward, he cast a spell, to hold me still and the door closed, locked itself shut, before I could get through to see Button. The magic he used filled me with that continuous invisible force of pressure like I am standing between two magnets, being crushed.
"Aurora?" Rhyiathe said to me in a low tone, "it's all going to be okay, and I'll be outside when you need me. I don't want to upset you but it's better you know the truth even if it hurts temporarily."
My eyes welled with tears, and I nodded. "Thank you," escaped my lips. A memory flitted across my mind of our first encounter. The pressure was released, the door unlocked, and I walked through.
The room I entered was vast, with a high ceiling and windows covering most of the outer walls. Moulded cornice and roof openings made out of the finest crystal. A lightness was in this room. Glass chandeliers dripped from the ceiling. Stained glass lamps were positioned around the apartment that glowed like precious gems. The suns were setting in the distance, projecting a golden light across all the soft furnishings, and the glow of it lit up a large tree, which stood proudly in the core of the building, growing out of the wall.
Sitting quietly on a chair with her back to me, was Dawn.
All was quiet and calm. A tranquillity settled in this room like a spell made of mist, lavender, and hope. The room was so different from our home life on Earth, it made me stand, subdued in the stillness, thinking about what could have been. My eyes prickled with regret about missed opportunities that I couldn't explain.
She was writing at the top of a piece of unfurled parchment. Gentle scratching came from the fountain pen as it glided across the hardened pulp. With softness, Dawn lifted her hand, in a practised way, to the inkwell

and dipped the nib in with a light *splosh* and a delicate *tap*, to rid the nib of its surplus ink, she placed it at the end of the sentence, to continue writing. I leaned forward, over the smooth wooden curvature of the desk, smelling of oiled wood, curious to see what she was writing about. She did not turn round. To my astonishment, she was writing letters on the crisp paper in a strange alphabet that I did not know. Tall and lean was the inky black writing, like spiders' legs nestling on the page. These were Vampire runes; elaborate, creative and delicate in appearance. They were of Tayre's language.

My head spun. I focussed, taking in each blonde and light brown hair strand, mingling together on Dawn's fair head. Familiar but not at the same time because there was a well-cared for shiny softness to the waves of her golden hair that hadn't been there before.

A sweet smell of pungent, full and rich roses blossomed into the room, it announced the lightness and sweetness of a life that Dawn had never known. We could never afford gold pens or flowers or writing desks with ornamental ink wells. My eyes were drawn to a bursting bouquet of summer meadow flowers that sat before her in an elaborate and exquisitely crafted large vase, on the writing desk. Alongside, sat a glass carafe of water with fruits to sweeten the taste and delicacies of strawberry pastries on a gleaming gold plate. *Dawn will want for nothing here. Why does she need me now?* Deluded, standing in a chasm of nothingness, the realisation choked me.

The polished floorboard creaked as I stepped back. Flinching away from the scratching and scribing coming from the desk, I wanted my legs to carry me out of this room. Away from this stranger who had hold of my sister's body.

I turned to look down the hallway, if I left now my brain's defences could keep pretending that she was still Dawn, and I was still me, and we were both unchanged – I could kid myself forever in this way. Dawn continued scribbling.

All this time, I had not realised what it meant to have someone who had lived through the years of the same experiences with me, who understood my strange characteristics and my responses to life's nuances. My darkness, my demons, my hurt and my shadows, everything about me that had protected us as small children. Through it all she had accepted me, loved me anyway, and the more for it. Dawn realised how brave I truly am, how brave I can be and the courage it had taken to live each day when you are born into absolutely nothing. Disadvantaged. To face down that despair and still roar – calling out life and shouting 'is this all you've got'. Dawn saw all this in me and believed in me, more than I believed in myself.

It was that feeling I wanted back, it's what I needed. It was me that was dead not her. The version of me that she saw. I shuddered in a deep breath. It turned into a sob in the back of my wretched throat.

Finally, her face turned, Dawn, my Dawn, stared out at me with the same familiar eyes from our childhood, but there were no dark circles there, gone was the gauntness, only soft soap-washed skin and a light, hopeful smile. My sister looked healthy and well for the first time in her short life.

"Hello, are you here to show me how to use the board over there?" she said in a familiar voice and then took her neatly bloused arm and pointed to a calendar board that set out her lesson plan. The board had a training itinerary, and the date circled when she would get to find out which dragon she had been paired with. There was a look of keen excitement on her youthful, smiling face. Gone were the years of neglect. They belonged to a different version of her. But there was no look of recognition for me in the depths of its folds. The pendulum swung; I was to stand in the darkness alone – I really was alone for the first time ever. A chasm formed between us.

It broke me.

I stared down at her and felt a crippling pain that started in my stomach. The swell of it was too big for my body. I had no hope of containing that feeling of absolute despair. It moved like a slithering asp upwards through my chest, a jagged pain pierced the back of my throat, like I had been bitten by the venomous snake inside me, my eyes prickled. I swallowed down hard. My windpipe felt like it was tearing open.

Remembering what I had promised Rhyiathe, that I would not worry her, I fumbled out a guarded,

"Actually, I just came to introduce myself because I'm new here too. My name is Aurora. We met the other day. I'll just go to get Rhyiathe who can explain your planner to you."

It took all my strength to keep my voice even, more than my little sister will ever know. I don't wait for a response. Turning away, leaving behind the past, the hope I had to be reunited with my sister, my eyes catch sight

of Rhyiathe subdued, hanging on the door, looking in on both of us. Lilly was behind him. They both had a sadness sparking out of their eyes – sorrow and pity. All for me.
Anger pulsed through me, and my two hearts were gladdened by it - I rejoiced. The gift of anger. It drowned all other emotions coldly like a psychopathic murderer, quickly disposing of all the other emotions that hurt me. They could shove their pity where the suns don't shine for all that I care.
My footsteps are thunderous as I made my way to leave. Dawn's voice carried towards my ear as I make to run away.
"Aurora, is it? How funny, my name is Dawn. We are both named after the sunrise."
My hand flew to cover my mouth, I choked back a scream, shoved my way past Rhyiathe's concerned gaze and the heartache in Lilly's eyes. They were both suffocating me, I had to get out of there - quickening my pace I bolted out of the apartment.
Downwards, I ran, covering the distance of the vast stairwell in a matter of moments, my feet barely touching each platform of the staircase in my haste. My hands glided over the polished handrail. I fled. Out of the building, I ran over the cobbles of the unknown streets of the city, heading for the treeline of the forest in the blindness of my tears. A blankness covered all my senses. Alone am I with this growing discomfort within me like a tear ebbing its way through my windpipe. Deadly and painful it pierced me, and I would never recover from it. Never.

***

After I had left his home, Rhyiathe and Lilly found the courage to get over their sadness and entered the room to start working through the planner with Dawn. They smiled and joked with her and she was wonderfully comfortable in their company.
They told her about the Academy for the Offered and why patrolling the Void was a great honour to keep both Earth and The Realms safe. The training plan had been tailor made for her. They had discussed her lessons, and told her of the exciting tournaments, and about the tests to choose a dragon to be paired with, as well as, what was expected of her in terms of patrolling the Void and the importance of adhering to the rules. Dawn had not been parented before, she never had the experience of a good parent;

one that she could look up to and she glowed a little brighter under Lilly's and Rhyiathe 's advice and tutorage.
Dawn said, "I am glad to be chosen as a protector but why was I chosen out of all the millions of people?"
Lilly smiled, smoothing the back of Dawn's hair and told her, "Because you have always shown incredibly special traits, even under hard circumstances. You and Tayre, the Vampire youngling, you are bonded into one with, you will share your unique gifts and strengths with each other to safeguard the Seven Kingdoms and The Void. You are now immortal. Tayre has shared this with you. You two will have each other and never be alone."
As they both got up to leave, to let Dawn rest, after her long day (she had yawned three times in a row), Dawn softly said,
"It's strange. I thought Aurora was going to introduce herself as Poppy. I really like the name. Thats what I will call the dragon I am paired with," she yawned, "Poppy is a really beautiful name, don't you agree, Lilly?"
Lilly laughed, "Yes, it is, but the Dragons will choose their own names and would not thank you for naming them. They are extremely proud and a little arrogant if truth be told but I would not say such things in front of one of them. They tend to set fire to things that annoy them."
There was a laugh from Dawn and a shared smile with Lilly. When Dawn turned back to her parchment, she let out another yawn, before beginning to hum an olde English cockney rhyming song. Putting pen to paper, she promptly started to draw a lonely, golden haired, floppy eared stray dog in a dark, blank street.
Very precise imagery for someone who had forgotten about their life on Earth, wouldn't you say governor?

Chapter Seventeen - The Lights

I ran in my comforting cloud of despair – to get away. It was familiar to me, I wore the desperate feeling like an old, worn cloak, as I tore away from the shiny new life all set for Dawn. A pain awoke in me of deep etched sorrow, it carved out a hole in my chest. It was cutting and slicing at me, knowing that I have nothing to offer her but darkness. The realisation of this like a scorpion's tail jabbing at my poisoned thoughts.
Rhyiathe was right. Why did I want to take her back to our life of hell on Earth?
Dawn would have everything she could ever wish for here and more besides. But why couldn't I just accept it. Why couldn't I shake this feeling that this place was eviller than back on Earth, if that were even possible?
Through the sandstone cobbled streets, I fled, brooding in misery.
It was a fine spring day and there was an aspect of calmness in these fair streets that I could just not enjoy. In my cloud of despair, I ran through the groups huddled together, mirth bursting forth from their gathered faces; smiling too much for my liking, on hot streets covered in sunshine, on this lazy balmy day.
"Hey, watch it. You nearly pushed me over," A tall, vampire female shouted out as I ran past.
I jumped over cats laid stretched out on baking flagstones, enjoying the mild weather.
I kept on running. I was too folded in on myself to even notice the bystanders nor the beautiful architecture of the city as I ran by, everything was watery and dull to me.
The suns shone down, the warm wind blew lifting tufts of my raven black hair, made soft from the water in this world, but all I could see was the darkness coming from within me that covered everything to a dull opal black.
My lost connections left me isolated, abandoning myself. I was no longer numb. The pain that had been locked away for years flowing out, undammed and breaking me into two. I had no practice at managing it on

my own. Last time this had happened Lilly was there to patch me back together, but this time I was on my own. The way it has always been for me. It felt right.

In my despair and panic, I reverted to my childhood ways of cancelling out any pain. A blanket shrouded me in a fine black webbing. I searched out the bloated black spiders of my youth. I would find them in the forest, where the trees are twisted and the air dense with damp and mould, my own brand of familiar decay. It would make me feel like I was home on earth in the poverty of the beginning with the ghost of my sister by my side - before all of this. Where nothing was expected, but just to survive.

Sweeping along the streets, I ran at speed to the outer walls holding in the vibrant city – defining it as a boundary to all intruders.

I smelt the scent from the trees before I laid eyes upon them and felt the familiar surge of the shift in energy from the large swell of nature; concentrated nearby in the forest. The Pericullions' called this place Tearswood, a place where dimensions collide and the dead can visit the living, or at least appear to them on the fine shimmer made by the mist from the lake – souls can be seen at the centre on the surface of the water. It is said to be haunted with spirits and souls that will not depart. Named Tearswood because the dead could never return home, never break through the boundary of the lake. Even so, it was soothing to my vampire senses and the human in me.

I came to a halt and entered the dense treeline, like I was entering a temple, hushed and quiet, footsteps and tears were the only things that gave me away. Forgotten and alone.

The canopy of the trees covered me in a cool shade and I bobbed under the branches of the densely packed trees. This was where I could finally abandon myself – revert to the primal. Find my lioness again. I went deep into the wood, it felt right.

I laid my body down in the crook of the first gnarled roots of an ancient oak tree that I found, curling up as if returning to the womb – to the beginning. Returning to the familiar and waiting for something - to be released. Or a rebirth; one of the two.

The Elder - Lights of the Seven Kingdoms

I must have fallen asleep, I had been dreaming of Dawn and I, playing with makeshift dolls in the dank basements of abandoned houses of London, when we were children and everything could be turned into a game.

How long was I asleep for, I don't rightly know. The suns were nowhere in the sky and the moons barely present either. A strange, liquid darkness was over this wood and the pressure of magnetised air pressed in on me. Magic was being performed nearby.

The wood grew still, a blackness seeped over everything. A dense quiet announced something was moving towards me. The rustling wind slipping through the dry, crinkled leaves was not the only sound in the woods. A great vacuum of nothingness, I couldn't quite explain it, loomed present before my vision. I struggled to see this invisible solid mass, but it was there, even the moon could not penetrate it, invisible but solid. Something within it had its great eye fixed on me, "Who is there," I shouted but the words landed heavy and bounced back towards me like a rebounded ball hitting a glass window. The pixelated shadows on the forest floor started to pool, collecting, drawing backwards to a centre point. Building into a thick black cloak. I watched in horror, unable to move away, as the hooded thing was materialising before my eyes – pulling itself together. The thing, without a name or face, lifted its hood with skeletal hands and I am looking into darkness. Thick, black, emptiness with nothing for a face. Two red eyes burning bright like the first atoms fusing together, like rolling fire for eyes, so burning hot that they were almost white. An ancient black tree, that until that moment, had stood silently, innocently, like a tree, burst open. A hissing sound started up, low at first, but then began to grow louder and louder. So loud that I covered my ears and began to scream at the horrors before my skinless eyes. I could no longer close my eyelids, as much as I tried. As much as I wanted to.

An eerie, thick smog descended, evil and obscuring, and then it became obvious, the black tree, was actually not a tree at all, but a rock of graphite, powdery and polluting the air around it. It rose ominously. I could hear a pounding coming from the inside of the rock, clanging, a booming sound, something was coming out of that hell hole. The red eyed monster was only a servant and I, and I, . . .I took a deep breath, and I just cannot bear to watch but I cannot look away either, I have to face it. Face this evil that

I know is coming, coming for the immortals, coming for humans, coming for the universe and if I don't do something it will swallow us all. A gloom descends across my vision and I opened my eyes with a start, hearts pounding in my ears, a sickness swilling inside me. The monster and the rock, gone. *Was it real?*

Voices I could hear in the distance under the cover of a group of thick yew trees. I had read in Rhyiathe's tome somewhere, the yew trees are the most ancient and wisest trees of the woods, holding within them a connection to the very gods and goddesses of the universe, The First. They can be used to invoke powerful incantations.

To me, the living woods have always been my home. It is bricks and mortar that make me afraid and uncomfortable. On this night, the ancient trees had been guarding me as sentinels against my pain. The smell of the forest fauna revived me. Their bark and root were rough to touch but warming to my weary, broken hearts.

I sat up, noticing the wind had blown crispy dead leaves into the grooves of my body. The crunchy children of the trees lightly fell to the ground from my clothing. Woodlice and ants had nestled into me, my only companions. Lovingly and with care, I shook them off. They had played the carer very well against my thin-skinned, upset and pain. I watched them with gratitude as they scuttled away.

Like an acrobat eager to perform, I moved to a crouching position and sat up onto my haunches, looking out over the clearing; through the peepholes made by little animals burrowing through the denseness of a bush. I found the source of the words that were being spoken. I could see clearly with keen eyes like a predator, in the absolute darkness surrounding this place.

Five beacons of fire had been lit, spitting and alive. The flames were flickering and smoking black in the unnatural night air. The air was smothered. A thick smog of velvety darkness, choking these woods.

The clearing was abundant with yew trees, the roots, knitted together fast, had created a makeshift bridge. Rushing water was running underneath seven joined sisters of these yew trees and a babbling river flowed through. The high notes of the water bounced between bark and branches. The smell of ripe acorns and promises of Spring faded in the dark foreboding of whatever was hovering in between these trees this night. Something disturbed them, so I waited and watched, just like the silent woods.

The hooded form of a Priest could be seen, standing near to four tall male Elves dressed in heavy armour and military gear. I followed their gazes. The assembled group were looking down at the river, drawn to the same fixed point at the water's edge.

The priest was worshipping the twisted Yew Trees and reciting words in a language unfamiliar to me.

Golden particles of light were floating down from the canopy of the trees, like shining beads gliding on wisps of finely spun yarn, falling from delicate leaf and sturdy branches. The lights landed lightly on the back of the head of a black-haired Elf lord. A halo formed. I couldn't see the Elf Lord fully. He was kneeling at the water's edge before the priest. The bystanders were silently watching the rite with expressions of awe on their hardened, arrogant faces. One of the tall blonde Elf Lords dressed in golden armour, was absorbed by shadows. He was unseen when he turned to excitedly whisper to another,

"The spell to stop the immortals from entering the Void is now broken. Even if the High Priestess tries to put it back, the spell cannot be remade but Gamone wants us to take no chances. We must kill the high priestess in the morning and our Priest will take her place."

A crippling and harsh reply cleaved out into the darkness,

"Keep your tongue in between your teeth, young Lord Tennison. We don't know who might be listening to your careless words," The Priest goes on to caution in an accusatory tone, glancing round "Gamone, the Light of the Elder has been summoned over the last few weeks and your bloodline is recognised as pure. The lights of Elenadril have marked you as complete."

A loud, heaving gasp escaped my lips. Understanding forms; of Gamone and the golden particles of light that have converged upon him; just as they had me. *What is the Light of Elenadril and why was I marked by it too? The Light of the Elders, eh?* This information had been pocketed in my mind.

There was an unnatural pause, and my chest quickened its rhythm. I couldn't help but think my gasp had been heard. I waited. A tension grew within me.

"Leave me. I want to bathe in the stream while I absorb the last of the Lights in this sacred place of The Elder beneath the Tree of Souls," The strong, deep masculine voice of Gamone shoots out of the recess of the riverbed, over the sounds of the babbling water. His words were hard and made to be heard - the water bowed before him.

"My Lord Gamone, I will wait for you," said a familiar voice of the female witch who accosted me earlier in the day. I shivered at the closeness of her vicinity, the blackness of her speech.

"Esmerall, if I wanted you to wait with me, I would have said. Now go."

Some of the golden lights hovering at the top of the branches of the yew tree, started to change direction, blown away from the mass of elves gathered and drifted lazily in my direction. Eventually, they would show the elves I am here.

No, no, no, no. The lights were going to betray me soon. I made to stand, and a few dried twigs snapped under my foot. The other Elves had hastily left the clearing, but I watched in horror as Gamone's great black-haired head turned around. His eyes were caught by the group of golden particles that were moving away from the mass of orbs. He stood, his violet, grey eyes illuminated in the reflections of the light, as he watched them float up. He was immensely tall and powerful, taller than any immortal I had seen in these lands.

In his hands, he conjured a white and gold sheaf of material. Wrapping it over his nakedness like a toga, draping him. It served to accentuate his masculinity. Unsheathing a sword, he followed the few renegade particles up the steep, dusty bank of the river and headed towards the oak tree, where I stood. His enthusiastic, hard eyes were watching the particles with a purpose.

"Come out or I will cleave you where you stand and take the tree down with you too. It affords no protection for you," his voice was silky, but his words were pure venom. I couldn't describe it. Lord Gamone commanded the world, it was made to bow and scrape before him on its knees.

Standing up, straight backed, I stepped out from behind the tree and the golden embers landed on me, absorbing into my skin; just as his were vanishing into him.

He stared at me for a long time, and I felt a type of fear that had my skin screaming for the protection of the woods, away from his prying eyes. His thick black hair blanketed his back and hang down his chest. His abdominal muscles well defined like he was a marble statue. On his feet were gladiator-style sandals and he stood towering above me with a look

on his face that denoted if he really wanted to, he might be inclined to snap my neck with his strong fingers. I shivered.
All was suddenly silent in the clearing, even the pretty chirruping insects and the sonar calls of the bats were quietly in awe of his presence.
He stood strong and tall, the Apex predator of these lands.
A throbbing sensation reached out to test me and every cell in my body was vibrating, aching for him to say something to break the spell. He did not comply. I doubted he was even aware of my need, as he stood still, full of a confidence that I had not encountered before. I stood very still, like I was being assessed by a tiger in its den.
"W-w-what are the golden lights?" I croaked out, my throat dry and cracked from the moisture abandoning my tongue. His eyes had ceased their interest in the lights and were now feasting, roaming all over my body. Stripped bare was I, scraped out by the spears of his gaze and aggressively so.
"Your name, is it Aurora? Tell me about your birth and do it quickly." His violet, grey eyes were penetrating me. I felt a cold longing for safety under that gaze, it reached out and placed a pressure on my mind. He was performing magic.
Digging in my heels with my head tossed back, I met the magic he was probing me with and concentrated - visualising a protective light around me, around those I loved, just as Rhyiathe had taught me. The golden lights responded and a translucent shield fell down around me Gamone could not break through. My mind screamed *Run, run, run, run,run,run,run, run. You are the hunted in this place. In these woods.*
The warning in my mind was speaking clearly to me, but I wanted to know more about the golden particles, so I ignored it.
"My birth? What? Why do you want to know about my birth?" my words were laced with uncertainty and confusion. I hated the sound.
His sizeable fingers gripped the hilt of his sword tight, with a heaviness of hand. The tip of the ice-cold blade shot up and burned me in the swiftness of its cut. I kept my chin lifted, allowing the blood to flow down my neck, dripping onto my chest, without moving my hands to it like I cared not. His swordplay was so fast, a blur. How do you best an opponent like that? It was unnatural. I decided it was best to watch and comply until a weakness of some kind was exposed. A hiccup of exposure and he would

be mine. My incisures slid over my lip. My confidence came into play. I had forgotten about my new freedoms, these new abilities. But then a dull ache ran rampant through my body. The restrictive potion throbbed in my veins, like a dog leash. If it had not been so, this dynamic would have been changed.

"Tell me now," He growled out in command. His stance is a sinewed story of his body performing great feats, an extensive list of conquests. So noticeably confident was he.

"I don't know about my birth, what do you want to know? My mother never told me anything. No photos. No birth certificate. She used to call me foundling come to think of it." I stood there, alone in the confusion of the shocking memory I had just recalled. Bearing my soul and oversharing with an alien barbarian was unexpected, unlike me. Fear does strange things to the mind.

He looked at the last remnants of particles sliding into both of us, splitting between us. Floating, the lights were separating, copying, doubling like atoms multiplying, creating new life and we were absorbing the power of them. We stood together watching in silence until there were none left, hypnotised, connected. The lights had changed our DNA structure.

We were becoming one and the same, Gamone and I. This was known to me and known to him like we were reading the same coding, and we could smell it on each other.

What comes next? I was left wondering while he was infinitely more self-assured and knew more than me.

"You have seen these lights before, haven't you?" A low growl of understanding escaped his lips in a way that I didn't understand.

"Yes, a few times before on Earth, and once when I landed on this planet. The lights were green that time. The other time was this morning. A large cloud of gold particles followed me, and I absorbed them. Your witch followed me and saw them too."

Did he just read my mind? I was straining to take a breath. *blank, go blank.* He raised his eyebrows and lowered his sword. Dropping the hilt at my feet, it clanged to the ground; a symbol of his defences sliding away. *Shit, I am no longer a threat.*

He moved swiftly towards me and lifted me out of the small hole made by the ancient roots of the oak tree, tossing me lightly aside. I was made of air

to him. Patting the dead leaves and detritus off me in a heavy-handed way and appraising me properly in the light made from the flames of the beacon, his fingers ventured to touch my face, but I stepped away and pushed his hands aside.
"Enough. I am not a toy." I inflated my chest, blowing myself up in an absurd pufferfish style.
With a glinting smile, he nodded.
"My name is Gamone, Prince Gamone. I have forgotten my manners. I am most pleased to meet you, Aurora. I was hostile before, and for that, I am terribly sorry. I was worried you were an assassin, sent by the vampires, to reclaim their Prince," he hesitated, "- who we had to take into the Elf King's *protective* custody, for his own good, you understand? To protect *him.* The Vampires, I mean the real vampires are vicious animals, cold and cruel." A smile formed on his lips.
This was strange. He seemed to have conveniently forgotten that he'd ordered Lindon to kill me when he tried to stop the Rite, but he seemed to have a protective streak – just like me. Protecting this vampire prince like that. Maybe I should give him the benefit of the doubt.
"Please let me make it up to you. To show you I am not a scoundrel. I'm different from my brother, from those I grew up around. I will pick you up tomorrow and give you a personal guided tour of the city," he said to me. His dark, handsome face was staggeringly attractive but there was a murderer behind his cheap smile with a dagger behind his back and an executioner's mask flapping in the breeze, but I could be wrong. My mind was only just gripping onto reality by a thread. I reasoned I'm often accused of being all those things - misunderstood.
"And if I agree you will tell me more about the gold particles of The Elder?"
"*IF* you agree?" He laughed loudly, like the most ludicrous of words imaginable have dared to be floated before him and he blew them away with a heaving of his chest. He moved conspiratorially forward with a gentle grace - practised and refined. Gamone pulled my hair away from my face and hooked it behind my ear, as gently as if he was unfolding the velvety petals of a rose. I could almost smell the scent of them on his skin – so sweet to me, was his smell. A faint breeze glided towards me and the

smell from the forest made me more alert. Danger screeched in the wake of his existence.

"*Aurora,* you will be begging for my company soon, I am Lord Gamone there are none that can withstand me."

Chapter Eighteen – Exposed

Standing in front of my favourite gilded, ornamental mirror in my large dressing room once more, back in my apartment, I mulled over what to wear for an afternoon with a potential monster. I weighed in my hands, my heavy, thick, comforting bodysuit, and in the other, a simple cotton shift dress. It would look lovely with golden bangles and sandals. There was a preference to appear unassuming, vulnerable, and silly, but a cold shiver of foreboding was on my flesh, screaming with a longing for my protective shield - the tan bodysuit.

Usually, it would be customary, to wear a dress on a tour of the city, especially when being escorted by Lord Gamone, a prince, no doubt. Something demure, like what the immortals wear. I sucked at a blood blister, one given to me by Rhyiathe, to stop any blood lust rising in me, while I am out on the tour of the city. I couldn't afford any mistakes or any bloodlust fuelled rage. I was taking precautions, and this was one of them.

Lilly was gently brushing my hair, humming to herself, when she suddenly leant forward, caught up in thought. The motion of hers shook me out of my contemplation.

"Where are you off to M'lady, this day? It is good to see your spirits lifted," Lilly said cheerfully, "you and Dawn will forge out a new relationship when your heart is less heavy." A warm smile settled on her lips, perking up my confidence a little and I smiled back.

With a small nod and a brightness in my eyes, I told her, "Lord Gamone has offered to collect me for a tour of the city this afternoon and I . . ."

Before I could finish my sentence, a vibration built behind me of silent screeching bells of warning. The force of it prickled the hairs on the back of my neck.

Lilly raked the harsh bristles through my long hair, harder than intended and my neck cracked. I pulled against the yanking, "Lilly!" I shrieked holding my head cradled in between my hands.

"M'Lady, I'm so sorry, my hand slipped and gripped you." Worry was heavy upon her words. "You cannot go. He is a monster," she said darkly.

"I will be going, Lilly. I must. He holds a secret to a riddle that has been plaguing me for some time."

"You cannot go. You must trust me on this. Stay away from him," placing the brush down, she talked intently to my reflection in the mirror with pleading eyes, "do you hear me?"

"Yes," I said, "but I cannot agree to what you ask so please trust me on this." I picked up the cotton dress off the back of my chair. The fabric was so very fragile, whispering as it was being unfolded. I held the skimpy layers up against me. A butterfly flapping its wings would have left more of an indent. I sighed, but I was determined. Pushing the bodysuit off my shoulders, it dropped with a comforting heavy *flump* to the floor and I stepped over the suit and into the cotton dress, into a new personality. Quickly, I realised this was something I'd never wear.

Lilly gasped at my choice of outfit. "It will afford you no protection. You are a warrior, and the body armour serves you true. You don't know what you are doing. You don't know the danger you are putting yourself in." she looked around in fear "He . . . he was in the games once. Killing is a sport to him," she lowered her voice, "each round hosted his wilful display of barbarism. He . . . he would be always thrilled by the bloodlust. Sees others as things. Objects we are to him. Ending each battle by tearing out intestines, battle warped and crazed . . . No one would fight him. The contestants had to be forced to fight him with the threat of a violent death."

The revulsion clearly showed on my face, but Lilly did not spare me any details, "You think that's bad? It gets *far* worse. He thinks werewolves, vampires and witches are lowly, not worthy to breathe the same air as Elves. Humans, even less so. I won't even tell you the rumours." Lilly screamed all this at me with the momentum of a runaway train, looking quite faint.

I couldn't help her here. Reassuring her means agreeing not to go and this was something I was not prepared to do.

". . . and The Elder. What does he think of the Elder?" This was the question I really wanted to ask.

Lilly's eyes widened, and a strange light crept across her shadowed face, turning to check the door first.

"Where did you hear that term?" she hissed, shushing me through her teeth. Livid, jaw clenching, holding her mouth shut.

"I heard it yesterday. In the market. Why, is it banned? What are the Elder, Lilly, please?"

A loud knock at my apartment door.

"M' Lady, Lord Gamone begs that you kindly join him in his carriage," A smooth-tongued elf footman announced, signalling the arrival of Lord Gamone. His master.

"Here, take this and attach the sheaf round your inner thigh so it is concealed, but it will not be enough. You are stupid. You have not even thought about the reason why he has asked you." Without another word, Lilly disengaged, anger clouding her face and goes to answer the door.

Oh contres, mon ami, I had my suspicions he knows we are one and the same – I shivered but I am not cold.

My ridiculous silk parasol fluttered as I put it up, against the suns gloriously brightness in the afternoon sky. The warmth made my dress sticky with perspiration. Little droplets of moisture formed on my lips and my chest, above my bosom. I licked the salty wetness off my top lip. At that moment, Lord Gamone leant forward, peering out of the carriage and turns, side glances lecherously at my tongue. *"Damn it,"* a whispered reprimand to myself. *Vigilant at all times* my mind warned.

"Good afternoon, Lady Aurora. You look unbelievably beautiful and . . . may I say, more open to new possibilities today." He was ensconced in the corner seat of the large, opulent, and gilded carriage, clearly built for his proportions but still, he looked as if he was perching rather than reclining on the red plush cushions. His thighs strained against the raw silk material of his trousers, muscles and bulges defined underneath. His neck and chest gave off the impression of a prized breeding bull.

"Good afternoon, Lord Gamone. You look more refined. I should say this is because you are *actually* wearing clothes today."

A snort of laughter came from the Footman while he opened the door for me. He was rewarded with Lord Gamone looking at him darkly. The footman flinched away.

Gamone nodded his devastatingly handsome head with a smirk growing on his lips. Raising one eyebrow, he lifted two crystal glasses of wine and handed one to me. His fingers brushed mine and he made sure we were touching each other. He was taking in my lips intently as he held onto the glass in my hand. A pressing sprinkling of pressure in the air and the glass in my hand was covered in thick frost, cracking and tinkling under the spell he had just used.

"My Lady. All for you. I am at your service today. If servicing you need, then it will be I, that will be at *your* pleasure."

Choking on the glug of wine in my mouth and dribbling down my chin unbecomingly, I snorted out a laugh. I was relieved that it was white wine dribbling from my mouth when I looked down at the wet patches pooling on the crisp whiteness of my cotton dress. He looked at complete ease, not noticing these minute details about me or about my behaviour.

"What? What did I say?" he asked puzzled, but did not laugh along with me. *This was going to be a very long afternoon.*

Once I was inside the carriage, and he was closer than was strictly necessary, we were off. The clip-clopping of horse-like creatures harnessed at the front of the transport, chorused through the noisy streets of the city. I was taken aback when a hand of his strayed towards my inner thigh and clutched at the outline of my knife, hidden there. In one swift movement, his hand darted up my skirt and retrieved the object, uninvited.

He studied the blade, "A remarkable Elven dagger, forged during the Crimerean era, I believe. Encrusted with moonstones and imbibed with wolf venom, so it can maim any immortal. A fine choice for a Lady." He placed it on his forearm to present it back to me in a mockery of a chivalrous gesture. His eyes were intent and dark. I did not laugh.

He said, "Relax, you have no reason to be worried. If I had wanted to hurt you, I would have done so in the woods when you were alone."

I most definitely do my brain cautioned me. "My Lord, the precaution was not against you, but a Lady can never be too careful." I fluttered my eyelashes and preened, or at least that is what I was hoping that I looked like.

"Very well. Driver, onto the gardens of Nebulous at speed."

We arrived outside a splendidly, brilliant white palatial palace. Exotic to the eye, the architecture was likened to human Persian design, intricate and decadent. The smooth white walls sparkled as if lit by moonlight, yet it was daytime here. Tinkling, opulent fountains were at the centrepiece of the lawn. Mosaic tiled pathways, awash with blinding bright colours, wound up to the main gates and enchanting, colourful dream-like creatures trotted their way by, as if floating on air. Succulent hydrophytes fanned out, and tropical plants claimed the grasslands, which encouraged a myriad of wildlife into the grounds, helping to shape the terrain by grazing and the natural order of things. Adding to the majesty of my surroundings, an ambience of a dreamlike world opened before me, and I could only gasp. My throat purred out in my efforts to contain my shaking excitement.

Two female servants swished forward, dressed in long maroon silks and feathered headdresses to open the door of the ornamental carriage.

"Let us help you, M'lady." They were not looking at me with their kohled and sultry eyes. All their attention was on the hunk of a mountain that sat at my side and they blushed at his piercing violet gaze. His presence was felt by all the occupants in that garden, even the gardeners stopped to watch him dismount the coach, like a prized racehorse. To look upon him appeared to make people feeble and enslaved by his power and handsomeness, but no one saw the disused, shrivelled black heart in his chest, as I did. He noticed nothing of his admirers, too intent was he on winning me. He took my hand and placed it under his arm, resting it on his large forearm, a flash of a dazzling smile, I was granted and we glided along, he thought I was his to command, along with all the other people in this place.

He talked to me lightly, in friendly tones, "I will show you the gardens my mother had made, where we can be alone." At these words, my throat dried out and the servants, eavesdropping, exchanged indiscreet glances and swooned at his sweet uttering to me, wishing it was them, but a cold stole over me. I pressed my thighs together, reassured that my blade was back in its sheaf.

So, we began to walk through the maze made of ten-foot-tall hedges - neatly maintained but hidden and dark. My flesh goose bumped. Made painfully aware, I would be unheard, should a scream escape my lips.

Screams would have been useless here anyway. The servants were all loyal to his family, under his control.

Fight or die, fight, or die, fight or die ran like a faulty projector flipping on rotation through my mind.

"So, is this your mother's. . . home? It seems far too grand to call it a home so apologies if I have not used the right words. You mentioned she created the garden here. In this palace."

"Yes, my mother is an elven queen, and this was her summer house until she gifted it to the city for the people to enjoy it." a rehearsed response. He acted like he cared, but he didn't.

"That is very generous. And your father? Is he a king?"

A look of icy anger slid over Gamone's eyes for a split second, this had not slipped passed me unnoticed. I have been able to read micro-gestures from years of honing myself to scan my environment for threats and risks. Although his face gave way to a charming smile, I knew there was something there about the father. At a guess, the king is not his real father, but I waited.

"Of course, yes, the King is married to my mother the Queen, after all." Coldly polite but did I detect a discernible sneer in amongst the vowels?

"So, then Lord Tennison is your brother? I would not have guessed this. You look so different. He is blonde and slender. You are black-haired and strongly built. I saw the King at the tournament and Lord Tennison is his double. Do you then take after your mother?"

"Yes, he is my. . . brother and what are you implying?" his jaw flexed, and his fists balled.

"Nothing, nothing . . . just an observation my lord. I don't look like my sister either," m eyes flickered to the muscle tension in his jaw. Contemplatively adding, "is this something that bothers you? That people will make this type of observation, about you."

A darkness crept over his eyes, that turned the colour pale grey. His eyebrows and forehead sloped lower forward. His neck strained against his shirt. *I am poking the bear, and the bear is debating whether to stand on its back legs to use its claws or charge at me and devour me whole.* My heartbeat quickened, adrenaline pulsating through my veins, but the potion's leash was still firmly in place. *Bloody hell.*

But all too quickly, there was a cunning gleam in his eyes and a message was sent from his brain to his body. A shift, a change in his countenance. Abruptly, he moved the gears of his personality into a type of carefree nonchalance. He shrilly laughed, carefully orchestrated, "I care not for what others and the court think of me. Now, to round off our afternoon, let me take you for a leisurely tour of one of the greenhouses. A particular favourite of mine to resemble one of the jungles of the Maldoom region of Tylerine, the elf home world. It is only for my leisure. No one else is permitted to enter, except by my leave. It's made of Elven Eliminum glass, where tropical vegetables and fruit are grown. Intensified by magic is the flavour. An aphrodisiac, encouraging mating and breeding by bonded and mated pairs."

As he walked away, I watched his back and Lilly's words of warning reverberated through my ears '*You are stupid. You have not even thought about the reason why he has asked you.*' I knew it had something to do with the Lights of the Elder and he was keeping his temper in check for a purpose on this trip, so I knew I was about to find out.

Gamone was in flight - feverishly, his footsteps once heard clearly ahead were now quite faint, nothing but a rustle and a whisper to my keen ears. A metallic door clanged open and then the doorway suctioned shut. He had entered the greenhouse up ahead.

Closing the distance quickly, my eyes were drawn to the top of the structure of the greenhouse. Dome-shaped and at least one hundred metres high, the top of the glass dome glinted in the afternoon suns, great waves of heat were coming off it, rippling in the air.

When I opened the sticky door, the humidity crept into my nostrils. A gush of hot, heavy air left a slick sweat over my skin. My clothes were heavy with prickles of dampness.

It was a jungle of bushes and trees. A jungle of noise, buzzing large insects, faceless hooting monkeys, and great exotic squawking parrots. The death knolls of the hunted prey. My eyes swivelled about looking for the animals, but I didn't see one, elusive they were, hidden by the density of the rubbery foliage.

The pathways were obscured, very little could be seen apart from wall-to-wall plant life and vegetation. It was wild in there – dangerous and overgrown. A haven, the environment was perfect for Gamone the hunter waiting for me inside. He had built this as an arena for his cat and mouse games. It was purposely chaotic to the senses, stripping his prey of any natural skills they may have, giving the advantage to him as the elf hunter in a replica of his home world.

I stepped away from the doorway, swivelling my head about to find an escape. There was none. My eyes fell on two of his guards, dressed in cream cloaks and gold armour, who were holding their swords with the tip pointing at me, indicating I go into the greenhouse or die on those blades. A trap. It was always going to be this way.

I chose to go into the arena and fight to the death once more – a choice I will always take, no matter the odds.

Ripping a slit in my dress with a cold defiance, all the way from the hem to my thigh, a loud tearing and cracking sound ensues as the thin, alluring cotton rips apart.

Sliding my dagger from my thigh, removing it, and placing it out before me, I walked in, armed ready for combat. It had been lurking between us since the first meeting by the river and it would be done this afternoon, wither way it panned out. I could imagine the pulse of battle racing stronger in his neck and it matched my own bloodlust – the killer in me ignited.

The squawking of parrots could be heard all around like an echo in a prism of glass, the domed greenhouse was distorting sound, but the birds could not be seen under the heaviness of the dense trees. Fan like ferns spread out, catching at my clothes. Warning me to get out of this hostile place, but I continued moving forward. The floor was squelching. Marshlands had formed in there, that gave way into deeper set water. Mangroves sprang up the deeper I ventured inside - *is this by magic?* The pressing sensation told me it was. I surveyed the entire landscape searching for another way round to the other side of the dome, where I could escape. There was no other way, so I stepped in the water, wading through chest height fetid warm water, I held my muscles taut, breathing quietly and every now and then, I cursed at myself for jumping back from a frog or some other creature submerged in the water, eyes peering out over the rim of the steamy wetness. The sound of the sloshing water battering against my chest is all that gave my location away.

I could feel his eyes upon me. It was a pressuring sensation that made my heartbeat vibrate in my ears, but I couldn't see him. He was trying to frighten me, but I would not be scared by him. I would not allow it.

Keeping my breath in a deep, slow rhythm, my heartbeat was steady. The sounds of animal chatter and birds calling had stopped. Deadly was the sudden silence and I knew why. He was near. *Splosh, splosh, splosh, splosh* went the small waves, much shallower was the water here, now lapping at my thighs, crossing the hot waters of the mangrove- I needed to find dry land. A poignant smell of sickly-sweet rotting bananas stung my nostrils and the surrealism of the situation bent at my mind. My lip trembled involuntarily. A sob weighed at the back of my throat. I smoothed my wet hair away from my face. The humidity in there was dulling my senses.

I was being hunted. This was really happening. *I am being hunted.*

He jumped down before me from the trees overhead, holding onto a thick branch, muscles rippling for a glimpse, then he dropped himself into the pools of water, in a controlled demonstration of his strength. Water crashed up his legs, as thick as tree trunks, in torrents. Crouching low in the warm water for a while watching me, before he slowly straightened up. His black hair dripped beads of moisture, like little hard gems, onto the straining muscles of his broad chest. He was power and I was the mouse. He had removed his clothes and stood before me like an animal, wildness in every line, in the primal, darkening of his eyes. All bleak, his pupils had leaked away from his irises. It was foul whatever savagery was on his mind. It was there written upon his screwed-up face.

Dagger drawn; blood dripped from the tip. He had already killed as a rehearsal for me. Bloodlines were drawn down his cheeks.

"Do you want to play, Aurora? Is this more like the afternoon that you thought we would share together? Of battle and revelations? Ask me what you have come to ask me and if you are honest, I will be too. Or stay cowardly like a Human, or act as a killer vampire, feral and filthy, or bringer of the light of the Elder, which one are *you*?" His jaw jutted forward in aggression and contempt was etched like runes across his face. He growled the last words out like an angry accusation.

"Well, my lord this afternoon *has* indeed taken a turn for the worse, but I am not surprised. You can only hold your behaviour in check for so long before your dark passenger emerges, is that right?" Cavalier, I said this, but

I was shaking from head to foot. He was a grizzly bear, and I was but a defenceless babe against his will.

With a look of complete concentration in his eyes, his lip curled venomously, "For all your pretty words and careful considerations, I could say the same of you. You see me and you recognise *you*. That's why you tremble and that's why I will know how to break you, little girl. Now spit it out, what do you want to know, and I may tell you why I am interested."

He held up the dagger and placed the tip, squarely to point at me. All pretence of the people we were both pretending to be that afternoon were gone in a blink of an eye. It was liberating and terrifying at the same time. I was truly naked in front of a man for the first time in my life.

We stared at each other, sizing each other up. I lowered my dagger an inch, but it remained in the tight grip of my hand, and I did not move forward.

"I want to know about the Elder and what it has to do with me. That's the only thing I want from you. But let's be clear, I no longer want to continue to be the parts of myself that I see in you."

Contemplation flickered over his face and a decision was made. He lowered his weapon but did not throw it on the ground. He was not done yet, but his tone had switched to more pleasing, I was struggling to keep when he said, "Right, right, you will have more questions when I tell you but I'm not here to give you a history lesson, more to put a proposition to you." He took a deep breath, boring into my eyes with a burning, urgent intensity. *So, he wants something from me.* Then he continued. "The Elder were a species of pure magical beings, immensely powerful and were able to complete great feats of magic. They were or are celestial. They lived in these realms before the half breeds or what we call immortals nowadays came to live in the outer realms after being displaced from Earth. This was part of The Clandestine Agreement. The Elders had vanished without a trace, before the immortals arrived and no one knows why.

It was once thought that the immortals genetically originated from the elder bloodline but became diluted from breeding with humans, which I think is true. The Rite you saw performed was testing my Elder DNA and it is very strong in my blood, less polluted from cross-contamination with humans and it would appear so is yours. The Lights congregated around us both. The Elder Lights have not appeared under the Rite for centuries.

You are one in a billion Aurora or even more precious than that. What can it mean? Two here now. A female and a male," he tapped his chest.

My eyes widened and I gasped, but I was rooted to the spot-on trembling legs, I wanted to hear it all regardless of the cost.

"How? How can this be?" The words escaped my lips, "I'm human. I am human. Or I *was* human, at least."

He shook his head, his eyebrows knitted together. "You most definitely are not human, but I don't know how this has come to be. It *is* correct. You *are* an Elder. The Rite does not provide a false truth. The test cannot be bent or tainted. You are an Elder, as am I."

My body loosened from the defensive position it was holding. The shock was making my arms and legs shake so violently that I was no longer safe holding my own dagger.

He took this as an act of submission. Without a moment's hesitation, Gamone dropped his dagger into the calmness of the water and waded over to me on strong thighs, rippling with muscles. Striding with purpose, he grabbed my arms holding me in place. He licked my neck. His rough tongue pressed lecherously on my skin. The slick of his saliva travelled all the way up to my mouth and he began frantically kissing me. It was softly at first, then more urgently, then insistently as he pulled my body under the water and into him. The skirt of my dress bubbled up with oxygen, floating on top of the surface. My legs and belly were laid bare. I was trembling, gasping for air as the palpitations of shock took over me. Numbing me.

He was pulling the bodice of my dress down, with breath that was laboured. His fingers were clumsy with excitement, eyes made primal with lust. Deliriously happy as he said, "Our offspring will be full Elders. We will bond now and then have a quick bonding ceremony in a few weeks' time. Tokenistic for my mother's sake and the royal family, we cannot have any scandal, then, . . ." he continued talking, but my mind was reeling and wouldn't budge past the vile words spoken *bonding ceremony... Mated partners for life* screamed in my ears. *Stupid, stupid, stupid.*

He had lured me here to complete the bonding and once it was done it would be done forever, that much I understood about the immortal culture. I didn't understand all of this yet, all the rules of this strange land

but I knew this was something permanent. *Get out* screams my brain *get out of the bloody water.*
I balled myself up, then threw my limbs outwards like a starburst, exploding from the water with the last of my strength, leaving him shocked; he did not move to grab me until I was out of his reach.
Springing onto my nerve bitten legs, I shot straight upwards. Out of the confines of the warm, stagnant mangrove water, I bound higher than I intended, higher than I thought possible, and I jumped from treetop to treetop like a wild spider monkey. Not once did I look back.
A roar erupted in the space I had left behind me. A deafening bellow of decibels of frustration. The sound of a tiger pacing the mangrove and all the animals quell before the call. Be it Alpha or apex, that roar instilled a primal response. All the animals stood frozen, fighting or fawning, in the wake of the decibels that screamed out death to the listener, or worse. Convulsing, my stomach emptied. The adrenaline was palpable in my veins now. I stood sopping wet, half naked and ready to run, to fight, to do whatever it took to survive. I vomited down the front of my dress in great luminous yellow streaks of bile from the fear of what he was going to do to me. *Still* wanted to do to me.
My brain jabbered in fear. A strange buzz in my ears. Horror froze on my dry, sticky eyes. I kept jumping, swinging from tree to tree.
Eventually, I found myself on the outer edges of the trees, when I hang-jump down to the ground, legs taking the full impact. With flashing, disjointed thoughts of the streaks of blood running down his cheeks, I ran as fast as I could to reach the dome walls. I smashed through the glass panels, not even using the doors. I could not even feel the glass rake, great red bloody welts into my skin. I was numb. Thank God I was numb.
"Aurora, I will find you, we are one you and I," he shouted, and his deep voice echoed throughout the dome: his hunting kingdom of freedom. It was a freedom from being anything other than a killer. It pulsated in my ears, making me run all the faster on my jerky, frigid legs.
Outside the dome, the cool breeze was dizzying. I stopped and vomited once again before darting towards the normalcy of the streets through the cover of the trees. I ran. Escaped. Immediately, I set my eyes on the blurred images of the guards. Their faces, span like a kaleidoscope of patterns in front of my eyes.

Jabbing and thrusting my dagger out blindly in my ruined state, I sobbed uncontrollably as they dropped, dead weights to the floor.

Great jagged gasps of breath I took into my painful lungs. Bewildered and afraid, I ran through the manicured lawns. My mind was warped by the normalcy of the outside of the dome when inside was pure horror. Cold sweats of terror leaked down my back. The trimmed grass, the colourful mosaic, the beautiful creatures, and the music floating in the air – it was all a grand charade. I was coated with blackness inside from my vulnerability. My shame at being used like a toy.

I heard a sound that lightened my soul, "Over here, stupid. Get in, get in the carriage." It was Lilly. She had followed me, and I wept hot tears of gratitude on that spot, running forward. Falling headfirst onto the open door with water dripping down me, she bundled me into a light, smaller lacquer black sealed carriage. Concealed and hidden at last, it whisked us away from the streets outside of the white stone palace. The palatial palace that had so very much impressed me at first sight.

Lilly had brought my tan bodysuit with her. It was folded up on the seat of the carriage. She knew me. Somehow, she just had known I would need it to protect me from the world, after my afternoon with Gamone.

My eyes brimmed over at the kindness of the gesture. I hadn't listened to her when she warned me about Gamone. *Why hadn't I listened to her?* I coloured at my own stupidity. A tough woman from London, sure.

I suddenly got the urge to scramble away, to place my body back into the hard comfort of the inner shell of my bodysuit, so I did so, immediately.

Lilly watched me silently. I tried to ignore my jangling hands, jerking to pull the fabric up over the slashes on my bleeding legs.

"Oh, Aurora, let me help you," I hated the sound of pity in Lilly's strangled voice.

"No, I must do this on my own." Eventually, I managed to put on the bodysuit, wincing and steadying my breath. Wrapping her arms around me, Lilly placed my head against her chest, her chin on my head and cooed out, "Do you want to talk about it?" all the while stroking my hair.

The pain stung in my throat. The acidic taste of bile coated my tongue and there was still fur on my teeth. My breath was coming in short bursts now, but the familiar smell of Lilly's hair and the comforting feel of my protective suit eased my pain some.

Tears streaked down the side of my nose, I anxiously held the terror in my chest and laid false iron bars over it and threatened my mind to comply, not allowing it to use my lips to utter a word of my distress.

I shook my head. “Not yet, I am not ready to talk about it. Can we go to see Dawn please?”

Lilly lifted her chin off the top of my head and moved her face level to mine. Her eyes observed the pain there in the spiralling blots of pupils reflecting my mind’s state and then she leaned in with her thumbs forward to remove the tears from my cheeks.

“Are you sure? She doesn’t recognise you. Won’t it be another blow and you've been through enough today already,” So tenderly she said this, and it was shocking. I didn't understand, a mother’s tender care makes me nervous, mistrustful.

“Please, please,” was all I could say. Lilly nodded at me, aching to look away and then yelled to the coach driver in Elvish, to take us to the Academy.

Chapter Nineteen - The Crown Prince of Vulldune

The Castle of Pericullious waited in stillness. The Suns, burning with red hot flames, are dominating the very centre point of the sky. The scorching heat of them pierced through the windows and coloured all the walls with a deep red glare, like the glowing of fierce rubies. The Suns understood what power they hold over the Seven Kingdoms, bleaching bones and burning skin, comforting dragons, with their blistering kiss. The Great Serpents would not bow to their beating flames, for these great Dragons are fiercest of them all.

It was High Noon on the day of the Night of the Full Moons, which comes but once every eight weeks. To explain this to you mortals, - there is a significance to it being High Noon.

High Noon is when the Vampires are at their weakest point in the day. They are a group of beings that draw power from the Moon Goddess, Nimwae, Mother of tainted light, Lover of the Damned. Virgin to the stars.

The castle waited to oversee a new custom that was introduced only recently by the Elf King and his two sons: Crown Prince Tennison and Prince Gamone. Both the Elf King's sons prefer the title of Lord in their day-to-day comings and goings. The term Elf Lord, they both deem to be mightier than the term Prince, you would do well to guard this knowledge.

A courtier steps forward, draped in his elven finery of frills, silks of over-zealous couture. Bowing to the Steward King – the elf king - sat on the Amber Throne of Pericullious, the mightiest of power seats in the Seven Kingdoms, he turns to the Crown Prince and bows deeply, then to the younger Prince, who shifts uncomfortably on his lesser golden throne.

The Courtier then stood on a crystal step in the centre of the room to unfurl a golden scroll with the intention of making an announcement. Flourishing one hand and making a show of overly exhibiting a silk handkerchief in the other, denoting a bad smell in the air, he spoke,

"Your esteemed guest, who may not leave these Lands without-" at this point the courtier makes a show of nodding in turn to each of the Elven Royal Family in the room "- M'lord's or M'Lord's or M'Lord's express permission, I announce the Crown Prince of Vulldune, Rhyiathe Bastion Maeerrillion the Tenth. Named after his Father King Rhyiathe and His Royal Highness Queen Maeerrillion of Vulldune." The courtier nodded, clicking his satin shoes together at the heel, and then stepped off the gleaming crystal step, bowing deeply on his way out of the Royal High Elves eyeline, with a simpering pomposity.

The Crown Prince of Vulldune, dressed in his family's silver armour; wrought from star light and moon rock, drew his sword. As ceremony dictated between two immortal tribes, he placed the sword hilt, facing up, under his eyes, blade towards the ceiling, and walked the length of the red carpet towards the raised platform that the High Elf Lords are seated upon – a show of power met by indifference. The Elf High Lords were dressed in all their regal attire, Prince Gamone wore a violet, grey suit of armour, with a crown made from platinum, simple of design, while his brother the golden-haired Crown Prince of the Elves, wore a splendid, armoured suit of pure gold – he gleamed and looked every inch a beautiful High Lord of the Elves. A great deal of effort goes into this ceremony by both parties. The High Elf Lords smiled and enjoyed the sport of humiliating the Crown Prince of Vulldune and insulting his family, by holding him here as a prisoner.

The Crown Prince of Vulldune bows to the Elf King, and slowly rose to resume a standing position and waited. Placing his sword down by his right side, which royal protocol indicated he had finished bowing and was ready for the battle, this ceremony would be repeated in eight weeks' time because the Crown Prince of Vulldune refused to bow to the two Elf Princes, a smirk playing over Rhyiathe's lips. The Elf Princes had taken great pains to shuffle forward on their golden thrones, leaning in their eagerness to see if he would bow this time around. He did not. Anger nestled in the corners of the room. The princes hissed between their polished teeth – demanding recompense. Crown Prince Rhyiathe saw wrathful stares before him. His neck was rigid with tension, barely able to contain his anger, but he put that aside, to address the king in appealing tones,

"My Lord Elf King of the united planets of the Seven Kingdoms, *current* ruler of Pericullious, steward King of the Amber Seat by the Immortals leave, who would you have me combat this time? I am most eager to get on with it. I have quite a lot to do this afternoon. I am a remarkably busy *Crown* Prince-" the prince's eyes slid sideways to *Prince* Gamone, who curled his lips with a nasty snarl "- of the Vampires, my Father waits for my letters, as Father's do. Should he not receive these then I do not like to think what would happen . . ."
The Elf King nods, "So you admit your father is busy again? I do hope not raising an army to try to overthrow the Amber Seat, and assuage the Elf's from the Amber Throne once more, My Lord Crown Prince of Vulldune, that is why you are our, . . . *guest* in the first place." Tinkering laughter from the courtiers, which pleased the king very much, then the Elf King continued, while the crown grew heavier with obsession on his head.
"So, you do not bow to my sons and swear fealty nor agree that the Vampires should abdicate the Amber Throne at the next turn of the Stewardship?"
A precise shake of the head from the Crown Prince of Vulldune,
"My good Elf King, my father consented to my *staying* at the leisure of the Elves to bring our tribes closer together, to align our values. The Elves have forgotten that immortals are not the enemy, we are stronger together, brothers and sisters – Guardians of the universe and Keepers of the Secret knowledge of Nature. It is with a heavy heart that I watch the fall of the ruined Seven Kingdoms all because of the spite and greed of one of its own kind. We *can* still come back together, but I see that we have some way to go, as your little *ceremony* still continues and there is a troll, ready and waiting in the corner, your champion, I take it, for this combat trial, this time? I do grow weary of the sub-standard champions your son's keep rolling out, but I will fight your champion, nevertheless. He grows restless waiting for my blade to slip into his neck."
The Crown Prince of Vulldune clicked his armoured heels together, bowing to the Elf King, then walked over to stand before the traditional elf spun, elaborate and thick-haired carpet, assuming a practised attack position – sword held aloft. He was very much ready and waiting.
Crown Prince Tennison placed his hand towards the intricately wrought hilt of his own golden ceremonial sword and moved to get up.

The Elf King steadied his son's hand and said in a low, discreet voice, "Stop, you know he cannot die by one of our hands, it will be war between the Vampires and Elf kind, but he can die in playful combat. This is why we hold this ceremony every eighth week. You know this to be true. Wait."

The Champion that the Elves had chosen this time, limbered forward. Tall, gangly, with battle scars on his cheeks and an eye patch covering a wet fleshy wound. An assassin, brutal killer, a murderer, twisted and cruel. The Elf Champion bowed curtly to the King then to the Crowned Prince of Elf kind and lastly to Prince Gamone, who sighed out his frustration at his position in the order of things. The Crown Prince of Tylerine, the Elf home world, flicked his eyes at his younger brother and saw there a hostility brewing – apparent in the lines of Prince Gamone's contempt which played around his down turned mouth.

Both the Elf Champion and the Crown Prince of Vulldune faced one another and a snarl unfolded over the lesser immortal's lips. The Crown Prince of Vulldune bowed, proud and true.

"Now, let us begin the *ceremony,*" The Elf King barked out. The Crown Prince of Vulldune, stiffened. A great shuffling was heard, as the Courtiers inside the throne room marched out of the chamber, dressed in powder blue and cream silks, striding double time. Closing the vast gilded doors on the inhabitants left inside the room.

The courtiers stood outside, anxiously waiting, avoiding each other's gaze, while the sounds of a battle to the death commenced inside.

War is coming, whether it be between Earth and Immortals, or between the tribes of the immortals. Either way, The Amber Throne glinting in the afternoon sunlight was far too alluring, and plots are being constructed to keep it or take it away; the very power seat of the universe allows none to rest. Noone can withstand the stealthy craven bloodlust of it, the Throne of Thrones, it would seem.

But for now, the castle's servants had to wait until the battle had finished, to drag the dead body out into the royal halls, freshly pristine and polished, knowing they would need a cleanup crew of their own.

Chapter Twenty - The Academy of the Offered

We came to a halt at a sprawling estate with multiple buildings made of glass; glistening like precious stones in the late afternoon of the brilliant suns. The planetary systems crowded into view in the colossal sky. I was engrossed. Temporarily distracted, looking out over the great expanse of this world, I enjoyed the diversion from my feelings. I felt most calm when I'm numb, feeling nothing, it was my preferred disposition.

"Come on Aurora," Lilly called out to me as I stood looking up at the sky. She run barefoot through the lush green, expansive gardens of the academy.

"Okay, I'm coming."

Groups of elves in full military regalia look around when they caught the sound of my human voice and begin to watch me carefully.

I squinted, placing my hand over my eyes to shade them from the brilliant light, to get a better view of the academy. There was a tall complex in the middle of the estate. The place had a campus of some kind too, with young people and scholars; mingling together on neatly laid out sidewalks. The cadets were walking in groups, dressed in black bodysuits like the one I wear, but these ones were heavier, reinforced for combat and had military motifs.

The architecture of the academy was of Old Prussian design like the Kremlin back on Earth. I later found out that the Academy was built to resemble the first fortresses raised by Premiere Leanndria and her war council of The Immortals, in the first wave of attacks by humans. The buildings held in them the stories of the militarised strategy; to protect the immortals and in homage to the war council, who negotiated the ceasefire. A lot of history was held in the strong lines of the design, held together with thick nostalgia and pride. The military cadets wore white cotton headbands with two red suns rising. It was some sort of emblem; meaning

they belonged here - together and bonded in their fight to protect the realms.
"Aurora, follow me. We are at the academy, where our young people are educated in the way of the Immortals and our ancient forms of combat. Separated into groups by their defined gifts. The Offered are trained here and kept separate from the other military cadets and young people in education. Did you still want to see, to observe Dawn? Rhyiathe will not want us to engage with her without him knowing though. Is that ok?" Lilly's voice was higher and more pitchy. She watched me closely, with a type of well-meaning care.
I nodded and then slipped out of the carriage. My suit smoothly glided over the velvet of the seat, making a luxurious rushing sound. A faint smell of gunpowder fluttered on the breeze.
I was guided along by the side of Lilly with her furtive looks, checking I was okay after my ordeal. Not a word was uttered about my afternoon with Gamone, but I was sure she could see the embarrassment in my gestures and my closed body language. The grim lines on my face and my quiet spoke volumes.
Walking under the solid pillars of the gold-veined marble archway entrance, I couldn't help but pause to take in its splendour.
Rhyiathe stepped out of an opening embedded in a grand marble hallway and he had a bloodied slash across his cheek. Our feet whispered across the floor towards one another, eyes meeting, mine glistened with sadness and his widened suddenly in response to my pain. Darting forward, he took my hand and curled his fingers to touch my face. My hand automatically moved upwards to cup his hand and to feel his gentle touch. It was quite the opposite of the barbarian this afternoon. It was an intimate moment and everyone else melted away in the hallway.
Lilly rushed off muttering something about finding Dawn, quietly, before she left us alone. We didn't hear her. We were consumed by each other.
Rhyiathe reopened the large door which he had just stepped through. "Please come inside. You can tell me what happened. There is no one in here."
"No, I don't want to. I just want to see Dawn." My eyes drifted to the hallway and anywhere but his concerned face. Then, at that moment I realised he was bloody and hurt. "What happened to your face?"

"Nothing, I was training with a sword and my opponent caught me off guard, is all. Anyway, that doesn't matter. If you want to talk, I am here to listen." He lowered his eyes and took my hands in his to kiss my fingers, softly. His green eyes were intense upon mine. The ice started to thaw, I leaned my head against his chest and listened to his strong heartbeat. It was comforting. The rhythmic beat allowed me to let go of the terror I was holding in my chest. He walked back inside, further into the room. It was dark in there. The coolness pressed in on my eyes.
But then came, a clattering and screeching noise from the corner of the room. An object dropped. A golden-musical disk, a cymbal of some kind, spinning round and round, before it settled on the floor.
"Rhyiathe, I thought you said we were alone in here?" His eyes looked startled and his head whipping around to peer into the shadows.
"I thought we were. Who's there?"
"It's me, Archibald Smythe-Wilkinson."
I would recognise that voice anywhere. The voice was etched and linked to my dead sister's body. It was the very same man who was in the funeral home and conjured the vortex in the first place. Archibald sidestepped out of the shadows.
In an instant, both of my blades were drawn out of the inside of my bodysuit. In one swift move, I jumped in the air landing on him with a full body slam dropping him to his knees. I tumbled down with him, but I was ready. My blade, I take to his moustache, and clip one of the elaborate wax corners off. His eyes widened in shock, but he did not flinch back or react in any other way than that. *So, we have a stoic.*
"What are you doing here Offered?" He demanded, glaring blatantly into my eyes.
"You don't get to ask questions, sir. Not when the last time I saw you, you threw a javelin at my head and tried to kill me, *Archibald.* What are you doing here and out with it now, Human." I yelled in his face, tongue lashing out with the hairdryer effect in full flow.
"You address me as human, eh what? But you're meant to be one too. I knew something was off *about you* when the javelin flew straight through your blithering head and bounced off the wall before my eyes. Before my very eyes. Who or *what* are you?"

I blinked rapidly. "The javelin flew through . . . my skull and didn't kill me? Is that what you are saying? How is that possible?" I straightened up, temporarily letting him go, astonished by the assertions being made.

My hands gripped back hold of him up by his shirt collar, all bunched fists and unrelenting, in my steadfastness to get to the truth.

"Well, it's obvious, eh what? You are bloody one of them. A bloody Immortal. What were you doing on Earth? You lot are not supposed to be there unchecked. Wait until I tell the Prime Minister. I bet he'll have something to say about it," Lord Archibald Smythe-Wilkins said, all stiff collared and terribly proper as the Emissary for the human governments of the world and Ambassador of Earth to the Realms.

"Aurora, put him down, please. He is here on behalf of Earth to uphold peace and support the academy's board to maintain the Clandestine Agreement, keeping the Void free from any breaches." Rhyiathe turned on his heel to face Archibald.

"My apologies my Lord Ambassador, Aurora is not familiar with our customs or with the current state of affairs to maintain the Agreement. Please forgive her . . .," Rhyiathe gulped, "*insolence* on this occasion."

As I stared at Rhyiathe in utter bewilderment, Archibald removed my hands quite forcefully from his rumpled shirt collar and said,

"Well, *quite,* on this occasion I will overlook this little. . . *indiscretion* but not again. Keep your dog on a leash, Prince of Vulldune." His crazed, bloodshot eyes were on me, and his finger pointed accusingly in my direction.

I snapped my teeth together and my hands fluttered to my daggers and Lord Archibald gave me a piercing look of contempt, but still looked wary before wriggling through the doorway like the slippery eel that he was. Rhyiathe steadied my hands.

I pointed my finger at the now empty doorway "*That* trumped-up little Coloniser tried to kill *me* on earth in front of the vortex and *you dare to* apologise to *him* for *my* behaviour. What the fuck is wrong with you immortals? And why'd he call you Prince of Vulldune, come to think of it?"

Rhyiathe sighed rather loudly and rubbed his hands over his eyes, trying to keep sleep away. I stood with my arms folded across my chest demanding answers in a silent way.

"Well, because. . ." His gaze flicked over my face and studied me carefully. A sigh escaped his lips, "Listen, Aurora. I'm sorry for apologising on your behalf, but it's pretty complicated here in the Realms at the moment. We need to keep Earth happy and engaged with upholding the Clandestine Agreement. There are a group of Immortal separatist terrorists that want to wage war on Earth, hell-bent on crossing the Void and want to subjugate all humans, taking back Earth. The Immortal military is defending the Agreement at present but there is a growing sense in the armies and amongst the generals that the immortals *should* head to Earth and take it back. The humans are not looking after the planet and immortals are guardians of balance and all living things, even the Elves, even though that doesn't seem quite true at the moment. Everything rests on a knife's edge and the only things stopping full blown war is the Clandestine Agreement, The Dragons and The Offered that patrols The Void. I'm hunting the separatists but I'm starting to think that the Royal family are . . . *involved.* The Elves are at the centre of all of this, I need you to help me and not start a war with careless words and acts of misguided revenge."
I stepped back, unsteady. It was a lot to take in. I mulled it over, the jigsaw pieces forming and slotting into place. An instant flash of images spun before my eyes and conclusions formed.
"I think you're right about the royal family. Gamone was in the forest, he said they are holding a Prince of Vulldune here, a hostage of some type to keep the immortals in check, maybe? ...hmm, how come you can say the full words . . . you know, the *Agreement* and the spell doesn't come *for you*?"
Rhyiathe's eyes filled with a flinching anguish of something left unsaid,
"Listen, Aurora, I have something else to tell you . . ."
He didn't get to finish the sentence nor did I get to hear Rhyiathe's explanation. I hadn't quite figured out where all the jigsaw pieces fitted at this stage, but I could tell he was keeping something from me. Something important.
Two guards barged in on us without so much as knocking on the door and Rhyiathe gave me a silent warning look with the urgent widening of his eyes.
Rhyiathe held his hands up to the guards.
"We are coming to watch the manoeuvres. Tell the General we will be with him in a moment." Rhyiathe's demeanour changed, when he

addressed the guards, he said this in a clipped tone, clearly comfortable giving military address and issuing orders. The two soldiers saluted, nodded, bowed, and left, quick smart.
"Listen Aurora, you need to finish the history book, The Tome of the Cold Ones, it's about the history of the Seven Kingdoms and why the immortals must return to Earth. You'll understand afterwards, but Archibald was right about one thing." I raised my eyebrows and he continued, directly looking at me with an expression I couldn't read.
"You shouldn't have been on earth, not with your powers. It's like someone or something had placed you there and covered it up so no one would find out. How that person or persons, got you through the Void, the magical space between Earth and The Realms undetected is a complete mystery to me. In fact, it's impossible. Let's stay vigilant, ok? Let's keep you safe. I'll explain everything when I can. Trust me *please*. Don't ask me anymore questions here," he said darkly, and I agreed before we left the room together to go to watch the manoeuvres on the battlefield.

When we arrived at our destination, there were the usual fanfare of sounds familiar to a military-practise combat zone, but it was the sheer scale of the area that I was not prepared for – it was huge. There were shouting cadets in the middle of training drills, hardened generals barking out orders, the grounds were shaking from the bombardment of heavy explosive spells and strange technologically advanced machines rumbling by, of the type I had never seen before.
The troops in military formations, wearing combat leathers of all assorted colours, denoting rankings, were marching past lush green fields outside the main building of the academy. The patchwork of fields were well-maintained, neatly cut, and precise in structure. The gardens bordering the grasslands were tamed, ornamental and kept trimmed. The entranceways to the vast forest on the other hand, were in stark contrast. Wildly overgrown, dense, and thick with plant life of every kind; this was intentional.
At a guess, it was kept this way for combat drills and teaching the cadets manoeuvres over harder terrain. In the distance were more combat training zones and beyond, some way off, a phantom outline of a vast grey and white dusted mountain range came looming into view. Jagged peaks

majestically rose butting at the clouds and wrestling for dominance over the sky.
Overhead and all around, the skies were filled with roaring and the loud beating of leathery wings, sounding more like a tsunami coming rather than that of a creature. The sounds rung all about of Dragons – their wings, their roars. The sky belonged to them.
Darkness and shadows consumed the Suns, as the dragons flew over them. There was no space above us, which was not covered in movement. An organised chaos ensued. Colossal shadows, the size of jumbo jets, streaked over the emerald-coloured waving grass. There were dragons in the sky, flying in pairs and landing all about in the fields, making the ground shake under their great and mighty landings. The sensation of the ground moving was making my body jolt up and down.
I stood in amazement, blinking rapidly. Wind rushed through my hair and kissed coldly at my neck as the gigantic bodies of the dragons took hold of the wind, flying above me. Landing heavily on the fields in large numbers, wave after wave, shaking the ground, it trembled under my feet. The deep bass making me shiver with excitement. Twenty pairs were standing together nearby, as tall as mountains, snapping their great snouts and smashing their horned tails to the ground, crushing the grass into the mud. My eyes reflected the wonder of the moment. My mouth opened emitting squeals of pleasure. Giddy, I was to see these great beasts of myth and legend. Real, solid, in living form outside of my dreams. The beauty and the majesty of the Immortal world was undeniable on this very hillside – how have humans lived without this wonder for so long, I don't rightly know. I can't find the words. All I know is that these creatures belong on Earth as much as they belong here with the immortals. They are a gift. A gift to us all. To the universe.
The dragons were beating their large wings, I watched with a great deal of pleasure as they tucked their heads under leathery wings to preen the huge scales of their golden or red or black or navy-blue coloured bellies. I stared; their mannerisms were so very much like birds back home.
Rhyiathe laughed aloud and was consumed by my wonder, sharing it with me– we gazed at each other. Kindred spirits at the joy of the universe opening before our very eyes.

Spellbound and beautifully puzzled by the miracles walking around me, the terrible wariness, which had plagued me for the last few weeks had gone up into the ether like a puff of smoke. I was left relieved from the flatness of grief. The stunned, shocked bewilderment of loss had left me. I was giddy like a child believing in magic and believing in this strange realm as tokens of it were walking around on taloned claws before me. They were the guardians of the Suns and the fire breathers of the sky. I wept tears of joy, my nerves once more covered – twined back together, undone from the tension I had been experiencing of late.

But then a blood-curdling scream came towards me on a freezing gust of icy wind from the mountains.

Where the clouds touched the tips of the mountains, was an assault course for cadets to test their very last shreds of nerve. Small blots were walking across the open expanse, while dragons wend and circle on leathery wings in the icy sky, filling up the space with their presence – the magic of the universe made me cry.

Rhyiathe's eyes saw something I did not, and his body froze in horror. In the distance was a terrible sight, that much I could make out on my own.

"Don't look, Dawn is stuck on the skybridge between the two towers. She is frozen with fear." He started running at superspeed and I looked around the field trying to spot the skybridge that Rhyiathe was referring to. I can't see her. Where is she? Where?

All the chins of the cadets were lifted, their eyes frozen on a moving object, hundreds of metres up in the air. It was a minuscule spot some way off in the distance.

It was Dawn, she was holding onto a rope, walking forward but it was swinging wildly in the winds – she was losing her balance. Being battered by the shrieking winds up where the clouds meet the crystallised water in the sky. I screamed.

The dragons were surrounding her, wheeling through the frozen sky, each of them taking turns to try to grab her into the claws of their back legs but they kept missing due to the wind's force and her violent swinging.

I screamed again, my useless legs were frozen to the spot, watching Dawn tumble limply back down to the surface of the planet. Golden hair streamed out behind her as she plunged headfirst to her death; a second death that is.

Gravity was brutally calling her home with the words of a siren's song. He was near - Rhyiathe. He bounded forward, firing up in the air like a blinding sun flare.

All waited, holding their collective breath with their eyes peeled back in terror.

The odds of him catching a tiny moving target, hitting ultimate velocity to mass, and intercepting at light speed was just unheard of, but I watched with faith in him anyway.

Straining my neck muscles, I waited carefully with prayers escaping my lips once again. I was unheard at the crime scene when Dawn died, and I feared I would be unheard this time.

I watched Rhyiathe's ascending path as he rocketed towards her. Dawn was near him, but too far away. He had overreached but he made a quick adjustment, of his rapidly moving, desperately splaying limbs. He grabbed her and pulled her to him at an awkward angle. It was not over. He still needed to descend but his careful cradling of her in his arms meant she now had a better chance. I watched, holding my breath in my chest, as they both plummeted like dead counterweights to the ground.

A shadow sped forward, explosive, straight across their path.

I closed both my eyes and instead of the splitting sound of bodies smashing to the ground, there was one careful, soulless crack instead.

Chapter Twenty-one - The Dragon at the opening of the mountain

Dawn sat up on her silk-covered fluffy pillows in a four-poster bed in the healers' quarters, after mostly healing from her ordeal. The room was beautiful. It was decorated with hues of blue forget-me-nots and smelt of lavender, chamomile flowers and of crisp cotton sheets. Tender care was nested in each corner, a warm light blanketing the room.

Walking in, my eyes were met with the sight of the Witch, Callen the Wise, sweeping dried flowers and herbs into a figure of eight before the upturned face of Dawn. The violet smoke of the dried leaves and petals settled lightly on the patient's cheeks. The witch stared at me with a blank face and I saw a twitch of nervousness under her eye socket.

"Hello, pleased to meet you. My name is Callen, and you are?" Her mouth spoke these words, but her eyes pleaded for me to play along. In my seconds of hesitation, the Elf guard at the door noticed something was amiss, stepping forward into the room slightly observing this microsecond gesture and reading it to mean there was a threat.

Co-conspiratorially, I said, "Pleased to meet you, my Lady Callen. I am Aurora. Thank you for looking after Dawn."

Callen's shoulders unhunched when the guard lightly stepped back out of the room. A heartbeat before Callen turned back from watching the guard and she dared to speak again, swallowing in moisture, "*you* are a Lady, my Lady Aurora, Elf-friend, but I am merely a . . . witch *here*," A silent set of information was transferred. Callen took great risks to let me know she was being observed. *For not being Elven, perhaps?*

I watched her in silence as she departed. She was staring at me with pupils wide with fear, while the folds of her full skirt rustled over the beating of her legs, slowly moving out of the room.

"I will be in the assault course fields when you are done here if you have any questions about . . . *Dawn's* recovery." Callen the Wise, wise beyond

me, curtsied low and then left the room. The room turned black, startling me. A dark and dense shadow crossed over the translucent glass of the window outside.
One large, great lizard-like eye pressed up against the pane of glass to look in on me. The amber eye was the size of the large window – it covered it. The eye boldly stared in and did not blink. The big black pupil slowly dilated into a slit and I was being taken in and assessed by it cruelly. I stood mouth open.
A soft voice spoke out from the bed, "This is Caemyre. Caemyre, this is Aurora, my friend," Dawn croaked out.
I should have been watching the dragon to make sure their reaction was one of alliance, but I didn't. I turned to my sister and repeated back her words for the sake of my own ears ". . . *friends*" It was comforting to hear, and my heart swelled against my ribs.
Eventually finding my voice, I asked, "He or she, is your Dragon then?"
Dawn softly giggled and coughed, wincing in pain while there came a cracking sound of her ribs resetting, crashed into the room. I lunged forward but she waved me away.
"It's ok. The magic is speeding up the healing process. Callen told me it would hurt. Now, where was I? Oh yes, Caemyre. *He* will not forgive you for referring to him as *my* dragon. He reminds me daily that he chose me, as is the way of it. Dragon riders, cadets even, have been thrown from great heights for insulting a Dragon, so I am most careful to be respectful and considerate to His Majesty, King of Golden scales, Prince of the rising Suns . . ." A smile crept across Dawn's face as these platitudes of overzealous reverence were given, most keenly and loudly. With each compliment, the dragon's chest swelled larger and a glistening twinkle in his eye grew like the first morning star. I softly laughed.
". . . Tamer of the Titans of the Sea . . ." Dawn continued, nodding at me to assist.
"Dawn, may I add, Noblest of his Line and more golden than the twin sunset?" I added, all honeyed of speech.
"Oh, yes, good one."
Dawn peered over at the window, and I saw that the great dragon had set his head on the ground outside. The wind picked up and the grass flickered around him as his eyes gradually covered over, nostrils flaring. Small flames

singed the dry patches of lavender moss, a blazing blanket surrounding him. Smoke curled up into the air. I was gathering the opinion that a sleeping dragon is best in my view.

Dawn's eyes became hooded too and slowly drooped. Stifling a yawn, she said,

"You'll need to take my place in the race, around the assault course, I mean. Caemyre will guide you. He's very skilful and the best at crossing the Fire Wall without getting the rider too burnt. Promise me you will?" Dawn lowered her head back on the unctuous silk, of the smooth pillow. Caemyre and me are left appraising one another through the window, looming between us, in the silence that followed Dawn's request.

Caemyre, the Great Red and Gold Dragon, stared at me through the window for a long time. He had only pretended to be asleep earlier. Dragons are sneaky; I pocketed that information. He pulled up his massive head and shook out his great neck and the crown of lethal horns, edged with sharpness, thudded against the building. The walls trembled. The great Dragon started to slowly lumber away, on thick and pointed claws, the size of the average household car back home.

"That means he's agreed to let you ride him," the Guard stationed outside shouts into the room from the hallway, barely moving a muscle when giving his advice. Giving me cause to note that Caemyre the Dragon was not the only sneaky one round here, I sighed. *Dragon riding for the afternoon's activity up a lonely mountain? But of course, sir.* The thought made me shake with excitement if truth be told.

The Offered and other dragon-riding cadets were milling around at the foot of the mountain, dressed in full leathers and metal riding helmets, titanium steel metal ballosh strapped at their backs. Apparently, a Ballosh is an elven traditionally made hooked sword that the elves imbibe with magic. Its aim is unequalled. It's bloodthirst unrelenting.

The wind was icy near the mountain, sheets of freezing razors blowing up a gale. The ground was frozen solid, the closer to the mountain I got.

Wintery ice-formed clouds rolled down from the mountainsides so dense, that it looked like one would rebound off it instead of walking through. A crashing sound of snow sliding down the mountain in great avalanches filled the air. I strolled through the valley and my feet felt light in the beauty of the surroundings.

The Dragons were in their element, rolling their necks, building furnaces in their great bellies, and roaring out licking flames creating torrential rivers of water that thundered down the raised ravines and jagged rocks of the great land mass. This created chaos at the foot of the rolling scenery below. Earth and mudslides collided in great rivers in thick sludge grooves, and the Elves were constantly on the move to stay out of the way. Dragons lifted off on their great wings should the mudslides dare to come near them.

Tall and proud was the mountain, the terrain fierce and unforgiving, everything was covered with thick snow. Treacherous was the cold.

Snowflakes landed thickly on my eyelashes as I looked up at the steep sides of the mountain but when I looked down, the warm winds blew in from the south, like a contradiction.

My eyes were mapping out the landscape, observing the bustling activities, searching for evidence of something triggered by Callen's words this afternoon. *"You are Lady Aurora; Elf friend and I am merely a witch."* Callen had shared this information. I am looking at each Offered, at every cadet, at the teachers and the dragon assistants with newfound knowledge and that's when it hits me, a burning truth. The immortals are a group, but the Elves are the masters here.

Other immortals, wolves, witches, vampires, and others not as clear to define are in servile roles in this society to that of the High Elf Lords.

Something was bothering me. Rhyiathe appeared to be treated differently, and the disgraced Lilly the elf too, of course. She was in a servant's role. They had both been close to me here and perhaps this was why I hadn't noticed the hierarchical culture before. There was a caste system at play with distinguished ranks. Rhyiathe was treated as a High Lord and I was starting to wonder why. He had been with Lord Tennison in the Forest the day I landed on this planet, so he must be a High Lord, but he is a Vampire. I had not asked him about Lord Tennison and his relationship to him.

In my musings, I failed to notice a werewolf female coming towards me holding a studded black dragon harness of enormous size, she stumbled under the weight of it. Her soft, kind eyes were speckled with golden brown, a smile was across her soft pink lips and a sprinkle of sweet freckles on her cheeks too. Just before she reached me, she lost her footing, slipping down the oiliness of the mud onto her knees, remarkably close to a strapping Elven cadet.

"Watch your footing, filthy dog," the cadet said as he wiped imaginary specks of mud off his pristine black bodysuit and went to kick the werewolf girl away – revealing his intention to do so with the underside of his boot.

"I would not do that if I were you," my words chilly as the frozen air they wrench through, "I would take my boots and walk away, in fact," Venomous are my words, laced with the anger I felt at the treatment of someone so harmless. Gamone swam before my eyes. Misplaced anger, spinning my senses out of control. I clenched my teeth and growled with my lip curled.

My robust response spiked fear in the eyes of the Elf cadet and he shuffled his boots together and waded away through the mud, but not before trying to save his handsome, arrogant face,

"Keep control of your dog, Shiv Queen," his words cleaved out to me but missed. I could tell he had shouted them out of embarrassment, which made him look like a fool.

My eyes glared at him. I gently pulled my blades out of the top of my tan bodysuit. The metal sang out in solidarity, that he should be afraid. The cadet tried to appear casual as his steps quickened away through the sludge.

A booming laughter caught on the breeze behind, from somewhere up high. I felt it lick my neck. I turned to see the large snout of Caemyre curling in merriment.

"*You*, I like," he said in a deep well of a voice that echoed around the mountain, "too long have The Elf lords ruled over these people and their treatment most unjust." His harsh eyes, narrow and soften. His horned brow slipped upwards, a lighter expression on his regal face. "I shall watch you with a keen interest."

I smile at the consensual words of the rebel; an accord was struck. We looked at each other, deeply appraising and seeing the same spirit deep inside one another. We were one, the Dragon and me, binding us together in our fates.

I turned around to lean forward and help up the mud-covered wolf girl, noting the hesitancy on her face about taking my hand.

"Please. I mean you no harm."

The Elder – Lights of the Seven Kingdoms

Taking her thin hand in my neat, clean gloved one, I smiled at how everything had changed for me. Once I was the girl covered in shit on the floor of Earth and now, I was able to help up others.

I heaved her up out of the mud-strewn ground, with one arm, a strength I was slowly getting used to.

"Thank you, M'lady, I am here to help you mount Caemyre the Golden Dragon of Taeyeon, better known as Mount Doom."

"No harness today. This one," Caemyre inclined his head towards me, "Aurora, needs it not, I can sense this. The Lights follow you, Aurora. Unseen to the many but not to the eyes of Dragon-kind." Caemyre stood proud and true, looking at me with a questioning wonder. "You have returned at long last."

The Dragon lowered his head, and I walked forward into the Abyss of the unknown, on shaking legs, in a dream-like state, but I trusted the Dragon, without knowing him, but he seemed to know more about me than I did. The magic and knowledge of the Great Ancient One, The Dragon Lord, I would come to hold dear.

The werewolf servant watched with wide-eyed fascination, as I climbed the great neck and slid down the broad ridge of the Dragon's iridescent scales, bumping me up and down in the process. I harnessed myself to the golden scales, nestled in at the back of the great mythical beast. Caemyre readied himself before leaping and spanning out his vast wings, summoning jets of warm air underneath him, sucking it up with the beating of his wings, then jumped forward into the air to take flight. I was buffeted around on his back and let out one or two choice swear words in the process, while he mounted the sky.

The assault course was far below us, we hovered in stillness on the winds blowing hard from the artic north. The apparatus was of military design, vast, set over many acres. I scanned the structure from my aerial view, Caemyre started descending to allow me to get a closer look. It was like he could read my mind when we were in flight. The course was practical, functional, and perfectly lethal; built with only the intention of training the Offered to manoeuvre with their dragons through the obstacles of the dense forest. Then, a short flight to the two black and bleak towers, high up in the distance above the mountain that had a huge ring of fire perched on the top-most tower. This was the racecourse.

As we landed, with him rearing upwards and me hanging on for dear life, before settling on the ground, a nearby cadet came running over. The cadet told me that there had not been a race that Caemyre had not won in terms of speed. The great dragon flicked his tail as he beamed with pride, and the ground shivered with the end lash of the stroke of his horned tail.

He softly said to me, "You are not going to hold me up Elder Star with your squeals of being a novice, are you?" Playful was his melodic tone.

"I'll try not to My Lord of Mount Doom," I replied, with a jaunty wink.

He lifted his great head and nodded, pleased. "Your kind have been Dragon Riders for aeons. From the first formation of the star protein, keratin that later became the material for dragon scales. Light as a feather, harder than the bones of the earth. You know this already. Open your heart and fly with me as the celestial beings we both are."

"And Dawn too?"

"At first, I must confess I thought so, but then I realised, she is covered in the hazing of The Elder from being around you for all those year,." He began to smoke as he said this to me. Great swathes of violet smog escaped from both his nostrils, providing him with a cover of mystique and majesty. Oh, the drama of a dragon speaking. It is hypnotic to behold – exciting too.

"So, Dawn was selected as the Offered because they detected the Elder on her from me?" I ventured, looking guilty once again.

"Perhaps, or maybe she has the qualities needed to guard the great expanse known as The Void. The universe selects for us what is right for us, who knows how this will turn out for Dawn," Caemyre said with kindness, but in truth too.

I nodded. There was a lot to consider interwoven in the riddles of Dragons. I found myself in later days sitting bolt upright in bed in the early hours of the morning, recalling the startling intellect of something the Dragon had said. He was actually very insightful, but he talked in riddles most of the time, so I never quite managed to figure out his wise words until days later. Most of the time he threw out words like a drunk uncle explaining the rules of a favoured sport - puzzling. I had decided to journal his speeches in a little book that I would keep about my person, because of this.

He turned his great horned head towards me that day,

"The vibration from you is strong. Your love for her serves you well and all will be good for the both of you. Time will show this to you."
"A foretelling?" I gasped out.
"My *wish* for you both. A Dragons' wish can be a foretelling or the maker of the fabric of the universe to twist and turn into a new beginning." He turned back around to face the mountain and flew towards the warmth of the Suns, his first ancestor – his mother.
Baffled and quiet, there was again a lot to consider yet I asked no more questions. My brain was overheating between my ears.
He leaped up again, launching us into flight. We were flying over the rich, green and arable lands of the immortals, Caemyre's dark shadow striping across the fields below as we glided lazily and comfortably overhead.
The wind whistled through my hair and my ears. The freezing climes and temperatures crested my frozen eyelashes. They were heavy with iced water. Chilblains formed on my cheeks, but I felt absolutely nothing. No pain. Just immense joy.
Soaring across the beauty of the pink, orange sky on the ridges of a great Dragon's back, I was secured only by the hooks of my feet under The Golden One's iridescent scales. Nothing but the vast sky above me, I looked down at the glory of the land. Waterfalls in the distance thundered and roared, chucking up rainbows. Mountain ranges with paths snaking through them, steeped tall out of the ice. The cosmos was above us and I was as free as the shooting stars that canon these dark nights.
Free. I was free. An intoxicating freedom. Joy was upon me, and I drank it all in. The very joy of life was mine, and I never wanted it to end.
I lifted both my arms to the sky, revelling in the feeling and screeched out into the frozen sky above releasing this magnificent feeling of my hard sought-after happiness. Caemyre belly laughed, and I was tossed around, bucking, and bruising my gluteus maximus, but holy shit. This was exhilarating. This was *everything*. This was where I was meant to be.
The Dragon, showing off, glided in a circle, and tumbled down for a better view of the horizon. I was giggling uncontrollably and complimenting his flying skills like a crazed drug addict.
Suddenly, Caemyre lurched to the left and I careened to the side so violently, tumbling onto my legs and arms, like an acrobat, until I grabbed

a tight hold of a large scale and pulled myself back onto the ridge of Caemyre's great back.
"What is it? What happened?" I yelled, my words whipped away and behind me in the onslaught of the winds, but still, he heard me.
"Down there, the werewolf girl surrounded, I think. She is in danger," Caemyre growled. Beating his wings furiously, he lowered his head to aerodynamically make himself faster and adjust altitude.
"Well, let's have at it," I said, pulling out my blades, biting down on my lip and relishing the thought of the fight ahead.
The Great Dragon, my twin spirit, started to descend onto the great plains below.
The sky changed above us. Great black and purple clouds rolled over us in quick succession.
All was darkness at our back. All was quiet, the stillness of the inhale before the coming storm. I shivered in the chaos and wildness of the weather, swirling with its grasping tentacles, pushing me back as I held fast onto the back of the dragon. Testing me to my limits, I rose in defiance.
"Aurora, you can share my magic as an Elder. Start by harnessing lightning bolts and then we will build you up from there," Caemyre threw out instructions behind him.
"Hmmm, what do I do?" my faced scrunched up, begging for any type of helpful tips.
"Figure it out, you must." Caemyre said, gruffly.
But then I recall the lessons given by Rhyiathe that day in the castle all that time ago and before I knew what was happening, my body took over. Intuitively, I knew what to do. I held a blade up above my head. The weather brutally buffeted my arm. Electric blue raw power peaked through the underbelly of the dark clouds attracted to my motion. The ionised atmosphere called to the lightning as it sizzled and zigzagged through the suddenly darkened sky. The lone steel dagger attracted it like a copper coil conduit. Hoisted up, the raw electricity struck down aiming straight for my blade. My only wish was to harvest the power and wield it to save the girl, and it was to be my ruin.
First, there was a white light from the streaking power of the lightning, then there was blackness, the total absence of light. Then there was just

me and Caemyre crashing forward through the darkness of the night sky, while the heavens opened above us.
My blade held onto that seismic, sizzling power and I harnessed it at my side. I tried to hold onto the snake-like coils of electricity as we darted forward into the planet's surface. Holding forth my blades, I moved to a standing position on the back of the Dragon, and as we neared the surface of the planet, I slammed the lightning bolt straight into the ground below us, sending flashes of brilliant and electric light through the night and all around.

Chapter Twenty-two - lightning and illumination

The lightning bolt hit the dry, powdery earth like a steel hammer smashing into a wooden nail. The blackness of the sky met the flashing lightning on the ground, driving through the crust, splintering, and throwing up boulders at the edges. We charged downwards following in the wake of the great beams of blue light from the screaming lightning bolts of electricity.

I jumped from The Dragon's back and landed softly on the grass, exploding forward on the roll. In the chaos that followed our arrival, I sprinted to stand and shielded the werewolf girl from what looked like a motley group of beings. Their weapons were raised to her.

Raising both my blades, I shouted out,

"Leave her be or death will come to you and fast."

Pivoting on my leg, I bounced on my thighs ready to attack. Caemyre in the distance bellowed out a roar of molten Dragon's fire. The fields alight, dancing all about with flames in the wake of his rampage.

Each one of the attackers, slumped forward to the ground, bowing their noses into the earth, kneeling, and waving the palms of their hands in the air in an act of submission. They begged to be listened to.

The werewolf girl screamed behind me, crying for me not to hurt her friends. Speechless, I turned to her as she held onto my arms and shaking me away "what the hell is going on?". The girl slumped forward to her knees begging me for forgiveness. Confusion was setting in. Gazing across the crowd, I saw a face I recognised.

"Callen? Callen, is that you? What is happening here?"

Caemyre paused, mid-stamping the ground. He had heard my words of recognition and halted, sitting up to listen in. The trembling of the earth's bones ceased. The Golden One listened to my shouts, waiting for the answer that would lift the confusion on both our faces.

Callen the Witch pushed forward through the crowd, and I was left wondering if this was some sort of weird Cult.

"Aurora, please. We mean the girl no harm. It was the only way to get your attention, get you here. Away from prying eyes. Please listen. Allow me to explain all."

Appraising her for a while, I eventually nodded and lowered my weapons. The tension left her body, gone were her tightly wound-up shoulders, but her eyes still pleaded for my attention.

"Aurora, I see you. I know you. Well, I saw a vision, that the Twelfth of the Offered would be the one to bring about a vast change to the Seven Kingdoms and that the one named The Twelfth, should not take part in the Offering because your powers would have been corrupted and you would have been destroyed. I went to the Werewolves and shared my vision. I asked them to protect you. They had taken a significant risk to travel through the Vortex in order to protect you that night. Dillion has been trying to tell you that you are in danger from the Elves. I know what you are. I prayed to Freya and Ingris for your return. To protect the Immortals." Her eyes searched mine. Her outstretched hand anxiously touched my fingers, testing me if I was real, "but I can't believe you are really here. It is a miracle. A great gift."

We were locked into each other's gaze. The intensity of my eyes squinted in the strange sight. These people had gone to such lengths to get me here, but why?

These people, look at them. What do you see? Callen's voice was in my head and a gentle pressure was on my face.

"Why would you take such a risk to see *me?*" I fumbled out, looking over the group and taking my time to really look at all of them. There was nothing obvious or anything that joined them together, but there was something missing.

No elves are here.

"Yes, that is right. There are no elves here," Callen responded. She must have read my mind. Her eyes were unrelenting, unapologetic.

"All is not what it seems. Our magic is taken from us and amassed by the high elf lords. *We* are their servants. *They* are the ones encouraged to populate, to live in abundance, but *we,* well, sometimes we can't even afford to eat or cloth ourselves let alone birth younglings. Our society is broken.

We are not exactly slaves, but we might as well be for all the good this society does for *us*."

The revelations astonished me, but my mind worked in a practical way, wanting answers to very mundane questions ". . . and me, what is it you want from *me*?" Caemyre blew air through his long snout. Smoke bellowed forth menacingly from his perfect nostrils. He placed his powerful claws forward, the tip clipping the floor making loud clacking sounds, as he moved into the middle of the circle, where we all stood. We fell back as the Dragon's chest swelled proudly; he sat up tall waiting to hear the answer. He is aware of how impressive he is and smiles slyly, in the safety of that knowledge.

"A champion to bring back equality to the lands of the immortals is all we ask of you. To protect us in the Elf lords' grand plans. We hear they are planning to take back Earth and I assume we will be the cannon fodder to deliver it to them. They would not choose to willingly spill Elf blood when other immortals will do, no doubt."

The group of immortals all nodded their heads, looking at each other morosely.

"But I don't understand. How am I to do this for all immortals, for a whole civilisation? There is so much to this . . ."

"Aurora, it is a fair question but perhaps for another time," Caemyre's voice floated towards me, the sound of his voice was fascinating and soothing, like watching effervescent bubbles of light float through the stars, "we must go now. The race it is over. The Elves will come looking and they will find this group here."

I took hold of Callen's hand and looked at the reflective pools of her watery eyes and in them I saw her desperation.

"You helped me once and I will do everything within my gift to help you and the other immortals. Come to my apartment with Lilly and we will talk more when I get back." I rested my hand on Callen's shoulder, squeezing slightly and she hugged me. The other immortals: walking trees, ragged werewolves, skeletal vampires, and crone-like witches, all looked at me with hope on their upturned faces. It was a devastating sight. I felt the responsibility of that hope to deliver them to the Light.

"Aurora, we must go now if we are to save these people from the Elf search parties that will come looking for you soon. These people will stand little chance of defending themselves against the elves," Caemyre said.

Hot tears streaked down my face, but I nodded out my agreement. Walking away was difficult but necessary. Leaping forward to mount Caemyre's great ridged back, I looked back at the crowd once again.

"Until next time," I saluted the group and then Caemyre bounded into the air with his great wings flapping to take hold of gusts of wind. We climbed upwards.

I watched Callen and the rest of the immortals in the field become little dizzying blots on the land, as we climbed in steep circles, until my eyes couldn't see them anymore. I turned my face towards the glowing light of the Suns. The wind whistled of adventure in the high altitude we were at, reminding us we could follow the suns and go anywhere – it was the sound of freedom, glorious to my ears. I sighed, but there was more to do.

Delivered was my resolve to help that small group of rebellious immortals, even though I knew the task ahead was greater than just those few. I pledged myself to the great planetary systems, above us, that this would be done, or my death would serve as a reminder that all must strive to protect the light of the universe.

Days later, I had blocked myself off from the immortal's world sitting quietly in Rhyiathe's study. Daily reading sprints had been my discipline; determined to get through the History of the Immortals book – The Tome of Cold Ones.

There was still so much to understand about these strange Lands that were so richly dense with wonder, yet fragile in its identity.

I looked in the mirrors and my own reflection showed the changes to my outward appearance as well as my inner world. My ears were growing pointed. *Am I one of them now, an immortal being? Am I completely changed?* I sighed. I was starting to look like one of them. I thirsted for the knowledge to answer these puzzles. Another sigh. But I was on the outside, shaking an elaborate, ornamental snow globe of the immortal's society and waiting for the first flurry of the artificial snow to clear so I could read the signs in a more settled landscape. I was an outsider trying to read bones, trying to see beyond the opaque veil deliberately closed to me, but so many of the immortals wanted me to be on the inside with them. Allied.

I did not know how to find the right way to do this, but I got the impression that until I understood their history and their complicated patchwork of coming together in more detail, then I would never understand the riddle of how to help them – to be able to find a way – to save the immortals under the rule of the High Elves. So, I hoped studying the book, would get me where I needed to be faster.

The hours floated by. My eyes took in the letters and the runes, forming visuals of battles and hardships. Letting the histories take solid form in my mind, I found myself on a page where the Agreement was being shaped and Earth was seeking compensation. There was a deep knock on the beautiful, limed oak door that smelled of a forest canopy. I noticed that the roots were still intact like the door was formed with the consent of the woods and trees.

With a smooth click of well-oiled and tendered locks, Rhyiathe entered with quiet consideration, as if opening a door to a church full of people praying.

His green eyes were dolefully on me. My stomach flipped over. A warmth spread throughout my core, and I clenched to stop it, trying to push down these uncomfortable feelings that spring up whenever he is near.

"Aurora, I must show you something. It is a vampire tradition and one that must be honoured now that you are one of us." He looked down at me, deadly solemn and serious. His hand was outreached to take mine and to lead us on our way. He looked different, more relaxed. My eyes roamed over him, spotting all the slight changes in the way he had dressed himself. Gone was the military black body suit, which made him look official – always ready for combat. In its place was a set of plainer, random selection of clothes, that he wore well – there was nothing that could diminish this vampire's handsomeness, but the clothes were trying ridiculously hard to. He was dressed in a silk shirt, tweed trousers and leather boots. The ornamental cape was gone and replaced by a simpler, more functional, woollen cloak with a deep hood, less expensive more standard set of clothes.

"Trying to blend in, are we?" I laughed out, he looked like an actor playing at being a peasant farmer, for a school play.

Rhyiathe's eyes crinkled at the corners, he laughed aloud too,

"Something like that, come on let us go." He took his broad hands and placed them on my shoulders to give me an excited shake, before taking them away to place his hood over his head, in such a way, it left me with a delightful sense of intrigue. I wanted to know where he was taking me and what we would find there – I was curious. I bit my lip. An evening out with Rhyiathe was just what I needed to forget about all this responsibility for a while. Stretching over the Tome to grab my cloak – I remembered it was far too big for me, I looked childish in it and it drowned me, when Lilly had made me try it on. I didn't want Rhyiathe to see me like that – its unattractive, lumpy, and old. Lilly had given me one of her own, but she had said at the time she would shorten it, size it down to fit me later but she had never gotten round to it.

Disappointment had clouded my features. "It's okay, we will do it another time, I've got a lot to do." My cheeks coloured; they were burning. Walking forward, Rhyiathe lifted my chin and pulled the warm softness of the cloak around my shoulders, leaning over me. He pulled the hood up and it flopped over the entirety of my face.

"There, a million times better. Now I don't have to see your grumpiness any longer, as beautiful as you are, your grumpiness is hard to look upon, especially the scowl," he joked.

My shoulders shook, then I had giggled out,

"You are ridiculous, do you know that Rhyiathe? Far too confident you are for your own good."

He picked up my fingers and brushed the tips across his lips, I shivered but pretended not to, straightening up a little too fast.

"Please, come with me, Aurora. There is something I have been waiting to show you."

I'm glad the thick hood swamped me and covered the expression on my face. I didn't want him to see my softness blooming across my cheeks. I let out a little sigh of bliss guarded under the hood. I had to bite down on my lip hard to stop myself from shouting,

"*I would follow you anywhere, you only have to ask.*" Fool as I am, but I had said instead, "Very well." A much more dignified response.

He took my hand in his, clenching my fingers tightly, and guided me at a brisk walk through his haberdashery of a bachelor's hallway and out into the cobbled streets of the beautiful city of Pericullious. The city was alive and brimming with immortals, hustling, and bustling, going about the city streets. I watched with a curiosity, admiring them like animals in a zoo, going about their lives. Exotic and frightening was this place, but I just felt at peace. Elves, werewolves, vampires, living trees, walking around on two feet and each one of them amazed me. I went to take off the hood and Rhyiathe stayed my hand, "No, we need to go incognito for this trip. It's like a vampire pilgrimage, you will see."

We slipped through the streets unseen. Usually, Rhyiathe draws the eye of all that pass him. He is tall and handsome, sweet, and kind. It shone out of him like pride. He is magnetic and people are naturally drawn to him. This time though, he is hidden under his pretend clothes and the cloak, that covers his beautiful face. I could smell him, wafts of sweet summer honeysuckle as he walked before me, that is how he smells to me. I trailed in his wake and felt comfortable and I was cared for, protected and cherished, not just my body but my mind and my hearts too. Again, I sighed out in bliss. For a second or two, I allowed myself to abandon my carefully constructed walls, peeking out beyond my dark shell – it still felt dangerous, but comforting just to be in his presence.

We left the busy, loudness of the city streets behind. There was a fish market in the square and the hollering of street traders was noisy, so I was gladdened when we started to walk down the quieter side roads for a while. The crowds were thinning, the greenery became more abundant and dominant as we saw the first smattering of the forest tree line – it's cool shaded canopy came into view. We zigzagged further and further away from the city, and it was so quiet in this part of town that I forgot we were in Periculllious at all. All I could hear were birds twittering and calling to each other, the sound of our breathing and the rustling of our feet through the crunchy leaves on the ground. A calm descended over us both, hearts beating in the rhythm of our footfalls and Rhyiathe rubbed his thumb idly over the inside of my wrist quite absent-mindedly, holding my hand and tugging me along. He was guiding us on, but I didn't want this walk to ever end. Its simple joy was intoxicating, it filled me with such pleasure, the like of which I have never known.

It's strange, isn't it? These tiny moments that mean so much, are so few, and that we spend our lives in a constant state of hunger; striving for the

bigger moments, the actions that we think prove we are special, the ones that come to mean nothing in the end.
We came to a stop in front of a tall, creamy sandstone building with vast stained-glass windows that covered most of the sides - the structure being more elaborate glass than stone. The bones of the temple ran deep into a steep hillside, and I was distracted by the panoramic views of the breathtaking city below. Tall building, copper rooftops, mixed in under the treetops, and glinting towers of castles spread out around the city, as far as where the land meets the swelling, glistening sea. Beyond that the deep blue water melted into the sky above. The location was selected to inspire the pilgrims, the non-believers, and the believers alike, into believing in something greater than themselves.
"Okay, now you can remove your hood." Rhyiathe stood to my side watching me carefully as I unhooded myself, but I had already been peeking. My hair was sticking up at all angles but gone was my self-consciousness. My eyes drifted upwards, into the light from the sky, to take in the great expanse of a temple, it had a large creamy stone statue of a woman guarding the entrance way. The stone woman looked like a goddess and had a carefully tapped out, moulded kind-looking face. The blank eyes of the statue looked down with love on those who passed under these gates. The statue stood guarding the worshippers with loving kindness, to shepherd them through the ornamental doors of the temple. Her children. The Goddess lives in the statue and fills the air with life and beauty of the ancient, the remembered and the lost.
"It. . . it's beautiful, Rhyiathe." I felt exceedingly small and insignificant, but the statue silently spoke to me of care, and of courage, and strength, without moving at all.
He took my hand and glided me into the main chamber of the temple. Through the light pine wooden doors of that place, we walked across the tiled floor together in devoted silence, up to the pulpit where another statue of the same woman was carved out of a creamy marble stone. At this, the second statue, he lifted a tarnished, golden oil lamp, it cast a warm beam of light over the statue's features. He took a moment to gaze quietly on her face. The shifting shadows, as well as the flickering candlelight made the statue seem to move, to bestow onto me a profound sense of love, devotion and there was something else, there was a growing sense of

expectation on me. Rhyiathe kneeled on a deep velvet cushion placed on the steps before the marble statue. He does not tell me to do the same, but the statue was hewn so beautifully that I chose to kneel before I fell. I was so taken by the ethereal beauty of the artwork and the kindness of the face that looked down at me, frozen in time, but it was as if I could hear her heartbeat in the stillness – she seemed alive.
"This is the Goddess of the Moon, Nimwae, these statutes of her are made from moonstone, sacred stone of the vampires," He spoke, while looking at her graceful face, like he was giving a sermon and I was listening with all my being, scared to breathe lest I break the spell of his words. This story was important to him, so I pay careful attention – in silence.
He continued, "This story is not repeated very often, only with those that share the magic of the vampires and even then, only amongst certain echelons of vampiric society, as it gives away too much information about how to harm our kind."
I gasped. He was trusting me with this knowledge, and I looked up at the face of Nimwae. For a split second, it seemed as if she smiled down at me and I bowed my head towards her. Eyes open, open to her guidance, as Rhyiathe begins to speak.
"Nimwae had a heart that beat vastly, she was a kind goddess, she loved life, all life, and honoured it greatly. Mother of the cosmos. She fell in love with one of the Gods of the Suns, Areace. He is powerful, continuous, eternal - burning in his own renewable flames of white-hot energy, but Nimwae was fortified by the power of the cosmic moons – all of them combined. She could withstand his searing heat and was unaffected by the touch of his blistering energy. Some say she was the birther of the universe and the beginning of the Elder, celestial beings of the Light. Nimwae fell pregnant, gave birth to a vast number of immortal children. Areace came to see his children and they fled from their father, they were made more from their mother, the moons, than from that of the furnace of his burning suns. His scorching heat burned them, and the moon children cowered before him. Areace was disgusted by his children. He perceived them as weak and set about destroying them, burning them into oblivion."
I let out a gasp and took Rhyiathe's arm, he was struggling to tell the story. He sighed mournfully. "Nimwae, searched through the wreckage burying her children and found a few of them alive, who had survived their father's

terrible wrath. Nimwae took them away to keep them safe and hid them behind one of the moons. Nimwae only came out with them, when Areace and his brother had left the sky. The moons and the suns never met in the same sky again. Nimwae died of heartbreak, of the heaviness of having to protect her children from their own father, and having to watch her children live in fear, those who could no longer look upon the Suns without terror in their heart of being burnt alive from the coming of the morning light. They stayed in the shadows and remained there to this day – the moon children of Nimwae. This is the true story of how vampires came into being. Loved but cursed. Each time a new vampire is made or born, we celebrate their life, and the vampire must pledge allegiance to Nimwae and make a vow to always protect those who cannot protect themselves, the children of the moon and stars. Do you make this pledge? Do you stand with us in our search for justice for Nimwae and her fallen children?"

My hand glinted, the moonstone on my hand glistened sadly. I now knew what the expectation was, Nimwae wanted me to save her children. I sat there in the quiet. A longing burst into my chest. My excitement came out in my loud breathing, as I looked on the remarkable, unseeing face of Nimwae. My breath was so loud that I thought the quiet chamber would crumble from under the force of it, but the temple and its foundations were strong, remained standing in its hushed stillness and grace, like it had for a million years, long before my being here. I cast my gaze around its mighty strong-hold and it gave me courage.

"I will honour Nimwae's memory, I will seek revenge for her. Yes, I vow to protect those that cannot protect themselves," I spoke in muted tones, the temple grew quiet, then the statue glowed.

Rhyiathe bowed towards the Goddess, faced me to bow towards me and he offered his arm to lift me up from my kneeling position. The rustling of my cloak was the only sound in that hallowed space.

"I have something for you." Sliding my moonstone ring from my finger, he gently replaced it with a much larger moonstone ring, surrounded with luminous glittering stones, that shone as bright as the moons at night. "My mother's ring, I gift this to you before Nimwae, I pledge myself to you if you will have me, to protect you and walk with you, wherever our paths take us, and your fate may lead us. In me, you will always find a home to return to, take this ring as my solemn oath."

I stood still, we gazed on each other, I stared in shock at first, not quite believing what he had just vowed. Fumbling for the right words to say, I began,

"Wherever our fates may lead us, within me, Rhyiathe, you will always find a home to return to," I repeated back his words, but I say them with a type of strength that I did not know I possessed. Rhyiathe broke into a slow smile and leaned forward and kissed my forehead, before he looked away, back towards the statue of Nimwae, as if asking for her permission. He was answered. A faint silver line floated down, like fine silver webbing from the ceiling and I watched it, eyes wide with wonder as it settled in circles around us, drew itself in and then slowly disappeared.

We stood facing each other for a while. He stroked my hair, smiling and then said,

"So, let us go and celebrate. Somewhere completely feral, maybe in order."

We both grinned and I say, "I don't know, I'm not sure you can handle my level of feral."

And he teased back, "Well, I think it would be a great deal of fun to find out. I love this side of you Aurora," he took my hand, and I gave it to him gratefully and gladly. Hand in hand, we swung our arms together as we walked out onto the streets, to find our own way, hoods down and free.

We found a ramshackle but lively vampire tavern near the temple and that night, I was introduced to Skoom beer, which is the traditional beverage of the vampires, made with special moonlight picked hops and barley, and frothy metallic blood – I tried not to think about that bit too much. I learnt some Vampire slang-words, which were very imaginative and extensively colourful and descriptive. We played games, partook in lots of dancing, until our feet were sore, and we laughed until we couldn't laugh anymore. We celebrated together, celebrated each other, and had a wild time of it. I colour just thinking about that night, the wildness of it. Rhyiathe had a fun, carefree playful side as well as being kind and true, and a little too serious sometimes – like the weight of the Seven Kingdoms rests on his shoulders. The funny thing is he had introduced himself as Dag'non and I played along thinking it was all such a blast, not thinking very much of it. I got very drunk and could not remember how we got home, but I remember shouting, *I think I've bloody well just married Rhyiathe* at the top of my lungs, at anyone who would listen.

The clumping of boots in the dance, cut across her words. Only a handful of vampires heard Aurora and of those that did, muttered out a low, "Prince Rhyiathe did she mean or this Dag'non here? This young woman tells tall tales," they chuckled, getting louder, "you only wish you could snag yourself a prince, lass." The crowd had jeered and shouted, but I was so drunk, I wasn't really paying attention to the other vampires in the bar and their strange mutterings.

Chapter Twenty-three – The Void and The Visited

"There is someone here to see you," Lilly expressed in a soft voice in the darkness of the bed chamber, I tried to open my eyes, but my head was throbbing. My palms moulded into the sockets my eyes. Safety against the brightness of the Suns flooding into the room. "You had *both* better get up," Lilly had said in a rather harsher, clipped tone.

"*Both, what do you mean?* . . . Who?" I sat bolt upright just as Lilly was leaving - catching a glimpse of her hand still on the door, as it was closing behind her. I stared down at the other side of the rumpled bed and Rhyiathe's half covered, naked form was spread across the bed. His hands strewn over his large, muscular bare chest. This wasn't my bed. This wasn't my room. This was Rhyiathe's house – I could tell by the tiny details littering the place. A fear gripped me, confusion at first then, a sensual longing for him and then, bewilderment. *Had we?* I looked under the cover, I was naked too. My head was pounding and I felt nauseous. I scrabbled for my bodysuit, which was strewn on the bed chamber floor, in amongst his clothes tossed on the floor. I ran with it into the bathroom, where I hurriedly dressed and got ready, brushing my teeth with some cloth, and pulling at my hair. Trying to look decent, but all I wanted to do was crawl into a ball and be sick. The blackness under my eyes was a whole new level of terrible.

When I came out, he was sitting up in his bed, as handsome and crisply clean as ever, like he'd just stepped out of an underwear advert – all beautiful and sultry. *Bloody immortals.*

"Good morning, how are you doing?" He grinned at me, and I slinked back against the wall. Petrified.

"Fine, erm, thanks, . . . I need to . . . get downstairs so let yourself out- or I mean, I will let myself out . . .". I ran for the door.

"*Aurora* – don't do this, " I heard him shout out, exasperated, but I kept going, running faster away, desperate to get out of that room and away from the expectations set upon his beautiful face.

Dawn entered the small room I had locked myself away in. She had a big mischievous smile across her light filled face. Her hair brushed up into plaits, crowning her head and her outfit was clean, and she looked well cared for, not worn, and frayed. I was glad, but sorrowful at the same time, that she no longer remembered me as her sister – no longer needed me at all. It was very confusing.

"*Aurora,*" she yelled and ran towards me, only managing to catch herself when a sharp pain dug into her side, and she crumpled in on herself.

My steps moved quickly across the floor, and I was upon her in seconds, helping her back up. Dawn looked up gratefully and I was caught in a memory of when she knew us as sisters.

She stirred and blinked up at me before fumbling out, "I'm so glad to see you. Caemyre told me you lost the race to help an old woman to cross a river, who had fallen in. What noble spirits you both are?" Dawn looked up at me in admiration and I hoped she did not notice the slight look of incredulity slipping across my face.

Yes, Dragons are devious. Not content with merely saying we were slow and lost the race. Caemyre fabricated a whole heroic act to save his arrogant skin. I smiled more broadly than intended.

"I take no credit. It was all Caemyre's doing," I explained, trying to hold the snorting laughter out of my reply.

"Yes, he said as much. In all honesty, he said you got in the way and thinks you need a learned and distinguished Dragon Lord to help you to become a tolerable Dragon-rider and he suggested that should be him. He's terribly experienced and knowledgeable, you know? I agreed. I hope you don't mind but it does sound like you need a lot of help."

I stood, glassy eyed, quite flummoxed, muttering darkly under my breath about understanding why Dragon's had gone extinct on earth, before saying,

"*Of course*, I do. He is far too charitable. Thank you, Dawn." I bent down and hugged her, smelling the scent of her hair. Remembering the times I had plaited it when she was a small child while getting ready for school, I sighed at the memory. Those days were long gone and Rhyiathe standing there behind Dawn brought me back to the present moment. Bowing his head, Rhyiathe was trying to look serious. However, he could not help

letting a snicker slip at Caemyre's obvious joke at my expense. I started fumbling and playing with my daggers.
"Aurora, we need to talk," Rhyiathe murmured barely above a whisper.
"Not now," I had mouthed back in reply, "I want to spend time with Dawn and not have to worry about what happened last." He sighed, but begrudgingly nodded. I flushed.
He placed his hand by mine, just out of reach, as a small gesture of solidarity.
Lilly was behind him with pink cheeks and mirth in her eyes too, still grinning at the dragon's mockery of me.
Dawn looked between me, Lilly and Rhyiathe and then said,
"Well, we'll need to go to the outskirts of The Void, where I can promenade before the remaining dragons to see if any one of them wants to pick me. You are going to love The Void, Aurora, it's unbelievably beautiful. The Celestial Body of star makers that separate the Earth from the other six Kingdoms is really something to see. Come on let's go."
A giddy excitement came over Dawn, she was bouncing up and down. I must admit, I was most intrigued to see an imagined Dragon-conveyor belt-come-selection-process up close, but to also, peer into The Void.
Our little group were all giddy when we rushed out of the room, marching after Dawn, and embarking on our journey to the far reaches of space and time. To the Star Makers, we go and beyond.

The swirling lights of a portal appeared in Rhyiathe's house. When we reached the other side and dropped out of the portal exit, I couldn't believe my eyes. I could do nothing else but to stare out over the stars and cosmic space hanging all around us. The stars were shining brightly and the heavens looked indiscernibly beautiful.
On the ground beneath our feet was a canyon of sorts, if I were to describe the alien landscape using Earth's language. The ground came to an abrupt stop. A deep cliffhanger opened with a dark nothingness below and on the other side even more of the nothingness.
I was told we must step out onto the nothingness to reach the other side – our destination.
"Huh? What? You gotta be joking? You are asking me to step out onto . . . nothing. What's stopping me from flying away into space?" I gulped at

the deepness of the chasm; a sturdier stomach was required than mine for the leap of faith that awaits.
The group stood and shook their heads. Rhyiathe patted my shoulder,
"Trust your friend's Aurora, please." Rhyiathe said, with a warm smile and I nervously smiled back.
"Trust you lot? but you are literally asking me to step out onto air and I'm supposed to believe you guys, that I won't plunge to my death?"
"Well, yes," Rhyiathe said with a cool calmness that made me want to scream. He folded his muscular arms over his broad chest and slowly smiled.
I searched for Dawn's face, she gave me an encouraging smile back and said, "I've done it and I lived." Then flipped her thumbs up, "now go on."
Petrified, holding on to the confidence of the others, who had been frequent visitors to The Void. I placed my foot in mid-air ready to step forward into the Nothingness. A fear gripped me.
I was asked to step out first for the sport of the others, no doubt. My foot hovered, held up in hesitation, bouncing on the thin air – testing it but I found nothing solid there.
I closed my eyes, "Here goes nothing," and stepped out, my heart lurched into my mouth as I land on . . . well, for a start, a completely translucent set of stairs that were limitless and covered the great expanse of The Void. *Not entirely what I was expecting.* The laughter behind me indicates that the others had experienced the same fear when they had first tried it.
"Yes, very funny." I rolled my eyes and then stuck out my tongue at Dawn, who laughed a little harder than the others at my childish antics.
My eyes surveyed the Celestial grace and vastness of the space enveloping me, while I stood on the glass staircase.
I had thought The Void was going to be an eerie, black space and, well, made of nothing - a literal void, but it turns out I was wrong. Very wrong. It's exactly the opposite.
The Void is a Celestial Body of matter. The Immortals describe space, matter, and time as living and breathing entities. The Void itself is a condensed, multi-versions of Space and time, shrunken down and contained into smaller dimensions. The cosmos and the star makers were all around. Great comets shot overhead so near that I felt the need to keep ducking my head down watching them pass by.

The Elder – Lights of the Seven Kingdoms

You couldn't just *see* the Milky Way; you could walk *into* the Milky Way - be a part of it. To explain it better, each part of space in the universe was folded into a flat record sleeve like structure and each record sleeve is leaning against another. The Void held all of this, and we were able to walk through each section or each record sleeve if you wanted to continue the metaphor. Each represented the distinct parts of the universe at various points of time – we were witnessing the past, present and future at the same time.

I was watching literal miracles happening.

The brightest living thing I or anyone had ever seen, a Quasar, powered by a black hole feeding on an enormous Sun, was hanging in the space above my head. Dimensions were being folded in on dimensions.

It was very dizzying to gaze upon and in truth, I felt like the top layers of the flesh of my eyes were being burnt away. Still, I had no choice but to keep gazing upon the miracle before me. Millions of stars and planets and miracles, crushed in on one another in one condensed space.

Rhyiathe explained that the average brain warps and spasms, it stutters to try to comprehend the scale of The Void, but my brain seemed to love the chaos, the alchemy. It celebrated the impossible - it drank it all in.

I could see the Seven Kingdoms. The six planets were folded in nearest to Earth and there was a great chasm between the two dimensions. This was the area guarded by The Offered. They were here to guard against The Immortals and humans crossing it, over into each other's lands.

I was still gazing around in wonder. It was like living in an oil painting of the Starry Night by Vincent Van Gogh, but instead of dark blue and yellow, all the colours in the universe were represented here, and they were defining the outline of about twenty different dimensions; all colliding into view, mixed in with brilliant bright gases. It was beautiful and terrifying with no clear end that I could see with the naked eye.

No one else seemed blown away by the sheer magnitude of the place and its startling beauty. Too used to seeing it, but I sighed out in blissful wonder.

Rhyiathe, Lilly and Dawn were walking towards a great purple volcano, striking out of a moving landmass. I had been left looking out over the vast expanse like a child watching the first sight of snow at Christmas.

Ahead of them, large Dragons were landing on the vast purple and green coloured rocks of the volcano. The dragons were warily watching us from the corners of their great, lizard-like eyes, assessing us but pretending not to be interested. They reminded me of the stray cats I used to feed back home – fierce, guarded, ready to fight for their territory, but frightened too.

A smaller black dragon with aquamarine eyes and smooth iridescent scales slipped into view. When the dragon moved, it changed colour like the rainbows on the slick surface of oil pushed up out of the road. The dragon was set back away from the group. It reached down its neck to preen its claws when a much bigger dragon of red hues snapped its fierce jaws at it. The smaller dragon quelled and withdrew back into the shadows carefully watching the big group of Dragons in fear.

A beating of wings thunderous and clashing, could be heard rumbling in the distance, coming nearer, moving into view. The great Golden One was flying fast overhead. Caemyre circled wide, then landed to perch lightly next to the small black dragon. He shook out his massive leathery wings. He could be seen conversing with the little dragon. Caemyre was the largest Dragon of them all, but the smaller dragon was not afraid. The other Dragons were watchful, eventually moving away from him.

Caemyre cooed and trilled in softer tones, issuing words of encouragement in his own tongue - I could tell by the way he nuzzled the little dragon to him. As Caemyre was communicating in dragon speak, the little black dragon whipped its head about, eagerly looking at Dawn – it looked at her with a hunger, before lunging forward to greet her new dragon-rider.

The Dragon chooses the Rider.

My heart was gladdened at the sight of the small black dragon nuzzling at Dawn, eyes closed with a deep contentment. Dawn was cuddling the female-dragon back and gazing with a bright love in her eyes. I could almost see the pink swirls of oxytocin settling over both of them. They were well-matched. They both had the same smile, the same temperament and were a better fit than Caemyre Golden One, Dragon Lord. Ruler of The Void and slightly covered in an imperialistic nature as if he has a right to act as overlord towards immortals and humans alike – in other words rather arrogant.

He silently conveyed to me that the black dragon is called Violaceae and that is her Elf-given name. Her Dragon name apparently was not comprehensible to me even if he deigned to share it. I watched the pretty dragon, Violaceae, for a fleeting time taken in by her story. Less regal, more bearable than the Dragon I was now used to, and the female exuded a gentle calm.

Caemyre could see me watching Violaceae. The Golden One hopped and took flight close to the ground. Gliding towards me, he landed with great land quakes rumbling underfoot. He was a glorious show-off.

He speaks, "Violaceae had a stillbirth recently. A fierce warrior she is but of late, vulnerable, and broken in her grief. Easy pickings for the other dragons. Her eyes are alight once more when she looked at Dawn. It is a good pairing would you not say?" He was self-assured, a curling smile playing on his ancient lips. In that moment, he reminded me of the statues of the dragons on display in Chinatown in London to mark the new year of the Dragon. In 1988, I had watched the parade winding through the streets of Soho in the thrilling mist of firecrackers and drums. Dragons on Earth are thought of as Wise and majestic, Giver of riches, Lights that guide us to fame and fortune, bestowing gifts of leadership and as mighty as the Sun.

They are all what is written about them and more, so much more.

My eyes flicked back to the little black dragon. I carefully watched her in her female nesting plumes. My head tilted to the side, knowing her without talking to her. I knew all too well the heaviness of her grief weighing down on her heart. We will both share this grief, in our turns, as ragged sentinels, presiding over the pain of the loss of a love so pure and true.

The light inside represents the intensity of a love like that. The grief doesn't heal but it continues burning us. Scorching. We bear it though; in fact, we welcome the pain and hold it closer to us as it serves as a reminder of a time when we experienced a love so bright, so strong, but we did not realise it or show appreciation for it at the time - when that love was alive. Alive in us.

I watched the female dragon from under my wetted eyelashes in my heaviness, my gloom. Great puddles of tears collected in my eyes.

Caemyre was staring again, "She is not lost. She is here with you, and all will be remembered soon."

My neck cracked from my haste to look Caemyre in his eye and to know if it was all true or some mad ramblings of a proud Dragon. He trilled, blew out hoops of smoke and smiled.

"Ahh, look lively, you have a visitor, I see."

Turning, I came face to face with The Elf King standing before me, bedecked in a brilliant suit of armour made from pure gold. An intricately wrought crown was upon his head of golden hair and a precise, manicured beard covered his handsome elven face.

"Your majesty." I curtsied and behind me, wave after wave of his Immortals lowered their heads in a silent show of respect to the Royal King of the Seven Kingdoms – at least, I think he is the King of all the Kingdoms, or a Steward King perhaps, but I am not so sure.

My eyes flicked over the lines of the King's face and made a mental note that Gamone looked nothing like his father.

Caemyre and the other Dragons did not bow but puffed their chests up, smoke curling from their snouts as a warning to anyone who tried to entreaty preferential treatment for the King.

"Arise Lady Aurora. I will see you back to your apartment in my castle if you please."

It was said not as a question but a command. There was no high inflection at the end, flat and full of sweet threats, is his voice.

"I would find no greater pleasure, your majesty."

I go to stand beside him. Out of the periphery of my vision, I saw the agape faces of Lilly and Dawn, but there was a shrewdness in the glint of Rhyiathe's bold and beautiful eyes. It was as though he had expected the King to appear and come to see me.

I tried to pry my eyes away from the comfort of Rhyiathe's gaze.

A slither of glass lightly fashioned into a sturdy yet flat step, flies to rest at our feet. The King stepped on and flourished his hand for me to follow suit. Two of his private guards moved to step on too and they were given a look of disdain.

"Catch the next one. Follow behind," Gruff was his command.

We were then whisked upwards, towards a fissure in space crackling with golden light and immense in power. My hair was blowing, lifting at the edges in the storm coming off it.

The King waited until we were out in the middle of space by ourselves before he spoke,
"Do not be afraid. This opening takes us back to the castle but on the other side is another opening that could quite as easily take you back to Earth." He said this all without moving his face towards me like a secret agent not wanting to be caught conversing with a person such as me.
"I am *not* afraid." There was a pregnant pause and silence. "That is very interesting information about a portal to Earth, Your Majesty, but why would it be of interest to me?"
He smiled knowingly. The maleficent King turned his face to look out over the cosmos like he had grown weary of the colossal, scenic view and wanted to return home to a beloved armchair just to enjoy peace and rest. Tall he stood, but his shoulders were slightly and imperceptibly shrunken in. The crown was heavy and the threats real from younger alphas, I would guess.
"Both my sons have a keen interest in you, Aurora. I don't know or care to know why that is." The King grimaced, thick with disdain for the imagined tastes of his two sons.
I went to scream accusations at him and accuse him viciously of raising two psychopathic killers, harmers of women and users of the vulnerable, but a bending, painful physical pressure slammed into my face. I bent my neck under the weight, then was made to bend to the knee. What he said next left me cold and numb. He inclined his head down, whispering,
"I take it you do not remember our agreement. The vow taken when you served as my lieutenant, my right hand?" He paused to turn and look me directly in the eyes. On closer inspection, there were beads of sweat dripped from his upper lip. My expert eye caught a peakiness to his creamy complexion. He hesitated and then relief flashed momentarily across his face. He felt assured by my blankness. With my jaw tightly clenched shut, my lips curling to try to pull my mouth open - shut it was and not by choice. The pressure of magic was thrust upon me. The king continued looking out over the great stars glinting in space,
"No, I believe that you don't recall a thing. Very good, because if it ever got out what we did, it doesn't bear thinking about. The damage it would cause. War would. . . well, I should not say anymore, but still, there is no harm as you will not remember anyway, because I intend to give you a

memory charm and seal shut your memories forever – Aurora, you were an Elf once, my most trusted guard, in fact. We agreed that we needed to test if Elves could be sent through The Void and reborn on Earth in human-form and then recalled, awakened in large numbers to form an attack. When you were a little hu-man girl, I tried to awaken the elf in you on many occasions, through performing the Rite. You were difficult to catch and each time we had to put memory spells on you to erase our interactions. It was a painful process for you. But alas, we could not awaken your Elf soul within the hu-man shell you reside in, and for that I am terribly sorry. I came here today to see if there was anything in you left of the Elf friend I once knew. I watched you at the Tournament and you have the same fighting style as Aurora the Elf. You move like her too and some of your gestures are hers, but you do not recall me or yourself, for that matter. I wanted to say how sorry I am. Sorry that I lost you as my most trusted friend."

My eyes are now so wide – peeled back in horror. They are dry and painful from staring in muted anger. I tried to wrench open my mouth with a great many questions, but I could not. It was in a small way, a mercy. I was dumbfounded, I had worked something out. All these years I thought my brain worked differently, talking to me, offering me advice – it is not so straightforward, there is an elf inside of me, one who talks to me, now and then. It is his Elf-Friend that he speaks of.

Good grief, I have been so very blind. I've been part of his cruel games all this time.

The King in his confidence at my inability to not be able to remember his greatest deceit, let alone tell others about it, took his time to casually raise a gloved hand. Under his command, we entered the bright, glowing lights of the opening, a tear in the fabric of space, while he was standing and I was bent down low, but in complete silence after his revelations.

I closed my eyes against the blinding glow of the opening. All was whitewashed. All was a brilliant type of blankness. It surrounded me. The pressure was still upon me, encompassing my head, this implied he was still using an invisible magic on me.

When I opened my eyes back up, I was standing in front of my bed in my apartment, inexplicably back at the castle. I spun around looking for the King, but he had vanished.

A painful pressure bared down on my face, there was a screaming in my ears and it was coming from my own mouth. My body swayed under it. An immensely powerful spell was swirling over me, then the golden particles vanished. What was left of the spell, was before my eyes in the images of the king opening and closing his lips, but I couldn't remember what it was he said. It was on the tip of my very tongue but out of reach - maddeningly near but unreachable.

Screaming in frustration, I slumped forward and smashed my fists into the mattress of the solid wooden bed. The frame wobbled and broke into two pieces of solid great oak. Duck feathers flew up in the air and settled back down, calmly around me.

Whatever it was that he exchanged with me, I knew this. It was especially important. The last piece perhaps of a riddle to unlock my muddled mind.

Chapter Twenty-four - The Tournament reveals all.

There was a chill air blowing in through my balcony window. It was my own fault for breaking my bed and now I had to make temporary sleeping accommodations on an exceedingly long, antique chaise lounge in the morning room, where the Suns rises each and every morning.

The Chaise lounge in question was built with a hardy sturdiness to it that accommodated the long limbed and robust elven folk. I tossed and turned still grasping with the silent image of the king as he opened and closed his mouth soundlessly like a guppy fish. I still couldn't recall what he had shared, but I knew it was significant. My fists slammed down either side of me as I laid restless with my back crushed up against the overstuffed chair; trying to coax my mind to chase at shadows and spinning yarns. Grating away at the enamel of my teeth, eventually I fell into a fitful sleep. As I laid there dreaming, the lights of The Elder emerged from my body, glowing like glass orbs, made from greasy olde English oil lanterns, like the ones used in the hazy smog of Victorian London. The little orbs violently swirled around my body - a vortex was opened in my minds-eye. A vision emerged and I was whisked inside...

I was floating above, observing unseen when the two noble and confident princes, Lord Gamone and Lord Tennison entered a long, dark chamber, a room of some kind. One dominated by the biggest fireplace I had ever seen. Six or more elves could stand tall within it and still, there would be space for more to join.

The fire was raging, blistering, ferocious flames-feasted on great tree trunks for fuel. Embers were ruined to white hot stones, ash corpses spewing onto the mount and dropping onto the carpet. Fire savage, ash as payment.

What can stand to be near such a blistering heat?

The princes entered and became less solid, more shadow-form, in the presence of that monstrosity of a fireplace.

Their tall and muscular bodies were nothing but creeping silhouettes, trying to stay away from the red lashing flames. They both knelt before a

densely cushioned, throne like armchair. Their eyes fixed ahead, tensely looking at someone sitting in the confines of the high-backed chair that I could not see.
I could not tell who it was in the chair, facing the fire as it roared and crackled joyously. The fire was devouring voices. I could just about hear the brothers speak. I strained forward from wherever I was floating.
"Tomorrow is the tournament. Battle hardened cadets will be in fighting mode," Lord Tennison said. There was an answer which they all laughed at. "Yes, I have been shaping the minds of the young cadets. They have become haters of humans and anyone different, 'Elves First' is their new purist slogan."
An answer was given again, then a curious look passed over Gamone's face. He knitted his eyebrows together, but it was Lord Tennison that answered.
"Yes, yes, they are ready to storm The Void while the tournament is happening. I will slip them the potion to intensify their aggression and then lead them out with the separatist military Generals to storm the opening and take it for our own. The offered will bend the knee or be slaughtered. When all is settled and the Crown of the Elven rules, dictates absolutely, then we can plan the attack on Earth. Occupation of The Void is only the beginning. What's that?" There was a pause while he listened. Lord Tennison leaned back and sighed, closing his eyes, and pinching the bridge of his well-defined nose.
Another murmur.
"Well, it's because you do not have faith in me. This line of questioning demonstrates you do not. I do not plan on there *being* any *shiv'ving* issues, but if there are then I have planted evidence of the rebellion coordination in Lindon's home. The Shiv Queen killed him, so, it will be easy to pin it on our poor dead elf friend, dearest Lindon. Still, he would be pleased he was still being useful to our cause." Lord Tennison then stood, curtly nodded with fingers twisting around his sword in anger and departed, under the cover of the hood of his silk cloak. A few heart beats past.
Gamone was alone with the shadowy figure. He waited for assurance that Lord Tennison had left, then shuffled further forward on his knee. He was intensely murmuring something. A hand was extended with a large golden ring wrought in the shape of a Dragon or a Griffin with some sort of

emblem stamped into it - hard to make out clearly, but the shape of the diamond in the ring was the size of a pigeon's egg and most unusual. Gamone took the hand, kissing the ring. Swearing fealty by the looks of it. While he was bent over, a hand was placed on the back of his large, black-haired head - a gesture of familiarity, or of sentiment even, of the kind that was not reserved for Lord Tennison earlier.
When Gamone stood, he stood so very proud and tall. Bidding whoever was in that throne armchair, a fond farewell and he uttered,
"Yes, succession and I will observe and not take part. Lord Tennison is disposable, I told you I agree. You know he is not my real brother. I don't care what happens to the fool, I've told you this a hundred times," With that he kissed the gloved hand, with the ring, on once more, then exited the chamber. Shadows fell, grey clouds obscure and the image swirls dizzyingly away.
Waking up out of my dream, I brushed my hand towards my cheeks and felt the heat of the fire still prickled out my face. The lights of The Elder were still hovering above me. Was I there? What can this mean? A military coup was being planned. An attack to take back The Void. That was all I could be sure of at that moment. But who would believe me? *Lilly would.* My mind replied.
I pulled on my tan bodysuit, packed up my blades and moved towards the door of my apartment shouting for Lilly.
She popped her head through the door.
"Hello, my Lady, keen for some breakfast, are we. We have fresh . . ." She stopped dead when she saw the expression on my face. A skillet she was drying came crashing to the floor.
"What is it? What is wrong?"
I began by shrilly saying,
"We need Rhyiathe, Callen, Caemyre, Violaceae but this is too dangerous for Dawn. She needs to stay at the Academy where it's safe . . .," I said.
"Well, good luck with that. An Offered will not be without her dragon, so think again." Lilly looked at me, a fear creeping over her face, and it was a mirror of my own. "Whatever is it? Please, do not spare the details for my sake!"
So, I began to tell her about my vision . . . she believed me without question.

After Lilly had listened to every word, all the blood drained out of her face. She only said one thing. "Here. Take my father's sword. Your blades will not be enough to stop the Princes, I'm afraid. If you do have to fight them, I mean. And Aurora, please keep it. He would have wanted someone like you to have his sword to stop evil from taking hold."

I took the sword from her outstretched hand and swung it in an arc, slicing through the air with a satisfying sound.

"It would be my greatest honour to fight with it, Lilly. Thank you."

My eyes were full of tears, warm and thick like honey. Her kindness was immeasurable. Her belief in me filled a hole left by my sister and I gently touched her shoulder. I hesitated, looking deep into the kindness of her eyes, I said "Lilly, . . . you never told me your story and about your family." I paused for a moment of reflection "and I never really told you mine, either."

"We will find another time. It does not matter really. I see your hearts and they are bright." Lilly nodded to herself and looked off with eyes seeing through the distant mountains and out into the far beyond – another version of time. There was a throbbing, palpable pain to her words, and I dared not push her any further through fear of breaking her.

"It's okay if you don't want to talk about it, I'll understand, but what happened to your family? Why are you now in servitude to the Elf King?"

Lilly's eyes welled and averted from mine, dropping to peer at the ground. Her sorrow was written across her face, I wasn't sure if she was going to speak, but I stood in stillness and waited to listen. The silence was heavy and continued for a while. To try and save her from any awkwardness, I got up to announce I must leave, when she started to whisper the words clasping at her throat,

"My father was a king of one of the Elf sub-kingdoms on Tylerine. It's a beautiful land, wholesome, cheerful just like its people. My father found out about Lord Tennison's Father, the Elf King's plot to declare war on the Vampires of the Kingdom of Vulldune. My Father had an alliance with the Vampires back then, our family was friendly with the King of Vulldune and his sons, the princes. My Father did not agree with the Elf King and stopped the plot by exposing it. You must understand, my father had tried to petition with reason and to the Immortal parliament, but these approaches did not work. The plan was not of warfare, but genocide, to release a spell and poisonous gases killing millions of innocent vampires. The Elf King found a reason to execute my father, my mother and my two sisters. I was left alive to live out my days in servitude and disgrace. In humiliation, a reminder of what happens to traitors of the Crown's iron will. On hearing of the plot, the Vampire King sent his first-born son, the Crown Prince of Vulldune to live with the Elf King, and Lord Tennison and Lord Gamone in order to reforge ties between Vampires and Elves – strengthen them. The King of the Vampires of Vulldune will ascend to the Amber Throne on the next cycle, which will displace the Elves from Periculious, they would have to return to Tylerine. It is this that the Elf King is resisting - he will not leave the Amber throne willingly. You will want to know who the Crown Prince of Vulldune is. It is. . ."

A courtier barged through the doors unannounced, dressed in raw silk and golden stitching, standing tall on heeled shoes, with mother of pearl buttons. Lilly and I both jumped out of our skin at the suddenness of the intrusion,

"The Tournament has started. Please Come now, Lady Aurora." The Courtier said in a clipped, uptight tone.

I hugged Lilly and held her close, whispering how sorry I was in her ear and then a little louder I announced,

"I guess, I better get to the tournament," I said, more determinedly but still in a hushed whisper as if talking to the gravely ill. I watched the Courtier exit the room. Lilly spoke as the door was closing.

"Yes, I think you need to be there to put an end to all of this at the beginning. Before it starts." Her eyelashes were moist.

"At the beginning . . ." I repeated not fully understanding any of this or how I came to be here, but I knew one thing for sure. I was going to make the princes bleed and regret ever having heard the name Aurora. . . Aurora . . . I realise, I can no longer remember my surname.

"Aurora, Aurora, Aurora, Aurora, Aurora, Aurora, Aurora. . . . "

Standing in the stillness of the cool tunnel before the arena, the breeze picked up and blew in tight circles through the enclosed space. Sand and dirt hit my face. There was a metallic smell of blood and bodily fluids mixed in with the squelching sounds of the mud. Hearing the deafening noise of the crowds chanting my name was surreal. Remembering last time I was here, when I was an unknown human Shiv Queen and now, I was a living fable. I clenched my hand around the cold metal hilt of my sword feeling the comfort that it brought. "For Lilly and her family." I whispered to the steel. It glistened.

The chanting was becoming louder, rowdier, announcing the audience was growing restless for the tournament of The Gathering and to celebrate The Offering had been a success.

In the arena, the cadets were sorted into groups by their magical abilities, elf, werewolf, vampire, witches and so on. How archaic the sorting was, pitting immortals against each other. In the distance, I could see the Elf King presiding over the tournament, dressed in fine gold armour with a thick lion's skin fashioned into a cloak draped around his shoulders. It was an odd choice as none of the other Immortals had brutalised an animal in such a way. It seemed to displease the crowds too.

Walking along the darkness of the tunnel on my way to the sunlit arena, I hugged the rough plastered wall. I blinked and looked down at the floor. The pathway was covered in a thick mat of deep brown and bright red liquid. I was shocked to discover these were wide lines of old and new blood, criss-crossing over the sand-covered ground, where multiple injured and dead warriors of the tournament had been dragged out of the arena on their backs or by their feet.

As I turned a corner, two elven guards round it. Before me, they were dragging a dead witch, freshly killed, out of the arena. I tried not to look, but my eyes could not help checking for risks constantly in this hostile environment, so I could not look away.

The shape of a young witch swam before me, ghostly pale with eyes frozen open in horror. Neck slit and blood seeping out in thick lines of crimson onto the floor, her life source was leaking out behind her.

One of the elven guards was casually telling a joke while the other rolled his shoulders, laughing. Both held a foot as the body was being dragged behind them. The body slithered over jagged stones and uneven sand, but those guards were completely unconcerned in their labour.

Disbelief burned at my eyes, but those elven guards walked by not noticing my malediction or intent. Eventually, they passed. When I was sure they were out of sight, the vomit came in waves, and I found a corner to be

discreet in. Callen was right. Elves treated the other immortals worse than can be imagined. *How did I not notice this before?* Change was needed.
That's when I stepped into the arena, out into the suns shine and into the rolling roar of the immortals. The Tournament is a killing field.
The arena was chaos and charged.
Motives and subtexts clung on the downturned faces of the crowds.
Elves could be heard chanting, "Elves First," from multiple points in the crowds, faces hidden. Werewolves growled, "death to killers," and witches and warlocks singing songs of old, of different times, when immortals were united in the spirit of tribalism - protective of one another. The tree people were fearful and set back. Vampires were quiet and elitist, not making a sound but observing with keenness attuned to the pulsating life force all around. I heard it too.
Uneasiness drenched everything like fine rain but unseen to eyes not looking. The air was thick and greasy with a tight tension. It made me anxious.
My eyes scanned across the great arena. The groupings of immortals stood separately; lonely distinct islands, where do I stand? What space is there for me? I was one, on my own not part of any group. Invisible poison ivy sprigs on me, untouchable I felt. Not belonging. I am not human, and I was not born an immortal either, although a vampire's curse is in my blood. I am something else.
"Aurora, over here. Come, stand beside me," I heard Rhyiathe's voice, warm and light at odds with the violence waiting to unfold.
My stomach flipped over and I was grateful for his attention. Walking slowly, I moved forward with outstretched arms to greet him with a hug.
My eyes scanned the arena and out in the front row on the opposite side facing me was Lilly holding the hand of a vampire female. They were both blushing and gazing at each other tenderly. I smiled at their warmth for one another.
Callen was by Lilly's side and Dillion was beside the witch. They were the only defiantly mixed group of immortals that I could see. The others were divided.
Dillon nodded to me and lazily smiled, giving me an encouraging thumbs up. I smiled back and knew I was forgiven for my behaviour after the Rite.
There was a young female werewolf. I spotted her in the crowds running

down the stairs to join him. They both had the same warm, brown eyes and golden copper, floppy hair like human labradors, one a pup. They were siblings.
Smiling to myself at my makeshift family, I turned back towards Rhyiathe, and he gently guided me in for a hug, under the pretence of a welcome but he lingered far too long for it to be strictly so.
"You look happy for someone who is about to be attacked by every wannabe contender in here," he said, green eyes reflecting back my own happiness with a broad smile. He touched my cheek. I wished we were somewhere else, somewhere clean, where I could wear a beautiful dress and he didn't have to wear battle armour. The sadness of this thought caught in my throat. Rhyiathe gazed down knitting his fingers through mine.
"I am happy, happy to be with you . . .I just feel really . . .," I croaked.
"Aurora, come over to this side right now. I have signed you up as part of my team."
All goes quiet and I daren't turn around. My hands involuntarily started to tremble and my throat dried out. Flashbacks. Disjointed images of the mangroves appeared in the chaos of my mind, and I was transported back in time. Looking down at my feet, I expected them to be covered in greyish unpolished, scuffed school shoes, just like when I was a small child unable to protect myself from monsters.
"You don't have to answer Gamone. Get behind me," Rhyiathe said in a whisper, eyeing me with concern.
"No, not this time." I straightened up and tightened my grip on my sword. Turning around, I used my fledging powers to coldly pull a thin crisp glass shield over myself.
"Lord Gamone, I am here with my friends. Let the best group win."
Defiantly, I stared into his eyes. We can all play games. I shouted into the centre of the arena, flinging my hands up in the air theatrically. Whipping the crowd up to get their support, using them as witnesses so Gamone could not hurt me or my friends. I got the crowds raucous applause.
Lord Gamone surveyed the crowd considering my response and he curtly inclined his head towards me, impressed at my subterfuge.
He feigned a mockery of a sad face.

"I see, alas, you have picked the under dogs. The best group is already here."
He lifted his massive arms. His chainmail barely containing him, links undoing under the strain as he lifted his hands to clap for his team members walking in a single line posing and playing to the crowd. All were elves, all were smiling, handsome and deceitful - like Gamone.
The crowds erupted and gasped out.
"Lord Gamone has entered the tournament this year."
The audience was standing to get a look at their mighty prince. Lord Tennison nodded his head at me, where he stood in a black leather-look bodysuit by the Elven cadets at the outer perimeter. A smirk was on his face, the same as his brother, Lord Tennison continued waving and smiling at the crowds - the consummate gladiator and people's favourite.
Then I watched, as Lord Tennison walked down the long line of cadets, giving each of one of them a tablet to swallow, turning to each one, before heading towards the exit. There was about sixty of them and they all followed the crown prince of Tylerine out of the arena.
It had begun.
Gamone turned sharply and strode towards me with thundering footsteps creating a distraction, keeping the crowds' eyes away from the Cadets. He slammed me into the dirt strewn ground, then playfully reached out a hand to pick me up.
Grabbing my hand in a crushing motion, he uttered, "I will protect you here because I need you, but mark my words Shiv, do not underestimate me or try to humiliate me again," Gamone said in a low whisper, with a sly smile on his face so the crowds thought it was by accident that I was knocked to the ground.
Rhyiathe bounded over, flying forward. His strong arms wrestling prince Gamone to the ground. Only I was close enough to see Rhyiathe's fangs sliding out of his mouth and talons growing long, while the crowd started booing and shouting, "Poor form. They have started fighting already" The luminous eyes of Rhyiathe the vampire, slid across and clouded his irises. The wind picked up around him, as if he had summoned it. The skin on his arms shrunk back and his muscles grew taut like a wild animal. Growling out a threat. Pure hatred was written across his features. Dark shadows upon his eyes.

Gamone lunged back up onto his feet. Rhyiathe and Prince Gamone glared into each other's eyes nose to nose. The commentator's voice filled the arena.
"Wow, it looks like the tournament has started for these two already. Keep it to the games please."
The commentator continued, explaining the rules and the various events lined up. Gamone looked up at the royal box, pleading silently with his Father, the king, peeled back eyes imploring him and the King shook his head – he would not let him hurt Rhyiathe in front of the crowd. A shared moment: debating the silent instruction, Gamone removed his gaze from the King and reluctantly stood down and barged his shoulder into Rhyiathe. Gamone made a show of dusting down his clothes and cruelly said,
"So, Rhyiathe you want the Shiv queen on your team. Think you can save her from all these Elves and immortals in the arena with us, do you?"
Gamone leaned in closer *"and from me?"* he said, with lecherous look on his face.
Rhyiathe squared up to Gamone. In tallness, they were equals. Gamone was bigger in bulk. Rhyiathe was tall, lean, and powerful in his own way.
Rhyiathe opened his mouth, fangs fully bared, but he did not get a chance to speak.
"I don't need anyone looking after me, I'm a *shiv'ving* nightmare on my own,"
Mt expert pronunciation, as well as the reclaiming of that particular insult, made the crowds fall silent, while I took the time to pull out my sword and my blade, twirling them in each hand, before I catapulted in the air. Twisting in a somersault and landing lightly next to one of Gamone's team; punching him in the side of the head, sword still in my hand, and out cold – a knockout blow. There was a *flumping* sound as the elf hit the ground and was sprawled out across the floor. The whole time my eyes were fixed on Gamone – daring him to confront me.
"Like the lady says, she doesn't need any protection from a *Cilena-ancae,* like you,"
Whatever Rhyiathe had said it was bad. I could tell by the look on Gamone's face and the immortals who stood with open mouthed disgust, surrounding them both, but before Gamone could reply, a loud gong,

sonorously clanged, in the middle of the arena followed by nine more gongs announcing the start of the contest.
When the last gong was struck, all was obscured by a smoke like mist that had descended, covering the arena floor.
The shape of the land changed instantaneously. My legs wobbled and I fell over, as the ground shook beneath me. The pressure on my face told me an enormously powerful spell was being performed. The pain was throbbing in my skull, but my thoughts bloom forth like flowers, fixed on stopping Lord Tennison taking The Void. That was all that mattered.
When my eyes flipped open, the environment had completely changed, magically, to that of a vast jungle landscape. I wobbled and fell down, but knew this place was lethal so pushed myself up onto my feet.
The sudden humidity heated the little hairs inside my nostrils. The air was warm, wet with uncertainty, as rain started bucketing down - torrential and driving like bullets. Thick areas of tightly packed trees were all I could see; the sheets of rain were battering rubbery foliage and the pelting rain was roaring – nothing else could be heard apart from that rain.
Dense and dank was the environment. The smell of hot vegetation lifted in waves so very pungent, from the jungle floor. Great ferns and hydrophyte plants gained the ground in some places and dust in others, only momentarily though - gushing water filled the landscape with thick, oily mud. A rampant river of it knocked me off my feet, pushing me into the undergrowth to tumble and slide for over forty feet down a treacherous hillside. Rolling and crashing, being thrust into rocks, I was forced away from Rhyiathe and his team.
I landed in a long stretch of darkness. Under the canopy of densely packed trees, the roots were twisted and knotted together in deformity, struggling against one another to fight for the light of the Suns.
Legs struck out before me, I sat nursing my bewilderment, all the while mud fell in a deluge above and onto me, trying to choke me with its incessant pounding. Covering my head in torrents, the weight of the heavy clay like mud was pounding me. I was made to bend under the weight of it. Struggling to breathe, I tried to stand and to wade out of the quagmire – both physically and mentally. Oily mud coated everything, my hair, my clothes, every pore of my skin. I'd scream out from the suffocation of it, but I daren't open my mouth. The force of the mudslide pushed me back

down. My muscles screamed, pulling on every sinew to hoist myself up. The monkeys in the trees laughed at my pain, howling out their desire for me to lose. The monkeys wanted to feast on my flesh.
Eventually, finding a tether made from a gnarled old piece of twisted jungle vine, I pulled myself free on muscles weak, trembling and I emerged out of the mud fall like a mewing newborn. On drier land, I crawled acting like the first amphibian to turn land mammal – awkward and wet.
I gasped to fill my painful lungs. Exhaustion was setting in, and I fell backwards with a splat, thanking the gods I had found dry earth underneath me. A hard fought for sigh before I took my hands and scooped the mud away from my eyes. A thick layer of terracotta mud, enveloped me apart from my eyeballs. I laughed maniacally to myself. *I must look a hideous sight.*
There was no time for sitting. I needed to get to the end and out of here to The Void to stop Lord Tennison from killing the offered and seizing The Void.
So very muddled was my brain. Whirling in the heat of this artificial jungle, my senses threw up fear in every direction, spinning me around and making my sight disjointed.
That was when I heard a gentle snap of twig behind me and I leapt up, spinning and looked directly at my two elven attackers, sneaking through the brush.
"Whatever kept you?" I smirked.
The thin line of my grimace greeted the two attacking soldiers. Swords aloft, they charged. Light footfalls quickly covered the muddy and fern speckled ground.
The first attacker to reach me was blonde, lean, and tall. He jumped forward, slashing a blade towards my throat. I pivoted, lightly bending, and arching my back. His sword missed my throat by the thickness of a coin.
Springing back up, I tutted arching my eyebrows at him, "No mercy" escaped my lips. Teeth baring viciously - an old habit - I drew my sword from its wet and heavy scabbard. The mud covering my skin was drying out, cracking at the joints. Flakes spun to the ground. Swinging the beautiful sword above and down in one seamless arch, the point of it slashed across the first assailants face, blood splattered and run downwards, cresting his neck.

The other attacker did not hesitate, running forward. Black haired and shorter but more muscular, this soldier had presence. He barged through me, shoving me viciously and then circled around to punch me in the ribs. Jabbing my sword forward, it sliced deeply across his chest. Bellowing like a bull, he grabbed at the cut across his chest left there by my blade and quickly cast a spell to heal it shut. They were circling me, searching for weakness, and figuring out a strategy. It's what I would have done.

When there came a rustling of leaves from the corner, Lord Gamone strolled into the clearing with an axe on his shoulder, all three of us held our breath, waiting for the savagery to unfold.

Chapter Twenty- five - The Separatists

Gamone took in the scene and laughed.

"Been hiding in the dirt, where you belong Shiv, was you? There is no way of escaping elves when we are hunting. Am I right soldiers?" He flicked his eyes mirthlessly towards the two soldiers standing near to me in the clearing.

"Yes, my lord, there are none that can withstand elves," The two elf soldiers nudged each other and laughed out, enjoying the sport.

A curious look slid across Gamone's face that I was not expecting to see. Abruptly, his features elongated, stretched inexplicably and his eyes slowly lost focus, unravelling, they were. Almost unseeing, those eyes took on a staring type of quality, filling the blankness in his flat pupils.

"You really believe that don't you, *boy?*" through the humid heat of the jungle, a chill settled over us – his victims. A vibration begun that changed to a shiver of our collective fear.

The soldier that was being addressed, grew goosebumps upon his flesh. The colour drained from his placid face. He darted a sideways glance at his companion, who looked away and gave out a gulp. His feet, moving off slightly to the side away from the soldier under the full force of Gamone's stare.

". . .and you. Yes, you, where do you think you are going? Stand back alongside your friend you filthy coward. So, answer me, both of you, do you think none can withstand elves then?" Lord Gamone gave them a crazed assessing gaze, which explored the expressions on the young elven soldiers. Lord Gamone's twisted face bouncing quickly between the two, while they stood utterly bewildered by the question. Opening and closing their mouths.

"But my Lord Gamone, forgive me, *you* are a high lord of the Elves, so I don't understand your line of questioning," the blonde-haired elf stammered out.

"oh, I am, am I? What would you say if I told you that is not the case by a long stretch? What would you say then, Elf?"

The two young soldiers exchanged bewildered gazes. The clever black-haired one, pivoted and silently raised his sword. Lifting his chin, he understood the challenge in the words of Lord Gamone and he reached a decision, it was apparent in the set, hard lines of his eyes. The look that made me weep - he had decided to not go so easily.

I stepped back, the heel of my heavy boots suctioned at the moist jungle floor as I lifted my boots. A loud '*puck, puck*' sound, but no one dared to move a muscle, except for me.

Gamone's frown grew wide, and his eyes were bulging in his head. His teeth bit down on his pronounced bottom lip. Seconds past, each one full of strain. Gamone chaotically reared back and pounced on the two soldiers like a deranged orangutan.

He was uncontrolled and disfigured in his madness as he was tearing away limbs, ripping at flesh, smashing bones to smithereens, and kicking in collarbones to a fine mulch like consistency, bundled up in skin.

I watched in horror as two beautiful elves were reduced to bloodied pulps. My body was shaking, my eyes fixed ahead in shocked disbelief.

That was when I heard the flapping, leathery wings of my saviour, Caemyre shooting through the sky. Caemyre was flying towards me, claws extended readying himself to pluck me out of that hellhole. Stretching my hands up, I hooked my sword over one of his long, curved talons. The dragon flew up, rising higher and higher above the canopy, my feet touched the tops of the trees – dangling down.

Gamone had not noticed at first, until there was no mistaking that a dragon was upon him. Wings clipping, gusts rolled over the trees and bush. Gamone was fighting to stand upright. Then, Caemyre's snout crumpled up at the tangy smell of blood on the floor of the makeshift jungle. Taking in the scene, The Dragon sneered at Gamone.

There was a flash of ferocious fire and snarling of teeth then curls of smoke as a stream of molten lava shot out of the dragon's mouth. Nearly smashing into Gamone but hitting the wall of trees instead. The bark exploded with the kiss of fire.

Caemyre flew upwards with me in his claws, then when the great dragon reached a safe distance, he flung me up and onto his broad back. His great wings expanded in flight, he climbed up and out of the invisible dome of the arena. Nestled into the comforting grooves of his ridge back, I glanced behind me. I watched the crowds gasps in wonder looking up at us, pointing, drawing all eyes away from the centre of the arena. At a terrible enclosed, spinning glass globe held up in the air. It was the spell holding the jungle in place. The spinning ball was gigantic. The spectators had been watching it, and the contestants inside fighting for their very lives – for the thrill of the entertainment.

The dragon had his keen eyes on the horizon as he spoke, "Dawn has gone ahead with Lilly, Dillion, and Callen on Violaceae. Rhyiathe has been told to leave through a portal conjured for him inside the tournament. I decided to come and get you myself." He flipped his neck, his great head turned to look at me. He watched me crumple forward, placing my cheek on his iridescent scales. I let out a long grateful sigh and said,

"I do not know how to thank you enough. There are no words." Tears started ebbing and flowing down my cheeks, dripping onto the hard scales of his back. He nuzzled me, scales shimmering with movement and light, lit up by the ethereal glow of the stars. Caemyre glided under the night sky, as silently as a long boat in the middle of an endless sea, in stillness, with the reflections of starshine upon him, he said,

"Do not cry, Aurora. How can you, when you can look up and see the wonder of the cosmos above you. Your strength is needed for the battle ahead. Call on The Primal, the embodiment of The Lioness, who helped you claw your way out of your grief. The Lioness is there for you always. Transcendence is needed, dearest one. Now ready yourself." Lurching forward, as sleek as an arrow, he flew through space, through time and onto The Void.

***

Lord Tennison was camped with the elf General, towering and intimidating, and his cadets, out on one of the stagnated, slow-moving asteroids, that bump along the outskirts of the region of the great expanse of space known as The Void. The shadows from the dwarf planet of Nepou fell in dark waves, a cloak of invisibility for the troops, away from prying eyes. The velvety darkness of the planet made the splattering Nebula of bright-matter above, shine brighter than was thought possible. So bright it was that all eyes were drawn to its glow. This was a welcome distraction for the troops, of which they very much needed. The young

cadets were scared, while they waited in the great expanse of The Void – readying themselves for the attack.
The Cadets were fidgeting, clipping, and unclipping their swords and held in their hands strange gems, used as weapons, to shoot out laser beams, aided by spells and military ware. Jagged, are their nerves like hairpin triggers. They waited in battle formation, gently chanting, "Elves First," to each other. The Elves had made up a secret salute associated with the terrible Elves First movement. They placed two fingers splayed over the right eye so followers could identify each other quickly. The two fingers signified the divinity of the Elves, Immortal, and their worship of the God of The Hunt - The Horned One. The Goddess Freya was frowned upon by those in the Elves First movement. The Goddess was considered as too weak and womanly to represent the 'Elves First' movement.
Lord Tennison's long, platinum blonde hair gleamed in the glow of the full moons. Moonlight, cast down in thick waves and stardust dropped, piercing through the space above. Staring up at the opening, the elf crown prince was mesmerised. Imagining the great battle with Earth beyond the gateway - where his fame and glory laid. His Legacy would be that of the conqueror that devoured Earth, reclaiming the planet for the immortals. He absentmindedly fingered a shiny, faded scar on his cheek given to him by his father for nothing more than showing weakness as a child – crying for his mother's care and arms.
His father would not be pleased. Words would not be spared by the king for his sons, but both Gamone and he, had devised this plan for the greater good together. Gamone had been clear about The Elder Light and the return of the true owners of the Seven Kingdoms and it would happen soon. Once the opening was seized and occupied by the Elves then it would be held as a symbol and all immortals would flock to it like a banner - the call to arms to take back the Earth and return as the mighty immortals. His father would thank him in the end.
The Generals were watching the skies above just as Lord Tennison was doing. Three red flares were fired and that was the sign to begin but he couldn't see his brother anywhere. *Oh well*, he thought, *the glory will be all mine.*
Lord Tennison looked out over the sea of young elf cadets. All tall, lean, and devastatingly attractive elves, who were in their first suns cycle.

Trussed up in pristine combat gear, barely tested. Young, stupid, idealists. The campaign had been all a bit too easy; to convince them to take the opening for all immortal kind 'Elves First' he had once said. The idiots had latched onto those words, coveted them, and then recruited others to its catchy banners. Malleable minds influenced malleable minds; Lord Tennison sighed. There was no challenge, it left a bad taste in his mouth - it had all been just too easy. He sighed.

Throwing his cloak over his broad shoulders, he stepped out before the troops, glaring down at them when he started barking, "Get ready and march out with General Idatain. On my command." The Crown prince dropped his hand. The troops fell in behind one another and started marching forward. The cadets were separated into three groups of twenty. They were moving forward at a pace, weapons drawn in steady hands, dressed in dull black bodysuits. The front of their hair plaited, twisted up in elven styles. The young cadets' eyes glowed from consuming too much potion. As soon as a surge of adrenaline spiked, battle rage would kick in. Warping and spasming the potion through each muscle, making their foreheads engorged and droop primitively. Making them insane.

"What you do now is for the glory of The Seven Kingdoms. Elves First."

Elves first, elves first, elves first, elves first, elves first, elves first, elves first, elves first, the simpletons chanted, while they grin out in their excitement and jeer at one another, as they keep pace.

The Generals, dressed in full battle regalia, capes fluttering and chests full of medals shining, looked on at the troops. The Generals swiftly began to ready themselves for the battle ahead. Unclipping their spell-powered, gem laser guns. Taking off their stuffy ceremonial hats that impressed the young cadets and made the oiks happy, they replaced them with functional titanium helmets. Strapping grenades with blast ranges of miles to their broad chests, they take out worn blades in their battle-trained, calloused hands. Secretly discussing tactics with the intention of making the cadets sweep through to take the void, while they hold back to clear up the rear.

"Keep the casualties to a minimum. Make it look easy," Lord Tennison said in a low tone, to General Idatain, who gave the lord a piercing look; enough to let him know that was not going to be a possibility.

"Sure," The General replied, with a slow smile.

"Get ready, death fast. Go, go, go," shouted the Generals to their cadets, each taking a squadron of twenty out into The Void, towards the Opening. The Offered were there, five of them at least, who were stronger, faster, with dragons and immense magic. Lord Tennison had devised a plan. The troops had on them glass gas balls, which were poisonous to the dragons and lethal to The Offered.
It would be all over soon.

***

Caemyre soared through the air above Violaceae. His great body, changed direction and careened to the side, linking wings with the black dragon and Lilly scrambled onto the ridge in between his shoulders, leaving Dawn, Callen, and Dillion on Violaceae's back. The dragons glided together, whistling through the skies, the riders scanning down towards the staircase for signs of movement ahead.
"We are nearly there. Callen, Witch of olden law, be ready to put up a barrier of protection around us. Moreso, Violaceae, I have my own magic," Caemyre ordered.
The witch Callen raised her hands. Glowing lights and particles emerged from her fingers and settled in a translucent sphere around the group.
The elf troops were running at speed, stealthily on the glass stairwell, heading directly for the opening to Earth. The handful of Offered at the Gates were guarding The Void, lazily looking the other way not expecting an attack from their own kind. Usually, the only action they saw were humans straying across the opening, quite unintentionally, or an immortal or two, trying to slip over to Earth for items for the black-market trade, that was big business. Occasionally, an immortal gets through to start a war on Earth pretending to be human and The Offered are sent through with a retrieval order, dead or alive. They would not be expecting a full-scale attack.
Lord Tennison watched on eagerly, counting on the element of surprise and the sheer numbers of cadets at his disposal.

Rhyiathe and ten of his fellow vampires appeared out of the portal gate, at the top of the glass stairwell, nearest to The Opening. They were looking out over the great expanse of The Void, trying to spot the elven troops.

The cosmos glowed in bright stillness, as beautiful as ever, but they were not here for the view. Spotting the elf troops running towards the stairwell from the south and watched the five Offered guards in their ignorance to the north, and Caemyre and Violaceae flying in from the east, Rhyiathe estimated he needed to get to the centre of the glass staircase to intercept the elven troops first. He had to be quick. Rushing commands out to his loyal vampires to form into lines, he called to alert the Offered with a spell that enhanced his voice, making it ripple across to their ears and that of their Dragons,

"Offered, you are under attack. Look to the south, look what is coming. Wake up your dragons, get up Dragon-riders. Fight, fight, fight now," Crown Prince Rhyiathe shouted, while he was running forward leading the charge, to join the glass staircase, then, he and his fellow vampires, would be in the middle of arm-to-arm combat on the stairs. A skirmish would be unfolding.

The elves spotted the vampires and saw the defensive manoeuvres and began speeding up to intercept the vampires. Their keen elven eyes were fixed on breaking through to open ground beyond the glass stairwell. The elves were running in lines of three, shoulder-to-shoulder. The Great Vampire Architects, who designed the glass stairwell made it narrow, so the design would limit the numbers crossing to The Opening – vampires are cunning.

Rhyiathe needed to dig in and hold ground until The offered and the Dragons, included Caemyre and Violaceca arrived, with Aurora and the others.

The vampires and the elves were feet away from each other and closing the distance fast. Aurora's stomach flipped over watching from her high seat on Caemyre's back. Her eyes were frozen in horror when the elf general spotted Rhyiathe, drawing his weapon as he leapt forward; sword swinging violently to cut Rhyiathe down.

"Caemyre, we need to get there faster. Our friends and our allies will be killed." Caemyre lowered his great head and let out a roar , picking up speed.

On the stairwell, arm-to-arm combat had broken out. The sound of battle was raising through the air, the clashing of weapons and the screaming from those in pain. Elves smashed forward into the lines of the vampires

and the seasoned vampire soldiers used their talons to shred the cadet's skin – blood pulsated, and bloodlust was being satisfied.
The Cadets were too young to be battle hardened and fell back in large numbers in fear but were being brutalised, forced back into battle formation by their own Elf Generals, who held up weapons against their own troops "Run forward or we kill you ourselves," growled the Generals.
Coming in, on the freezing northernly wind, the Offered had mounted their dragons and were flying along the stairwell, closing ground and would soon be upon the skirmish.
The five dragons carrying The Offered stopped in midair, great wings expanded out, holding themselves up while the dragons' flames were let loose. They roared through their powerful jaws.
The Dragons came together, their flames aimed at the same point, burning a hole cleanly through the glass stairwell. None would be able to crossover to The Opening, the melting of the glass had ensured that.
While all about battle reigned down, Rhyiathe was fighting the lead Elf General, looking around at the burning white flames as the stairs collapsed behind him. He realised there was no escape for his vampires, but to fight their way through the elves.
The dragons descended on the Elves, grabbing them in their huge claws and throwing the shrieking Cadet elves into The Void, where they would fall through time and space for all eternity. Never to be seen again by those they loved and held dear.
Once the stairwell collapsed, the Dragon's fire was refocused on the combat zone. Molten flames licked out at the cadets, flaying their skin on their bones. The screaming out of pain and despair would have turned the stomach of the most hardened soldier who witnessed it. The cadets staggered forward on slowly burning limbs, covered in a clinging hissing fire. Some of the elves were throwing themselves over the stairwell voluntarily, choosing the abyss rather than be caught by dragons' fire and die a painful, horrifying death.
Caemyre and Violaceae arrived, Aurora jumped from her ride onto the stairwell behind Rhyiathe and pulled out her sword. Hand-to-hand combat was her speciality. Rage was in her eyes and every sinew of her being demanded she fight to the death. Her blade sang out and cut down the elf

generals, like the metal was attuned to their vulnerable signatures, seeking it out to obliterate and destroy.

On the staircase below, Rhyiathe was in full fight mode, with one of the Generals. His blade slashing and piercing the great soldier's chest. Rhyiathe lunged forward to take hold of General Idatain's throat, crushing his windpipe, in his hand,

"Call the Cadets off and we will let you all go. They are too young to be here. You have my word."

The general croaked out a dry laugh and shook his head, shoving his face forward, with spite, he said,

"Tell me Prince Rhyiathe, what good is the word of vampire scum."

Rhyiathe's eyes blazed, as he clenched firmer, tightening his grip, and the general gurgled out his last breath.

The last of the cadets took out the small glass phials of gas from hidden pockets and volleyed them at the dragons. Most of the dragons swerved but a large red dragon was hit directly in its chest. Its smouldering eyes closed, it started to drop out of the sky.

"They have dragons-bane -" screamed Callen " - get the dragons out of here now. We must finish the rest ourselves."

All jumped down apart from Dawn on Violaceae, she remained on the dragon's back, buffeting and too scared to move. A cadet, bloodied and wounded, grabbed the last of his potion and hurled it at the little black dragon.

Violaceae dived and managed to lurch out of the way, Dawn as her rider, could be seen careening to one side, barely able to hold on - quickly moving out of the way. Dawn lost her balance and tumbled, landing with a great cracking sound on the glass stairwell. She laid deadly still.

Aurora rushed towards her sister, crashing to her knees as the fight continued, quite furiously around them. Holding her sister's head in her gloved hands, she spoke,

"Dawn, Dawn. Are you…are you okay?" Aurora watched as blood ran down her sister's temple.

"I'm okay, I'm okay. My head feels funny. Where is Poppy? Rory, where is my dog?"

A gasp escaped Aurora's lips; she had remembered. Dawn had remembered. The two sisters embraced each other in amongst the chaos

of the fighting on the broken and split stairwell, but their reunion was still intense, nonetheless.
"I will find Poppy for you. You have my word. I will find our beautiful dog Poppy even if it means travelling through hell and back. She will be with us." Thick tears of joy fell from my eyes and I kissed my sister's forehead. All around the battle ensued but was moments away from being lost for the terrorist elves; all was unravelling and ruined that day for the princes of the elves.
The generals had been killed and the remaining handful of elf cadets, turned and started to run back towards the shadows of the dwarf planet of Nepou. The young cadets in their fear charged back to their base camp, towards safety. But on drawing near, one of the cadets stopped dead in his tracks with a look of abject horror on his fine young features, staring in astonishment as Lord Tennison raised a gun,
"Lord Tennison, please . . .we only wanted to serve you. I want my mother. What have we done. What have we done. I want to say goodbye to my mother. . .," The young cadet pleaded, with a despair growing thick on his words, only realising now the error he had made that the natural order of the elves is to preserve life not take it.

Lord Tennison from his place hidden in shadows, slowly drew out a weapon. Lining up the target, without hesitation he coldly pressed the trigger. Three laser pulses hit his own troops. Disregarding, the shock on their unlined faces when the prince had stepped out to line up his aim. The cadets had been a disappointment and had tried to turn and flee, when the light expounded out of the gun's nozzle but it was over too quickly and they were too late. The prince would say he had been merciful, killing them on impact. No survivors, no witnesses. And then Lord Tennison, the crown prince of the Amber Throne and of the elf planet of Tylerine then turned to the darkness of the shadows and fled, unseen.

Lord Gamone watched in disbelief, some distance away, as his brother sent the laser pulses to kill the last of the elf troops. His simpleton brother was defeated, the plan had not worked. Gamone smashed his hands into the wall, breaking, and crumpling the solid mass into dust, floating up in the liquid like air. The wall had offended him with its existence, just like his brother.

It cannot be! The plan had been perfect. His brother's execution of it was sloppy, pathetic elf lord that he is. Gamone the terrorist was disgusted by the defeat. A rage slipped over him. The Opening, the gateway, still stood guarded by The Offered. Their great dragons circled the devastation of the staircase, carrying between them their injured dragon-kin. The cadets hadn't even been able to kill not even one of the stupid lizards, even with the Dragons-bane.

It was his brother who had suggested young cadets. When he had cautioned and advocated for mercenaries. Lord Gamone's anger sizzled as he watched Aurora and Lilly break off from the group to scout out the shadows of the planet Nepou looking for the leader, while the others celebrated the departure of the elves.

Gamone took out his hunting knives, gripped them in both hands, and silently followed in the footsteps of the two women, as they circled the abandoned base camp, further and further away from the group they wandered, on their own.

Chapter twenty-six - Death fast

"I have never *shiv'ved* a *hu-man* before. We are told they are too fragile for us to enjoy, but I have a different reason to abstain. I see them as less than dogs. But you, Aurora, I will make an exception for. We are alike, fated in a way. You, under my spell, I would find intriguing, especially as I know Rhyiathe has an interest in you. I would find it quite exciting, in fact." Gamone's eyes were intense, penetrating.

He had many different voices, just like he had many different versions of himself that he carefully shared with the world, and this was cold and cruel. Reaching out his large fingers, his eyes were deep into me as he grabbed both my wrists, they looked tiny in between his fingers. His slow, cold smile, tod me he intended to drag me to his bed chamber, any time now. The hostility was written on his heavy-set face.

Before I replied, my eyes slid sideways towards Lilly. Her face was bowed in profile to me. I could see she was frightened for me. He was a wild male grizzly bear, and I was her small, new cub. Her eyes were wide like saucers and her breathing quick in her chest – panting out her distress. Every woman's worst fear was what he had planned for me, what he tried to do before, and she knew it – I had told her of my last encounter with Gamone, eventually, late one night when we were alone.

A fear settled over me. I had accepted I was not in control here and if he wanted to hurt me, there was nothing to stop him from doing so. He had the power of an Elder. Don't poke the bear my brain told me. My eyes did not move away from Lilly's. Panting, I was too afraid to even look at him, too comforted by Lilly's presence, even though I knew something terrible was about to happen.

"*Relax*, you will enjoy it. I will make sure of it. To impregnate you is my intention." Gamone said in a low quiet voice. Humiliation coloured my cheeks at the way he talked to me like I didn't have a choice like it was only his to make and that to overpower me was his right. He stood up from the table to remind us of both how excessively tall he is - extremely tall even for an elf and muscular, well built. He began to disrobe in front of both of us. It was a display of dominance and power. Sickness tickled at my throat. The bile tinged my flaring nostrils. He undid his long black, sleek hair from its band. The thick strands fell down his back and reached his defined buttocks. Next, he removed his weapons from across his chest and then, unbuttoned his shirt, a show to divest himself of all garments. I tried not to look at the power of him as he stared down at me primally. Tears slid down Lilly's cheeks as she bowed her head low, her hands bound together with thick leather ties. The truth is, Gamone could have any female he wanted. He was highly desirable, and he knew it. Nearly every immortal I had seen with Gamone fawned over him, but there was something about him that made me think he needed to prove he could have anything; taken by force if necessary. Wanting only what he couldn't have, he was a sadistic bastard.

My breath was difficult to draw into my chest if it even came at all. There was a lump in my throat, strangling me.

He leaned over me, his hair touched my face. Each strand prickled at my skin as if the ends were made from cactus needles - dry and lethal. *Is everything about him evil?* He then took a knife that he had used to cut fruit - the sweet smell of mango made me want to cry for its ordinariness - and he severed the bonds holding my hands together. I could hear the excitement in his laboured breath as he released me. He wanted me to struggle, and he would enjoy it even more.

My cold, hard shell slid over me and that's when I decided I would rather die or be unconscious than be taken against my will by a barbarian like him. I gritted my teeth and snarled ready for the pain of a fight to the death, but I would die gladly knowing that I went out fighting like the warrior I am, undefeated and undefiled.

Fight or die, fight, or die, fight or die, fight or die, fight or die. Fight or die, fight, or die. Runs through my brain – calling out to my Lioness, who sashays into being. *To Fight or Die* rang through my head. I was first born into chaos, and I was reborn to be a killer in the lands of the Immortals. In both realities, I have been hewn from stone and lived through it all out of sheer spite. It would be my truth until my last breath. I would not succumb or be dominated.

He slowly pulled the table away, dragging the huge furniture to the side effortlessly, so there was nothing, but empty space left between us. My body shrank back involuntarily.

He leaned down and gently lifted me up onto my feet. Lifting my chin to his face and pulling back my hair with his fingers, he lowered his violet, grey eyes to mine. Touching my mouth roughly.

"I will observe the niceties and you will enjoy this, *hu-man*."

He leaned forward to kiss me, pushing my lips apart with the urgency of his bumpy, rough tongue. I pulled my head back in a feeble attempt to stop him. He, holding it in place all too easily, smirked, pulling my body into the curve of his own. Stealthily, I started creeping my hands up to the small, throwing knives in the hip pockets of my suit.

He began to laugh out loud. "Looking for your knives, little human? How sweet. Please do try. I like your feistiness." He roughly moved the tip of his index finger down my neck, between my breasts and pushed down hard. "Now, let's move into my chamber. Goodbye Lilly traitor of Elf-kind."

A sob sounded out behind me.

"Lilly!" I screamed, trying to run back towards her, but he grabbed me by the front of my hair, summoning a guard with a loud snarl.

With that display over, he picked me up and flung me over his shoulder and started walking away down the hallway. One of his guards stepped forward to grab Lilly. A glinting knife in his gloved hand.

Gamone had my arm pinned behind my back, to stop me from wriggling like an eel, and getting away back to Lilly. He reached the door of his bed chamber. The door creaked open; it was dimly lit inside Gamone's chamber, a vast array of flickering candles positioned all around. His attempt to seduce me no doubt.

He grabbed me by my hair and tossed me inside. Landing on a thick fur rug in the centre of the room, I smashed into the hard floor with the weight of my full body. Tumbling a few feet more and rolling to a stop, I smacked my cheek on the floor. I could feel the blistering inflammation and the bruised flesh of my skin stretching over my cheekbone. Pushing myself up onto my knees, I made to jump up, but he quickly closed the door, locking it from the inside and strides towards me removing his trousers in the process.

I averted my eyes and ran for the balcony door, and he intercepted me. Pushing me back down to my knees on the rug. He was grinning and I was burning with a vicious hatred – the vibration of it pounded in my ears.

Looming over me, a talisman settled in between his huge chest, bouncing on his well-defined abdominal muscles as he speaks,
"Why do you fight? It was *YOU* that wrecked my plans human. I am taking my *compensation*. You will give me a son that can live in both worlds. You will be bonded to me, Aurora, and we will have a son that is half you and half me. The ultimate warrior. Purest of immortal DNA. The rebirth of the Elder bloodline." he says this with a charming smile, standing naked before me. Like I was lucky in some way.
He pulled me up by my arms and then slammed me into the wall, taking a knife off a treasure chest. He then slowly cut the front of my bodysuit open and peeled it from me like preparing a grape. He looked all over me and touched my stomach.
"We will have a lot of children because I plan to enjoy each other as often as I can. You will stay in my bed chamber. You are a quick study so I'm sure you will learn all my little favoured ways fast," He laughed in my face, narrowing his eyes and pinched harshly at my flesh.
I wiped the spittle away from my face and my response slipped out of my mouth and cut him down,
"You will feel nothing but my rage cutting into you before this night is out, you have my word," A challenge that rung deeply into the quiet of the bed chamber, we stood glaring at each other. I was waiting for the right opportunity to strike when he lunged forward and pulled me to the floor and pinned me down under the weight of his body.
A skirmish ensued on the floor. I am not so easily taken. A shadow slowly crept into the bed chamber, flying in from the open window, made out of the vast ornamental masonry – dedicated to the elves and their love of angelic elven figurines. It looked like an odd choice for Gamone.
A gust of wind announced the shadow's arrival to Gamone. Candles hissed out all at once, leaving a pale curling white smoke behind, licking coldly at the hairs of the back of his neck. Gamone's eyes glowed bright green in the sudden blanket of darkness. His face was horribly close to mine – blinking, staring down at me. He had just managed to roughly pry my legs open. "Stay still and on the floor," he commanded me, his excitement abated none as he stood up.
The shadow was in the corner of the room staring at me laying naked on the floor, crushed into the fur rug. I leaned up onto the backs of my

elbows, peering into the velvety place inhabited by two eyes, which blinked down at me out of the soot like shadow. I went to jump up but then I stopped. I was watching in stunned silence, as the shadow took out two silver blades and in a hushed whisper incantated a spell. The green glowing eyes of Rhyiathe glared out of the gloom, all familiar to me, like a lighthouse beaming with care, calling me to rise.

"Aurora, the spell removes the potion from your bloodstream and brings on the quickening," Rhyiathe yelled out, in a voice thick with emotion. "Stand ready, combat is upon us or Death Fast."

Gamone grabbed at the shadows, prying Rhyiathe away from the wall by his neck and smashed him into the ground. The flagstones of naked slate cracked and shattered under the weight of Gamone's anger. Strangled sounds of choking bounced between the stone walls and into the liquid black night.

I heard the yells of Rhyiathe as he was being choked to death, but my body was nonresponsive, shaking, writhing on the ground, as the potion was being removed, forcefully. Ripped away from my blood vessels. Being pushed out through the air, the lights of the Elder exploded out of me with the energy of a thousand stars. My body was shaking violently. Rhyiathe's choking was becoming quieter; his gasps were growing further apart. Gamone's laughter grew loud,

"Oh, little Prince of Darkness, no one is coming to save you. Not even my father can stop me this time."

I scrabbled from the floor to stand in one swift move. I strode forward landing a kick in the centre of Gamone's broad back, with my Elder and Vampire strength combined and finally unleashed. He jolted forward letting go of Rhyiathe, who started gulping in huge breaths of air. I caught a glimpse of his gasping form, and his eyes were filled with wonder at the light of the Elder, hovering above us.

"What *is* this? Why are the lights here now?" Gamone said, all the while swinging around, watching the lights of the Elder were grouping overhead. Picking up a sword from the wall of Gamone's bed chamber, I aimed the tip at his broad chest and summoned the Lights to attack him with a flick of my hand. The lights hovered, he grinned at the Lights at first.

"I command them too," he raised his hands, but they did not respond nor obey him. A cold fear grew in his hard grey eyes, and he conjured a great

black snake and threw its muscled coils at me. I slew that scaly demon with the piercing darts of the lights. Then, I changed direction and threw my hands forward. With this gesture, each one of the lights took turns to dart at Gamone like a seabird plunging into the water diving for its next meal to devour. In no time, Gamone was consumed by the winding fire of the lights circling him. Charging, I positioned my weapons to attack and swung the sword in an arc to slash the blade across Gamone's thigh before reversing back to slice through the back of his tendons in his heels.
The man made of mountain and stone, fell forward with a terrifying crack to the floor, giving me enough time to drive my dagger through the back of his ribs and there I held it, while I questioned him,
"Who is behind all of this? Who was the person in the chair in front of the fire who was giving you and Lord Tennison orders? What was in the shadows in the wood banging to be let out?"
Gamone stared, with wide eyed astonishment at me, fumbling out, "Impossible, . . . impossible that you saw that. Are you some kind of a witch?"
"Tell me now, tell me the truth." I drove my dagger a little further in, catching a nerve in the process. His back arched and spasmed, bellowing came from the wide, bull-shaped Barbarian, his eyes ablaze with pain and fresh anger. Lunging forward at me with his clenched fists, as big as fish bowls, we were near the open window of his bed chamber, scrambling for chokeholds on one another. Landing punch after punch and kicking out in our ferocity to kill one another - brutal, primal to observe. I was fuelled with hatred and all thoughts of revenge were hellbent upon him. Killing was on my mind.
That was when it arrived. When the thirst in the back of my throat caught me, I stumbled back. The plumes of Gamone's scent wafted over me. This sweet scent sparked a burning bloodlust upon me, and I shivered in exhilaration, as my incisures slowly pushed down to help me partake in the meal. His pulse quickened in his neck, and I rejoiced. It was an unholy beacon calling me home. I grabbed his neck, crushing his windpipe in my haste to have at the sweet nectar pulsing through him. I wanted to taste Gamone - in the worst way possible. He was frozen under my strength. There was fear in his eyes for the first time and I stared at those grey

soulless eyes while I darted forward to bite and sink my teeth into his skin. I took out my dagger and shoved it into his arm to hold him in place.

"*Noooo,* Aurora, don't bite him. You'll make him into a version of you," shouted Rhyiathe weakly from behind me. Hand on my shoulder, slumping forward, as he collapsed into me. In that split second when my attention was elsewhere, Gamone shook free of my hold.

He lurched over to the window but turned,

"I will tell you this, Aurora, the Darkness is coming and there is nothing that can stand against His will."

Gamone jumped out of the window into a thousand-foot drop becoming a speck, assumed broken and dead, somewhere in the minuscule river below.

Chapter Twenty-seven – Poppy

Gamone's body was not found anywhere by the outer walls or on the lands of his castle, nor in the clear river that run through it, or its bedrock. I was fearful he had escaped. Fearful because I might not get a chance for him to die at my hands.

Hunting him, I would do later. But for now, my attention was needed for another matter. I had to get Rhyiathe and Lilly out of Gamone's castle, unseen. After Rhyiathe and me, escaped Gamone's private suite, we had to take a journey through his territory, that I must say, I am not proud of when I reflect back on it. I will explain. . .

I had dressed quickly and sprinted down the hallway to rescue Lilly first. Now, without the potion in my veins, I did not have the leash-on and my rage was roiling out of me.

I crept silently through the castle, slipping from shadow to dark shadow. The guards stood in the hallway, not seeing me as I came for them; each one in turn. I watched as a few of them were busy pushing Lilly to one another, enjoying the sport of torturing her before defiling and killing her, no doubt.

I slithered out of the darkness and reared up, eyes glowing, from being hidden inside the shadows. I was made of mist and vapour, gliding down the halls. When I was upon the three guards who had Lilly, my anger overtook my actions. Fury unleashed. Lilly kneeled and put her hands over her eyes and cried, she had not wanted to watch, while I devoured and drained the blood of the elf guards, in turn. She handed me her father's sword. Pools of the liquid-of-life were allowed to seep onto the floor, over my full belly. The Primal One, The Lioness was hunting– my rage was upon me. I dipped my fingers in the crimson elven flow, splaying my two fingers, and colouring two blood lines over my right eye. A terrible mockery of the Elves First movement. Making the rest of Gamone's elf guards flinch back in maudlin, I rampaged through his castle. They could

smell the blood of their dead kin on my hands, my face, and its macabre tattoo.
Eventually, I managed to get Rhyiathe, who was gravely wounded, down the stairs, heading towards the castle gate, with the aid of Lilly. She had sustained injuries too. In zombie states, they both wandered forward guided by me, stumbling, holding each other up. Stopping every now and then, on their hobbling feet, they held their stomachs, while I noisily dispensed of a guard or three. The numbers did not matter, the bloodlust was upon me. The crimson liquid dripped in torrents from my fangs and the sword in my hands. Incensed, so enraged, was I, that I could not seem to control myself. I wanted the guard's blood to be Gamone's and I attacked again and again in a fitful rage. But every one of those elves did not satisfy me, they made me feel bad and ashamed. I hated myself and my wrath all the more for it.

As we neared the large, wooden main gate, a felonious sound of cracking could be heard from the outer walls. A golden glow was building. The gate began cracking and bending under the heat of it. The wooden gate warped and its metal fixtures blew out. Steel bolts propelled through the air. The guards that remained behind, cowered under the weight of the looming threat growing from behind the walls. Finally, the last remnants of the castle gates blew inward with plumes of dancing red, orange and white-hot Dragon-flames. They announced Caemyre the Great Dragon had arrived, like great trumpets sounding at the coming of a monstrous royalty.
The Castle-Gates flew up in the air and smashed against the inner tower of Gamone's Castle – wreckage and rubble, made a path for our escape that day. The remaining Guards fled, running before the terrible roars of a Dragon with no master, except for himself. He did with them as he pleased.
I rushed towards Caemyre. There he stood, glittering and Golden, seated on the bountiful lands across from the drawbridge, waiting for me.
His golden flecked, amber eyes were wide open, his pupils like slits and bearing down on me in cold judgement. A terrible sentinel, guardian of my soul. Piercing me with his stare, prodding, and provoking me silently to take care. Be warned. Do not lose your soul. His eyes were pleading me.
I looked away afraid, while the elf blood dried over my face, building up in the pores of my skin. It served as proof of my failure to control myself.

"I think you've had quite enough death for one day, wouldn't you?" Smoke curled out of his nostrils, while he sat, blinking at me. Caemyre's ancient, knowledgeable eyes, looked tired. Weary of his long years and of seeing the mistakes of immortals and humans alike, repeated time and time again. The dragon sighed reliving shadows of bygone years, that he didn't share.

I nodded, but only once. That was the only sign of acknowledgement of my wayward behaviour, he would extract from me that day. I did say, stubbornly, but sheepishly,

"I am in my trial-and-error period of my journey. Do heroes not get to commit great savagery and then vow to redeem themselves? Isn't it the way this goes?"

He looked at me carefully, watchfulness in His large eyes, while his tail smashed on the ground in his annoyance,

"I do not think you get this at all. The Elder, they are nothing that you can comprehend or *so it would seem*." His eyes were heavy with revulsion, raking over me like slashing blades, as he continued,

"They are celestial. Do not incline to think that you can pollute yourself in your own brand of idiocy without consequence, *little one*."

I stirred at the tone of his reprimanding voice and the way I was spoken to, mostly because of the shame that covered me with each one of his words spoken.

In my humiliation, I screamed, "Gamone is an Elder, but look what he does . . . why has he been given the Elder Lights? He is disgusting. It makes me believe being an Elder is a curse. Celestial beings? He is a *killer*."

Caemyre stared at me for a long while and said nothing. I stood hunched over, bathed in blood but holding up my friends. A contradiction if there ever was one.

"Perhaps, but Perhaps not. What if I told you of a story. Of Light and Darkness. For The Elder to return, a great sacrifice must be made. There is a Prophecy, and it foretells of an Immortal marked, who will bring about the return of The Elder through blood. But the thing is The Elder are a peaceful race, so the Prophecy must be recovered to understand it fully, I do not believe The Elder would be born of blood and ruin, more so, of Light, we need the prophecy to understand it better, do you not see?" Caemyre looked at me, patiently waiting.

I paused and looked at him. He trilled, blowing smoke in the air, playfully. I shook my head, too exhausted to listen to riddles – my head was too foggy for the sport of Dragons. I did not respond to His words, other than to say, "This Prophecy is *none* of my business, I helped to stop the elves from crossing over to Earth. I am done. Do you hear me? Done."

I stood there, in the silence that unfolded, knowing that what I had just said hadn't sat well with me, but I refused to take those words back. I was too tired to see beyond getting my friends to immediate safety.

Caemyre leaned forward into my silence and eyed me with a look of interest, "hmmmmm, yes, well, we will see. You are a *little one* if these acts of barbarism are what you truly want to be . . .There is always a choice even in the darkness of despair of the Last Night of the Soul. Maybe you are sad because you can no longer act as a vigilante without understanding the toll that it takes on you. Maybe it is you that has grown, changed perhaps? We will see."

The Dragon had me stumped so I pretended not to have heard the light of knowledge in his words. Although, I knew that his advice was given in kindness, he was guarding me against my own self.

The Guardian of the Vulnerable and of the Light is what a Dragon is, after all. What I took away from the conversation was, I needed to find that Prophecy. Caemyre was hinting that I have a part to play in this in some way.

I staggered forward placing Rhyiathe and Lilly onto the great dragon's ridged back. At least now they were both safe. I wiped my forehead of blood and sweat and let out a long-drawn-out sigh. A whimper too, but Caemyre pretended not to have heard it.

Laying on the back of Caemyre, Rhyiathe suddenly started talking nonsense in his feverish state and burbled out,

"Thank you, Aurora. Thank you for saving us, for saving me. I believe in you. I believe you are destined to save the Seven Kingdoms."

His eyes were unfocussed as he opened them looking up into the sky, "My love for you is stronger than you will ever know. I have pledged myself to you. My life is yours forever, for the taking. Do what you will with it," with these last words, his eyes closed, and he slipped further into unconsciousness; pale, drawn and immortally beautiful. I stroked his thick black hair with my hand, my finger dropping down, over his neck to trace

the angles and lines of his strong chin. My eyes filled with hot tears, Caemyre had gone silent, looking back at me staring down at Rhyiathe.
"It is your destiny to save the Seven Kingdoms, as much as you try to deny it, you know it is true. He will come to understand that in time. His heart is pure and true. Maybe he will help you and that is what he is meant to do too."
My jaw was set, I clutched away the tears sliding down my exhausted face. I burned as I looked at Rhyiathe with an unquenchable love for him, that pulsed through my veins, but my thoughts drifted to what I needed to do, to what I needed to become to save Earth and the rest of the planets of the Seven Kingdoms. The sacrifices that I must make along the way. I didn't know what they would be but knew there would be many. There always are.
For a while, I gazed down at Rhyiathe more objectively.
If only I was different, if only I was the type of person that followed their heart, hearts in my case. The longing didn't leave my eyes, but my body detached and went through the motions of disengaging. I stood up tall, straighter. Bounding onto the back of Caemyre and taking up my Dragon-Riders seat, I weighed up the great Dragon's wise words – his previous words of wisdom gnawed at me.
Blowing out my cheeks, I knew I was not ready to be a bonded pair. I knew I was too muddled, too unfinished, and incomplete. My searching was not over for the treasure trove of who I am and what this prophecy has got to do with me.
I put on my riding gloves, looked out over the horizon. The morning sky was coming into a brilliant dawn. The first pink light of the twin rising suns of the seven Kingdom were peeking out over this world and I watched those suns rising with a heaviness in my hearts. But then I sat bolt upright, remembering that I still had one more to save before I could rest and I yelled,
"Caemyre please deliver them home, back to the city, and on the way drop me off at The Void please. I have some unfinished business on Earth."
A Dragon does not need to say a word, to object to a chosen path. A Dragon can make you feel alienated from yourself by the tone of His silence. Something I would learn to live with. I will keep my own will for myself, I decided that day.

That day, I left Pericullious and The Seven Kingdoms, Caemyre and The Immortals behind, but what I did next, I did for my returned sister and the need to protect the innocent – I was going to find Poppy, our dog.

Caemyre flew away and I watched him for a time, before I walked through the Gateway back to Earth. Beforehand, I meditated on my destination of choice and visualised it with such vivid detail, that as soon as I stepped through the Gate, the image on the other side matched my mind's eye perfectly. I knew I had returned to the place I spent my miserable childhood. The smell of hell polluted my nostrils.

The smell is so bad and the thickness of the atmosphere here is heavier, more densely packed, unlike the dimension that was now my home in the Seven Kingdoms, where I always felt at risk of flying away into the Great expanse. My body not quite securely anchored. There is always a fear of lifting off from the surface of the planet of Pericullious. Never to be seen again - gravity is lighter in the outer dimensions. Perhaps that is why they are all so tall? Come to think of it.

I walked along the bleak London streets of my childhood. It was startling how different Earth is to the Kingdoms. There is no honour to the beauty of the natural world here on Earth. Sprig like, ill looking trees lined the streets, fortified, and hemmed in by concrete blankets. Bowing and scraping their magnificent branches in their misery against the air pollution, hanging down - defeated.

Nature is subjugated here, mocked. The last remnants left for humanity to look at rather than revel in. This concrete prison looks like the very worst version of hell to my now knowledgeable eyes. I long to be back in the lands of the Seven Kingdoms, to be at one with nature and the universe – connected to the divine. Not only has my DNA changed but my world view - I see the warrens, the cages humanity has built, and humans are the battery chickens that are no longer 'free' range. They are stupid and don't even see it.

It was night and I strolled along. In my tan coloured bodysuit.

I meandered forward through those familiar, yet far away streets. I must have looked odd. A majestic sword sheathed in my intricately woven scabbard, but in all honesty, I believe the petrified looks from the humans

I passed-by, were more to do with the dried and congealed elf blood about my person – on my face.

I tutted out, "Oh well, I'm here now, better get on with it," to myself.

Walking through my old neighbourhood, I heard a familiar sound, which sent my hearts soaring. It was Poppy barking weakly and I went to her at a run. Elven-made shoes covered made my footsteps light, soles tapping on the cold-hardness of the grey cracked, unforgiving pavements of the poorer parts of London.

Brushing my hands over the ripples of mortar and cheap crumbling orange bricks of the dilapidated old houses, as I ran alongside them. I remembered when I used to hold a marker pen in my hand as a little girl, marking the brickwork with a line as I ran by.

I stopped; *I wonder if the lines are still there.* I started peering at the wall to look for the pen marks. I felt too tall, too visible, too *seen* walking these streets, it made me question if I was really here back on Earth at all.

I found a faint line of blue marker pen, my fingertips instinctively touching it, reaching out to cross the divide of time, to connect the woman I am now with the last remaining parts of the little girl I once was.

She did exist after all, and she deserved protection too. "I am so sorry," I said to myself.

But then Poppy's barking became more insistent, a yelp and a yowl. I dashed forward, running towards her distress on scrambling legs. *"I'm coming Poppy, don't give up hope, I'm coming for you."*

There in a back yard, tied with a rope that was burning great welts in her neck, she stood, starved, with her ribs-showing and haunches bony. Mange was ravenous on her skin and her eyes were dull. A haunting despair wallowed in them. There was my Poppy, worse for wear, but there was our diamond.

My hearts jolted under the ribs of my chest as I saw the state of her "*Poppy, Poppy.*" I called out. With a crack of her neck, the beautiful Poppy lifted her head staring at me in a type of shocked disbelief.

"I'm here to take you home, girl. Oh, Poppy. What happened to you?"

A movement between the wreckage of the back garden near where I was standing. A large, beer bellied brute came lumbering towards me with a piece of old pipe in his hands.

"Bloody dog. Worthless it is. Woke me up barking and I'se going to make sure it doesn't wake me up again." He tapped the old pipe in his hand. The brute peers at me,
" 'ere, I know you. You're that scruffy little street urchin that stole my old leather coat and broke my leg. You shittin' better get out of 'ere, before I set about you, gel." Pointing the piece of pipe at my chest, I recognised him as the street trader from the market all those years ago. *A reckoning perhaps?*
"Thats my dog and I'm taking her. The state of her. You better move back, sir or I'll enjoy taking you down." My lips drew back in a growl and my teeth clenched and bared, but the ape did not heed my threats.
"You bloody well are not taking my mutt anywhere. 'Ere why are you covered in blood, like that?" Leaning his face back to squint at me a little closer, he shrugged and took a swing at me. The old piece of pipe clanged for my head.
I tutted as he clumsily tried to hurt me,
"Apologies, Poppy. I will be with you in a moment, my dear sweet one. Then . . ." I ducked my head as he swung the pipe a little too close for comfort,
". . . we will go and find Dawn. Okay?" I looked around and Poppy was looking at me with a kind of brightness growing in her dull eyes. "I'll take that as a yes."
While the brute shouted with a sneer "Stupid bloody idiot talking to a fuckin' dog."
"I assure you my good sir, it's a far superior conversation than talking to a great buffoon like you."
His smirk dropped from his face faster than a bunch of coins, thrown down a gutter. I cracked my elbow into his nose and the bone broke with a satisfying *crunch.*
A howl of pain ensued from his fetid mouth, then I drew my sword. It sung through the air as I slashed him across both arms – blood dripped freely. Then, I started shoving him backwards into the backyard of his own grimy little house.
The neighbour watching me over her fence, ducked her head in alarm, trying to remain unseen – too late.

Once we are both inside, the ape and I, I threw my small knives, immobilising both his knees. "Help, help, help." he started to scream. Moving forward through the dirt covered hallway, I grabbed a piece of the washing line cord off, where it had been strung up between two metal pulleys. Hesitating at picking up a weirdly marked tea towel, I grab it anyway taking it off his mouldy old kitchen table and gagged him with the foul rag. Then with the cord, I tied a loop round his neck and some around his hands. Throwing the end of the coil, over an exposed beam in the kitchen.

I felt nothing for the revenge I was about to exact. Caemyre would have been disappointed and cross if he had been there. I shrugged, "but he is not."

"mmmm, mmmm,mmmm" muffled alarm from the street trader.

"What was that, eh?" I said, "Speak up man. Cat got your tongue?" I coldly laughed.

His eyes bloodshot, staring at me with open hatred. I hoisted the heavy man up and he dangled off the floor slightly, I hoist him up some more. About three feet, *which should do the trick.*

I kicked away the chair that he had been trying to support himself with and looked directly in his bulging red, bloodshot eyes as his ugly and putrid heart gave out. Then, there was a silence as the light in the room swung backwards and forwards. *Shadow and light, shadow, and light,* over his still body.

Bounding outside with some fresh drinking water in a cup. I took the ropes off my Poppy, and she gave me a tiny lick with her swollen and dry tongue. I rubbed her head gently, lifted her up trying terribly hard to avoid her open sores, and started to move out of the back garden gate.

There were blue lights silently flashing across my eyes and memory freezes me to the spot. A car door slammed shut and an officer's walkie-talkie crackled to life.

I swung my head around, over the fence to glare at the neighbour, who ducked down behind the collapsing neglected pieces of wood adjoining the two backyards. "He nearly killed my dog and beats up little kids and did far worse things. He was a monster," I shouted to her.

"Aren't we all in some way 'ere?" a muffled, dried out husk of a response came from fag-ash Rita or Karen. Some such name like that, I imagined.

I reflected on what the neighbour had said. *No, we are not all monsters*, but I decided and made a promise to myself that day, looking down at the sorrowful state of Poppy, that I would use my own brand of monster to make these worlds a little better. To save all the Poppys out there – animal, human, immortal alike. The universe needed saving. Call it revenge for what had been done to me over the years, for all that I had seen and what I had done. I would be the Bringer of Pain to those who inflicted it on the vulnerable – the Gamone's of this world will pay.

I had my purpose.

Maybe Caemyre wouldn't approve of my decision. I think he had something nobler in mind for me. I would just have to show him there is no Light without some Darkness.

The landscape of London was grey. A dirty dusky line of humanity's failure but I stood tall, ready for the fight ahead. It was a bit of a shame that I was going to prison. Bit of a dampener really. Come to think of it, that just won't do.

The police officers placed me in handcuffs and carried Poppy to the back seat of the police car. Handling us both like convicted villains, only Poppy showed any remorse and bowed her head, we all went for a short drive through the back streets to the Police station.

"Sorry, for the inconvenience, Pops. We'll be home with Dawn soon," I muttered to Poppy. The officers' eyebrows stretched up into their hairlines as they looked sideways at each other without saying another word.

Several hours had passed by in the police station; a few of them taken up by being interviewed by incompetent police officers, more than any skilful art of interrogation. I played along and bided my time, while I plotted my escape.

"There you have it. My story is done." I peer over at the police officer in the interview room with me, Poppy still on my lap – where she has been for the duration of the interview. The police officer and his bitten down pencil had stopped moving over two hours ago as I was telling my story. He stopped asking questions about one and a half hours ago. He had not moved an inch in the last hour. I'm going to have to pause - I wonder if I have broken him, maybe.

"Ahem," I clear my throat, waving my hands in front of his eyes. No reaction from the officer.
My gaze drops while he sits there. Taking notice of the fraying of his shirt cuffs, bloodshot eyes - cracked lips and hangdog, defeated scowl on his face. I recognise that look. I'm looking at another scruffy, uncared for kid looking back at me. His staring unseeing eyes, with his mouth open in shock. Dazed and confused, but I could tell he wanted to believe in fairytales and Happily Ever After, more than anything else in this world. The sad child in him wanted to believe that dreams do come true – it made me like him that little bit more so I couldn't really feed on him now. I sigh, I was getting hungry. Licking my lips.
He snapped to attention - furtively checking the door, scanning out his exit route and wanting out of this room into the hallway. I see it there in his piss-holes-in-the-snow like beady eyes. But he daren't move - he needed magic to be real, to believe in something greater than him.
Poppy was curled up on my lap, content, after eating some dog chum and had drunken her fill of water. The police officer's, who had drove me here, had asked if they should they take Poppy to the vets. I had replied to leave her for now as I'd take her straightaway after I left here. The Police constables had looked at me with wide eyes at the time, incredulity shining from their faces and reminded me I had killed a man or two.
"Just leave her with me for now," is all I said, quite vexed, snapping. They had agreed. Not wanting to cause a scene. In their mind, I wasn't going anywhere after all.
The police officer sat across the desk from me in that Interview room, cleared his throat, The Police Officer in him slipped into place. All business. Face hard - hope drained away.
"So, where was I? What you're saying is there is another dimension folded into Earth, called the Seven Kingdoms and it's there, you fought off a man with the strength of a" he looks down at his cheap, lined notebook and finds the words he was looking for "Elder, who are mystical beings not seen for centuries. You have been living in a world, in another dimension, time and space, and there are vampires, elves, witches, warlocks, talking trees and so forth and that you escaped to come and rescue your dog for your dead sister?" He stared at me with a large question mark on his face.

I nod emphatically with a smile. Then I squint an eye in deep concentration. "Well, not escape per se. I came back to Earth of my own accord and intend to go back and take Poppy with me," I flick my head towards her and Poppy's ears prick up slightly at the mention of her name. "-and also, there are dragons. Did you write down there are dragons? Mine is called Caemyre C–A- E-M-Y-R-E pronounced kai-mire in human dialect. It's a really interesting language, elven." I stroke Poppy's ears while casually conversing about Dragons.

He looks at me and scratches his head,

"Mental illness runs in your family, don't it? On your mother's side, ain't that right?" before I could reply, a confident rapping on the door with bold knuckles, announces two men in pristine, tailored black suits.

They don't wait for an invite, before they barge into the room, shoulder to shoulder with sunglasses on that do not leave their faces. The Metropolitan Police Chief Commander walks in after them.

"Lloyd, erm, a quiet word in my office please. The young girl must be let go. I'll explain what I *know* . . ." his eyes drift accusingly to the two men in black suits.

"Woman and dog." I shout out to all in that room.

"I beg your pardon," the chief commander says to me in baffled tones. Shiny, polished buttons on his regally cut deep navy-blue suit, showing us his pride in his work.

"*I said* I am a woman, and this is my dog, and we are *both* leaving here."

"Well, I say, I will not be addressed like that by the likes of *you* . . ."

He is cut off mid-sentence with a withering sunglasses-reflective look by both men in black. Lloyd is dragged up, out of the hard orange chair opposite me and unceremoniously thrown out into the hallway along with his commanding officer. The door is slammed shut on both of their shocked faces. Angry words are exchanged out in the hallway, rattling at the locked door. Ignored.

Two seats are dragged back and wiped down "Hello Aurora, we will get straight to the point. You'll need to feed soon so we don't really want to be your next meal if we can help it." The Black guy says in a thick London accent, smoothness and confidence etched into each syllable. He carries on. "You were a human and now you are in the seven kingdoms, and we don't need to know any more than that. It's your duty to Earth and

Humanity to spy for us. Gather intelligence about the Immortals, so we are prepared."

"Prepared for what?" I say, Poppy flicks her ears up and I lean forward.

The other agent, an Asian guy, in a very plummy British accent laughs in a public-school boy kind of way "For war, an uprising. Hell, to be unleashed on earth, wouldn't you say?"

Into a camera affixed to a wall, I lean forward, eyes bright, pupils dilated, grinning without laughter from the stress of the last few days and say, "Well, okay . . .let's have at it then." Whoever is offering me this deal is not in the room. The real high-up bosses never are, they are watching me on a screen somewhere, but I play along, for now.

A deal is struck, and the finer details of an agreement worked out. A specialist vet is brought in and after all is said and done, I am given access to a shower before we, Poppy, and I, are both given our leave to go.

I had asked for a couple of special tasks to be completed by the agents, as part of the deal I had made in exchange to spy for humanity.

For the teenage girl that witnessed me killing The Cook, I asked for her to be found and offered help too. They had reluctantly agreed. The Cook's victim would receive an allowance and a home – be looked after, that sort of thing. The very least I could do really. There had been other witnesses, to my other crimes, but this seemed like redemption for them all and for me – to help the girl. My mother was to be looked after in her residential care home - she had suffered a terrible stroke, lost her mobility, and had dementia. Her last days were to be spent in comfort and she would be given the absolute best medical care. I felt relieved. A clean slate. Some of the debt paid for my life of brutality. The remainder would be paid by my keeping on the straight and narrow from now on, dedicating myself and using my powers to save those poor souls, who needed it the most.

The men in black tore up the police officer's notepad. Then took out a weird gadget and zapped the paper into ash. I waited. The agents told me that my records would be deleted, and I would be just like the agents, a ghost, a spook to the world with no paper trail leading back to Aurora the little girl or assassin I once was. The human, Aurora would not exist anymore. A cleansing of sorts.

"Understood, but how do I contact you?" I ask.

The agents grin, "Aurora, we are always watching."

The shock of this statement overruns my face temporarily – I stood, head to the side wondering how long they'd been watching me and how much they had seen. I suppose it doesn't matter anymore. Not really. I was heading back to the Seven Kingdoms and these agents or the agency they worked for, were the ones asking me to act as a weapon for Earth. *They* needed *me.*

Me and Poppy get up to exit the room, ready for our fresh start.

I am escorted through the pared-down public-funded building, scooting down the bland hallway in a crisp white shirt and dark blue trousers of a police uniform. I had asked for a police helmet, to complete the ensemble, but quickly declined was my request. The verbal equivalent of the arm quickly withdrawn – like I told you before, there are other ways to be shown they think you're dangerous, insane without telling you so. Poppy treated and bandaged up. My bodysuit, sword plus scabbard and small knives placed in a mundane, battered plastic carrier bag - at my request. I love the thought of it – me carrying a plastic Tesco bag back to the Seven Kingdoms. *Hilarious. I still had my humour, right? Worn like a badge of honour.* It's what got me through all of those long years of hell, but now I sense a change on the wind, and I want it more than I have wanted anything before in my life.

I am taken to the back door of the square, bland building. The two agents open up the fortified doors for me, with Poppy for company, and see me through it. "See you soon." They offer a firm salute, crocodile smiles firmly in place, before the heavy riot-proof door is clanged tightly shut in mine and Poppy's faces.

I look out, around me, over the rear courtyard of the Police Station. The car park is empty of police and their black and white vehicles. Shadows are creeping forward, and the faint breeze stirs at crispy leaves being swept into abandoned corners of the baking tarmac.

The last rays of Earth's single sun are beating down and piercing over the buildings of London, shining against the backdrop of the City's skyline. This is when I notice a crisping sound, a sizzling, accompanied by the smell of smouldering flesh. It rings in my ears. I am sniffing, trying to make out the smell and where it is coming from.

Quite suddenly, my cheeks are searing with white-hot heat. I dart into the pixelated shade of the first shadows forming. Scrabbling to give myself

respite under a bush nearby – trying to save my cooking skin, from the blistering sun, but finding it hard won.
Urgently, I set my mind on the Seven Kingdoms, calling into being a portal, while the burning intensifies across my face. A swirling, effervescent portal comes hurtling into life, on the surface of a plain brick wall. I pick up poppy in my arms, cradling her gently. I run fast, legs like a locomotive, holding the ground, to close it faster between me and the Gateway; back to Pericullious.
I jumped, feet first, spinning through the air, flying in rotation and then I enter the brilliant, peachy-pink maternal light of The Void. Poppy's eyes aglow in wonder looking all about, ears pricked up with joy. Both my feet struck out, readying to land gently on the renewed glass stairs of the entranceway to the Seven Kingdoms with a *Thud, thud.* The Gateway closes and I watch it pop out of existence; Earth is closed to me.
What did I learn? What didn't the agents see from behind the locked door? The burning of my flesh tells me the Immortals can no longer return home to the warmth of Earth's single sun.
I started walking.
I had already saved my sister, kept her safe on Earth until she was able to cross over to the Lands of the Immortals, where she now has a much better life, more than I could have ever dreamt possible – she has been resurrected. Dawn is renewed and strong, and she will be reunited with Poppy soon. Underneath her healing wounds, Poppy was still the same loving, kind, and loyal dog she always was. Dawn would manage to coax out any residual nightmares Poppy may have, with her abundant heart and naturally kind disposition. I was sure of that. She reminded me of the Goddess, Nimwae, in a way.
But, what about me? Yes, I realise now there is a *me* to look after too, not just my sister. There is so much *to me*, more than cobwebs and shadows, of what I had to become to live in this harsh world, and so much more *for me* to do; to protect the innocent will become my life's purpose. The Elf King and his two Son's, Gamone and Lord Tennison must be stopped from destroying the Seven Kingdoms and breaching the terms of the Clandestine Agreement, which I am apt to do with these new powers I have. I need to find out more about this Prophecy and The Darkness that Gamone referred to – it sounded like he was referring to a person, rather

than anything else. The prophecy is important, it is something that is linked to me – I feel it deeply in the pounding of my two hearts.

Also, I must ask Rhyiathe what a *Cilena-ancae* is too.

I carefully hugged Poppy to myself and walked down the glass staircase of The Void, into the deep, heart of the unknown, and I no longer feared my life and that is the one thing that I had truly wanted was to be free.

The End . . .

A note to readers

Dear Reader,

I hope you thoroughly enjoyed reading this book as much as I did writing it. I have included the fuller extract of The Tome of the Cold Ones, that Rhyiathe and Lilly wanted Aurora to read to bring her up to speed, - it follows this note. I didn't want to include it in the prologue as it gives away some information that was revealed in the latter part of the story.

Currently, I am drafting book two in this dark fantasy series, it's called, The Elder – Legends of the Cold Ones. It's about the planet of Vulldune and the vampires. Each book will focus on one of the immortal home worlds.

I'm in love with writing, completely obsessed with it - have a head full of book ideas so please do follow my author page on Amazon and Goodreads for more details on my books and works in progress.

Thank you from the bottom of my heart for all the love and support I am shown by my lovely readers.

INSTAGRAM: phillipa_readsbooks

TIKTOK:@peppaaub

Phillipa x

The History of The Seven Kingdoms

Book one: The Tome of the Cold Ones

The first recordings of the existence of magical beings in our civilisation, was believed to be through the telling of fables that were then translated into a range of different texts, across the world. Before the Clandestine Agreement of 2026 BC, on Earth, it was a time of discovery; development of empire states and colonisation of the discovered continents of Earth. Each country on this planet is organised around a set of natural resources and minerals, and these natural occurring elements were traded for equal value between nations in early 3000bc. This Free Trade enabled the setting up of transport links connecting the globe through trade routes. Specific countries in the West, like Briton developed skills and crafts that enabled great expeditions, which included vast armies and weaponry. Ship building and engineering was the centre of Empire-building civilisations, during this period, with one mission in mind; to colonise. Colonising and expanded territories through the treaties of offering education, sanitation and infrastructure to smaller countries and tribes. Whenever smaller groups resisted this offer and wanted to continue arrangements of fair and equal trade, then the empire would become aggressors and occupy lands in territories, organising into campaigns to subdue resistance. The British Empire colonised many parts of the known world from 2860 BC through to more recent years, AD, creating systems of control such as mass slavery, oppression, and death penalties to those that did not cooperate. Although this was a dark time in the history of the world, it also connected smaller communities and tribes to one another. This is when it became apparent that magical beings existed and, due to the established transport links, these communities started to gravitate to specific areas of the globe and consolidate.

Magical beings were already organised and more secretive about their own abilities, due to the real threat of persecution, and were often found settled in regions of the planet that were considered as less hospitable plains of Earth – away from their human counterparts.

The Elder – Lights of the Seven Kingdoms

Magical beings lived together in peace and harmony, safety in their combined numbers. As a society they had cause to become more militarised in response to colonialism.

The beginning of the world finding out about the existence of magical beings on Earth, was brutal, during a barbaric time in the history of the world. It is recorded that magical beings could not be distinguished from humans without them being in the act of performing magic in some way. Their abilities were unique to each of them - no two had the same powers, but elemental and celestial groupings were evident. For example, all the immortals were able to channel and draw on nature to conjure fire from their hands and manipulate the elements. Most Immortals were discovered when they were in a heightened emotional state or provoked or trying to protect themselves in some way. Immortal looked exactly like humans at the beginning, and it was not until much later, until they crossed over to the other planets that make up the Seven Kingdoms, that they grew in tallness and in strength. it is typical for an immortal to grow to be over seven feet high. In the beginning, their discovery rate was minimal, so their existence was interwoven with folklore, myth, and legends. As their numbers grew, along with a tendency to converge into settlements more commonplace, Leaders and kings of humans became very wary of their potential. Humans believed they could absorb the powers by eating the flesh of a magical person. A gruesome black-market trade started, and stone tablets have been discovered on archaeological digs of evidence of sales of immortals and their body parts. Those who were not killed were enslaved, performing magic for Kings, Queens, and leaders, and supporting armies through performing spells. Children were kept as pets on occasion.

It is recorded as early as 3000 BC that a woman of magic called Leanndria started to travel the countries to band the magical communities together. Leanndria, a high priestess of the Light of the Elders, preached strength in unity, and safety in numbers and started a school for the gifted. The curriculum was devised to support the honing of skills and enable magical academics to study magic more comprehensively. The humans were greater in number than that of the immortals, thus not threatened nor coordinated in their efforts to contain the magical uprising when it did eventually occur, and the Great City of Prussia was formed. Substantial numbers of magical beings flocked to the city in what is now referred to as the great migration of Floderen, who was the second Lieutenant to Leanndria and her bonded life partner.

It was not until the Floderen Era, that humans necessarily saw the magical beings as a threat to their existence. Until that time, magical beings cohabited with humans, diluting their potency and some humans even sought out magical beings as shamans for their tribes. It was not until the city of little Prussia was established and magical beings started to procreate together, which created stronger and more powerful bloodlines, splintering off into subcultures of witches, werewolves, vampires, and elves, were seen by Humans as a substantial threat.

The human world watched The City of Little Prussia, and the Earth waited. When the Immortals emerged from their great fortresses, they were organised, coordinated and lethal. The immortal leaders had developed infrastructure and society that supported procreation at scale. Part of their design was worshipping female deities of fertility and celebrating bonding ceremonies with stronger pairings being revered – all pairings were celebrated; same sex couples would be encouraged to use their magical abilities to breed and raise a family or adopt. Single People too. It was abundant pro-procreation that was key to the survival of the Immortals.

Food was in bountiful supply and good health was prioritised. The magical population exploded. Immortals sent their emissaries to human cities accompanied by vast armies, demonstrating great powers and their might. The Immortals openly and quite aggressively showed the world their abilities, as a warning, through taking part in tournaments and organising great Olympics, where they bested humans in every field. Their agriculture progressed by magic, their infrastructure accelerated their civilisation through keen development of medicines, art, engineering, and weaponry, - the humans were left behind. The immortals' advancements were beyond anything the human world could comprehend or replicate.

At this point, the human leaders met in secret and plotted against the Immortals. It was agreed that the magical beings needed to be stopped at this juncture in time, as they were not yet as many in population. The human armies converged on the Immortal City of Little Prussia in a coordinated attack. The Immortals were ready.

Little Prussia was fortified when the armies of the humans arrived at the walls. A magical shield protected the ice kingdom city. Human scouts on reconnaissance were either paid off or killed. Little intelligence was gathered prior to the human's arrival. The frozen climes outside of the walls were treacherous, humans went in blind and had underestimated the magical community and their military strategy. The human generals had strategically planned for an attack on a civilian settlement rather than a heavily militarised city located on treacherous terrain. This is when the humans realised that they had not been monitoring the evolution of the magical communities as closely as they perhaps should have been. Great battalions of the immortals were already in attack formation when the humans entered the vicinity of the fortress. Five hundred thousand human soldiers entered the lands of the immortals that day and none returned home.

The Elder – Lights of the Seven Kingdoms

All communications with the human leaders were blocked. Radio silence sent a deafening message of the power of immortals to the humans. By the fifth day when not one soldier returned nor messages were received, the human leaders declared war on the immortals. Great armadas were sent forth and again, and again, the same pattern followed. Communications ceased first and no soldiers returned or details from surveillance equipment could be gathered. The humans were in turmoil. They knew from lack of contact that their armies were being obliterated but had no detailed intelligence as to how or what resources and weaponry the magical communities were using. The human leaders resorted to base tactics to secure information. Magical beings were hunted and found, and their families were held hostage until information was secured. They learnt of new, unstable energy sources created by magical spells. The humans-built prototypes based on this innovative technology. Civilian magics were held hostage and tortured to produce magical weapons of mass destruction that could be used against the enemies of humanity.

The next time a human army ascended on little Prussia, the human-assault was prepared, with military precision. Breaching enemy lines with ease, the infantry took down one of the fortresses and killed as many magical beings - civilians and soldiers – just as humans were killed during that skirmish. The humans learnt that inside the kingdom of the great city of Prussia, was a tropical terrain, amidst the ice and snow. The Immortals had the ability to transform any inhospitable lands, into a liveable tropical environment yielding many opportunities for terraforming, agriculture and stability of infrastructure, a highly desirable set of gifts.

Warfare continued back and forth for over three decades and there were huge losses sustained on both sides. The war became all-consuming, impacting world economics. Pushing the world into a state of collapse in terms of systems outside of the war, thus it became unsustainable and unaffordable. This is when a cease-fire was called and world leaders met with Premiere Leanndria and her war council of The Immortals.

The war council of Leandria were convened. It is noted in reference journals of the serving Councillors of the time, that there was a great discontent at her willingness to parley with the human leaders, but Premiere Leanndria stood firm. The Immortal's war council were inclined to believe that the humans had sustained heavier losses than the armies of The Immortals and human frailty was at the core of their own demise; in fighting and greed, creating chaos throughout the human ranks. Premiere Leandria did not trust her Council's arrogant words and believed the losses were too great to bear on both sides. Immortals were being killed to the brink of extinction. The humans were sustaining heavier losses but had a larger baseline population. The Premiere knew the immortal's time was running out and looked for a solution beyond her generals, to strategy and negotiation her eyes fell. What she found led her to look to the Realms of the outer dimensions. Earth was an abundant planet, but her magical explorations had scanned far and wide, locating the planets that now form part of the Seven Kingdoms. These vast worlds were inhabited by a smaller number of ethereal beings, referred to only as The Elder. Not much was known about The Elder, no history books or divination could help her ascertain more information. She brooded long and hard. Her War Council needed a distraction from their bloodlust and their plans to exterminate the humans. The worlds in the outer dimensions where the Elder lived were bountiful, arable, and unguarded. This was the answer to her prayers, or so she thought. The human leaders of Earth were asked to come to the dimensions later known as the seven kingdoms, to discuss the details of a treaty: away from any distractions or plotting. It was also a show of power by Premiere Leandria. To demonstrate the might and majesty of magic, far beyond human comprehension.

Premiere Leanndria arrived with a diplomatic party to scout the outer dimensions. The Elders of the Seven Kingdoms recognised the Immortals as a form of their children and they being their ancestors were humbled by the wonder of the divergence of their bloodline and the remarkable, uniqueness of the elder line mixed with humans. They agreed to protect the Immortals. Altruism foreshadowed their actions. To leave the seven kingdoms in the present day and go back in time to live in the lands once again, when they were but once new blots of land mass in the universe. The Elder cautioned that when the two-time lines meet once again, The Immortals will need to give back what was gifted to stop a terrible war: a tragedy of useless destruction. Premiere Leandria had agreed knowing The Elder were the Immortal's origins – their ancestors, in some way. She would work on a plan to ensure that when The Elders returned, the Immortals would be strong in number and magic. Enough to return to Earth and take it for their own.

The military and government leaders of Earth and The Immortals met in the realms to work out a peace treaty. The Clandestine Agreement began to take shape over a matter of days. Earth would be compensated, but how would they protect the Agreement?

Premiere Leanndria invited Earth's Leaders to the outer realms to negotiate the Clandestine agreement in late 2027bc. This was a task in of itself. Her own family agreed to stay with one of Earth's principal leaders in exchange for the humans agreeing to be transported to another realm. Her powers of persuasion formidable even back then. Premiere Leanndria was insistent upon the humans coming to the realms and the seven kingdoms. Her scribes catalogue her intention to demonstrate that the war would be over by the immortals agreeing to settle in lands, much more suitable and far superior to the provisions on Earth - not a defeat at all but a compromise. The Humans who attended the negotiations described the outer realms as 'ethereal', 'beautiful', 'harmonious with the pure essence of the universe', 'majestic and profound'. The human General Kilmore's journal goes into eighty odd pages of detailed descriptions of what they saw on their two-day visit there. This journal is restricted, held in the pentagon as agreed by the Global Clandestine Agreement Agency. Earth's leaders agreed to support the mass migration of the immortals to the Six planets of the seven kingdoms. The compensation for warfare exchanged on both sides, mostly art and cultural objects stolen during the war and the perpetrators of prolific war crimes resulted in executions. It was then discussed how the secret would be protected of the existence of the immortals and of outer realms. Agreement was reached that all parties should contribute to offering resources to protect the secret and uphold the foundations of The Agreement, which would be inter-generational and binding. Premiere Leandria had her chief witch devise a Ritual that would place the soul of an immortal into the body of a human - later known as the Offered. Commitments were made that each century; twelve tributes would be put forward to demonstrate both parties unwavering commitment to uphold The Clandestine Agreement. The document specifically details that any crossings without permission would be seen as an act of war.

The Clandestine Agreement was drawn up, signed and sealed. The mass migration of The Immortals started. A portal was opened on the day of the summer solstice on Earth. Humans were kept away, distracted by celebrations and firework displays. A spell was placed on the largest cities. The Immortals left earth under cover and were welcomed into the lands of The Elder. Taking up their dwellings, coveting their places of worship and adapting their civilisation and infrastructure for their own. All is at - The Seven Kingdoms, of which Earth will always remain part of to ensure peace. The Immortals set about planning to grow back stronger and in number. To be prepared when The Elder return. To be prepared to take back Earth.

The Elder much smaller in number, with no need to procreate due to their exceptional gifts and immense powers – longer lives by being of celestial nature, did as they had agreed and left The Seven Kingdoms, but instead of travelling back in time to live in the outer dimensions once again. They left to travel through time and space. To explore the universe and to discover the origin of their own power and have not been seen since. Turning from history to myth and then to fable, then to legend.

Glossary of Terms

Word	Definition	background
Rhyiathe	In the vampire dialect, Rhyiathe means strength, honour.	Rhyiathe is the name of the Vampire King of Vulldune. It is a custom that all his sons are named after the king, but only the Crown Prince can use the name. The other Princes use their second names.
Periculliious	One of the planets or home worlds that form part of the Seven Kingdoms	Periculliious is the pinnacle of the Seven Kingdoms, due to its location – the planet sits at the very centre of the universe. The point of creation. Abundant in resources and the heart of all magical power.
Twelfth	The Twelfth are so called because this is the number of beings / people that take part in the magical Rite called the Offered.	This is part of the agreement between Earth and the Kingdoms. The Offered are representatives of Earth and the Kingdoms
The Offered	The name for the rite that is completed to place an Immortal into a Human.	These combined beings are guardians of The Void. The area of time and space that has multiple Vortexes and Portals to Earth and other planets
Rite	A religious or other solemn ceremony or act	This is a scared custom to the Immortals and Humans, honoured to maintain the Clandestine Agreement
Shiv'doress	Vulgar Immortal Slang meaning infested	This slang is used for humans and, for

	Human whore (gender neutral term and non-binary) of no value, which has relationships with low class animals. Verb Shiv'ving	implying that a particular immortal is lower or equal to a human – a very deep insult.
Cilena-ancae	Vulgar Vampire Slang – the worst insult in Vulldune Lands of the Vampires. Meaning: crabs that live on genitalia. A deeply unpleasant or stupid person.	Vampires are descriptive in their created insults and have a vast array of slang and expletives for insulting other immortals.
Caemyre	Dragon names converted to Immortal languages: meaning Golden One	To the dragons Caemyre means King, but to the Immortal who do not fully understand Dragon customs, this means Golden One
Violaceaca	Dragon names converted to immortal languages: meaning the scent of violets	To the dragons Violaceaca means Guided by the heart, but to the Immortal who do not fully understand Dragon customs, this means scent of violets
Ballosh	The Ballosh is an elven traditionally made hooked sword that the elves imbibe with magic to heighten its battle prowess	The weapon is large and unwieldy for those that are not trained in the art of Balloshery. These weapons tend to be used for ceremonial purposes but there has been a rise in their use, with the coming of the Elf First movement.
dwarf planet of Nepou	The plant of Nepou is not one of the giant planets of the seven kingdoms, but is part of the solar system, of	The Dwarf Planet of Nepou, is a home world to some of dwarf kind, discovered by King Tur'ok of Attraides, who claimed it as an

	which there are many lesser planets.	outer dimension for the Werewolves, of which the Dwarves consented as they would be protected.
Pressure	Continuous physical, but invisible force exerted on or against an object by magic being used	A helpful indicator that someone or something is performing magic nearby

Printed in Great Britain
by Amazon

45618827R00162